IMPERIAL GHOSTS

Ashes of Empire #5

ERIC THOMSON

Imperial Ghosts

First paperback printing July 2022

Published in Canada
By Sanddiver Books Inc.
ISBN: 978-1-989314-77-7

PART I – AWAKENING

—1—

Angelique Mission
Celeste

Seconds after the last light of day vanished from the far horizon, the rhythmic thump of a solitary drum echoed across the still night air. Moments later, dozens more joined it, encircling the besieged abbey with a wall of sound. Though they were hidden in the dense forest, Friar Haakon, prior and chief administrator of the Angelique Mission, could sense hundreds, perhaps even thousands of natives swaying to the beat, letting the madness of bloodlust rise within them, erasing any trace of humanity. A rotund man in his fifties with a bald head and a salt and pepper beard, Haakon's grandfatherly face showed more despair than he knew, but few would have commented under the circumstances.

He heard a gasp behind him and turned in time to see Verica, Leading Sister of the mission, crumple to her knees. She shook under the full psychic force of the envy, hatred, and barely suppressed blind rage emanating from the natives encircling the ruins of the Angelique Abbey. Thin, tall, and dark-haired, Verica was in many ways Haakon's opposite even though they were of an age. But Haakon could easily imagine Verica's plight as she fought to shutter her mental barriers.

Before the friar could help her, a figure emerged from the shadows, put his hands under Verica's arms, and lifted her effortlessly. Centurion Cord Loumis, officer commanding F Company, 1st Battalion, 1st Guards Colonial Marine Regiment, was a slab of a man, tall, broad, muscular, with an even temper and a stoic disposition that rivaled Haakon's own.

No lights shone within the abbey's old walls, hastily repaired by the Marines, and neither of Celeste's moons had yet risen into the cloudless sky. However, Haakon could still make out the grim expression on Loumis' face thanks to what little came through the bell tower's open windows.

"Sensors are picking up over six hundred life signs within a kilometer of our perimeter, Friar," the Marine said in a rough voice. "And more are moving up from the city. Hundreds more. Where they're coming from is a mystery."

"I guess the attacks of the last two nights were merely rehearsals, ways of probing our reactions and our defenses."

Loumis nodded once.

"Or perhaps more like recons in force than rehearsals, but the result is the same. They know more about us than we about them. The true them."

Haakon scoffed. "The wounded in our infirmary and the lingering smell of the fires they set still stand proof of their intentions and ferocity. They mean to destroy us."

"Without a doubt. And they've now pinpointed our exact dispositions, the range of our weapons, and how many bodies it takes to overwhelm my Marines in any given section of the defensive perimeter." He shook his bare head in despair. "But at what cost to them. How can so many offer up their lives against modern power weapons and trained Marines and come back for more?""

A sob escaped Verica's throat as she stepped away from Loumis and leaned against a stone wall.

"They decided we're the sky demons of their legends, Cord, no different from those who murdered their ancestors and destroyed their golden paradise. And we proved them right by killing hundreds in short order, even though it was self-defense against their mindless rage."

The Marine let out a snort. "If the histories are accurate, Celeste was far from a paradise for most people."

She shrugged with the weariness of someone who'd accepted her mortality.

"Be that as it may. Once their priests decided we were anathema, destroying us became a religious duty. If you haven't noticed, they hold life cheaply around here. Appeasing their gods is worth every sacrifice." Verica let out a long sigh. "We were wrong to set up our mission here without doing any sort of preliminary outreach. But there's no use complaining about it now. What are our chances of repelling the next assault, Cord?"

"Ammunition stocks are dwindling. Some will get through if they pour enough bodies at our walls, and although our armor is proof against their spears and arrows, a Marine beset by eight or nine crazed fighters will go down. It would be different if we'd brought augmented battle suits, but HQ thought we wouldn't need them, so we didn't. In other words, I'm afraid it's not looking good, Sister."

"There's no way out?" Haakon asked, eyes roaming over the walled-in abbey grounds, where containers dropped from orbit filled most open spaces. Many held the stores vital to help rebuild a failed civilization. Others formed a small field hospital, a kitchen with refrigeration, something unknown on Celeste for over two hundred years, and barracks for Brethren and their protectors.

The Marine gave him a listless shrug.

"Where would we go? It's dense forest around the old abbey fields. Except for the one headed into the city, the roads are gone, overgrown like most of Angelique other than the underground networks where the locals live. That leaves the Harmonie River. But to get there means passing through countryside held by thousands of crazed natives, and they'll cut us to pieces before we even make it halfway down the hillside. And once on the river, then what? No, I'm sorry, Friar, but this is it. We either repel them and pray *Caladrius* returns before they finish the job or prepare to join the Infinite Void."

No one spoke for almost a minute while the drums sounded their death knell, stroke upon stroke.

"When?" Verica finally asked.

"When will they attack?" Loumis stared out the north-facing window where a black curtain was blotting out the stars. "Not for a few hours. They may be savages, but the Angeliquans can read the sky as well as we can. They'll wait until the coming storm crashes on this benighted land. Or at least until there is no more starlight to help us see them."

"But doesn't your night vision gear work even if there's nothing but total darkness?"

"Yes, but your Brethren aren't so equipped, and they're part of our defensive array, if only as ammunition carriers and medics. The few carrying our spare long arms won't be able to aim at anything until the savages are on top of them."

Verica raised her hands to her temples. "If only those damned drums would stop."

"They won't, Sister. Psychological warfare. Even the most primitive societies understand the efficacy of driving their enemies mad before striking." Loumis turned his eyes back on the encroaching cloud front. "I wonder whether your Old Order cousins faced this sort of problem on worlds Lyonesse recolonized."

"Certainly not on Hatshepsut, but the ones staying with us have been less than forthcoming about their experiences with missions to other fallen worlds."

The Marine let out a bitter bark of laughter.

"If I were a prisoner, I wouldn't humor my captors with stories about my nation's exploits. Especially if we faced failures."

"Such as what we're now facing," the friar said softly.

"Isn't despair a sin?"

"Being clear-eyed about our situation isn't despair, Cord. If we're destined for the Infinite Void on this night, we'd best prepare ourselves to meet the Almighty. Will your troopers welcome a service before the last stars vanish?"

Loumis nodded.

"If you can make it two services, each of them short. I'd rather leave half my Marines standing to at all times. The natives might strike earlier than I figure if one of their priest-commanders gets a sudden urge to spill blood. None of us want to die, but if that's our fate, we'll make each death count so they never forget the cost of attacking Wyvern Hegemony Marines. In any case, I've prepared a cache for our war diary and records. Once action is imminent, we will trigger the container's beacon and bury it. When *Caladrius* returns, they can retrieve it and figure out what happened. That way the next mission won't make our mistakes, the biggest of which was being friendly with what we learned too late were irredeemable remnants who put on sly smiles while they sized us up."

Verica turned a sad smile on the Marine. "And when will *Caladrius* return, do you think?"

"In truth, Sister, it won't be for weeks, if not months. They'll be sniffing every wormhole in the neighboring systems to rebuild our navigation maps."

Another sigh. "This is what it feels like when hubris meets nemesis, I suppose."

"Sister?"

"We landed on Celeste bursting with pride in our superiority, advanced technology, and knowledge. But we didn't bring wisdom and humility, two qualities that might have tempered our zeal. Instead, we settled in the ruins of the star system's principal abbey, near the largest concentration of natives, and immediately started work without understanding who or what we faced. We wanted Celeste for the Hegemony as fast as possible. But Celeste isn't Santa Theresa, which suffered less during the Great Scouring, and whose people still retained generational memories of the past instead of legends blaming sky demons for their ancestors' expulsion from paradise. Now, that pride faces its downfall. I hope whoever comes after us will heed the lessons we learned."

A gust of wind laden with the promise of a monsoon-like downpour swept over the old abbey and made the shadows around it dance like demons from Angeliquan lore. Except those shadows hid humans, albeit of a branch unrecognizable even to the Order of the Void Reborn Brethren, who understood history better than most. If Friar Haakon wasn't facing his imminent demise, he might have pitied them for their brutishness and ignorance and prayed for their salvation. But at the moment, he was entirely preoccupied with his own salvation, that of the other thirty-nine monastics and the one hundred Marines who were both their protectors and field engineers.

He should have seen the peril coming, but his zeal blinded him to the truth that they were unwanted, although the natives coveted the items they brought. None of his Brethren were trained in anthropology or any other discipline that might have given them insight into the Angeliquans' strange, twisted minds. And now, they would pay for his mistakes. May the Almighty forgive him.

"I should give you a copy of my diary and our logbook." Haakon turned toward Loumis. "After I make one more entry."

"If you would, Friar. And the services?"

"In fifteen minutes."

"We'll assemble in the chapter house." Loumis vanished into the night, his footsteps silent on the stone stairs.

When he reached the bottom, his first sergeant materialized out of nowhere, the soft rumble of his voice going no further than Loumis' ears. "Those damned buggers are multiplying, sir. Never seen the like before. We can pick up over nine hundred of them by now, but they're staying well within the tree line. What I wouldn't give for a mortar platoon right now. Or a frigate in orbit with precision kinetic rods."

"You and me both. The Brethren will conduct services in fifteen minutes in the chapter house, one half of the company at a time."

"So we can make our peace with the Almighty, eh?" Loumis could picture the older man's ferocious frown. "Just as well. It doesn't matter what weapons we have because it won't be enough with ten to one odds. Not with our depleted ammo stocks. And at this rate, it'll be more like fifteen or twenty to one when they finally launch. They'll wait until the wee hours when the heavens pour warm piss in solid curtains."

"Aye. After the services, arm all booby traps."

"Already done, Skipper. I can read the omens as well as you, and so can everyone else. The chapter house in fifteen it is."

Like every one of the abbey's main buildings, the chapter house had no roof, doors, or windows. However, it provided a clear space where believers could assemble, and there was no shortage of them in Loumis' unit. He didn't consider himself a man of faith but would attend with his Marines if only to cover all possibilities should he die in battle this night.

As Haakon and Verica officiated under a rapidly blackening sky, the drums provided a somber counterpoint to the Brethren's plainchant, and Loumis wondered whether the Angeliquans could hear them. And if so, what they made of it. Loumis, along with most of his Marines, had come to see them as belonging to a different human lineage than Wyvern Hegemony citizens. Perhaps another species altogether. Even though only little more than two centuries had passed since their ancestors were imperial subjects, just like his, living parallel lives under the same banner, albeit under different suns.

Once the second service concluded, Loumis and his first sergeant walked the perimeter, speaking with each Marine in turn and those of the Brethren who'd chosen to hoist a plasma rifle even though they had no armor, helmet, or night vision gear. All sounded grim but determined to sell their lives dearly. Perhaps enough casualties might make the Angeliquans withdraw and abandon their project of wiping out the sky demons. But those who ventured the thought didn't sound convinced it was a realistic outcome.

At around oh-two-hundred, the first fat, greasy drops of rain landed on Marines and Brethren alike. Moments later, lightning split the sky asunder, followed by a roll of thunder that might well have heralded the end of all things. Then, the heavens opened up, releasing a deluge that would have drowned someone looking upward with an open mouth.

Each flash of lightning showed nothing more than waving grasses around the abbey grounds, although sensors could make out dense masses of human life in the woods no more than a hundred meters from the waiting Marines. Loumis desperately wanted to open fire with his automatic weapons and slice through the ranks before they took a single step toward the abbey. But he realized that would precipitate an all-out assault, and a tiny part of him still hoped the natives would stop at mere intimidation tactics.

Just before oh-three hundred, the rain let up as the storm front passed, and without warning, one drum shifted from a steady rhythm to a frantic staccato. The rest followed seconds later, and a wave of shadowy figures emerged from the tree line around the abbey. Pinpricks of flickering light appeared, signaling that the first wave of Angeliquans was lighting arrows, atlatl darts, and spears. They began moving toward the perimeter, bouncing up and down as the natives ran. Loumis, on the wall, along with every other Marine capable of handling a weapon, lit up the company frequency.

"F Company, take aim." He inhaled deeply as he settled his rifle's crosshairs on a silhouette holding a spark and released half of his breath. "FIRE."

As the Angeliquan sparks rose into the sky, more than a hundred plasma rounds, each of them whiter and deadlier, streamed out, their trajectories utterly flat. As they struck, screams of pain erupted, but those were drowned out by a sudden release of war cries as fire arrows, and flaming darts plunged on the abbey. After the two previous assaults, nothing flammable remained out in the open. Still, the burning missiles negated the Marines' night vision advantage and lit them up from behind as they struck ground softened by the downpour.

Each volley by the defenders dropped over a hundred attackers. But the human wave kept coming, urged on by frantic drumbeats and the loud yelps of people driven over the edge of reason into a form of mass insanity that negated individual will and survival instincts.

Another flight of missiles rose into the air while Marines kept shooting until their weapons ran dry. Working in pairs, one firing, the other reloading, they swapped out power packs and magazines and resumed their volleys, but the human wave kept moving forward, stepping over its dead and wounded as if they were minor obstacles.

Then, the first ranks reached the abbey's stone walls, and despite the merciless fire from Marines and Void Reborn shooters who couldn't miss at this range, the Angeliquans poured over the top. They carried long knives, axes, machetes, and other implements, many of them donated by the mission over the previous weeks, and swung them wildly as they sought targets for their rage.

Even as Loumis ordered the defenders to withdraw to the central cluster of buildings, the first of them were swallowed by a human carpet. Hands tore off helmets and bits of armor while others seized weapons and still more bashed heads in with savage glee. Primitive the Angeliquans might be, but within moments, they were firing back wildly at the retreating Marines and Brethren with captured rifles and carbines even while many died under what was now an endless crackling of plasma fire.

In short order, the abbey's forecourt, garden, and other open spaces teemed with ululating Angeliquans in a press of bodies so dense those shot and killed by the defenders remained upright, held in place by their still-living comrades.

Inexorably, they pushed the defenders back, overwhelming and killing them one after the other by sheer numbers. When the field hospital fell into their hands, they massacred both patients and medical staff in an orgy of blood and gore that presaged the mission's end.

Loumis and his first sergeant, holding the door to the abbey's main administrative building with a handful of survivors, finally succumbed. But they would suffer one final indignity as recognized leaders of the troopers who'd killed so many natives. Even while the attackers hunted down the last living Marines, their priests decapitated F Company's commanding officer and first sergeant and raised the heads on spear tips to victorious howls.

In the old bell tower, Haakon and Verica, along with a handful of surviving Brethren, attempted to barricade the stairs as they retched at the overpowering stink of blood and voided bowels wafting through the open windows. All were praying loudly as they fought to keep a shred of sanity in the face of imminent death.

When Haakon glanced out to see Loumis and the first sergeant's heads on pikes, he realized his and Verica's end would be equally undignified — both were also well known by the Angeliquans as leaders of the mission, and now, to their priests, as top sky demons.

The barricade held a few minutes before it crumbled and blood-smeared, grinning natives brandishing machetes climbed up the stairs, followed by a priest who wore a carved wooden mask and a necklace made with what Haakon recognized, in a last burst of clarity, as human teeth. Then, they fell on the surviving Brethren and bundled them into the chapter house where more priests waited, surrounded by warriors who seemed preternaturally calm compared to their fellows capering outside.

The priests pointed at Haakon and Verica, and a half dozen warriors descended on them, removed their clothes, and tied them to stone pillars that once held up the chapter house's roof. At a further signal from the priests, they stripped the four other surviving Brethren as well and hogtied them as the warriors carrying the heads of Loumis and his first sergeant entered.

"Behold what we do to sky demons who curse our lands," one of the priests intoned in heavily accented Anglic. He pointed toward the men and women staring up at him with terror in their eyes. "They took away what was ours and destroyed the paradise of our ancestors. For that, they must pay by never being able to meet the father demon again as entire beings. It is the punishment decreed by our gods."

"Praise be to them," the assembled Angeliquans replied.

"Let the punishment begin."

Two warriors fell on the first of the hogtied Brethren and methodically removed her toes and fingers one by one while the sister, a gentle and devout woman who'd believed in the natives' innate goodness until the very end, screamed in pain before she lost consciousness. They kept amputating her limbs as her blood poured out on the ancient flagstones. Verica suddenly gasped, and Haakon understood she'd just felt the sister's soul leave her body to merge with the Infinite Void.

The priest who seemed to be in charge gave her a hard look, then pointed at one of the two surviving friars. He also suffered atrociously as the warriors dismembered him and died much like the sister. The remaining Brethren soon followed, and the head priest walked to where Haakon and Verica stood, transfixed with horror.

"For you, the leaders of the sky demons, we will perform a special exorcism."

He gestured to one side, where Angeliquans, arms loaded with firewood taken from the mission's supplies, were streaming through the other door. Under the priest's direction, they placed a ring of split logs around Haakon and Verica, created a pile of kindling between them, then stepped back and waited. The remaining priests approached, and an intricate ritual ensued as they took bits of kindling one by one and primed the firewood rings until the pile was gone.

To the relief of what little sanity still remained in Haakon's mind, he and Verica remained silent even though they could see the horrible fate awaiting them. Instead, they prayed softly, repeating the universal mantra, their souls reaching out to the Almighty, asking for a final bit of strength.

After a while, all but the head priest stepped back. One of the warriors produced a lit arrow and reverently handed it to the priest. He, in turn, touched it to the kindling at Haakon's feet and then at Verica's.

As the flames reached up into the night sky, the surviving Angeliquans celebrated their victory over those who'd come to desecrate the soil of their ancestors a second time. But by then, Haakon and Verica had merged with the Infinite Void after their souls left their tormented bodies, unable to withstand the excruciating pain.

—2—

Wyvern Hegemony Ship Caladrius
Celeste System

"Good morning, Skipper."

Captain Newton Giambo, *Caladrius*' commanding officer, looked up from his breakfast — oatmeal with dried fruit — and smiled at his first officer, Commander Evan Kang, as the latter placed his tray on the table and took a chair across from him.

"Good morning, Evan. Everything is well?"

The wiry, dark-haired man with hooded brown eyes deeply set in a craggy face nodded.

"She came through the wormhole transit with nothing knocked loose. I don't know about you," Kang took a hearty gulp of coffee, "but I'm glad we're back in Hegemony space after weeks of probing dead ends."

"If you consider this system part of the Hegemony." Giambo spooned up a mouthful of oatmeal. "But yeah, I'm not unhappy that we're headed home. After making a little dogleg to check up on the Celeste Mission."

"That'll prolong the trip by a day or two." Kang took a bite of his toast, eyes on Giambo.

"What's another twenty-four to forty-eight hours? Or do you have a hot date waiting for you back home?"

"Me? A date? Perish the thought. I wouldn't know what to do in polite company, considering I'm spending most of my time in space. Ah, the life of a naval officer conducting surveys on behalf of the Colonial Service. There's nothing quite like it." Another gulp of coffee. "At least we ride the big honking starships with antimatter fuel reservoirs to make heroic interstellar crossings like no one else in this part of the galaxy since time immemorial."

Giambo snorted.

"Then you'll suffer from ship envy once we dock. *Alkonost* should be done with her post-refit space trials by now and re-entering service. She's bigger than our *Caladrius* by at least ten thousand tons, with correspondingly greater autonomy. Last I heard just before we left, Derwent Alexander is getting her or should be in command by now. You met him?"

"Yep. Good man. A few years ahead of me at the Academy, lucky dog." Kang grinned at his captain. "*Alkonost* is the first of a new class, and the Almighty willing, I'll command one of her sisters once you write up my next performance rating. There are at least three more in the yards who still don't have a crew or captain. Amazing how far we've come in the two and a half years since President Mandus renewed the Oath of Reunification."

Giambo took a sip of tea and nodded. "We're only starting the expansion, so don't worry about your future prospects. I'll be finalizing the department head ratings before we arrive. I expect we'll be in port long enough for the career manglers at HQ to put through reassignments and promotions as they believe fit. You've been my first officer for three years, which means this is likely our last cruise together since you're in the zone, and the rating I'm giving you will put you over the quality control line for captains."

"Why, thank you kindly, sir."

"You earned it, Evan." Giambo wolfed down the rest of his oatmeal and drained his tea mug.

"Any career prospects once the admiral signs your performance rating? It's been a good cruise."

"A star on my collar?" He snorted with amusement. "Not just yet, but I'll probably get a task force with *Caladrius* as the lead ship until she goes into refit." He stood. "I'll be in my day cabin. Once everyone finishes eating, we can go FTL for Celeste, check on the mission and call this one over, but for the return wormhole transits."

"Roger that. Still, it's a shame we didn't find Pacifica."

"Sure. But we're the first to find hard evidence wormholes that have been stable for more centuries than we know can suddenly shift. So at least there's that. And we didn't run across any Lyonesse ships in the bargain. The daily reports, most of which are yours, beckon. Talk to you later."

Moments after Giambo settled behind the desk in his day cabin, which sat halfway between the bridge and the combat information center, his communicator chimed softly for attention.

"Captain here."

"Officer of the watch, sir. Course laid in for Celeste, all systems green. We can go FTL whenever you give the word."

"Execute."

"Aye, aye, sir."

Moments later, the warning klaxon sounded, and Giambo braced himself for the mercifully brief explosion of nausea that accompanied every transition between sublight and hyperspace. Once his stomach settled, he drew a cup of tea from the samovar sitting on a sideboard and read the daily reports, his soul at peace with the universe.

Sailing one of the Hegemony's upgraded cruisers through the wormhole network on what Archimandrite Bolack had blessed as a Holy Mission — what could be better for a professional Navy officer? Perhaps commanding an entire squadron or battle group as a rear admiral. That might happen if the fleet kept expanding at a breakneck speed. When President Mandus opened the floodgates, she'd created the biggest boom in the Hegemony's history.

***

"No answer from the abbey, sir," *Caladrius*' signals chief reported when Giambo entered the CIC shortly after they dropped out of FTL at Celeste's hyperlimit. "It's morning there, so someone should be awake and listening."

Giambo dropped into his command chair and stared at the image of the planet on the primary display. "Keep trying. Maybe they're experiencing atmospheric interference."

"Aye, sir."

The minutes ticked by while Giambo scanned the duty log, and the signals chief did what he could to raise the abbey on the standard Hegemony radio frequencies.

Finally, he turned to face Giambo. "No luck, sir. I can't even pick up a carrier wave. The abbey isn't emitting, let alone transmitting."

"Thanks, Chief. Sensors, scan the abbey and its surroundings and put up a visual."

The duty combat systems officer nodded once. "Aye, aye, sir." Then he and the sensor chief busied themselves. After a bit, the former turned around.

"Um, sir."

Giambo looked up from his chair's virtual display. "Go ahead."

"Sensors aren't picking up any life signs in or around the abbey, although there are plenty at the site of the former capital, Angelique."

Giambo made a noncommittal face. "Maybe the entire complement is in town for festivities."

"Perhaps, sir. But we took a baseline of Angelique's population before leaving. There are over a thousand fewer life signs in and around the city. Almost half the people seem to have simply vanished. And there's no evidence of electronic activity or functioning power sources at the abbey either."

Caladrius' captain sat back with a thoughtful expression, eyes on the planet's image, as a sense of deep unease wormed its way through his gut.

"Visuals?"

"Coming right up, sir."

The planet faded out, replaced by an aerial view of the Angelique Abbey's ruins, clear enough and close enough to show hundreds and hundreds of decomposing bodies strewn across the fields and within the walls, like carpets of rotting flesh. The combat systems officer let out a soft grunt of disgust.

Giambo, not a squeamish man at the worst of times, felt his stomach lurch as he unconsciously tallied up the number of dead. Many within the abbey precinct were naked or stripped to what seemed modern underclothes, while most of the bodies were clad in rough homespun rags. He immediately understood the former were the remains of mission personnel, meaning the locals now had Hegemony Marine Corps armor, weapons, and equipment, along with whatever they'd looted. Because they'd surely taken everything that wasn't welded in place, judging by the wide-open container doors.

"I don't think any of our people remain alive, sir," the sensor chief said in a quasi-whisper. "What the hell happened?"

"Sir." The signals chief raised his hand. "I'm picking up something — a faint log buoy beacon, or whatever the ground pounders call their version. It's coming from the abbey precinct."

"Thank you." Giambo rubbed his square chin, dark eyes fixed on the image of innumerable dead where they'd last seen a thriving mission protected by a company of the finest fighting troops in the known galaxy.

"How did those primitives overrun an entire Colonial Marine company?" Commander Kang's hologram at Giambo's elbow asked. As per standard operating procedures, he occupied the bridge command chair when the captain was in the CIC. "Those troopers are among the best the Corps offers."

The latter scoffed. "By disregarding casualties and sending wave after human wave against them. The better question is why they did so? And for an answer, we'll need to recover that log buoy, Evan. Have the second officer organize a large and well-armed landing party. Fully pressurized armor. I don't want them catching anything nasty from that killing field. Their orders are to find the beacon, identify our dead, and bury them. A mass grave will do under the circumstances, so they may bring all necessary tools and explosives to quickly make a large enough pit. Any natives come near, they may open fire in self-defense. Better more of them rotting in that field than another Hegemony citizen."

"Will do, sir."

Lieutenant Commander Jana Venkov, *Caladrius*' second officer, was a thorough veteran who'd been commissioned from the rank of chief petty officer third class. She took every precaution as she prepared her fifty-strong landing party and briefed them on the cruiser's hangar deck, near the armed shuttles that would fly them to the surface. The spacers, bosun's mates with plenty of experience, listened to her in grim silence as she outlined the situation, aided by visuals of the abbey projected on the hangar's large traffic control screen.

One of them, a grizzled petty officer first class, raised his hand when Venkov opened the deck for questions.

"How about the skipper drop a few rods on Angelique to make sure the locals can't get excited again and try us on while we're running the burial party? Might not do much for what's left of civilization on this crappy ball of rock, but it would sure make me feel better."

The other landing party members greeted his suggestion with widespread, albeit silent, approval.

"As satisfying as it might be," she replied, "we're not quite to that point yet, especially since we don't understand what happened. But if the CIC detects a threat against us, you can be sure the captain will have our backs. And I'll keep two shuttles in the air flying cover while we're working. They can head off any enemy column coming at us. Swamping Marines with sheer numbers is one thing, but standing against a couple of thirty-millimeter plasma calliopes at close range? We'll be okay, PO. Anything else?"

When no one spoke up, Venkov clapped her hands once.

"Put your suits on, draw your personal weapons, and be back here in thirty minutes. Dismissed."

At the appointed time, four of *Caladrius*' shuttles nosed through the force field, keeping the hangar pressurized while the space doors were open and began a spiral descent. Two carried the landing party's fifty spacers, while the other two were rigged as gunships and would provide top cover. The latter had enough ammunition to flatten what was left of Angelique and everyone living in the ruined city's underground network.

As per the second officer's flight plan, the shuttles came down a hundred kilometers north of Angelique and covered the remaining distance flying nap of the earth so the natives wouldn't see them arrive and mount an encore. Or so she hoped.

Finding one or two clear spots to land proved more difficult than expected. Decomposing bodies, all showing signs of animal predation, covered most of the open area between the tree line and the abbey walls. The pilots eventually settled near the forest and asked permission to lift the moment they'd disgorged their passengers for fear of ambush by the natives. Not that buttoned-up shuttles had anything to fear, but things could still turn messy.

The first of the bosun's mates to climb out retched at a closeup view of the corpses. Unfortunately, his radio was on, and the entire landing party heard him curse as he struggled to keep his breakfast. Several more retched in sympathy while their chiefs and petty officers urged them on.

A section tasked with finding a suitable place for a mass grave moved off to one side, carrying excavation gear. The remainder, who towed antigrav stretchers, stepped over and around the piles of remains, which proved not a little unnerving. But they soon reached the abbey, where a dozen spread out to stand guard while the rest entered via the main gate, broken open by native axes, the same given to them by the mission.

Inside the walls, they found their first dead Marines, men whose helmetless heads had been bashed in with such ferocity their skulls seemed flattened. One of the petty officers assigned as registrar scanned the Marine's ID implant and nodded when the data appeared on his sensor screen.

Two bosun's mates lifted the body and placed it on the nearest stretcher at his unvoiced command. Then they retraced their steps out of the abbey compound before heading to where the grave diggers had set up their excavation gear and were busily opening a deep trench a few meters from where the forest began.

"Shit." The raspy voice of *Caladrius*' bosun came over the radio. "Commander, you need to see this. I'm in what they call the chapter house, behind the building with the bell tower."

Venkov made her way through the piles of corpses and found the entryway where a spacer, visibly green behind his helmet visor, waved at her.

"In here."

She took one step over the threshold and froze as her eyes found what had caused the chief to swear. An unknown number of dismembered corpses were strewn across the flagstone-covered floor, each bit sitting in a congealed dark red puddle. After repressing a brief surge of nausea, she counted the number of heads and came up with four.

The chief reluctantly pulled out his sensor, approached the segments that appeared to be lopped off arms, and scanned for ID implants.

"Brethren, sir." Then, he stepped around the dried blood stains and approached the blackened skeletons lying in a heap of disjointed bones at the foot of two adjoining pillars, sensor pointed at the remains. "Friar Haakon and Sister Verica — the mission's leaders. Looks like the natives burned them to death. Gonna be a bitch to collect these remains for burial."

"Find us something we can use as shrouds, and we'll do it, you and I, Chief."

"Roger that, sir."

The chief returned with an empty antigrav stretcher, and all they could do was load the six sets of remains on, bit by bit. The resulting pile struck the second officer as utterly obscene. Her anger at the natives, which had been growing since they landed, reached a crescendo just as one of the shuttles flying top cover reported a column of approximately a hundred and fifty locals coming up the road at double time. Three scarecrows wearing masks and feathers led them, and many wore scavenged Marine armor. Some even brandished power weapons.

"Mow them down," Venkov ordered through clenched teeth. "Do it now before they get any further. Fucking animals."

"Aye, aye, sir. One strafing run apiece should do it."

She looked up at the shuttles just as they broke out of their figure-eight loop and dropped to strafe the road at as shallow an angle as possible to make every round count double or triple, if not more. Then, they vanished from sight as they headed downhill to meet the enemy column. The same shuttle pilot voice came through her helmet speakers a few minutes later.

"Done. A hundred and fifty crispy critters littering the road."

"Good."

Ordering the death of the natives didn't make Venkov feel any better, but it bled off much of the anger that had been building.

After checking to make sure the identification and burial process was working smoothly, she and the chief helped move bodies to the mass grave one after the other until they'd counted one hundred and forty — the mission's entire complement. That done, she led a party to dig up the buried log buoy, a small cylinder no larger than an adult's forearm, and assembled her people by the mass grave for a quick yet solemn service before they filled in the trench.

A long sweep with lasers fused the top layer of soil so animals, both of the two and four-legged variety, couldn't dig and commit further desecration. Belatedly, Venkov wished she'd thought of bringing or building a memorial marker, but the grave's coordinates would have to suffice.

The transport shuttles landed at her orders, and the spacers, weary beyond belief, trudged aboard silently, stowing their antigrav stretchers. Along with the pressure suits, the latter needed thorough decontamination once they were in *Caladrius*, something she'd made sure the first officer would organize before their return.

No one spoke during the flight back to the cruiser.

***

"The natives must have really hated our people, sir," Venkov said around a mouthful of her sandwich. "The Marines and Brethren were either mutilated before death or their bodies desecrated afterward. My bet is on the former."

"The CIC is going through the log right now, so we should know more shortly."

Giambo and Venkov were alone in the wardroom, though the members of her landing party, or at least many of them would be eating a late lunch in their own messes. The moment she came through decontamination, Venkov had felt ravenous, and Giambo, never a man to stand on senseless protocol, joined her in the wardroom so she could give him a verbal report while eating.

He and the rest of the CIC crew had watched most of the operation unfold via helmet and shuttle video pickups, but they only gave a superficial impression of the reality on the ground.

"I'd be happier if we simply wiped the entire site off the planet's surface with a few rods. The evil that happened there will never dissipate. I'm pretty sure most of us sensed it even through our suits."

Giambo grimaced.

"That's not something we can do lightly. The Void Reborn owns the abbey and the surroundings, not to mention it's an archeological artifact of the imperial era."

She gave him a grim smile.

"Screw archeology, Skipper. I don't understand what happened to the people down there, but they don't belong to the same humanity as you and I. If I had my druthers, I'd bomb Angelique out of existence."

Giambo let out an indelicate snort. "That I certainly cannot do."

"Will I be in trouble for ordering a strike on that enemy column coming up the hill before they openly demonstrated hostile intent?"

He shook his head.

"No. As far as I'm concerned, that was per our standard rules of engagement covering force protection. After all, we saw what they did to our fellow Hegemony citizens, as evidenced by the plundered military equipment they carried."

"Boo-yah, Skipper." Venkov suddenly released a massive yawn as the last of the morning's adrenaline vanished. "Burial details sure take it out of you."

"Finish your after-action report and hit the rack. You're relieved of watchkeeping until tomorrow. Evan will cover your department for the rest of the day."

"Thank you, Evan."

"We'll be breaking out of orbit shortly anyhow. There's nothing left to do here." Giambo finished his tea and stood. "Well done, Jana. That'll go on your performance rating along with the rest."

As he walked along the passageway to his day cabin, Commander Kang, on his way to the bridge, intercepted him.

"I've been wondering. Does the mission's annihilation mean the Celeste system slipped back into the badlands, beyond the Hegemony's sphere? Or were we never really its masters?" He gave his captain a strange look.

"Why do you ask?"

"Watching the video feed from Jana's landing party this morning, I was reminded of an adage — those who can destroy you, own what you desire."

"You think our way of initiating reunification with Celeste was wrong?" Giambo stopped at the door to his day cabin.

"The Colonial Service certainly didn't place the mission in the right spot to ensure success. If you ask the shades of the dead Brethren, I'm sure they'll recommend a more thorough reconnaissance the next time. Less haste, more thought."

—3—

New Draconis
Wyvern System

"Ah, Crevan, Ardrix, please come in and sit." Admiral Johannes Godfrey, Commander-in-Chief, Colonial Service, waved Brigadier General Torma, the Colonial Service's Inspector General, and its Leading Void Sister to their usual chairs around the conference table.

Godfrey, a distinguished-looking man in his late sixties with thick, white hair and intelligent eyes, wearing a Navy blue uniform with four stars on his collar, didn't give them his usual welcoming smile. Torma, as tall as Godfrey, but dark, brooding, and in Commission for State Security black, glanced at Ardrix with a cocked eyebrow.

The latter, a pale, ageless redhead in a Void Reborn monastic's flowing dark robes, gave him a faint shrug. She was one of the few Void Reborn Sisters whose talent was so developed she could sense another's emotions, though not actually read their thoughts. But, she would never dare try with her Colonial Service colleagues, let alone the admiral.

The conference room was on the second floor of the Colonial Service Headquarters building, previously known as the Blue Annex, on the grounds of the Wyvern Palace, home to the Hegemony's President. It was a temporary arrangement while the government built a new HQ. But President Mandus enjoyed having her Colonial Service C-in-C close at hand as she plotted the Hegemony's expansion, so the mysterious and fast-growing Republic of Lyonesse did not catch them flatfooted.

"I'm waiting for the President, Chancellor Conteh, and Archimandrite Bolack to join the conference call. Admiral Benes and General Sarkis are already in attendance."

After taking their seats, Torma and Ardrix looked up at the primary display opposite Godfrey's chair and inclined their heads politely at the Chiefs of Naval Operations and Ground Forces. The latter returned their greeting in the same fashion. Moments later, Commodore Saleh, Godfrey's chief of staff, entered and sat on the admiral's right.

"So, I hear the news isn't good," Sarkis said to no one in particular.

Godfrey shook his head. "No, it isn't. Ah. Here we go."

Three faces, those of the Hegemony's Executive Committee, joined those already visible on the primary display. In the center a lean, platinum-haired woman in her seventies whose icy demeanor had become legendary — President Vigdis Mandus, the Wyvern Hegemony's head of state. To her right, a heavy-set, bald man with a salt and pepper beard, dark hooded eyes, heavy eyebrows, and a large, flattened nose — Archimandrite Bolack, who headed the Order of the Void Reborn. And finally, to her left, Chancellor Elrod Conteh, the Hegemony's head of government, a bland-faced, dark-haired man in his late sixties whose cool patrician features hid a biting sense of humor and a sharp intellect.

"Good morning, everyone," Mandus said without preamble. "I understand the Colonial Service received dire news concerning the Celeste Mission."

Godfrey inclined his head.

"Yes, Madame President. A report from the survey cruiser *Caladrius* arrived an hour ago. Her captain — Newton Giambo, a solid officer by the way, ready for his first star — sent it the moment his ship reached the Santa Theresa system and came within range of its subspace relay. In short, the Celestans massacred the entire mission and its Marine complement and looted everything they could carry. All of our people suffered mutilation, likely while they were still alive.

"They hacked four Brethren into small pieces, and burned the leaders, Friar Haakon and Sister Verica, alive. Captain Giambo sent a landing party to retrieve a log buoy the mission hid just before the final assault and bury our dead. A copy accompanied his report — you'll receive it momentarily. As the burial party was working, almost two hundred natives charged up toward the abbey from Angelique, Celeste's former capital, several wearing captured armor and carrying captured weapons. The shuttles flying top cover neutralized them permanently and extracted the landing party without suffering casualties."

"My Lord," Bolack said in a whisper. "Of all the possible bad news, I wasn't expecting this. The Brethren we sent to Celeste were the flower of our abbeys and priories."

"And the Marines were among the best," General Sarkis added. "Damn. I personally approved Cord Loumis' appointment as CO of the Celeste garrison. He was slated for promotion to major once his tour ended. What the hell happened?"

"We don't know yet," Godfrey replied. "I barely had a chance to go through the recovered logs and quickly scan *Caladrius*' visuals before calling this meeting. Once we finish here, I'll ask General Torma and Sister Ardrix to analyze the data and see if they can reconstruct the events that led to this catastrophe. In any case, I'm declaring Celeste off-limits to Hegemony citizens. The Navy may still transit the system, but no one shall land on the surface until further notice."

"A good precaution, certainly," Chancellor Conteh said, "but we must keep ownership of Celeste, which means landing a new mission somewhere else. Perhaps one with a battalion of Colonial Marines rather than just a single company."

Godfrey nodded. "Of course, Chancellor. And we will do so within the next few months. *Caladrius* also reported that they didn't find Pacifica. One of the wormholes leading to it shifted at some point in the last two centuries and now ends in a red dwarf system, which *Caladrius* tentatively identified as ISC00045, also known as Barnard's Star. Its only planet was never colonized, and our forebears rarely visited the system even at the height of the imperial era. But, if nothing else, we now know formerly stable wormholes can shift."

Admiral Benes let out a grunt. "You're full of good news this morning, Johannes, aren't you? That'll make remapping this part of the galaxy much more exciting for survey ships. Good thing they'll be carrying enough antimatter fuel to come home the long way around."

Godfrey grimaced at Benes. "Be glad that was it, Sandor. Once we finish analyzing the logs, you'll receive a full report. Anything you'd like to add, Madame President?"

Mandus shook her head. "No. Let's not make this public for now."

"I wasn't intending on it." Godfrey turned his eyes on Bolack. "How about you, sir?"

"Perhaps Sister Ardrix should speak with the Old Order Brethren and see if they experienced something similar. They have been helpful on a few matters since they settled in the New Draconis Abbey and began enjoying the same freedoms as my flock."

Godfrey glanced at Ardrix, who said, "I shall do so once we finish with the logs."

"Chancellor?"

"I'll withhold my comments until we know more, but perhaps we didn't spend enough time making sure the Celestans in Angelique were the sort who'd welcome a mission. Maybe we might recall the ancient adage that time spent in reconnaissance is seldom wasted."

"True," General Sarkis replied. "But sadly, many a good reconnaissance is wasted by commanders who decide the facts don't meet their expectations. Not that anyone in the present company would do so."

"Any last comments or questions?" Godfrey looked from the display to his three closest advisers around the table. "No? Then, with your permission, Madame President, I'll adjourn this meeting."

One by one, the faces on the display vanished until Godfrey was left with Torma, Ardrix, and Saleh.

"Alright. Let's find out what went wrong on Celeste, so when we send a new mission, it won't get massacred."

Only later did Crevan Torma realize no one had offered a prayer for the dead on Celeste, both Hegemony and native. He thought of mentioning it to Ardrix, then figured she might construe his words as criticism of Archimandrite Bolack and kept silent. But it left him wondering about the radical shift in the Hegemony leadership's way of thinking since President Mandus decreed they would abandon extreme isolationism for headlong expansion.

Not everyone was handling the abrupt reversal that well, not even in the armed forces. His colleagues in the Commission for State Security had seen an uptick in cases over the last two and a half years, citizens unhappy with change, fearful for their security, and in many cases, finding their sinecures under threat. Awaken, Citizens of the Hegemony! A grandiose slogan, but it wasn't to everyone's taste. Perhaps the existential change offered by the Celeste Mission struck the natives as the sort of overwhelming threat that could only be alleviated by ruthlessly erasing it.

***

By late afternoon, Torma had read the logs and reports at least three times, and he felt his eyes protesting. He stood, stretched, and wandered over to the tall office windows. As usual, during the monsoon season, a late afternoon rainstorm was brewing on the western horizon, the clouds low, black, and heavy with moisture picked up from the ocean as the system moved toward land. The coastal communities, several hundred kilometers away, had already received their due, and now it was New Draconis' turn.

After a bit, he wandered over to the open door connecting his and Ardrix's office. Sensing him before he even appeared, she'd turned away from her display and was waiting.

"What are your thoughts?" Torma asked without preamble. They'd worked together long enough by now that small talk was not only unnecessary but wasteful.

"We evidently chose the wrong surviving remnant to raise up."

Torma dropped into one of the chairs facing her desk. "Evident in hindsight, at least."

"It should have been so from the outset." Ardrix ran both hands through her thick hair and sighed. "Based on our initial survey of Celeste and its history during the late imperial era, I'm convinced the current population of Angelique descends from what were called residents back then, as opposed to what they termed citizens. Angelique was a massive city, founded over fifteen hundred years ago, and built both upwards and into the depths. But only a minority of its inhabitants, the citizens, enjoyed a prosperous life above the surface in gleaming towers surrounded by hanging gardens in the late imperial era.

"Some, the luckier among the residents, who lived in the shadows of those towers, served the high-born, yet more than half of the resident population lived in underground warrens, unemployed and, in many cases unemployable. They subsisted on what the ancient Romans called bread and circuses — a basic living allowance and endless entertainment. The more enterprising left Angelique to find a more fulfilling life in smaller cities or the countryside, but most stayed. And even with severe population control methods imposed on the residents, their numbers weren't dropping much by the time the Ruggero

Dynasty ascended the throne thanks to sabotage in part committed by citizens who used residents as a form of quasi-slave labor."

"Fascinating. I wasn't aware some imperial worlds had developed a form of serfdom."

Ardrix smiled at him.

"A few were always like that, even under the old Commonwealth. Celeste was one, along with many of what the ancients termed the Home Worlds, those colonized by Earth during the first great migration to the stars, such as Pacifica, the first extrasolar colony. Like most of Celeste's cities, Angelique was destroyed during the Great Scouring, which would have wiped out most citizens who lived above ground. But the ill-educated, low intelligence residents who lived underground would have survived in much greater numbers.

"Oh, most of them would have died in the following weeks or months because they'd never learned to feed themselves, but enough, the toughest and most adaptable, survived. Their numbers eventually expanded to what they could sustain with basic agriculture, hunting, and gathering. Yet because the survivors lacked education and awareness of politics, history, and galactic matters in general, legends must have arisen around the destruction of Angelique."

Torma nodded.

"Hence a tribe imbued with stories of mythical sky demons destroying paradise rather than the sort of preindustrial society like what we found on Santa Theresa. People who'd remained aware of the empire's civil war and collapse because their ancestors, survivors of the Great Scouring, kept history alive and rescued what they could."

"That is indeed my theory. If I am correct, we should find places on Celeste more receptive to a Void Mission. I would suggest looking not for large population centers — the mistake made in choosing Angelique — but for ones, be they ever so small, with evidence of established agriculture and basic manufacturing. Economies of scale are fine in many settings, but not, I'm afraid, in restoring civilization on fallen worlds."

"Quality over quantity. I agree. We're getting carried away with our zeal to expand before the Republic of Lyonesse comes knocking." He gave Ardrix an ironic grin. "Quite the effective bogeyman, that."

"Too effective. The Hegemony is making mistakes it cannot afford." She paused so she could study her friend and colleague. "This impetus to find Earth and claim it for the Hegemony is another bit of zealotry that worries me, Crevan. Yes, Earth was part of the imperial Wyvern Sector before the fall, but so were many other inhabited worlds, and we only occupy six at the moment, two precariously. Until Santa Theresa and Novaya Sibir become self-sustaining, we can hardly consider them fully integrated."

Torma made a face. "Speak with your Archimandrite. He's the one convinced the only way that old prophecy of his will come true is by reclaiming humanity's birthplace."

"You mean Sister Jessica's vision? *When both halves of that which was split asunder merge once more under a new, glorious Crown, humanity will fulfill its destiny in the Infinite Void.*" She gave him an amused look. "Yes. Some of my Brethren have debated whether humanity can only reunite on the world it sprang from. I consider it arrant nonsense, but I do not make policy."

"Neither do I." He climbed to his feet. "I think we can call it a day. Please include your theory in our analysis. If nothing else, it might ensure they take good care with the location of the replacement mission."

"Of course."

"Can I give you a ride back to the abbey?"

"Please. I don't relish taking public transport once the heavens open and soak us sinners." Ardrix swiveled her chair to look out the window as fat raindrops spattered against the Blue Annex. "Which it just has."

That evening, after the New Draconis Abbey's regular service, Ardrix sought out Sister Hermina. She, Friar Metrobius, and the other six Old Order Brethren were, at their request, occupying a separate dormitory wing where they could live by Lyonesse traditions. Moreover, despite no material differences in the liturgy, they worshiped in the small chapel and not with the rest of the abbey in the chapter house. Ardrix knew it was simply their way of ensuring no one forgot they were quasi-prisoners on Wyvern, taken from their mission and their people by the Hegemony's security forces, which had included Ardrix.

She found them in their small common room, reading or holding low-key discussions among themselves. A large representation of the Old Order's Void Orb, created by one of Hermina's Brethren, hung on one wall, while the Republic of Lyonesse's coat of arms, a double-headed Vanger's Condor — as Ardrix had discovered — hung on another.

As a mark of respect, Ardrix stopped at the threshold of the open door and bowed her head.

"May I impose on your time for a few minutes, Sister Hermina? The subject I wish to discuss might be of interest."

Hermina, the former prioress of Lyonesse's Hatshepsut Mission, a slender, ageless, gray-haired woman of average height with a narrow face and intense eyes, examined Ardrix in silence as if the latter were a previously unknown specimen of insect. It was her usual way of greeting Void Reborn Brethren, even Archimandrite Bolack, although they were unfailingly polite to her and her comrades.

All wore the same robes as their hosts in the same fashion, differing only by the content of the small orbs pinned to their breasts. The Old Order's was a field of stars while the Void Reborn's was a phoenix rising from the ashes.

"You may enter, Abomination."

The pejorative name Hermina gave Ardrix upon their first meeting had stuck, though she spoke it with less asperity and more in jest these days, mainly because the latter had ignored it all along and hadn't entered their minds since.

"That would be Sister Abomination if you please, Prioress Hermina." Ardrix allowed herself a mischievous grin none of the assembled Lyonesse Brethren could miss.

Friar Metrobius, former chief administrator of the Hatshepsut Mission, a jovial, stocky, white-haired man with an equally white beard and perpetually amused blue eyes, let out a hearty burst of laughter.

"She's got you there, Hermina."

The prioress gave Metrobius a look of mock despair though a faint smile creased her face.

"Et tu, Brute?"

"Uh oh. You'd better come in, Ardrix. When Hermina speaks Latin, things happen. Eldritch things from humanity's distant past. Perhaps even a discourse from Marcus Aurelius' Meditations, of which I found a leather-bound copy older than the Commonwealth in the abbey's library. Printed on Earth, if you'll believe it. Only the Almighty knows how that venerable tome survived the wars and destruction we inflicted on each other since then."

Hermina pointed at a chair across from her. "Sit and speak your piece, Ardrix, before Metrobius develops too great a sense of self-satisfaction at his questionable humor."

"Thank you, Prioress."

Ardrix sat in a respectful posture.

"You're aware we recently established a mission on the fallen world of Celeste."

"Yes."

"We received word today from one of our survey cruisers passing through the Celeste system on its way home that the locals massacred the entire mission and its protection complement in a most disturbing manner." Ardrix recounted *Caladrius*' report, summarized what she read in the logs, outlined her theory about the root causes, then asked, "Did you ever experience the like?"

Instead of replying, Hermina and Metrobius exchanged a glance heavy with meaning. The Old Order Brethren had refused to discuss Lyonesse's expansion and their Order's missions on reclaimed worlds, deeming such conversations to be treasonous since they considered themselves somewhat like prisoners of war. But they had been quite open with theology, religious practices, and the routines of an Order of the Void house. And they did their fair share of work alongside the Void Reborn Brethren.

Finally, Hermina shook her head.

"No. Our missions have encountered hostility, but we simply relocated them to another remnant community before things got out of hand." She hesitated for a second. "I think I speak for us all when I offer you my condolences for your Order's loss and that of the Marines. I'm reminded of John Donne's great wisdom at a moment like this. *Any man's death diminishes me, because I am involved in mankind. And therefore never send to know for whom the bell tolls; it tolls for thee*."

Ardrix bowed her head. "Thank you, Prioress."

"Your theory as to the root causes of the massacre seems quite cogent. Nicely done for an Abomination." When Ardrix looked up at Hermina, she saw a hint of playfulness rather than the usual mixture of irritation and contempt in the older woman's eyes. "But if you came looking for advice, we have none to offer beyond relocating if necessary, something you already know. Pray that the next time, whoever heads the mission and her superiors here on Wyvern understand it as well and act before the situation becomes irretrievable. It does no good settling near the largest community if its inhabitants suffer from intergenerational trauma caused by the Great Scouring. Sky demons, indeed. Now let me ask you a question in return."

"Certainly."

"The survey ship that passed through the Celeste system was searching for what? Are there not closer habitable worlds to claim, or did I lose my star map reading skills?"

Ardrix gave her a sly look. "Wouldn't that be telling, Prioress?"

Metrobius guffawed again. "We really should have you visit more often, Sister. Your fellow Void Reborn Brethren don't provide us with nearly as much entertainment."

Ardrix winked at Metrobius, which merely caused him to laugh with gusto again.

"The ship was remapping the wormhole network in that part of the old empire."

"You mean the part where Earth can be found?"

She nodded. "Among others. After the empire supplanted the Commonwealth, what they once termed the Home Sector became part of the Wyvern Sector. The Hegemony's goal is reunifying those worlds under Wyvern's leadership once more."

"So you're not specifically seeking Earth?"

A frown creased Ardrix's pale forehead. "Why do you ask, Prioress?"

"Might as well tell her, Hermina," Metrobius rumbled. "They're much closer than we are and will find it first."

Ardrix shot Metrobius a questioning glance.

The friar jerked his chin at Hermina. "I'll let her speak of it if she so desires."

"I suppose it can't do any harm," she replied. "You may recall me mentioning we always produce one mystic per generation at the Lyonesse Abbey ever since Sister Marta joined the Order in the years following the empire's collapse. No one's ever figured out why or how, but these sisters possess a terrifyingly powerful talent which supposedly includes a form of precognition, or as some would have it, the gift of prophecy."

"Yes, I remember. The Archimandrite showed great interest in the matter since we too have had a few sisters who were considered prophets."

"Sister Jessica among them, right?" Metrobius asked. "She who declared something concerning humanity's reunification?"

Ardrix nodded. "The most famous and eldritch of them. Archimandrite Bolack has studied her life and times with great interest."

"So you know what I'm talking about," Hermina said. "Good. Our current mystic began speaking of Earth as the locus for the rebirth of a unified humanity across the stars and through the Void a year before we left Lyonesse for Hatshepsut. Historically, we've never paid much attention to the mystics when their visions seemed a little too outrageous, although a surprising number of them materialized in some form or other. Of course, skeptics will say you can interpret prophecies any way you like and make them match subsequent facts. Many books were written over the millennia debunking prophets, seers, and the like."

"And are you a skeptic, Prioress?"

Hermina made a face and shrugged.

"No more than the rest of my Brethren. But we experience things beyond an ordinary person's ability to comprehend and we understand the psychological importance of symbolism. Precognitive visions and prophecies generate potent symbols for a people like ours. We retain a clear memory of the past and are raised to believe in a single purpose, that of making whole again what Dendera rent asunder. Whether those visions come true is beside the point. What matters is how they influence people into creating movements that can sway the course of a society's development. Our students of applied foundational psychohistory have a grand old time comparing prophecies to their own predictions."

"And do they sometimes match?"

Hermina snorted. "More often than you might think, but many on Lyonesse believe applied foundational psychohistory is no more scientific than a mystic's wild visions. Perhaps the latter are merely intuitive psychohistorians. Now, circling back to the question of Earth. Since we've been away from Lyonesse for several years, I couldn't tell you how our mystic's pronouncements have evolved. Still, I wouldn't be surprised if they received added impetus by the discovery Lyonesse isn't the sole space-faring survivor of the empire's collapse."

Ardrix chuckled. "Without a doubt. Our finding out about Lyonesse's existence transformed a sleepy autarky of four star systems into a hive of frantic imperial rebirth and expansion overnight. You do not know how frantic and exhausting."

"And you're at the very center of it, aren't you, Leading Sister of the Colonial Service?"

"For my sins, Prioress."

"Now that I've told you about Lyonesse and Earth, is the Hegemony also on a mystical quest to annex Earth so your people become the anointed who'll lead us into the promised land?"

Ardrix nodded once.

"Archimandrite Bolack and a few Brethren in his immediate circle think Sister Jessica's prophecy might only be fulfilled on humanity's original home. A return to our wellspring, if you like."

"Fascinating," Metrobius murmured. "A form of parallel spiritual and social development in societies separated by two centuries of divergent evolution."

"Proving we have more in common than one might think," Ardrix replied. She stood and bowed her head. "Thank you for taking the time to speak with me, Prioress. And you, Friar. Enjoy the rest of your evening. Until tomorrow."

And with that, Ardrix swept out of the Old Order's dormitory, conscious of eight pairs of eyes on her back.

—4—

"I trust everyone had time to read and absorb the very cogent report on the Celeste massacre prepared by General Torma and Sister Ardrix."

President Vigdis Mandus looked around the long oval table occupying most of the presidential conference room next to her office. As usual, the other two Executive Committee members, Chancellor Conteh and Archimandrite Bolack, sat on either side of her. The four Service Chiefs — Admiral Benes, General Sarkis, Chief Commissioner Nero Cabreras of the Commission for State Security, Admiral Godfrey — and Hal Cadotte, Wyvern's ruling consul, occupied the remaining chairs. The consuls of Dordogne, Arcadia, and Torrinos were attending via subspace radio, and their images stared back at Mandus from the primary display at the room's far end.

"Both are waiting outside if anyone requires clarification or has questions."

They nodded, knowing she'd tear a strip off them if they confessed to not having read one of the most stunning reports produced by the Colonial Service since its inception. Even though Mandus no longer wore a uniform and styled herself as President rather than Regent, she remained the Wyvern Hegemony's iron-fisted ruler, a dictator in everything but name. Conteh and Bolack wielded power in their respective domains, one secular and the other spiritual, and debated decisions with Mandus. But she still held the final say for now, though reforms were underway.

The rest, whose positions were once part of the defunct Ruling Council, now only held their posts and fulfilled their responsibilities at the Executive Committee's pleasure. That wouldn't change once the Hegemony's Conclave, the closest thing to a legislature it had, became a senate with say over more than just the nominations of Council members. But the creation of the senate was still in the future while Mandus waited for those opposed to tire themselves out and concede victory. The Hegemony's awakening upset too many entrenched interests whose neutralization would take time and energy best used to reunify human worlds.

"Good. Then let's discuss the fate of our attempts at elevating the Celestans so they can eventually join the Hegemony as full citizens."

"Remove the bastards and open the planet for colonization by our people," Consul Cadotte growled. "No sense risking more Brethren and Marines for the sake of irredeemable savages."

Cadotte, a former Ground Forces general, was well known for his blunt views and his opinion the missions were a waste of time. He was the unofficial leader of what Mandus privately termed the secular colonization faction, which advocated simply taking over former imperial worlds without the local population's say-so and making them Hegemony possessions. By force if necessary. The locals could adapt or perish for all he cared. Once a world became self-sufficient, it might get its own consul, but Cadotte preferred keeping newly annexed worlds as colonies forever. Why dilute his own standing as *primus inter pares*, first among equals?

"They remain the Almighty's children, Consul," Bolack said gently. "Children whose lives are still damned by Dendera's evil. They have a right to be angry."

"And murder your Brethren?" Cadotte scoffed. "Some rights you give those savages."

"I know the dead would not wish us to take revenge on the living, Consul. Although I will be the first to insist the next mission land far from Angelique, in some place where the remnant population isn't violent and deeply superstitious."

"What if they're all bloodthirsty, irredeemable savages?"

"I can't believe that would be the case. Provided Sister Ardrix's analysis is correct, and I believe it is — she's exceptionally perceptive — then the descendants of those who survived in smaller communities, where the social strata were less starkly defined during late imperial times, won't have faced the same overwhelming disadvantages."

"You mean they'll be less bloody-minded and primitive?" Nero Cabreras asked. "Let's hope you're right, Archimandrite."

"I'm leaning toward Consul Cadotte's views," Chancellor Conteh said. "Why risk more of our people needlessly? Colonize Celeste outright, away from existing population groups, and let them adapt or perish. This idea of elevating fallen societies like the Republic of Lyonesse does can only work if you're dealing with people who haven't forgotten their heritage and can grasp what it means to bootstrap themselves back up the technological ladder. Hunter-gatherers have sunk too low. Let them live as they wish, so long as they don't attack our colonists. And who knows? Maybe a good percentage will eventually be fit for interstellar civilization — in a few generations. I'm sorry, Archimandrite, but there's a limit to how much even your most dedicated missionaries can do."

"There's just one problem with the idea." Admiral Godfrey let his eyes roam around the table as he leaned forward. "Getting enough colonists to establish something self-sustaining and worthwhile. Our people aren't particularly interested in leaving the safety of our four core worlds and facing the perils of undeveloped star systems. Novaya Sibir's imperial era population was wiped out, and it is, in many respects, a virgin planet, yet finding volunteers to resettle there has been a struggle."

Admiral Benes chuckled. "The cold climate might be responsible, Johannes. Folks prefer warmer places."

"Perhaps, but the take-up rate for Santa Theresa has been little better, and it's a warm, welcoming world. Fortunately, we won't need many colonists if our missions succeed, and the local population expands as it absorbs new technologies, more advanced knowledge, and modern medicine. I'm afraid the principle of gradually bringing locals up to our level and turning them into Hegemony citizens is the best way of repopulating and expanding, short of rounding up current citizens and moving them against their will."

"And that won't happen," Mandus said. "Although we must eventually discuss the idea of turning habitual criminals into colonists, voluntary or not. But that'll wait until our infrastructure on new worlds is better developed."

"Still." Sarkis rubbed his chin thoughtfully. "I don't want to lose any further Colonial Marines in such a fashion. That's not what they signed up for in the first place. They're volunteers, just like the colonists, and the idea of dying on a backwater world at the hands of primitives will see many troopers remaining with their current regiments. And then where will we be? Forcing transfers to the Colonials? That'll make for low morale garrisons at the end of a long supply chain. Historically, those never found a good end."

"Oh, understood." Godfrey nodded. "No one wants a repeat of what just happened, but throwing out the entire program — at least for Celeste — because we didn't conduct a proper reconnaissance and found out what sort of locals we were dealing with? That would be ill-advised, in my opinion. The Hegemony simply doesn't have a surplus population that would be glad of new lives on new worlds and won't for at least a generation — probably more like two or three. Looking at the matter from a purely utilitarian angle, we obviously need the people who already live on the planets we intend to annex. And that means sending another mission to Celeste, along with a larger Marine contingent and landing them where the locals aren't blaming sky demons for their miserable existence."

The head of the Colonial Service turned to Archimandrite Bolack.

"I'll seek your pardon in advance for this, but the Order made the decision to land the mission outside Angelique based on the native population size as the deciding factor, without studying that population for suitability. I'll write it off as excessive enthusiasm — this time. But that haste precipitated a disastrous mistake. As a result, the Colonial Service will decide where the replacement mission goes after conducting a thorough reconnaissance led by my people and assisted by your Brethren. Not the other way around." Godfrey shifted his gaze to Mandus. "That summarizes my recommendation to you, Madame President."

"Thank you." Mandus let her gaze settle over the assembled officers and consuls. "Are there any further comments or questions before I issue my decision on Celeste?"

When no one spoke because they knew she'd already decided, Mandus nodded once at Godfrey.

"We will establish a new mission on Celeste, with a stronger Colonial Marine contingent — a battalion initially — and greater means of living off the land. The Colonial Service will send a survey team to determine the location of the new mission while the Brethren and the Marines assemble and prepare their contingents. I want the survey team off as soon as possible and the new mission leaving in no more than six weeks from now. The survey team can meet the new mission's leaders in Celeste's orbit and guide them down."

She speared the three military commanders with her piercing gaze and waited until they nodded in acknowledgment.

"Next item of business — *Caladrius*' exploration cruise and what follow-up we should carry out." She turned to Benes. "Admiral?"

"We've been refitting cruisers with larger antimatter fuel containment reservoirs and upgrading hyperdrives to give our survey ships greater autonomy if they encounter wormhole problems and face lengthy interstellar crossings. Longer than what Task Force Kruzenshtern did on its initial leg. But the ships are under orders to stay within the wormhole network, since we must remap and prove each connection. As you read from *Caladrius*' report, one wormhole mapped during the imperial era shifted in the last two hundred years, leading her not to the expected star system but a different one. As a result, we no longer know which branch of the network will connect the cluster of worlds in that part of the former Wyvern Sector, including Pacifica, Farhaven, Meiji, Han, Sarasvati, Shambala, and ultimately, Earth. We can identify their stars and make the crossing through interstellar space. But remapping the wormhole network is more critical in the long run.

"You may remember we put restrictions on the number of wormhole transits away from the Hegemony our ships could make in a given branch as a precaution. When *Caladrius* arrived unexpectedly in what we now know is ISC00045, also called Barnard's Star by the ancients, she had reached the end of her allowed transits. There they mapped the detectable wormhole termini and turned for home. The crew now needs rest and the ship a quick pass through the orbital yard before taking on routine patrol duties. The most recent refit, *Alkonost*, is even now preparing for a survey cruise, and I propose we send her to continue *Caladrius'* work.

"*Alkonost* is larger, with more antimatter carrying capacity, and thus enjoys at least fifteen percent greater range under the most conservative estimates. The shipyard, of course, is more optimistic and gives her twenty-five. Be that as it may. I think we should continue mapping the wormhole network in that part of the old Home Sector. If it lets us reconnect the former core worlds and even reach Earth, so much the better. But the aim should not be finding those systems at any cost. Let them be rediscovered via the remapped network." Benes gave Godfrey a polite nod. "And in keeping with the spirit of making Celeste a success, I suggest *Alkonost* accompany the transport carrying a new, expanded mission in six weeks and remain in orbit as top cover for a few weeks after the convoy's arrival before proceeding on her survey."

Mandus looked around the table again. "Questions or comments? No? Adopted. Make it so."

She turned her eyes pointedly on Benes and Godfrey in turn, silently telling them they'd better work together nicely, or she'd know the reason why. Not that both admirals were frequently at odds. On the contrary. Most days, they formed a mutual admiration society. Otherwise, Benes wouldn't have recommended Mandus appoint Godfrey as head of the Colonial Service. But since naval units engaged in survey, exploration, and colonization came under the latter's command as force employer, they sometimes had different priorities. They could forget the sole priority that counted was the Executive Committee's.

"Yes, Madame President," they replied.

"Now on to other business. Chancellor, if you'd please go through the latest economic report and discuss the next steps in our shipyard expansion effort."

—5—

Wyvern Hegemony Ship Strix
Celeste System

"Hello, Celeste, my old friend," Commander Jutta Pernell, captain of the frigate *Strix,* muttered as the image of the planet appeared on the combat information center's primary display. A thin, dark-haired woman with a narrow face, aquiline nose, and deep-set eyes, she was young for her rank, but anyone who spent more than a few minutes in her company could feel her boundless energy and drive.

Strix had dropped out of FTL on Celeste's hyperlimit a few minutes earlier, after a quick passage from Torrinos at Admiral Godfrey's orders. They'd barely had forty-eight hours to prepare for the trip, but in this new Navy, those who tarried found themselves beached. Pernell didn't mind.

Until President Mandus reversed two centuries of isolationism, naval service was, mostly, unrelieved boredom with the odd war games as a distraction. Commanding a survey frigate under Colonial Service control was more interesting, even if the upgraded cruisers were now getting the longer-range missions. And sadly, by the time *Strix* went into refit so she matched or exceeded the cruisers' autonomy in interstellar space, her tour as captain would be over.

Pernell's ship had conducted the original survey a year earlier and pinpointed the locations of human life sign clusters. But her landing parties hadn't visited more than a handful of the larger ones. And then only to find out — from a distance and secretly, of course — what level of technology the natives possessed.

After what happened at the Angelique Abbey, sixty-five Marines belonging to B Troop, Reconnaissance Squadron, 1st Colonial Marine Regiment, would look for a new site where the locals weren't apt to massacre sky demons. Pernell, along with her department heads and the officer commanding the troop, Centurion Garth Lee, had read the doomed mission's logs, *Caladrius*' report, and the Colonial Service Inspector General's report. Based on their analysis, Pernell and Lee knew as well as anyone what danger signs they should look for and what characteristics proved a site was likely safe.

Lee entered the CIC moments later and slipped into his usual seat at an unused workstation behind the throne-like captain's chair in the center. Square of body and face, with features hewn from granite, hooded blue eyes, and short blond hair, he was a former command sergeant commissioned as a centurion and brought two solid decades of experience to the operation. He'd also been part of Major Vinh's company during the Hatshepsut expedition and had broader horizons than most of his peers.

"Let me just repeat I'm glad we'll not be landing near Angelique, Captain," Lee said as he studied Celeste's image. "Seeing video of the killing fields around the old abbey was enough."

Pernell glanced over her shoulder. "No kidding."

"My people are conducting their final preparations. We'll be ready to head down the moment our orbital passes confirm the designated sites still appear workable."

"Impatient?" Pernell smiled at Lee.

"While we enjoy the odd cruise across the stars, staring at bulkheads and doing parkour runs around your hangar deck get boring, Captain. This sort of recon is why we volunteered for the Colonials. And once we're done here, the universe is our oyster — if *Alkonost* finds the way to Earth. Which is why we must be done by the time she arrives with *Yatagerasu* and the new mission's personnel."

"Always a treat seeing enthusiastic professionals at work."

***

By the next morning, ship's time, Centurion Lee was satisfied the secluded mountain glen he'd designated as the emplacement for his forward operating base sufficed. It was large enough for his unit and their shuttles, clear of any sign humans had visited it in the recent past, and wasn't approachable without being seen. A pair of drones launched from orbit, and *Strix*'s sensor suite had ensured that.

From the FOB, Lee planned on inserting observation posts around three of the settlements that showed many of the right signs, such as evidence of post-imperial collapse buildings, extensive agriculture, cottage industries, and defensive walls.

None of the three sat right on top of city ruins, though each was within a few kilometers of one in much the same way as New Draconis on Wyvern was built almost within sight of the former capital's sparse remains.

Lee and his Marines would wear light scout armor and carry sidearms with non-lethal loads. However, they were also bringing the usual sort of weapons designed to kill quickly and efficiently, including the organic mortar team, to defend the FOB, just in case. No one wanted to suffer F Company's fate, which was why the locals could only reach the FOB via a narrow pass easily transformed into a deadly killing zone. Natives overwhelming sky demons by sheer numbers wasn't going to happen this time.

Pernell met Lee on the hangar deck as the Marines of B Troop were loading their gear — everything needed to set up a fortified camp that could be broken down and removed quickly once the mission was over. The four shuttles would remain at the FOB, deliver the observation posts to their targets, and then switch them out regularly for rest and recuperation. More importantly, they would serve to evacuate B Troop if the worst of all scenarios happened and the locals attempted a repeat of the Angelique Abbey massacre.

After a final inspection by Lee and his troop first sergeant, Kanwar Anand, a stocky, dark-complexioned man, with a short black beard and a pugilist's nose, the Marines climbed aboard their craft, and Lee faced Pernell formally.

"Permission to leave the ship?"

"Granted."

Lee raised his hand in salute, then turned on his heels and vanished into his designated shuttle. Moments later, Pernell and the hangar deck crew withdrew behind the airlocks. As soon as the latter were sealed, a red strobe flashed, and the space doors opened, leaving the faint film of a force field behind to prevent the hangar's air from escaping.

Then, one after the other, the sleek armed shuttles nosed their way out and disappeared from sight. From this point on, *Strix* would orbit Celeste until *Alkonost* and *Yatagerasu* arrived and watch over Centurion Lee's command as best they could.

A trio of satellites spread around the planet in geosynchronous allowed them to see the area of operations, but arranging for fire support might take time. Hopefully, B Troop wouldn't need it. Besides, shooting from orbit generally left indelible marks on the countryside.

Pernell returned to the CIC and watched the shuttles descend while monitoring the surveillance drones currently hovering above the secluded glen, just in case interlopers arrived at the last minute. And though it was now night on that part of Celeste, the drones saw as clearly as if it were daytime.

Eventually, they detected the four shuttles coming in over the treetops after dropping to the deck several hundred kilometers from the nearest cluster of human life signs. That way, the chances of any insomniac spotting them were as remote as possible. Moments after the shuttles landed, the drones did so as well, this time under Centurion Lee's control. He and his Marines now owned them.

***

By the time dawn broke over Forward Operating Base Loumis, named in honor of the late officer commanding the Angelique Abbey garrison, they had laid out a ring of sensors. Temporary shelters were springing up among the trees, where they'd be quasi-invisible from a distance, and camouflage nets hung above the grounded shuttles. One shelter, rigged as a command post, was in service before the sun rose above the hilltops, with B Troop's battle AI watching the sensor network.

At First Sergeant Anand's signal, the Marines and shuttle pilots broke out rations and had a hearty breakfast in shifts, so there was always a section watching the perimeter. Once they'd eaten, Lee and Anand climbed up the steep hills, first on one side, then the other to see what a casual onlooker might detect. Then, they entered the narrow pass connecting the glen to the outside world and headed out for a kilometer before turning back and approaching FOB Loumis from that direction.

Declaring himself satisfied, Lee ordered the rest of the base set up before sending his troopers to rest so they'd be ready come nightfall when the shuttles flew out the first observation post crews. Every hour, under command post control, the drones rose into the sky for a quick look at their surroundings, but the only life signs they picked up were those of wild animals.

And that's how Centurion Garth Lee, Officer Commanding B Troop, Reconnaissance Squadron, 1st Colonial Marine Regiment, liked it — sneak and peek. The locals should never know they were around. Practicing on Santa Theresans who still hadn't been contacted by the Rosalito Abbey had helped hone their skills to quasi-perfection.

Shortly after last light, the Marines of B Troop ate supper in complete darkness — at least to eyes not enhanced by combat helmet night vision visors. Then, Lee reviewed the observation post orders with each patrol sergeant before sending them and their troopers on roller-coaster nap of the earth rides aboard their shuttles to the designated drop-off points.

Two OPs, each made up of six Marines who'd stand watch in pairs on and off for forty-eight hours, would observe every targeted settlement. The tactical AI responsible for continuously recording in the visible, infrared, and ultraviolet spectrums as well as tracking the number of human and livestock life signs, would help them.

The OPs would stay in radio contact with the command post, reporting every four hours with a data dump from the AI. B Troop's other half, less the command element, would take care of the FOB's security while resting between rotations. Theoretically, they could keep this routine indefinitely, given a continuous flow of consumable supplies, but Lee knew too long and even the sharpest troopers lost their edge.

So, they needed to collect the necessary data quickly before mental fatigue caused mistakes that might betray their presence to the locals. Besides, no one knew when the replacement mission was arriving. President Mandus had become quite a motivator since she reaffirmed the Oath of Reunification, so it might not take long.

As the sun rose over the western coast of Celeste's primary continent, Baune, over a thousand kilometers from Angelique and hopefully well beyond the reach of the former capital's sky demon legends, the six observation posts were in place and recording what they saw.

Very quickly, they established that the three settlements targeted by the Colonial Service were surrounded by wooden walls and vast fields and that they carried out large-scale animal husbandry as well as inshore fishing activities. The one built a few kilometers upstream of Havre de Grâce, a ruined seaport that once dominated the Harmonie River estuary, seemed the most promising.

A half-destroyed priory sat on a hilltop a few kilometers northeast of Havre de Grâce, within easy walking distance of the village, and the initial scans showed it was unoccupied. Once they'd developed a feel for the area, Lee planned on sending a foot patrol to examine the priory under cover of darkness.

The other settlements had no Order of the Void ruins that might serve as a focal point for the new mission, but since it came with its own instabase, containers dropped from orbit that turned into buildings once emptied, it didn't matter. This time around, sentimentality about Old Order ruins wouldn't play any role.

If necessary, a new priory or even abbey could be built in due course. The first step was gaining the local population's acceptance. And before that could happen, Centurion Lee had to recommend the most likely settlement.

—6—

New Draconis Abbey
Wyvern System

"Please come in." Archimandrite Bolack rose from behind his desk and waved at chairs around a simple wooden table in front of it.

His office, on the second floor of the New Draconis Abbey's main administration building, overlooked the Motherhouse's extensive grounds, fields and orchards, and the Hegemony's capital in the distance beyond. Bolack never tired of the sight, but now, he watched the two he'd summoned enter the austere, though spacious room.

Friar Shakku, a wiry, beardless man, with short black hair, dark, watchful eyes, and smile lines on either side of his mouth, stepped through the open doorway first. Ageless, like the sisters, he bowed once, then stepped aside to allow Sister Maryam in.

She also was tall, slim, with dark eyes and dark hair, though hers hung in a thick plait. Like most sisters, her smooth features belied many years in the Order of the Void Reborn. Between them, Shakku and Maryam could claim well over half a century of monastic service and witnessed the Hegemony's long decay followed by an unexpected revival because of Crevan Torma and Sister Ardrix's expedition.

When both had settled across from the Order's supreme leader, Bolack studied them in silence, looking for signs of trepidation, excitement, or other badly suppressed emotions, but found nothing other than the serenity so prized by the Brethren.

"Is your team ready?" He finally asked.

Friar Shakku nodded once and replied in a surprisingly deep baritone, "They are. We can leave the moment *Yatagerasu* is ready for us. However, we must still inspect the supplies and equipment before loading."

He glanced at Sister Maryam, who said, "I'm still holding debates with the Colonial Service concerning the field hospital configuration, which remains unresolved. I prefer using what the Old Order built on Hatshepsut as a baseline rather than what the earlier mission brought. Sister Hermina and her people make very cogent arguments about more being better when befriending the locals. But the Service's logistics people are unconvinced."

"I agree with Sister Maryam." Shakku inclined his head toward her. "Unfortunately, Sister Ardrix's position in the Colonial Service's Inspectorate General makes her a resource of last resort if we face obstruction from the logistics department, one I'd rather not involve at the moment."

"Let me know how it goes," Bolack replied. "*Yatagerasu* and *Alkonost* can't sail until we sign off on the mission stores, and President Mandus is impatient we return to Celeste and resume our mapping of the wormhole network. And I, as you know, am keen on our re-establishing a connection with Earth, where many of us believe humanity's future and fate await."

Both friar and sister bowed their heads. "Yes, Archimandrite."

What they thought of Sister Jessica's prophecy, or Bolack's interpretation of a vision that didn't explicitly mention the cradle of humanity, wasn't apparent, nor would it ever be. Unless the Order's Doctrinal Conclave made Bolack's belief canon, it remained his opinion and that of many, though not a majority of Brethren.

The Void Reborn weren't overly inclined to mysticism. The Order's rebirth from the ashes of Empress Dendera's downfall made it much too hard-bitten and realistic for vague pronouncements by sisters who could just as well have been mad rather than visionaries. Still, Bolack enjoyed universal respect for his wisdom, quiet leadership, and decency and the Brethren gave him much leeway to pursue his notions.

"Both of us are meeting with the Colonial Service this afternoon, and we hope we can finalize matters then," Maryam said. "Once that happens, it'll take a few days to reconfigure the field hospital aboard the containers and load them in *Yatagerasu*."

"Thankfully," Shakku added, "Both she and *Alkonost* are almost ready for departure."

"Excellent. Please let me know how your meeting goes." Bolack raised a few more minor points related to the mission's administration and outreach protocols, then let Shakku and Maryam carry on with their preparations.

Alone in his office once more, he returned to the windows and gazed out at the misty landscape around the abbey, each tree delicately draped in tendrils of fog that swirled gently, pushed around by the faintest of breezes. He saw no sign of New Draconis but knew the city lay out there, bustling with activity.

A faint rumble reached his ears, signaling a heavy shuttle or small ship lifting off from the military spaceport, headed for a ship in orbit or Starbase Wyvern. Perhaps it even carried personnel or equipment for the new Celeste Mission or *Alkonost*'s exploration trek into what was once the heart of the pre-imperial Commonwealth.

Would that he was young enough and without leadership responsibilities so he could accompany them. Yet the Almighty decreed he should live through these times as one of those with his hand on the tiller of state rather than as an explorer.

***

Captain Derwent Alexander, commanding officer, Guards Navy cruiser *Alkonost*, raised his hand to attract the attention of the woman who'd just entered the Starbase Wyvern wardroom. She wore four gold stripes topped by an executive curl on the collar and an FTL ship captain's wreathed star on the right breast, just like Alexander, a stocky, broad-shouldered man in his early forties, with short dark hair, piercing blue eyes, and a square, honest face.

He turned a lazy smile on Gelsa Vitt, *Yatagerasu*'s skipper, as she headed for his table. They were of an age and Academy classmates but physical opposites. She was tall and lean, almost rangy, with medium-length fair hair and a narrow face dominated by a patrician nose and hooded green eyes.

"How are you, Der?" Vitt asked as she dropped into the chair facing him.

"Getting a little impatient, if you really want to know. We've been docked since our readiness evaluation, waiting for the Colonial Service to finalize things."

"And how did the eval go?"

His lazy smile returned. "As well as I had hoped. We got full marks. Raul Vitez was the team leader, and he's no pushover, so I figure we're good to go."

"Yeah, I hear that about Raul, although some of our colleagues use different words to describe him."

"Hah." Alexander guffawed. "They must have shown lacuna during their evals. He's fair, but he doesn't mince words if you don't meet his standards. At least not in private."

"In any case, congratulations. Why are we still docked? That's easy. The Colonial Service is still working on details with the Void component of the new Celeste Mission. I have most of the containers aboard, and the Marine garrison is on twenty-four hours' notice to load. But there's one last snag concerning the field hospital." She gave him a helpless shrug. "Speaking of Marines, I hear you're taking on the bunch currently in the Celeste system with *Strix*."

"Yep. A sixty-five strong recon troop. Celeste is supposedly their last practice run to prepare for landing on the worlds we'll remap."

She cocked an amused eyebrow at him. "Including Earth."

"If that's our destiny. Shall we order?"

Holographic menus appeared, and they selected their meals, along with a glass of wine each. The wine arrived moments later on a tray carried by a trundling, cylindrical serving droid.

"To your health." Alexander raised his glass.

Vitt imitated him. "And yours. May we both have successful yet uneventful missions."

"So," she asked after carefully putting her glass down, "is your ship's counselor one of the mystics?"

"Taina? No." Alexander shook his head. "She's as level-headed as they come. I don't think there are any mystics in the Navy. They wouldn't be suitable, and if the Void has learned nothing else about the Hegemony Guards, it knows better than sending folks who can't integrate with a rough-and-ready crew."

"True." The droid returned with two plates and placed them on the table, then vanished again. "Looks good."

"They eat well on Starbase Wyvern. Comes from getting fresh ingredients shipped up every day on the orders of a rear admiral who enjoys eating and keeping his people contented."

"The Almighty bless him." Vitt took a forkful of her chicken, chewed, and swallowed. "Nice."

"I have to ask, so don't take this wrong, Gelsa. Will there be problems with my taking on the senior officer role while sailing together?"

She snorted with amusement.

"Why would there be problems? You're senior to me by promotion date, and you command a cruiser while I have a replenishment ship."

"That's what I thought you'd say, but when people don't talk with each other, things can go sideways."

"You and I are good, buddy. And if a Lyonesse battle group shows up looking for trouble, *Yatagerasu* has plenty of teeth hidden away. My port and starboard secondary cargo holds are stuffed with missile launcher modules." She took a sip of wine. "Not that we know what a Lyonesse warship looks like, let alone carries."

"And you still have enough room for an entire instant base, supplies to last three months, and a Colonial Marine battalion with its gear?"

"Easily. *Yatagerasu* was the biggest civilian hauler in commission when the Navy bought and refitted her. I also carry containers for Santa Theresa, which we'll drop off on the way. And I'm still not one hundred percent full."

"And an air wing's worth of shuttles."

"Of course, but that's the hangar, not the holds, so they don't even count against cargo space. There was talk of making her a space control ship early on, but the needs of transporting and resupplying colonies won out, and by the Almighty, we do that job better than anyone else."

Alexander took a sip of wine.

"And if Lyonesse proves aggressive, we might regret not having a space control ship capable of interdicting one of our newly acquired worlds."

A broad smile lit up Vitt's face. "Turning her into a space control ship simply means converting one part of her primary cargo holds into hangars and filling the rest with missile launchers and reload packs. She already has a fearsome array of antimissile guns. Admiral Benes made sure *Yatagerasu* could turn from a beast of burden into a fighting dragon at a few days' notice."

"Good to hear."

"And how's *Alkonost* post-refit?"

"Same armor, better ordnance, vastly greater autonomy. She's a throwback to the pre-wormhole FTL warships of the early empire. Until the next cruiser sails out of the shipyard under her own thrusters, *Alkonost* is the most powerful in the fleet, if not the fastest. I'll have no qualms taking her into the wormhole network without an escort, Lyonesse or not. Besides, we haven't yet detected any of their ships in our expanding sphere. News of our existence must have been just as shocking to them as theirs was for us."

"No doubt. Still, let's hope we don't shoot at each other over a misunderstood message. Repeating past mistakes will only ensure neither of us has a future."

Alexander raised his glass.

"Here's to that. I'd rather not end up in a running battle with other humans several dozen wormhole transits from home if we can have a reasonable conversation and sail away unharmed."

—7—

Hegemony Starbase Wyvern
Wyvern System

"We won't lack for protection, it seems." Friar Shakku and Sister Maryam, at the head of the Void Reborn contingent, halted a few paces after passing through the airlock to the spacious docking compartment, eyes drinking in the rows of Colonial Marines standing at ease beside orderly piles of gear, waiting to board. The replacement mission's Brethren had landed on Starbase Wyvern's shuttle deck, ten levels up, just under twenty minutes earlier, courtesy of the Guards Navy. Their possessions, loaded on a few antigrav sleds controlled by junior friars, took much less space than those of the Marines.

Maryam nodded. "Four hundred troopers for a mission of sixty Brethren. One cannot truly appreciate that number until one sees it arrayed in full martial splendor."

"That sounded surprisingly sarcastic." Shakku gave her an amused glance. "Considering what happened to our predecessors."

"Their fate ultimately stemmed from that most ancient failing — hubris — and not from a lack of firepower." She turned a sardonic smile on her colleague. "But the practical missionary in me can appreciate how much more clearance work will get done by four times the usual number of pioneers."

Movement near the Marines caught her eye.

"Ah. There's Dozier the Dozer, and he spotted us," she muttered in a voice pitched only for Shakku's ears.

"Be nice, Maryam. We'll be living cheek-by-jowl with him during the next six months."

For reasons Shakku couldn't fathom, Maryam had taken an instant dislike to Major Redfern 'Red' Dozier, commanding officer of the 2nd Battalion, 2nd Colonial Marine Regiment. Built like an armored earth-moving machine — bald, massive, square, and powerful, giving the impression he could clear anything out of his way — the dark-eyed Marine was the antithesis of a monastic.

Maryam didn't let on, of course. Only Shakku could tell. He suspected Dozier's ribald sense of humor and lack of piety were in part responsible. Though Maryam was as tolerant as any other sister, she was more serious than most, be it about life or faith. And Dozier, though no doubt serious concerning his duties as a military man, seemed blessed by an outsized lust for life. Or perhaps there was something only a sister with a powerful talent such as Maryam's could sense.

Dozier's rough-hewn face split into a smile as he neared, and he raised a hand.

"Friar. Sister. Glad to see you. We're waiting for *Yatagerasu* to complete loading so we can board."

He gestured toward the station end of a large docking tube where containers were vanishing one after the other every few seconds.

"Somehow, they got the timings a little mixed up, but that's the Guards for you. Hurry up and wait."

"It is not much different in the Order," Shakku replied with a small smile. "But we use the time to meditate, so we waste nothing."

Dozier nodded at his Marines.

"And they use the time to engage in their own forms of meditation. Some of it even resembles yours, although most engage in what we call the fine art of shooting the shit."

Shakku sensed rather than saw Maryam's reaction to Dozier's crude words.

"But make no mistake," the Marine continued, "you won't find a finer bunch of pioneer-trained infantry troops in the entire Guards Ground Forces. They'll build you a priory with the same skill and dedication as they'll use if ever the locals go stupid and try to fuck us over."

"No doubt," Shakku replied, hiding his amusement at Maryam's unvoiced and, hopefully, unnoticed distaste. Before he could add any further comments, Dozier raised a hand as he tilted his head in the unmistakable way of a man wearing a communicator ear bug.

"Hang on, Friar. I just got word we'll be boarding in five minutes. We can continue this conversation in the passenger mess once we're underway."

He gave both a polite nod, then turned on his heels and, with an energetic and determined stride, headed to where his second in command and the battalion's sergeant major waited.

"I think I'll take my meals in my quarters for the entire trip," Maryam murmured.

"Might as well get inured to our friend Red. There will be fewer possibilities of avoiding him once we're on Celeste. Think of it as the Almighty testing you in novel ways." A mischievous grin appeared. "And you testing us in turn."

She gave him a smirk so faint that no one but Shakku would have noticed, but it only broadened his smile.

Maryam's eyebrows twitched as if in mock irritation.

"Instead of waxing philosophical, maybe we should send one of the young friars over to where those Navy people are standing by the docking tube and inquire about our boarding."

***

"Nice of them to give us a room we can use as our itinerant chapter house." Maryam made a full circle as she surveyed the large compartment at one end of the passenger section occupied by the Brethren. "Let's put up a sign, so no one stumbles in while we're holding services."

"Yes, Sister," one of the younger and more junior friars replied before turning away to carry out her orders.

The arrangements satisfied Maryam. She and Shakku enjoyed private berths while the sisters and friars shared cabins at two per. It still beat the squad bays the Colonial Marine rank-and-file occupied on the decks below them.

"Put the sign up permanently and never leave this compartment, and you won't see Red Dozier at all during the trip," Shakku murmured, repressed merriment crinkling the laugh lines around his eyes. "One of the juniors could bring your meals and give you sponge baths."

"If I tell you why I'm not comfortable around Major Dozier and then accept the Almighty's test, will you stop making snide comments?"

"Snide? You wound me, Sister. I'm merely attempting to pierce that cloak of righteousness you use as a protective shell."

Before Maryam could give Shakku a pungent reply, the ship's public address system came to life.

"Now, hear this. All members of the 2nd Battalion, 2nd Colonial Marines, and the Void Brethren mission to Celeste will assemble on the main hangar deck in fifteen minutes for a farewell from President Mandus and the Executive Committee. Floor indicators in blue will guide you there beginning now."

"You can tell me about the source of your discomfort with Red later on." Shakku pivoted on his heels and headed for the door. After a few moments, Maryam followed him.

As they stepped down the circular stairway connecting the ship's decks, joining the rest of the Brethren along the way, Shakku and Maryam soon found themselves among throngs of Marines in rifle green uniforms, chatting among themselves.

When they reached the entrance to the main hangar deck, a bosun's mate directed the Void Reborn to one side, where the mission's deputy chief administrators were organizing them into orderly ranks. Meanwhile, the 2nd Battalion's sergeant major, helped by the company first sergeants, formed the troopers into serried ranks facing the giant display normally used for traffic control instructions.

Shakku and Maryam joined Dozier and his second in command on one side of the formation as befit the mission's joint leadership team.

"Friar, Sister." Dozier bowed his head respectfully.

Shakku returned the gesture. "I trust you're settling in as well as we are, Major."

"Easily. Barracks are barracks, even in space. I consider our current berths as a last bit of luxury before landing in the wilds of Celeste, where we'll enjoy our own, much more austere, encampment. As my old CO used to say, never seek discomfort before its time."

"What a wise way of looking at it."

A sideways glance showed Maryam keeping an impassive expression as she chatted with Dozier's second in command, a tall, lean, hatchet-faced man in his early forties. He and his commanding officer were a study in contrasts, but they worked well together from what little Shakku had seen during the preparatory meetings.

Shakku and Dozier made small talk until the hangar's display lit up with the phoenix sigil of the Wyvern Hegemony.

"Stand by for President Vigdis Mandus, Archimandrite Bolack, and Chancellor Conteh," a disembodied voice announced, echoing across the vast shuttle hangar.

With a quick nod, the Marine officers walked off to take their positions in front of the battalion.

Once there, Dozier called out, "2nd of the 2nd, atten-SHUN!" Then he turned on his heels to face the display.

As if prodded by Dozier's command, the Brethren also turned and adopted a respectful stance — heads raised, backs straight, and hands joined at the waist.

Moments later, the phoenix disappeared, replaced by Vigdis Mandus standing on a stage in the Wyvern Palace's ballroom, one backed by the flags of the Hegemony, the Navy, the Ground Forces, the Colonial Service, and the Commission for State Security. The other two Executive Committee members and the four Service Chiefs stood behind her. All wore solemn expressions.

"Good afternoon, members of the Void Reborn's Celeste Mission and the 2nd Battalion, 2nd Colonial Regiment."

Her eyes roamed over the assembly, proof she saw them on a display in the ballroom just as *Yatagerasu*'s passengers and crew saw her.

"You're aware of the fate that befell the first Celeste Mission, Brethren, and Colonial Marines alike. Their loss is a tragedy that should never have happened." A pause. "But it did. You know what went wrong on Celeste and what we must do to avoid a repeat. An ancient once said the fault is not in our stars but in ourselves. And by replanting the Hegemony's flag on Celeste, but near people who can understand our undertaking, our faith, and our values, we can redeem that fault. And you will do so."

Mandus paused and scanned her audience again. Throughout, the worthies standing behind her hadn't so much as twitched.

"The people on Celeste are humans, just like us. And they're not far removed from contact with our ancestors. Less than ten generations, by the old reckoning. Unfortunately, the inhabitants of Angelique diverged from humanity's norm to the extent they could no longer recognize their kin. But their ancestors suffered more than most on that world. The Almighty will surely see fit to grant them forgiveness.

"However, your mission will find and elevate those who haven't forgotten the stars and will reach out to join the Hegemony as full partners so they may rediscover their patrimony. Yours is a Holy Mission, one you undertake because it is necessary, because we must repair the incomprehensible damage wrought by the Mad Empress. And therefore, I ask Archimandrite Bolack to invoke the Almighty's blessing on your undertaking."

She stepped aside, giving the Hegemony's top religious leader the place of honor.

Bolack, sober in black robes with his chain of office as sole adornment, raised both hands, palms facing upwards.

"Oh, Almighty in your Infinite Void," he intoned in his rumbling basso, "we ask you to look kindly upon those headed for Celeste where they will do your holy work. Give them the strength and wisdom they need to succeed so that our fellow humans who live there in obscurity may once more find the light of civilization and peace. The Void giveth, the Void taketh away, blessed be the Void."

Hundreds of voices on *Yatagerasu*'s hangar desk repeated the incantation, then Bolack bowed his head at them and moved back to his spot.

"I will not wish you luck," Mandus said, "because you will create your own as necessary. Of that, I'm convinced. You represent the best the Wyvern Hegemony offers, and you will bring Celeste back into the interstellar human family. Fair winds and following seas, my friends."

She, too, bowed her head formally, then the video feed ended, Mandus replaced by the Hegemony's phoenix emblem.

In the ensuing silence, Shakku wondered whether she and Bolack had spoken the same words to their ill-fated predecessors at the moment of departure but decided the answer didn't matter. All that mattered was what lay ahead.

— 8 —

Celeste System

"Bridge to the captain."

Commander Jutta Pernell placed her tea mug on the day cabin desk and touched her communicator.

"Pernell."

"Two contacts dropped out of FTL at the hyperlimit. Beacons make them as *Alkonost* and *Yatagerasu*. Visual scans confirm."

Pernell bit back the first word that came to mind — finally — and replied, "Thank you."

Complaining about the long wait while mapping Celeste down to the last square millimeter wouldn't have been seemly, although she was sure the officer of the watch shared her sentiments. He'd likely voiced that same thought when the CIC called with the information.

Try as she might, Pernell couldn't remember who between the two captains was senior, and she hedged her bets rather than consult the Navy list. Besides, a quick conference call might be more efficient.

"Please open a link with both captains and suggest the leader of the Void Mission and the CO of the Marine battalion join in. I'll take it in my day cabin."

"Aye, aye, sir."

"And ask Centurion Lee to join me. Pernell, out."

The Marines of B Troop had completed their reconnaissance mission without being noticed by the locals four days earlier. Instead of staying on the surface, they'd torn down their forward operating base and rejoined *Strix*. Lee had privately admitted to Pernell they looked forward to their next mission aboard *Alkonost* after what he'd deemed a straightforward operation on what wasn't exactly unknown ground.

The troopers from the 2nd Colonial Marines aboard *Yatagerasu* could have done the same job in the same amount of time, setting first contact back by two weeks. But President Mandus had wanted action to regain the momentum on Celeste after the deadly setback.

Lee showed up in Pernell's day cabin before the new arrivals joined in and silently poured himself a tea from her private urn. He moved one of her guest chairs to one side of her desk and sat, facing the primary display, which came to life soon after with the feed from *Alkonost* and Captain Derwent Alexander's solitary figure.

"I trust you had a pleasant trip, sir?" Pernell asked by way of greeting.

"Uneventful, Jutta. How are things?"

"Equally uneventful." She nodded at Lee. "I don't know if you've met your soon-to-be embarked Marine reconnaissance contingent leader."

Recognizing his cue, Lee sat up straighter. "Centurion Garth Lee, B Troop, Reconnaissance Squadron, 1st Colonial Marines, sir. I have sixty-four troopers under my command."

"A pleasure to meet you, Centurion. You come highly recommended by General Sarkis."

"The general is too kind, sir. I was a lowly corporal in his battalion when he was a major. I'm surprised he remembers me."

A smile danced on Alexander's lips. "You never know who's monitoring your career, Centurion. May I assume you'll be ready to shift over as soon as we're in orbit?"

"Yes, sir."

"We'll use our shuttles if you don't mind," Pernell said.

"Not at all. I would have suggested it myself. Our first officers can take care of the transfer." At that moment, the primary display generated a second feed, this one from *Yatagerasu*. "And here are the rest of our merry band."

"Hello, Jutta," Captain Vitt raised a hand in greeting. "Everything is good?"

"As well as can be, sir. Welcome to Celeste."

Vitt nodded in reply, then gestured at the three people sitting around what was probably the replenishment ship's main conference room table.

"Major Dozier, 2nd Battalion, 2nd Colonial Regiment, Friar Shakku, Chief Administrator of the new Celeste Mission, and Maryam, the mission's leading sister."

Both Pernell and Lee inclined their heads, a gesture those in *Yatagerasu* returned. Then, Dozier broke out into a big grin.

"How are they hanging, Garth?"

"Upside down from the trees, Major. And you?"

"Same, same. Job's done?"

"Yep. Ready to move on." A slight grin appeared. "After we see you fine folks settled in a nice place where the air is clean, the water pure, and the natives seemingly sane. By the way, we scanned Angelique and the old mission site, both from orbit and low-level drone overflights."

"And?" Dozier asked.

"Lots of life signs beneath the city's ruins and traces of the tech they took after overrunning the mission, which looks pretty damn eerie now that predation has stripped the flesh off the corpses of the native casualties and dispersed them. A field of bones, you might call it."

Sister Maryam's face tightened as if she were repressing a shudder. "A field of evil, more like, Centurion."

Lee inclined his head in acknowledgment. "No doubt. Fortunately, the sites we reconnoitered are over a thousand kilometers from Angelique. If the Angeliquans hear about your presence, you'll see them coming from so far away. Major Dozier's people will enjoy a pleasant week or two of range practice with live targets."

"They're still human beings." Maryam's tone held a hint of reproach, barely noticeable, but neither Lee nor Dozier missed it.

"As you say, Sister." Lee let his eyes meet those of Shakku and Dozier. "Shall we discuss the sites we observed now or when you enter orbit?"

He gave Pernell a brief glance to see if she objected to his taking the lead. But *Strix*'s captain merely shrugged.

"No reason why not now."

Captain Alexander, as senior officer present, nodded. "We have little else to do while we're on final approach. Please go ahead, Centurion."

"Sir. As per our mission profile, we scouted areas near the mouth of the Harmonie River on the western coast of Baune. The first site was the second choice for the original mission, centered on the semi-ruined priory serving the old city of Havre de Grâce, which was flattened. The new settlement, which we dubbed Havre Two, is about five kilometers upstream of the old city's eastern outskirts. We detected nine hundred and forty-two inhabitants and took as much biometric information as we could record from a distance. The settlement is surrounded by a three-meter-high wooden palisade, and they close the entrances at sunset."

"Meaning there are threats."

Lee nodded.

"Likely, but we saw nothing more than wild animals capable of entering barns and making off with domestic fowl, piglets, lambs, and other small things. The village survives on farming and fishing, the former using draft animals and the latter sailboats. None of the farmers or fishers carry anything more than large knives, although we spotted hunters with lances and bows and detected animal traps in the woods. They use candles and tallow dips after dark, but no one stays up long.

"Compared to the records left by Centurion Loumis concerning the Angeliquans, these people seem peaceful and almost civilized, albeit at a definite preindustrial level. Still, they have a forge, a cooperage, cloth manufacturing, and other cottage industries," Lee smiled, "and a distillery along with a brewery. However, we saw no evidence of religious practices or activities hinting at violent behavior. And finally, there is regular trade along the coast and upriver. You'll find the details in the package I'll transmit shortly, both raw data and refined analysis. As a site, it seems promising. More so than Angelique in any case, even though it's not a large community."

Shakku stroked his chin while nodding.

"If there's regular trade between coastal settlements and inland up the river, it has built-in transmission channels." He glanced at Dozier and Maryam. "Questions?"

"How are the defensive possibilities?" The Marine asked.

"No better and no worse than anywhere else we checked out. The old priory is on a low rise, and once you clear out the brush to put in fields, you'll have excellent lines of sight and fire. More importantly, there aren't enough humans in the village to present even a minor threat, and you'll easily notice large numbers of outsiders entering the area. This one is probably the best of the sites we scouted, if only because, as Friar Shakku noted, it has lines of communication with several other settlements, including the alternate sites."

"Any sense of how they'd react to the arrival of strangers?"

Lee shook his head.

"Negative, sir. We weren't spotted. But for what it's worth, they strike me as reasonably peaceful and hardworking. Friar Shakku and Sister Maryam will have to figure out whether they're just as xenophobic as the Angelique natives or ready to receive their long-lost cousins from the stars."

"Tell us about the other sites," Shakku said.

"Certainly." Lee described settlements differing from Havre Two only in details such as the number of inhabitants, variety of cottage industries, and distribution of food sources.

As before, Shakku glanced at Dozier and Maryam when Lee finished speaking, then said, "I think we'll land a first contact party near the village you call Havre Two and see how the locals react. If they accept our presence, then those inhabiting the surrounding settlements should also do so."

Alexander leaned forward.

"It's your show, Friar. We'll stick around for a few days after taking Centurion Lee and his people aboard, just in case you encounter trouble. In fact, how about you let me know when you feel safe enough you no longer need *Alkonost*'s presence? *Yatagerasu* isn't helpless." He gave Vitt a quick grin, which she returned with a wink.

"That she isn't, Captain," Shakku replied as he allowed himself a small but serene smile. "Captain Vitt gave us the grand tour, and *Yatagerasu* is indeed an impressive vessel. I'll feel more than safe with her in orbit while we go through the delicate process of first contact. I think you may depart at your convenience."

"And miss the show?" A broad grin split Alexander's face. "Not a chance."

"The *show*? You think first contact will be entertaining?" Shakku's face took on an unmistakable air of inscrutability. Alexander couldn't tell whether the friar was irked or amused.

"I prefer the term enlightening."

"No doubt." The friar's tone was as dry as Wyvern's Central Desert, where it rained once every thousand years, proof he was teasing Alexander. "Then, by all means, please stick around and watch us make first contact."

"And what's the plan for that?"

Shakku knew Alexander was asking as the senior Hegemony officer in the Celeste system. Therefore, he lost his inscrutable air and leaned forward.

"A shuttle will land Maryam, myself, and four Brethren along with a section of Marines at a hidden site near Havre Two an hour before dawn, exact coordinates to be determined based on Centurion Lee's data. After daybreak, we will approach the settlement on foot, leaving the Marines to guard the shuttle and stand ready to assist if needed, something I hope will not happen. From there, we shall play it by ear. If the natives remember the empire and the Great Scouring, they should have no issues understanding that we come from another human world."

"And if they turned those sad events into sky demon myths like the Angeliquans?"

Shakku gave Alexander a slight shrug. "As I said, we'll play it by ear."

"Wouldn't it be safer to have Marines with you? Maybe a company's worth?"

"No. If we're not safe without the Marines, we won't be safe with them. And the mission fails before it begins." When he saw the doubt in Alexander's eyes, Shakku smiled. "The Almighty will provide."

"The Almighty didn't provide for the people in the Angelique Abbey."

A sardonic expression lit up Maryam's face.

"That's because the Almighty will not protect those guilty of hubris from the ensuing nemesis. We wanted the largest population center because we felt capable of handling such, based on the Old Order's experience with the Hatshepsut natives. Worse yet, we didn't take the time to study the natives' suitability."

"And you think the ones observed by Centurion Lee's unit are suitable?"

"More so than the Angeliquans, without a doubt. Any society practicing large-scale agriculture and cottage industries, never mind trading peacefully, will have greater potential than hunter-gatherers, scavengers, or herders. But we'll have to see for ourselves."

"That's basically the plan, Captain," Shakku said. "If the people of that settlement are amenable, we can reclaim the old priory, set up the field hospital, and begin spreading modern medical practices to gain their trust. I don't doubt that they experience their share of injuries from hard physical labor, especially those engaged in fishing."

"Didn't the first mission do the same?"

"Yes, but the Angeliquans weren't interested in our healing. They wanted tools, implements, and technological items with no strings attached. What medical care they accepted was more a way of studying us and confirming we were sky demons. Or at least that's what our late Brethren thought."

"Then let's hope your ministrations will win this bunch of natives over."

— 9 —

Friar Shakku couldn't have wished for a better night to land in the woods north of Havre Two. The low cloud cover and heavy rain reduced visibility to almost nil for standard-issue human eyes. He figured there was no chance any of the locals saw their shuttles — in the end, Captain Vitt had insisted on a backup to escort them — and the rolling thunder over the open ocean would have masked the noise of the thrusters. So far, so good.

By dawn, the rain let up, easing to a drizzle under a glowering gray sky as they walked down the shuttle's aft ramp after getting the all-clear from their protective detail. A slight chill hung in the air, but their practical black tunic and trouser combination beneath equally black cloaks kept them warm and, more importantly, dry, although they went bareheaded. Sturdy boots, waterproof, of course, completed the Void Reborn's new expeditionary clothes, along with small packs holding everything a friar or sister might need for an extended stay among friendly natives.

Mist was rising from the fields and the slow-moving Harmonie River as the party of Brethren emerged from the forest, leaving a squad of Marines inside the tree line for long-range protection. They could make out the ghostly silhouette of the old priory's ruins a kilometer and a half to the east, on a low promontory. It struck Shakku as not merely desolate, but sad. He briefly looked at Maryam, but her expression remained as composed as ever.

"If you're wondering whether I'm sensing any echoes of the past," she said, having noticed his glance, "then the answer is a faint one coming from the old city. The priory merely feels empty. No souls imprinted its remains."

"Unlike the old abbey near Angelique."

She shuddered.

"The psychic echoes of our Brethren's tortured deaths must be terrifying. I'm glad we're not near that dark, haunted place."

Soon, they could see the indistinct shape of the village spread out along the river's edge on a slightly higher piece of ground where it was probably sheltered from seasonal floods or storm surge coming up the Harmonie estuary, currently hidden by the fog. A few faint bird trills overhead reached their ears, but otherwise, sounds were eerily muted, as if the entire planet was swaddled in cotton. Soon, however, the mist began to glow and it evaporated rapidly under the rays of the early morning sun.

Any villager watching the fields to the north would have seen six black-clad Brethren appear out of nowhere, less than half a kilometer from the main gate, which was now swinging open with a low creak. At Shakku's command, they halted in a loose formation on the rutted track and composed themselves to wait until someone approached.

Based on the heads popping up over the palisade — perhaps the village guard checking the fields as the mist lifted — someone would come out shortly. As it happened, several villagers appeared after approximately ten minutes, four in all. They were stocky, fit-looking bearded men in their thirties, dark-haired, tanned, and wearing homespun clothes and appeared unarmed save for the ubiquitous knives Centurion Lee's report had mentioned.

"Who are you?" The one in the lead called out in understandable but accented Anglic as they neared. His voice, deep and rough, matched his solid figure. "And why are you just standing there?"

Shakku raised his arms slightly, palms facing upward.

"We are servants of the Almighty in the Infinite Void and are standing here because we did not wish to come nearer to your home without permission. My name is Shakku." He gestured at his colleague, standing beside him. "This is Maryam."

"Oh, aye? Void?" The man frowned. "You'd have escaped from the lot massacred by wildlings upcountry in the Forbidden Zone, then?"

Shakku and Maryam exchanged a glance. News had traveled far in the intervening weeks, further than they expected.

"No." The friar shook his head. "They died. We're from the same Order as they were but newly arrived on Celeste."

The man squinted at them as he scratched his beard. "So, you're from beyond the sky. And why are you here? What do you want in Grâce?"

"Is that the name of your town, Grâce?"

"Aye. Our ancestors lived in Havre de Grâce before the Great Scouring. Those who survived the madness by escaping into the countryside rebuilt here and elsewhere along the coast. And where are you from, servant of the Almighty?"

"Wyvern."

Unsurprisingly, at least to Shakku's eyes, an air of astonishment mixed with fear and a little anger overtook the man as he heard the name of the old imperial capital.

"Then the devil of a Mad Empress survived if you came across the stars?"

"No. Dendera died along with the rest of her dynasty and government. Wyvern also suffered from the scouring. But not so much that our ancestors who survived lost the ability to travel between worlds. The empire is gone forever, as is the mad dynasty that destroyed most of humanity. We now seek to reunite the descendants of those who survived and rebuild what was destroyed by evil."

"Oh, aye?" The man repeated, skepticism writ large on his tanned face. "And how will you perform such a miracle?"

Shakku allowed himself a rueful smile. "With much hard work, prayer, and time, sir. May I inquire about your name?"

"Yann. Yann Faranz at your service, Friar — is it?"

Shakku inclined his head. "It is."

"Do you seek to reoccupy the old priory, perchance?"

"If we may."

"None of our business, that. It's an ancient, empty shell to which we lay no claim, but having Void Brethren in the area after two hundred years of absence will disturb many people here in Grâce and along the coast."

"Why is that?"

Faranz hesitated, then said, "I'd best let you speak with our elders, Friar. I'm just the man in charge of the militia. I make no policy and take no decisions beyond my remit."

"It would honor me to speak with your elders. If I may ask, what else do you do in the community?"

"I'm the blacksmith, Friar." He thought for a moment, eyes roaming over the six Brethren. "Best if you and one other come with us. The rest can wait here."

"Of course."

Another glance at Maryam confirmed she sensed no danger, and she fell into step beside him as they followed Faranz, boxed in by his three silent companions. The remaining four Brethren remained motionless, practicing their meditation discipline in the growing warmth of the morning sunshine.

As they approached the gate, Faranz made a hand signal above his head. A stream of people with draft animals pulling farm implements emerged, ready to work fields still bare after the last harvest, an event witnessed by Centurion Lee's Marines. According to the recovered records, this was a fertile region, warm year-round, capable of supporting at least two if not three plantings. That the previous mission chose Angelique, with no good arable land within a day's walk, remained a mystery. But then, hubris was never reasonably explained in the first place.

An array of smells reached their nostrils upon entering the village itself, and Shakku's mind separated them into their various points of origins — manure piles, latrines, kitchens, byres, and humans living cheek to jowl on the shores of a slow-moving river. Though initially unpleasant, the mixture soon revealed a place full of life, hard work, and possibilities.

The houses, small though they were, gave the impression of being sturdily built, with many boasting stone walls and slate roofs, though the majority were made of wood and topped with either thatch or clay tiles. Open doors and window shutters gave them glimpses into simple rooms with wooden furniture and bustling inhabitants, including many children.

Shakku noticed, here and there, materials that were surely scavenged from Havre de Grâce or other imperial era structures over time, such as laser-cut granite blocks and metal ornaments of a complexity well beyond what a village blacksmith could produce.

Grâce's streets were straightforward, though, only packed dirt with the occasional patch of gravel in front of dwelling stoops. At least they didn't boast open-air sewers into which the villagers tossed the contents of human waste containers, such as those the mission on Santa Theresa had found in some places.

They emerged in the small central plaza Shakku remembered from the aerial views of Grâce and headed for the most prominent house among those fronting its four sides. When they reached the open door, Faranz held up a hand.

"Wait here." He vanished into the shadows while his three companions remained in a loose formation around Shakku and Maryam.

Passing villagers gave them strange stares, and a few even made what the friar guessed were gestures to ward off evil, based on his study of ancient superstitions. He gave Maryam a sideways glance, but she wore a serene expression, which he took as a sign she still didn't sense danger. Of course, neither had the first mission's sisters until the moment the Angeliquans struck for the first time.

Shakku hoped the after-action report — based on the recovered logs — blaming the natives' unusually chaotic minds for the sisters' inability to detect the growing hostility was correct. History was replete with incidents of populations turning on new arrivals without warning and massacring them merely because they came from somewhere else, Angelique being the latest case in point.

Finally, Faranz reappeared and ushered them into a stone-floored room approximately six meters square, whose sole illumination came through open windows on two sides. It took a moment for Shakku's eyes to adjust, and he made out a large yet simple wooden table surrounded by equally simple chairs. A clay pitcher with clay mugs sat at the table's center in front of a white-haired woman whose clear blue eyes, set in a wizened face, studied Shakku and Maryam with an unusual intensity. Though she appeared ancient, Shakku suspected she wasn't much older than his own sixty years. Hard labor in preindustrial societies wore a human body out prematurely.

"I am Britt Urriga, Chief Elder of Grâce," she said in a surprisingly steady and robust alto. Her accent was as evident as the blacksmith's, but her words were just as understandable. "Yann tells me you're Void Brethren come from the stars, like those massacred by the wildlings far to the east."

Shakku and Maryam bowed respectfully at the waist, then the former said, "We are, Chief Elder. Thank you for agreeing to receive us. My name is Shakku, and this is Maryam. We belong to the Order of the Void Reborn."

Urriga frowned. "Reborn?"

"Our forebears in the Almighty arose from the ashes of Empress Dendera's destruction after her downfall and the Great Scouring. The Order of the Void was, in that sense, reborn."

"I see." Her eyes narrowed in thought, although they never left Shakku's face. Another might have found Urriga's gaze unnerving, but not the friar. "And you've come here to help us rebuild?"

“To help Celeste regain its place among the stars, Chief Elder. But such an undertaking must necessarily start with one small step, one small community.”

A burst of raucous laughter escaped her throat.

“No doubt. And the wildlings were the wrong community, weren’t they? What makes you think Grâce is the right one, and more importantly, why would we wish your presence, let alone your help?”

—10—

"May I ask your age, Chief Elder?"

Another frown. "Why?"

"I would take it as a kindness if you'd humor me."

She didn't immediately reply, as if searching for the reasons behind his request.

"Sixty-two, by Celeste reckoning. I know there once was such a thing as a universal age, but we no longer bother with such calculations."

Shakku, who'd expected an answer of the sort, had memorized the formula to convert Celeste years into universal years. Urriga was barely sixty by Wyvern reckoning.

"What would you say if I told you I was sixty and Sister Maryam fifty-nine?"

Urriga let out a muffled oath.

"You look no older than Yann Faranz, and he's forty. Either you lie, or you are sky demons, as the wildlings believe."

"We neither lie nor are we anything more than ordinary humans just like you, Chief Elder. Before the Great Scouring, your ancestors were like us because backbreaking labor, the sort that prematurely wears out a body, was unknown and because they enjoyed advanced health care, something the Mad Empress' killers destroyed on this world. On average, your ancestors lived well past a hundred, and we on Wyvern and the other three worlds that survived still do. That is why our apparent physical age is less than you expect from our years, according to the calendar, whether universal or local."

Shakku let her absorb his words for a few moments.

"The first small step we would take to help you regain what your ancestors lost is the benefit of advanced health care. We count many physicians and other medical specialists among us. Sister Maryam, for instance, is a highly regarded medical doctor and surgeon."

He saw a spark of interest in Urriga's eyes as they briefly shifted to his colleague. "And you would do this in return for what?"

"Nothing, Chief Elder. We are here on a mission given us by the Almighty so we can help you, our fellow human beings, and reunite you with the rest of humanity. For that, we brought a small but complete hospital. We will treat the people in Grâce and any other community existing on good terms with yours. We also brought tools and teachers who can help increase your agricultural output while reducing the effort, help make fishing more efficient and safer, and give your blacksmith and other craftspeople the ability to create more while doing so faster."

Urriga scoffed.

"You expect nothing in return? Nonsense. No one simply gives away such things. What price will we pay if we take what you offer?"

Shakku spread out his arms, palms facing Urriga.

"None. We dedicate our lives to doing the Almighty's work and helping Celeste regain its rightful place is what the Almighty requires of us. Celeste is not the only world where we've sent missions. We are truly here to help and not otherwise interfere with your lives, the way you govern yourselves, or live as a society. We do not require belief in the Almighty or any other deity, but merely open ears, open minds, and acceptance."

"What if I say no, thank you?"

"Then we will offer our services to another community along this coast."

The moment his statement registered with Urriga, he knew he had her hooked.

"But before we continue, Chief Elder, may I ask why Yann Faranz said having Void Brethren in the area after two hundred years of absence will disturb many around here? I noticed some of your people makings signs to ward off evil when they saw us outside your house just now."

Urriga let out a grim chuckle.

"As you may have noticed, unlike the wildlings upcountry, we remember much of the past and those awful times when everything was destroyed. It is knowledge passed down the years both orally and in writing. Yes, we keep written records, and our forebears rescued some books from destruction, but not enough to rebuild with what remained. One of the things we know is that the Void Brethren abandoned their houses and the people they served, vanishing into the night, never to return. Stories grew from their disappearance at our peoples' greatest hour of need, none of them flattering. No doubt some see your return as a bad omen recalling the dire times of the Great Scouring when the Order of the Void last occupied that priory on the hill."

"I see." Shakku nodded once. "I cannot presume to speak for those long dead Brethren, but the Mad Empress nearly extinguished our Order in her paranoia. Her minions hunted our forebears down and murdered them. Whether the friars and sisters in this part of Celeste fled for their lives or were taken and massacred is a question without answer. As I said, if the people of Grâce don't want us here, we will leave and look for another community."

Urriga raised a gnarled hand and made a dismissive gesture. "The past doesn't matter, Friar. The future does."

"Do your finger joints ache?" Maryam asked, startling her.

"Of course, they do — the penalty of a hard life and old age."

"We have simple treatments that reduce swelling and remove the pain, although repairing arthritic deformation will require surgery. If you like, I can offer you something that will ease your discomfort." When Urriga gave her a suspicious stare, Maryam smiled. "I have a few ointments in my bag. One of them should bring instant relief."

She produced a small, round, white plastic container and placed it on the table. "Just twist off the top and apply the ointment to your joints. The relief will last for a good day or so."

"And what do you seek in return?"

"Nothing, Chief Elder. As a servant of the Almighty, healing is my vocation and reason in life. If you allow us to work with you and your community, we can discuss longer-lasting options that will ensure those joints not only heal but never bother you again."

Urriga's eyes narrowed again.

"Ancient legends speak of demons bearing gifts. Only later do they reveal the price. And if payment is not prompt, they take their due in flesh."

"Legends, Chief Elder. There are no such things as demons. Merely soulless humans who take advantage of the weak, the needy, and the gullible. Why don't you try the ointment?"

After a few seconds, Urriga reached out, took the container, and examined it, arm outstretched.

"Are your eyes no longer capable of seeing details close up?" Maryam asked.

"Indeed. And you'll tell me next you have an ointment for that as well."

The sister smiled. "Not an ointment, but we have a few ways of helping your eyes regain their ability to see both near and far."

It took Urriga a few tries, but she eventually opened the container. After another arms-length examination of the contents, she took a few sniffs.

"Doesn't seem like anything more than the animal fat we use on burns, but with no odor."

Urriga cautiously dabbed a misshapen finger into the little pot, scooped up a small dab, and rubbed it against her other hand's index finger knuckle joint. Almost at once, an air of wonder transformed her face. She spread more ointment over her left hand and then treated her right without saying a word.

"This is a miracle, Sister. The pain is gone."

"Reapply it tomorrow at about the same time. When you run out, let me know. I have more."

Urriga gave her a sitting bow.

"Thank you, Sister. May you enjoy the Almighty's blessings. Now tell me what you intend in detail before I decide whether the community will accept you."

"Certainly," Shakku replied, taking the lead once more. "We are sixty Brethren, twenty of whom are medical personnel. The rest are skilled in various disciplines, including agriculture, metal working, masonry, engineering, animal husbandry, and more. Four hundred pioneers who'll provide our labor since we do not intend to call on your community's resources accompany us. They'll also protect Grâce and us from hostile forces, such as the wildlings, and help with any construction projects we might jointly embark upon."

Another questioning squint. "A sort of militia, then?"

"We call them Colonial Marines, military personnel who specialize in helping missions such as ours succeed. They will live with us at the priory and only interact with Grâce's inhabitants on your terms. If you wish them to help train your militia, they will, of course, do so. That being the case, we can discuss providing your militia with better equipment and weapons." Shakku paused. "If I may ask, is there a lot of call for the militia to defend Grâce from outsiders?"

Urriga shook her head.

"No. A few years back, a group of wildlings tried to raid us, but we fought them off with only a few wounded on our side, though they suffered half a dozen deaths. They've not returned since, but we hear stories from communities further upstream of nomadic bands engaging in razzias."

"I suppose word of the massacre of our fellows in Angelique came to you the same way — via riverine settlements in the interior."

"It did." Urriga shook her head. "I may regret this later, but my regrets might be even deeper if I turn you away. I shall discuss the matter with my fellow elders shortly, and we will put your proposal before the assembly. You'll have a definitive answer by this evening."

Both Shakku and Maryam bowed their heads.

"Thank you. In the meantime, we will visit the remains of the priory and see how we might rehabilitate it should you allow our presence."

"Please return at sunset."

—11—

"So?" Shakku asked once they were on the path to the priory ruins, well out of earshot of the militiamen who'd escorted them through the gate.

"Suspicion, a little fear, but also curiosity and maybe even hunger for things they knew existed in a bygone age. As we spoke, I gave her and Faranz a few nudges, but the outcome remains in question since we didn't meet the other elders, let alone the community. That being said, I'm cautiously optimistic. I felt no hostility or ill-will among the militia guard or the population, not even those making signs to ward off evil, only suspicion mixed with interest. They're certainly not a fundamentally brutal or violent society, seeing as how Urriga presented us her genuine self, which is as decent as it appears."

"From your lips to the Almighty's ear." Shakku pulled his communicator from a hidden pocket and switched it on. "*Yatagerasu*, this is the Celeste Mission Chief Administrator."

A few moments passed, then, "*Yatagerasu*, here. Captain Vitt speaking."

"First contact went reasonably well. The village elders will seek approval from the community to collaborate with us at the end of the day. Until then, we're reconnoitering the priory ruins so that if they accept our presence, we can begin landing the rest of the mission and the containers."

"So it's looking good."

"Angelique looked good in the eyes of my late predecessor." Shakku gave Maryam a sardonic grin. "But the people here in Grâce — that's the settlement's name, by the way — retain generational memories of the days before the empire's collapse and weren't taken aback by visitors from the stars, not even Void Brethren. I'll call again once we have a firm decision. Considering the hour at which we will hear it, we may spend the night in Grâce, seeing how they close the gates at sunset."

"Fair enough. Thanks for the update."

"Shakku, out."

***

Shortly after the sun first kissed the western horizon, far out to sea, the six Brethren found themselves back at Grâce's main gate. They stood to one side and watched the farmers stream back in with their carts, plows, implements, and draft animals, followed shortly thereafter by the community's herds of sheep and cattle. Soon, the off-worlders were the only ones left beyond the walls, but the four militiamen standing guard, stone-faced and silent, gave no signs of welcome.

Shakku's keen hearing picked up the rumble of many voices coming from the direction of the central plaza. But he couldn't make out any words. A glance at Maryam left him no wiser. She merely shrugged, indicating her senses picked up nothing worthy of note.

Celeste's sun slowly slipped away, leaving ripples of light on the gentle waters of the Harmonie River estuary. The air was cooling quickly and tendrils of mist rose from freshly plowed fields as they surrendered their stored heat and moisture to the oncoming night while a thin layer of condensation settled on blades of grass. Even so, voices wafted over the walls and through the gate while the militiamen watched them with their impassive gazes.

Just as the last burst of sunshine vanished and stars filled the cloudless sky in multitudes seldom seen over the New Draconis Abbey, Yann Faranz appeared around a corner, striding toward the gate with a determined step and an inscrutable expression on his square face.

He halted among his men and bowed his head.

"The Council of Elders extends the hospitality of Grâce to the Brethren of the Void Reborn and asks that you join them for tea and a night under a solid roof."

"Does this mean our proposal was accepted?"

"Elder Urriga will answer your questions, Friar. Please follow me."

Candles and tallow lamps were dancing in open windows and doors while torches lit the street at regular intervals, keeping the darkness at bay for a little longer. The people they passed watched them with solemn countenances, but Shakku saw no one making a sign to ward off evil.

When they entered the central plaza, it was empty, though people peered at them from open windows and side streets. Faranz brought them to the chief elder's house and ushered them through the door. Urriga was in the same spot as before, but two men, also of advanced years — at least for Celeste — sat on either side of her.

Urriga indicated the two chairs facing them.

"Friar Shakku, Sister Maryam, please take your ease. Faranz will lead the rest of your party to the guest quarters, where they can prepare your evening meal and your beds."

The Brethren did as they were bid, wearing serene expressions, though they remained silent as they returned the interested gaze of the elders. Both men were likely Shakku's age but seemed older than Archimandrite Bolack, who was approaching his ninetieth year. Neither he nor Maryam could see their hands, but he suspected they suffered from arthritis as well. Perhaps Urriga had shared Maryam's gift, and it helped sway them. If so, it was a minor effort well spent, one they hadn't rehearsed but notable enough for future missions to remember.

"These are Elders Marcus Borland and Yun Neva," she said, pointing at her companions.

"Honored." Shakku and Maryam bowed their heads.

"We discussed your arrival among us and with the citizens of Grâce and came to a consensus." Urriga paused for a few heartbeats. "We bid you welcome. But with conditions."

"Thank you, Chief Elder. And what are the conditions?"

"That you leave when we ask you to do so; that you not engage in religious preaching — those among us who are curious may seek you out in the priory; that you consult us elders before extending your blessings to other communities and abide by our decisions in the matter; that you conduct no teaching without our approval, and that you extend your protection over this community and its lands without hesitation."

Shakku inclined his head again. He'd expected stipulations of the sort and would go along with them in the name of leaving the Celestans their autonomy while guiding them back to the light.

"Agreed, Chief Elder."

"And finally, that your soldiers do not engage in romantic or sexual relationships with our people."

"Agreed."

"Then please occupy the priory and make your dispositions. We can discuss how you plan to transform Grâce into a community destined for the stars once you've settled in."

"Thank you."

"Here in Grâce, we seal agreements with a cup of tea, Friar, Sister. I hope you'll enjoy it."

As if Urriga's words were a signal, a young woman in a homespun dress appeared from deeper inside the house, carrying a wooden tray with five steaming clay mugs. She placed one before each of them, then vanished again.

Urriga raised hers, imitated by the others, and said, "May we prosper as friends."

The tea was dark and bitter, but Shakku, attuned to many things, figured it had medicinal, if not mildly narcotic properties. Maryam could likely tell him more, but he figured if they wanted to drug or poison them, she'd have sensed it in their auras and warned him. It warmed his insides rather pleasantly, and the speed with which he'd downed the hot liquid surprised him.

The elders peppered them with questions, and they did their best to respond in ways people whose ancestors were cut off from advanced technology and knowledge two centuries earlier could understand. Finally, Urriga stood, a sure sign of dismissal. Shakku, Maryam, and the two male elders climbed to their feet.

"It is time to retire. Dawn arrives faster and faster as I grow older." The young woman reappeared as if on cue. Urriga gestured toward her. "She will take you to the guest house. I wish you a good night's sleep."

A deep silence had settled over Grâce while they were with the elders, and few lights shone other than the occasional torch. A short walk saw them at the door of a two-story building near the main gate. It alone still stood open, as did its ground-floor windows. The woman ushered them in, then bowed.

"A good night to you." Then she vanished around a corner.

They walked through a sitting room and into a corridor where Shakku spotted what he recognized as the glow of Wyvern manufactured light emitters coming from one room. There, they found the others sitting on wooden cots, chatting quietly among themselves. All four jumped up when they spotted their leaders.

"Everything is well?" The senior among them asked.

Shakku smiled. "As well as can be, Sister."

"We have some bread and cheese for you and water we purified, just in case."

Their full-spectrum inoculations should make them resistant to water-borne illnesses, but being careful always paid off. Shakku nodded his approval as he approached the table where the food and flasks waited. The food appeared simple but hearty. He and Maryam ate their fill, then Shakku pulled out his communicator and reported a successful first contact to the rest of the Celeste Mission and Captains Vitt, Alexander, and Pernell.

The advance party would land at the old priory shortly after daybreak the following morning.

—12—

Torrinos System
Wyvern Hegemony

"Attention. Emergence signature detected at Wormhole Torrinos One."

The dulcet androgynous voice of the tactical AI, chosen by the recently formed 4th Fleet's chief of staff for operations, cut through the quiet conversation between the night watch duty officers who'd congregated by the coffee urn. Although Starbase Torrinos never slept, the so-called graveyard shift saw most personnel asleep in their quarters, and it felt like the middle of the night in the operations center, even though the vast, spindle-shaped orbital station was currently bathed in sunlight. The station observed the same time zone as Torrinos' capital below, and there it was the middle of the night.

"Attention. Emergence signature detected at Wormhole Torrinos One," the AI repeated. It would do so until one of the duty officers acknowledged, and the young Guards Navy lieutenant responsible for wormhole traffic control buoys drained his coffee mug and headed for his station at a quick pace. He dropped into the chair facing a half-shell workstation with a large, curved display and touched the control surface a fraction of a second before the AI spoke again.

A constellation of subspace radio-equipped traffic control buoys surrounded each of the Torrinos system's four wormhole termini. They warned 4th Fleet HQ of incoming starships without delay as soon as the latter crossed the event horizon.

Two of the wormholes saw regular naval and civilian traffic, now that Santa Theresa was a going concern, with the other connecting to Wyvern. Of the remaining two, one led into a branch the Navy's survey ships had not yet remapped, and one into a part of the old empire visited by Task Force Kruzenshtern. There, the latter encountered a Republic of Lyonesse outpost on Hatshepsut, many dozen wormhole transits away.

Now, something had come through that wormhole, and it wasn't a Hegemony ship. Since President Mandus ended the Hegemony's isolationist policy, those who'd traveled in that direction had returned on schedule encountering no other sentient life.

Which could only mean…

"Do we have telemetry and visuals?" The senior duty officer, a Guards Navy commander, asked as he made his way to the lieutenant's workstation.

"Not yet, sir. The buoys detected an emergence signature from the wormhole terminus but couldn't find what came through. It must be running silent and with really tight emissions control. Naval grade, I'd say."

The commander spoke the one word that was on the mind of every officer in the operations center since the AI issued its first warning — Lyonesse. Finally. The Hegemony had been expecting an incursion in response to Hatshepsut for over two years.

"It has to be a Lyonesse naval unit, sir. No one else has a reason to come through Wormhole One unannounced and then hide from our sensors."

The commander nodded.

"Agreed." He turned to his deputy. "Warn the nearest task force and see that it heads for Wormhole One at best possible speed. I'll call the admiral."

"That'll be Task Force Four-Four, Captain Newton Giambo, sir. On it."

Vice Admiral Nora Kutani, Flag Officer Commanding 4th Fleet, lived on Torrinos Station. She synchronized her day with its day, meaning she was fast asleep when the senior duty officer called the flag quarters at the heart of the residential section. But she had a reputation as a light sleeper and answered — audio only — after little more than ten seconds.

"Kutani, here. What's up, Commander?"

"An unscheduled arrival through Wormhole One, sir, currently running silent with the sort of emissions control you'd expect from a well-maintained and properly crewed naval unit. Task Force Four-Four is receiving orders to intercept. We can't tell who the intruder is, but there can only be one rational answer."

"Lyonesse. Hammer the area with every sensor in range, Commander. I don't care if the intruder notices the entire wormhole traffic control buoy constellation. Should Task Force

Four-Four make an intercept, they will not, I repeat, not fire unless fired upon. Instead, the commanding officer will make every attempt to open a communications link while keeping a non-threatening posture, meaning no targeting sensors."

"Aye, aye, sir. I'll tell Captain Giambo myself."

"Keep me apprised of developments. Kutani, out."

That was one thing most of the 4th Fleet staff liked about their new flag officer — she didn't breathe down anyone's neck and stayed away from the operations center until her direct involvement became necessary. Considering the time and distances involved, that wouldn't be for a few hours yet, certainly not until well after the day shift took over at oh-eight-hundred. The commander and his team would be fast asleep by then and miss the denouement, if there was any.

Too bad the shipbuilding program took away resources from developing the hotly debated wormhole forts. A fort at Wormhole One might not only have spotted the intruder immediately but made him stand down and open communications. Yet the need for new cruisers and frigates took precedence over any other construction except upgrading the current inventory and converting civilian freighters into replenishment ships.

***

"A what now?" Captain Newton Giambo, commanding officer of the Wyvern Hegemony cruiser *Caladrius* and recently appointed commander, Task Force Four-Four, sat up in his cot as the bridge relayed orders from 4th Fleet Operations.

"An unknown intruder running silent."

"Has to be a Lyonesse ship. They're the only ones with FTL capability we've encountered since the empire collapsed. I'll be in the CIC in five. In the meantime, have navigation plot a synchronized jump to take us," Giambo paused as he thought, "five million klicks from the center of the event horizon. The task force will drop out of FTL running silent."

"Synchronized jump to five million kilometers from the center of Wormhole One event horizon, coming out of FTL running silent, aye, sir."

"Captain, out."

Task Force Four-Four wasn't much by any standards, one cruiser and three frigates with even more time in space since their last refit than *Caladrius* — the Mythos class ships *Scylla, Abaia,* and *Monocerus*. But if the buoys only counted a single intruder coming through the wormhole, that would suffice. Besides, his orders forbade him from opening fire first, which was a relief.

Everyone in the Hegemony knew the Hatshepsut story, and no one wanted to go down in history as triggering the next all-human interstellar war. Of course, there was still a tiny chance the newcomer came from a non-human species, but neither the Shrehari nor any minor space-faring races had made contact since the last days of the empire. And the Shrehari were on a decline as bad, if not worse, than humanity's.

The jump klaxon sounded just as Giambo was pulling on his boots, and he nodded to himself with satisfaction. Patrolling the Torrinos system instead of remapping the old wormhole network and reclaiming star systems might be tedious, but his crew could react as quickly as the best of them. He waited until the jump nausea dissipated before standing, then made his way to the CIC, where an updated tactical holographic projection waited.

The combat systems officer relinquished the command chair and pointed at an expanding, transparent red blob growing from the wormhole terminal's green disk.

"Based on the data from the buoys, probable exit vector, and standard wormhole emergence speed, the intruder is somewhere in this segment if he stayed sublight. And that's what any sane scout ship captain would do for a long time after entering a new star system. We're out of luck if he went FTL before reconnoitering the area."

Giambo grunted softly. "Assuming it's a Lyonesse ship, he'll stay sublight until he knows whether this system is inhabited and, if so, what's there. It's what we would do, and we all descended from the same damn Imperial Navy. If we kept many old doctrines alive simply because they made sense, they would have as well. Some things just shouldn't be messed with."

"No doubt, sir."

Giambo sat back, eyes on the projection, and let his mind wander. The Navy had played many a what-if scenario around Hegemony ships meeting Lyonesse ships in deep space, none of them conclusive. Task Force Krusenshtern's abduction of Old Order Brethren from Hatshepsut had been a hostile act, but nothing to trigger another ruinous war.

In fact, Giambo suspected that if a Lyonesse task force showed up on the Hegemony's doorstep and demanded the return of the kidnapped monastics, President Mandus would do so without argument. The Hegemony's quasi-absolute ruler could be accused of many things, but being foolhardy wasn't one of them.

He glanced at the countdown clock and decided there was more than enough time for a quick bite in the wardroom before they dropped out of FTL.

"You have the CIC, Commander."

"I have the CIC."

***

Task Force Four-Four dropped out of hyperspace with barely a ripple and immediately vanished, its ships' emissions dampened like only naval units could manage. As Giambo expected, they detected nothing. No coherent emissions, let alone a sublight drive signature.

After an hour, during which they would have picked up anything artificial shed within the ever-expanding area of space that should encompass the intruder — provided he hadn't gone FTL — Giambo ordered his ships to go up systems. He hoped his sudden appearance would trigger a reaction. Maybe a sudden course change. Anything. Otherwise, they might spend the next day chasing sensor ghosts and in all likelihood moving further apart.

"Signals, make to the task force, go up systems in five, I repeat five minutes at my signal, and hammer the area with active sensors."

"Up systems in five minutes at commander's signal and hammer the area with active sensors, aye," the signals chief said.

Caladrius' new first officer, whose holographic representation hovered at Giambo's right elbow — the former had the bridge while the latter was in the CIC — said, "Acknowledged, Captain."

The five minutes passed as they always do, one at a time, yet Giambo found himself impatient. When the countdown timer finally reached zero, he glanced at the signals chief.

"Make to the task force, up systems."

"Up systems, aye, Captain."

Within seconds, three blue wedges joined the one representing *Caladrius* in the tactical projection, all in perfect formation, and Giambo allowed himself a brief smile of satisfaction.

"We are at full power, shielded, weapons charged, and active sensors searching, sir," the combat systems officer reported moments later. "If the intruder is sublight, he can't fail to notice us in the next hour or two."

In the end, it took eighty-three minutes until Task Force Four-Four's sensors picked up a sudden surge in emissions on a vector leading straight away from the wormhole terminus.

Caladrius' combat systems officer pumped his fist in the air as telemetry began filling one of the side displays.

"Gotcha, you sneaky bastard."

Giambo leaned forward as if urging the sensors to refine their scans and was quickly rewarded by a visual on the primary display.

"Power curve and apparent size indicate something in our cruisers' range," the sensor chief said. "There's nothing like her in our database, but her hull and hyperdrive configurations are definitely of human origin, according to the intelligence AI. She could well be descended from what we once called a fast attack cruiser in the last days of the empire."

"Signals, ping the intruder with our subspace radio. Let's see if her captain wants to talk."

"She's changing trajectory away from us, sir." A few moments passed. "Looks like an emergency about-turn. Perhaps the captain decided discretion was the better part of valor and is headed back for the wormhole terminus."

"If their job was finding us, then mission accomplished."

The minutes ticked by but without a response from the intruder, although Task Force Four-Four was gaining on him, though he only needed minor course adjustments to reach the wormhole.

Finally, Giambo said, "Signals, get me a link with 4th Fleet Operations."

Admiral Kutani surprised him by taking the call herself, but he reported events calmly and methodically.

"If the intruder — sorry, Admiral — make that when the intruder enters the wormhole, shall I pursue?"

Kutani shook her head. "No. Let them go. We won't engage in a hostile chase if we can't establish communications. As you said, they probably found what they were looking for. Let's leave it at that. High Command on Wyvern can decide the next steps."

And so, over the following few hours, they watched the Lyonesse Navy ship claw her way back to the wormhole terminus, her identity no longer in doubt. The visual sensors eventually made out a national ensign — a golden double-headed raptor on a green background — a name, *Seeker*, and a hull number in numerals used by humanity for millennia.

But *Seeker* never replied to *Caladrius*' hails on any frequency. Inevitably, she reached the wormhole terminus just ahead of Task Force Four-Four and vanished, leaving Giambo both puzzled and frustrated.

"Why do you think they didn't want to talk, sir?" The first officer asked.

Giambo shrugged.

"Beats me. Would Task Force Kruzenshtern have answered Lyonesse hails when they were in the Hatshepsut system?"

"We'll never know."

"No, we won't. Please have nav plot a course back to our patrol route."

—13—

New Draconis
Wyvern System

"I suppose it was inevitable." President Vigdis Mandus sat back in her chair at the head of the conference table after Admiral Benes finished relaying the report from 4th Fleet. "But why not open a dialog? We've known of each other's existence for over two years."

When Benes opened his mouth to reply, Mandus shrugged irritably.

"It was a rhetorical question, Admiral. We could spend the rest of the day speculating without finding an answer. Instead, let's discuss what, if anything, we should change in our naval posture and the control of Wormhole Torrinos One."

"Might we also discuss the wisdom of sending an embassy to Hatshepsut, along with the Old Order Brethren who should be returned to their people, now that Lyonesse knows where we are?" Archimandrite Bolack asked. "A gesture of goodwill which might help prevent future grief."

"A fine suggestion." Chancellor Conteh gave his colleague a seated bow. "And one whose time will come, though it may not be at this very moment."

"The Chancellor is right," Benes said. "We should deal with our defensive perimeter before trying to make friends with Lyonesse. What if they plan on eliminating the Hegemony before we become a threat to their ambitions? One of us will reunite humanity, and I'd rather it not be them."

"And your recommendation would be, Admiral?" Mandus arched an eyebrow at the Navy's commander-in-chief, first among equals in the Hegemony's second tier of leadership and, therefore, the most powerful after the three Executive Committee members.

"Move the Wormhole Torrinos One defense to the other side, so nothing gets through without warning again. A full buoy constellation, the first wormhole fort once it's built, and a task force from 4th Fleet that'll rotate through every two or three weeks. Of course, we'll also need a powerful subspace relay in that system, something like the ones keeping the Hegemony's core worlds in constant communication."

"Additional and unexpected expenditures," Conteh said in a slightly disapproving tone. "The Hegemony's industrial, financial, and human capabilities are already stretched to the limit, as you're undoubtedly aware, Admiral. With the pace of shipbuilding and colonization, we face rapid inflation for the first time since the end of the empire."

Bolack gave the Chancellor a beatific smile.

"Yet the people are enthusiastic and hopeful about the future for the first time since the end of the empire. Isn't that worth any price?"

"Up to a point, Archimandrite. A bankrupt state that cannot protect its people will find generating enthusiasm and hope an insurmountable challenge."

Mandus raised a restraining hand before the debate between the head of government and the head of the Void Reborn went on any further.

"We will do what we must to secure our future. Chancellor, find the funding to support Admiral Benes' plan. However, the wormhole fort will continue to wait its turn in the shipyards. Our priority remains building modern starships. Approaching Lyonesse on a diplomatic footing will also wait until we're stronger and more secure. They outstrip us in ships if they're colonizing Hatshepsut, an entire sector away from the Coalsack and Lyonesse itself. Yes, I know it stretches their forces, but still."

Benes raised a hand.

"If I may, Madame President. Would you entertain reciprocating with a reconnaissance mission of our own, say our newest and fastest starship running the wormhole network to Hatshepsut so we can see what they've done these past two and a half years? Strictly sneak and peek, no communications, and no open hostilities. It'll be detected, that's a given, but if it turns and runs the moment the Lyonessers light up sensors, just like their ship did, we accomplish two goals. First, we show that we're monitoring them and second, that we're not aggressive." Benes paused. "Make that three goals. Third, we find out whether they've established outposts past Hatshepsut."

Mandus looked around the table. "Comments on Admiral Benes' proposal we sent a reconnaissance mission to Hatshepsut?"

They shook their heads one after the other.

"Approved. When can you have a ship on its way?"

"A few weeks, Madame President. It will be the cruiser *Aethon*, our most recent Hegemon class refit, capable of bypassing wormholes and making long interstellar voyages. She's under the command of Captain Evan Kang, who ranked in the top five percent of the commanders promoted to captain during the last boards. He was the first officer in *Caladrius*, the ship that found the massacred Celeste Mission on her return from mapping the wormhole network in the old core sector. *Aethon* just finished the first phase of her operational readiness evaluation and passed with almost perfect marks."

An appreciative air lit up Admiral Godfrey's face as he nodded. "Almost? High praise indeed. I can't remember getting more than an entirely satisfactory in my day. Your Captain Kang must be a paragon of efficiency."

"Does anyone ever get perfect marks for anything in the Navy?" Chief Commissioner Cabreras asked in a semi-sarcastic tone.

Godfrey turned a sardonic grin on him.

"Have you ever met the flawless human being, Nero? No? Not even in the Commission for State Security? There's a shocker. Well, neither has anyone in the Navy. The last time captains got perfect scores at the end of readiness evaluations was in Dendera's day, and they weren't earned honestly but based on favors, titles of nobility, payoffs, and other forms of corruption. One more thing that helped drive several admirals who'd kept a shred of integrity to revolt, triggering a cascade that tore our thousand-year empire asunder. Never underestimate the deleterious effect cheating has on loyalty and morale when it means the lives of honest spacers might be lost."

"Something just struck me," Archimandrite Bolack said in a pensive tone when Cabreras didn't comment on Godfrey's brief history lesson. "You noted the emblem on that Lyonesse ship, yes? A double-headed avian of some sort. I still recall studying the ancient origins of the Hegemony and our Order's symbol, the phoenix, when I was a young friar with a keen mind thirsty for knowledge. Many references speak of such double-headed birds not as eagles or the like but as phoenixes standing for empires, the sort that lives for centuries, then dies in flames only to be reborn. Curious that a republic would choose such an emblem, but even curiouser, we might see parallels between Lyonesse and Wyvern's rise from the ashes of the old empire in terms of symbology and an almost identical Oath of Reunification."

Godfrey shrugged. "Maybe the Lyonesse people don't know about the references you mention, or they attribute a totally different meaning to their sigil. I wouldn't read much into it."

"All right." Mandus looked around the table. "Let's move on to other business."

***

Later that day, Godfrey summoned Torma and Ardrix and informed them of the cruiser *Aethon*'s mission as a reply to the Lyonesse starship visiting Torrinos.

After giving Ardrix a knowing look, Torma said, "Would it be unrealistic to hope we might return the Old Order Brethren aboard *Aethon*? It could help dispel Lyonesse's impression we're a hostile power. There's nothing they've learned that could harm us in the short and long term. On the contrary, they might tell

Lyonesse about us and perhaps defuse hostile intent before it raises its ugly head. Neither they nor we can afford a confrontation. Not now. There's not enough of us, and it will take the Hegemony at least a generation to ramp up capacity. I suspect Lyonesse is in a similar position. Best we make peace, if not forever, then for now."

Godfrey chuckled. "A definitely unpatriotic opinion for a general wearing the Commission for State Security uniform, Crevan. But a sane one, though I'm sure Chief Commissioner Cabreras would object most strenuously."'

"And do you think returning the Old Order Brethren is a good idea, sir?" Sister Ardrix asked

Godfrey gave her a searching look.

"What might the Archimandrite's views on the matter be?"

"I've not broached the subject with him, knowing the idea will find vigorous resistance in many quarters, but should President Mandus and you agree on repatriation, I'm sure he would as well. Keeping Brethren on Wyvern against their will grates on his sensibilities. Of course, that leaves the Chancellor, whose opinion I couldn't even fathom." She paused for a few heartbeats. "We're in the wrong here, Admiral. Best we repent our sins and make restitution the only way we can. Our so-called guests belong with their own people. As Crevan said, nothing they've learned can harm us. On the contrary, once Lyonesse discovers we're a determined people, its leaders will be less likely to take aggressive action."

Torma nodded once. "Indeed. We can put them aboard a sterilized civilian pattern shuttle and release them at Hatshepsut's hyperlimit. I'm sure Lyonesse stationed naval units there by now, and they can recover the shuttle. If not, we'll ensure it has sufficient autonomy to land safely at their priory. An AI can take care of the controls."

Godfrey considered both in turn. "What would you expect our guests to tell their people?"

"The truth, which harms no one and the Almighty willing, might prevent unfortunate consequences."

"President Mandus and the Executive Committee might not take such a sanguine view of your proposal."

A faint smile softened Torma's severe expression. "We were hoping you'd use your almost mystical powers of persuasion, sir. Or failing that, your powers of dissimulation to smuggle the Old Order Brethren aboard *Aethon* with secret orders for her captain."

"I'll approach the President — quietly — with the proposal. If she says no, then no, it shall be, understood?"

—14—

Celeste System

"Impressive." Captain Alexander pivoted on his heels to study the field hospital's half dozen intensive care units clustered around a central node. Each was separated from the others and the node by transparent aluminum windows and sliding doors. "And to think you set it up so quickly."

"Major Dozier's people are invaluable. We couldn't have done the job by ourselves, at least not without a lot of effort and time," Friar Shakku, who was giving Alexander the grand tour, replied. "The idea of forming Colonial Marine units trained as military pioneers who can turn their hand to any task that needs doing was a stroke of genius."

"You can thank Admiral Godfrey. He came up with the idea."

In record time, a small village had sprung up in and around the priory ruins, complete with water and waste treatment plants, its own fusion reactor, greenhouses, barracks, storerooms, electrical and mechanical workshops, and of course, the ultramodern field hospital.

Every citizen of Grâce had visited by now and came away with awe written clearly on their faces. Those who'd sought medical treatment were even more impressed. For the last two days, visitors from neighboring communities had shown up, wondering what was going on at the old priory and why the Void Brethren had returned along with a veritable army. Shakku and the rest showed them the same courtesy but let Chief Elder Urriga deal with the leadership of those settlements.

"I'll make a note to send him my thanks. Did Major Dozier mention he plans on a broad sweep of the region, with elements going upriver on the boats they brought?"

Alexander nodded with approval. "A wise precaution. I doubt word about new sky demons has reached Angelique yet, but there will be people in the wilds to the east who've regressed further than those inhabiting the coastal towns, and they might present a threat."

"Precisely what Major Dozier figures." They stepped back out into the watery afternoon sunshine. "And that's it, Captain. As you can see, we're well along."

"Indeed, although I question the wisdom in not setting up an actual defensive perimeter. The fencing you've erected will keep marauding wildlife out but won't do much to stop humans bent on entering whether or not they're welcome."

A smiling Shakku glanced at Alexander. "Neither do Grâce's walls, and our long-term goal is becoming an integral and indistinguishable part of the broader community."

Alexander chuckled. "Point taken, Friar."

"Besides, Major Dozier will keep us safe day and night thanks to the perimeter sensors, drones on aerial watch, patrols, and troopers on standby. He assures me no hostile force will get within a kilometer of the priory." When Alexander made to speak, Shakku raised a restraining hand. "Yes, the Angelique mission also saw the hostiles coming from a distance, but they were overwhelmed by numbers, not victims of insufficient intelligence. We won't face a similar problem here."

"Let's hope the Almighty sees it that way, Friar. Thanks for the tour. Once I'm back aboard *Alkonost,* we'll leave for our wormhole mapping mission. Who knows? Maybe the Almighty will guide us to Earth this time."

"Ah, yes. Earth. Take care you don't encounter the ghosts of humanity's turbulent past, my friend."

Alexander gave Shakku a curious look. "What do you mean?"

"Places that saw great suffering and death retain an echo of the souls who perished. The greater the horrors, the stronger that echo will be. Many Sisters of the Void, those with strong psychic abilities such as Maryam, can sense them. But even we who cannot pick up the imprint of long-vanished souls will feel unease in such places. Some may perhaps be influenced into making decisions and taking actions they would normally avoid simply because of psychic pressures they cannot detect, let alone define."

"Huh. Can't say I ever encountered such a situation, Friar. I'm not even sure I believe in the idea souls leave imprints that the living can sense. But why caution me about Earth?"

Shakku studied Alexander with solemn eyes for a few heartbeats.

"Though Dendera's downfall resulted in the deaths of countless billions, they were diffused across worlds our species had occupied for little more than fifteen hundred years. By contrast, every human being who ever lived since our species appeared until it left Earth during the First Migration at the start of the 22nd century died there. That's a lot of souls on a single world. Well over a hundred fifty billion by the time the empire was born. And so many perished in terror during the almost continuous warfare conducted by our forebears. Or because of political upheavals, genocide, and catastrophic natural disasters. Add to that the hundreds of millions who were massacred by Dendera's Retribution Fleet, and you have an entire planet capable of making a sensitive sister blanch with the weight of the past."

"Well." Alexander shrugged. "No offense, but as I said, I'm not much of a believer. Still, I'll keep an open mind and see how finding the cradle of humanity affects me. If we get there on this cruise. With one of the old primary wormhole branches disrupted by a wandering wormhole, we might remap uninhabited star systems until we reach the limits of *Alkonost*'s autonomy. Surveying is not a glamorous job, but as the wandering wormhole proved, we must do it before we can race headlong into other parts of the old empire. And on that note, I'll take my leave. By the time I reach my ship, she'll be ready to break out of orbit. Please pass my farewell along to Sister Maryam and Major Dozier."

Alexander stuck out his hand. "Take care, Friar. I'm sure you'll make this mission a success."

"And I am sure you'll make your survey a success as well, Captain. Fair winds and following seas."

They shook, then Alexander turned on his heels and, with an energetic step, walked back to the shuttle landing pad behind the priory proper where his pinnace waited. Shakku watched him go until he vanished from sight behind an old, ivy-covered wall remnant, then headed for the container that served as the mission's administrative offices. As he was about to cross the threshold, a sharp whine followed by a muffled rumble reached his ears, and he turned in time to see Alexander's shuttle rise straight up into the clear morning air on a column of pure energy.

With *Yatagerasu* having left the previous evening to return home and *Strix* long gone, once *Alkonost* left, they'd be alone in a star system light-years from the nearest Wyvern outpost without the means to leave Celeste and no way of calling for help. *Yatagerasu* or another Navy replenishment ship was due in approximately eight weeks with their first resupply, provided everything went according to schedule. Much could happen in those eight weeks, and Shakku offered a quick prayer that what happened would be per the Almighty's plan.

***

As he sat beside the pinnace's pilot — the Navy did not permit starship captains to fly themselves and hadn't since time immemorial — Alexander pondered Shakku's words concerning souls and the ghosts of the past. He was a career officer with solid credentials and an average starship captain's imagination. Or so everyone thought.

The Wyvern Hegemony Guards Navy and its sister services, the Ground Forces and Commission for State Security, weren't keen on officers with too much imagination. At least they weren't until President Mandus removed the shackles keeping the Hegemony's people imprisoned in their four star systems. Alexander figured out why it was so early on, and he'd spent his entire time in uniform coming across as stoic and dispassionate.

But Shakku's words touched upon questions he'd asked himself repeatedly without finding answers or even someone with whom he could debate them without risking the opprobrium of his profession. Alexander figured it was the price he paid for being inquisitive, curious, and well-read in a society where such things weren't considered particularly praiseworthy. Now that the Hegemony was transforming at breakneck speed, they could only be helpful, but changing attitudes took much longer, and he'd keep his thoughts private, probably for the rest of his life. And that meant if he encountered the ghosts of humanity's past on Earth, he'd deal with them on his own.

Or he could open up just a bit to his ship's counselor, Sister Taina. He didn't know whether she was of a sensitive disposition and might glimpse more than others, but they would get to know each other well over the coming weeks and months. So far, she'd been nothing but pleasant, helpful, competent, and a delightful conversationalist. Like every other Sister of the Void on assignment with the Navy he'd met over the years.

Alexander had always entertained good relationships with them. Still, he'd never confided in one or used her skills as a counselor — only as a medical staff member who dealt with physical ailments. However, he promised himself he'd listen if she sensed anything out of the ordinary or beyond what an average Navy officer considered rational.

The shuttle's switch over to artificial gravity pulled Alexander out of his reverie, and he saw *Alkonost* growing rapidly on the flight deck's primary display, her starboard shuttle hangar doors opening to receive them. Thirty minutes later, the cruiser broke out of orbit and accelerated toward the hyperlimit for her first FTL leg to where human history had begun.

Not that there was any guarantee *Alkonost* would reach it before she had to turn around, but after Shakku's sibylline words, Alexander hoped they did, if only so he might absorb more of humanity's past than any other officer before the inevitable shiploads of researchers arrived.

Later, as he sat in the empty wardroom at his usual table beneath the ship's crest, a mythical bird with a fierce beak surrounded by a ring of eight-pointed stars, Alexander was about to lose himself in a whirlpool of speculation when his first officer entered. Commander Reena Prince, a wiry woman in her late thirties with short black hair and intense brown eyes framing a narrow face, drew a cup of coffee from the eternal urn and dropped into the chair across from him.

"A cred for your thoughts, Skipper. You seem preoccupied."

"You're overpaying, Reena."

"Try me." She took a sip, then cocked a questioning eyebrow. "Generally, your thoughts are more cred-worthy than those of most admirals. Not that you ever heard me say so."

He related Shakku's words as closely as he could remember them and his impressions of the friar.

"Hmm." Prince took a sip of her coffee, brow creased in thought. "One thing you can say about Void monastics — they cover many possibilities with the same eldritch words, hedging their bets. But that low-level overflight we did of Angelique, the destroyed abbey, and the mass grave yesterday left me feeling lost for almost a day afterward.

"Lost?" It was Alexander's turn to frown. He'd sent every small craft in *Alkonost* out on an atmospheric practice run, so pilots got one last chance at nap of the earth flying before they headed out. "What do you mean?"

She didn't immediately reply. Instead, she chewed on her lower lip as she searched for the right words.

"Like something brushed my soul and numbed it, taking away my ability to feel positive emotions."

"You didn't mention it after the flight."

Prince shrugged.

"It isn't something a first officer casually discusses with her captain. But after Shakku's warning?" She let out a soft sigh. "I'm no more a believer than most Navy officers, but you and I both know there are things in the galaxy that defy rational explanation. You need not be a Void mystic to realize that."

Alexander chuckled. "I think you've just answered why we still have religion in this day and age — so we can account for the unaccountable. Our species doesn't suffer uncertainty with much grace, let alone stoicism."

"True. Still, I wish I hadn't taken part in that overflight. I'm still not sure whether I've retrieved all of my soul from wherever part of it went. But it was my last chance to get off the ship for the Almighty knows how long."

"What's done is done. Do you know if anyone else aboard the dropships and shuttles were affected?"

She gave him a wry smile.

"It's not something crew members casually discuss with the first officer or Marines with anyone outside the Corps. Was there less banter when we returned? Possibly, but I wasn't paying close attention to the behavior of others at that moment. Maybe I'm just more sensitive than most and didn't know it. The Angelique Abbey was the closest I've ever been to a site that saw such evil and violent death."

"There are plenty on the Hegemony's four home worlds from the days of Dendera's downfall."

Prince's eyes narrowed.

"Well, that would explain my depressing sadness at visiting memorials erected over places where so many died from orbital bombardments by the Mad Empress' killers."

"You should have joined the Order and become a sister."

"I don't like people enough to be a good monastic whose sole purpose is serving others."

Alexander let out a bark of laughter. "So instead, you serve the state, which embodies the collectivity of others."

"Sure." She smirked at him. "But the state doesn't force me to like people. First officers should always be misanthropes, at least while so employed."

"Or, you could have become a sister and requested employment with the Commission for State Security, where misanthropy and service to the Hegemony unite as one."

Prince was saved from replying by the public address system. "Now, hear this. Transition to hyperspace in five, I repeat, five minutes. That is all."

Both officers drained their coffee mugs and climbed to their feet.

"You have plans for physical training once we're FTL?" Alexander asked.

"I figure I'll join the cox'n's aikido group. A little sparring might knock what's left of that strange feeling out of my thick skull. Especially if, as I expect, Garth Lee's Marines take part. Aikido is one of their favorite martial arts."

"Sounds like a good idea. I'll join you."

A smile briefly lit up Prince's narrow features. "I always look forward to your graceful way of conceding defeat."

***

"Sir?" The duty sensor operator, a grizzled petty officer first class, raised her hand to attract the CIC officer of the watch's attention.

"Yes?"

"I could have sworn I just saw a sensor ghost near the hyperlimit several million kilometers to starboard."

"What does the intelligence AI say?"

"The usual. There is no way of telling whether it's a natural phenomenon or a ship running silent."

The officer of the watch reviewed the sensor log and shrugged. "We're the only Hegemony ship out here, and I doubt Lyonesse has come this far. It has to be a natural phenomenon. Not that we'll have time to investigate. We're going FTL in sixty seconds. Log it for the captain."

"Aye, aye, sir. Besides, whatever it was is gone."

Moments later, the transition warning sounded throughout *Alkonost,* and the incident was quickly forgotten. Sensor ghosts were a rare but known occurrence in other star systems. Why not Celeste?

PART II – SEEKERS

—15—

Hatshepsut System

"Operations to the captain."

"Morane."

"Traffic control buoys report *Seeker* emerging from Wormhole Two, sir."

"Finally. Get me a subspace link with her before she goes FTL.

"Already on it, sir. Wait one."

Captain Lucas Morane, commanding officer of the Lyonesse Navy's Hatshepsut Squadron, put away the weekly maintenance report for Starbase Hatshepsut, his headquarters and home away from home. Although calling the small, prefabricated orbital a starbase was a bit grandiose in Morane's opinion, it still served the same purpose as its larger siblings around Lyonesse, Arietis, Yotai, and the republic's other core worlds.

The Hatshepsut Squadron wasn't much — two Lannion class frigates and three Frater class corvettes. It was all the Navy could spare. The republic's shipbuilding industry was still confined to Lyonesse itself, and even with a dozen orbital yards for large starships and another dozen on the surface for small combatants, it barely met the needs of both the Navy and the Merchant Service.

And hard-pressed Void Ships, such as *Seeker* and its sisters, who patrolled the wormhole network, kept the republic's outposts connected with the home system, and escorted replenishment convoys? They were almost constantly on the go. Fortunately, the Navy's policy of double crewing meant time ashore between missions, so the men and women aboard didn't burn out.

Squadrons protecting outer star systems weren't quite as lucky with home leave while on station, but their crews could still enjoy a few days ashore on the world they protected every couple of weeks and breathe fresh air.

"Commander Byner for you, sir."

His office display lit up with the narrow, angular face of a pale, copper-haired woman in her early forties. Keen blue eyes met his, and Morane couldn't help but see barely contained excitement.

"We found them, sir," Julia Byner said in her rich alto before Morane even opened his mouth. "Torrinos. A single wormhole transit from Wyvern, according to the old navigation charts. Full buoy constellation around the wormhole terminus and a task force of one cruiser and three frigates within easy FTL reach. They must have spotted us emerging even though we came out running silent and sent the nearest ships to investigate."

"Or it was a coincidence."

"No, sir. They knew we were there because they came out of silent running a few million kilometers from the terminus and hammered our most likely vector with every bit of the sensor power they had. Since my mission was to find and report, I went up systems and turned back. They pursued, but we reached the terminus ahead of them and broke contact. One notable thing, though. They didn't use targeting sensors — at least not that we could tell. But they hailed us on every frequency, normal and subspace. As per my orders, I didn't reply."

"Well done, Julia. Send me your report, and I'll push it home via the relay network, which, as you'll be pleased to know, is now operational. The Chief of the Defense Staff can have your commendation ready and waiting when you dock."

"Thank you, sir. I just hope my mission didn't trigger something we might come to regret."

"If they didn't show an aggressive posture and tried talking instead, I'd say we won't face an invasion anytime soon. Do you want to spend a few days here to catch your breath? The station is still a little small for a Void Ship, but with Thebes now boasting an operational spaceport, you can send liberty parties down directly. I'll sort it with the garrison commander. The locals are quite happy to make money off visiting starship crews, now that they've adopted Lyonesse Creds as a secondary currency along with an official exchange rate."

"You've been busy since I passed through on the way out."

"Not that you stopped to take stock, let alone spend a day or two in orbit." Morane's smile took the sting out of his words. "Always on the move, those Void Ships. I should know after three years in one. But the credit belongs to Abbess Rianne and Chief Administrator Horam, and they've been busy for the last two years." When he saw the look on Byner's face, Morane chuckled. "Yes, it's been going so well. The Motherhouse upgraded Thebes Priory to an abbey a few weeks back. That means they can establish subsidiary houses elsewhere on Hatshepsut, provided they produce enough local Brethren to staff them."

"And when do the locals get a senator?"

"Not just yet. First, the Thebans must set up missions in the other large population centers and extend their influence to eventually bring everyone under a single government. Once they unify this place, we'll offer them membership in the republic as a sovereign star system. But a Lyonesse ambassador arrived on the resupply convoy yesterday to formalize our relationship with the Thebans. In fact, you'll probably catch up with that convoy. It headed back a few hours ago and is in FTL between our hyperlimit and the wormhole terminus."

"Considering I'm faster than a replenishment convoy, I'll sail right by with no one noticing. Do the Thebans know what we've planned for them?"

Morane nodded. "Yes. It gives them the incentive to absorb every bit of the technological progress they can manage as quickly as possible."

A sly smile lit up Byner's face. "It's part of your ancestor's master plan, no doubt?"

"More or less, adjusted for local conditions, such as another interstellar polity, if not on our doorstep, then within a Void Ship's reach. But we can discuss that around a cup of coffee, perhaps spiked with some Theban rum, if you decide to stop for a bit."

Byner grimaced. "As much as I'd enjoy that, my people can almost smell the upcoming crew change and a stint at home. I'll send you my report for onward transmission and make for the exit wormhole directly."

"Pity. But I'm here for a while, so we can always have our chat the next time you visit."

"It would be a pleasure, sir."

"In that case, I'll wish you an uneventful trip home and some well-deserved rest."

"Thank you, sir."

"Starbase Hatshepsut, out."

Morane sat back as a view of the planet below replaced Byner's face. Responsibility for the safety of Lyonesse's furthest outpost was an honor. He would watch history being made in real-time as Jonas Morane's plan went into overdrive so Hatshepsut quickly became a self-sustaining bulwark against the Hegemony about which they still knew little.

But he still envied Julia Byner. The Void Ships traveled to places that hadn't seen a human spacecraft in over two centuries. Long journeys, indeed, but the dual crewing system also meant they spent a lot of time at home between cruises.

A soft chime announced the arrival of Byner's report. As promised, Morane put a priority tag on it and made sure the signals officer funneled it into the longest subspace transmission chain in existence. He then made sure both the new ambassador and Abbess Rianne received a copy before he settled in to read it himself. If he couldn't travel beyond the republic in person, at least he could do so vicariously.

***

"Ambassador?"

Currag DeCarde, the new Republic of Lyonesse envoy to Hatshepsut's Thebes Republic, turned at Abbess Rianne's voice by the garden door. Tall, muscular, with a square face, sandy hair going gray at the temples, and his family's deep blue eyes, the fifty-five-year-old had been a Lyonesse Marine Corps officer for a quarter-century before donning a diplomat's sober business suit.

The two and a half decades in the Defense Force hadn't been optional — every DeCarde had served since the 21st Pathfinder Regiment arrived on Lyonesse aboard Jonas Morane's ship *Vanquish* over two centuries ago. Even if only for a single hitch as an ordinary spacer or Marine private. It was not just a family tradition that went back to the days before the empire's founding, but an obligation.

And those aspiring to high government or political office had better put in a good twenty and reach senior officer rank at the very least. DeCarde, in keeping with his ambitions, had left active service as a lieutenant colonel after a stellar career culminating in command of the 3rd Battalion, 21st Pathfinders. However, he still held a reserve commission as a colonel.

"Ah, Abbess. I was just admiring the embassy garden. How did you find such a sumptuous mansion this close to the Presidential Palace?"

Rianne, an ageless blonde with intelligent blue eyes, prominent cheekbones, and a serene smile, shrugged. "We didn't so much find it as it found us when I told President Freeman that an ambassador would arrive in Thebes to represent Lyonesse. It was once the property of the most prominent shipping magnate on this island, one who profited greatly from our teaching them to build motorized surface vessels of useful tonnage. He offered it to the government, which, in turn, sold it to Lyonesse through Friar Horam's office."

"I should like to meet that shipping magnate."

Rianne let out a throaty chuckle.

"Oh, you will, Ambassador, have no fear. He, along with every other industrialist and entrepreneur in Thebes. Their hunger for technology they can use to improve the industrial infrastructure is insatiable. Let's just say the last two years, since President Hecht put Hatshepsut on an accelerated path, have been interesting."

"As in the old Earth curse, may you live in interesting times?" DeCarde asked, eyes twinkling with mischief.

"Not quite that dramatic, sir, though some days we might feel like the Almighty is testing us in novel ways. And we haven't yet established priories on Aksum, which will give me a whole new batch of headaches."

"Ah, yes, the main inhabited continent. You've been there, I understand."

Rianne nodded.

"To a city called Mazaber." She grimaced. "Not particularly salubrious. While Thebes is clawing its way back to industrialization, Mazaber and the other Aksumite cities have been heading in the other direction. Hopefully, we can get the Thebans to establish their first offshore mission soon and arrest the slide into barbarism. Motorized surface ships will help. Until we pacify the Saqqara Islands, the trip to Aksum remains lengthy and fraught with peril for sailing vessels."

"So I read from your report. Shouldn't the problem correct itself in due course, however?"

Rianne made a so-so gesture with her hand.

"That's my belief, but we've never captured Saqqarans and examined them for the rapid deterioration leading to premature death I noted when our ship sailed through the Central Passage. Still, the motorized vessels using the North Passage will reach Mazaber faster than the sailing ships did by using the Central Passage and without the risks."

"Perhaps the Marine garrison might run a few expeditions into the Saqqaras," DeCarde suggested.

"I'm not sure their commanding officer would be in favor of such an operation."

A wintry smile played on his lips. "As ambassador plenipotentiary, I can direct local Lyonesse military activities to support our government's aims."

If Rianne was taken aback, she showed no sign. "I wasn't aware of that."

"It's a rather unusual arrangement, I'll grant you. Since Hatshepsut is at the far end of our supply lines, even though the relay system lets a message from us reach home in relatively short order, the President granted me enhanced powers. You might say I'm something like a colonial governor managing Lyonesse affairs to bring this world into the republic as an equal member, as well as an envoy to the local polity we've chosen as the future star system government. Especially since we now know where this Hegemony's sphere begins, confirming Hatshepsut is the closest to an interface with it. In practical terms, we shall leave the locals to advance their affairs on the planet's surface, under our guidance, of course. Anything beyond their reach is ours to manage as we see fit for both republics, from here to this star system's heliopause."

Rianne didn't immediately answer. After a few moments, she inclined her head in acknowledgment.

"I see. Is the abbey also under your remit, Ambassador?"

"For non-ecclesiastical matters affecting Lyonesse's interests."

"And you will define what those interests are, I suppose?" She asked in a neutral tone.

"Such are my instructions from our government. Of course, we shan't speak of my purely Lyonesse responsibilities with the

Thebans. The details don't concern the locals even though my administrative duties are for their long-term benefit."

"As you wish, Ambassador."

— 16 —

"Ambassador, Abbess?" DeCarde and Rianne turned to find the former's principal and only aide, David Raney, standing at the garden door. "We're expected at the Presidential Palace in five minutes."

"Thank you, David." DeCarde turned to the Abbess. "Shall we?"

As they walked through the embassy, he asked, "You read *Seeker*'s report, I assume?"

"I did. Finding a Hegemony that would rather talk than shoot is encouraging. We still long to see our eight abducted Brethren return one day."

"Ah, yes. Of course. Hopefully, they're being treated as kindred spirits by what passes for the Order of the Void in the Hegemony."

"If they have an Order of the Void, Ambassador. All we know is that one abductor, a woman wearing a quasi-military uniform, displayed the talents of a sister. Nothing more."

They stepped out into the bright midmorning sunshine beneath a fluttering green and gold Lyonesse flag atop a tall white pole, then walked across the embassy's forecourt and through open gates where a pair of Lieutenant Colonel Thomas Salmin's Marines stood guard. The troopers, wearing khaki tropical uniforms, low boots, blue berets, and black gun belts with holstered blasters, snapped to attention and saluted. DeCarde returned the compliment with a nod and an equally formal good morning.

The Marine guards were more ornamental than anything else, and DeCarde didn't know whether he'd bother keeping them in the long run. Once modern security measures wrapped the embassy grounds in a quasi-impenetrable and invisible barrier, the Marines at the gate could sit in a small operations room and monitor everything remotely. Besides, the Thebes City police kept criminals in check with the sort of effectiveness that might draw condemnation from some of Lyonesse's more radical politicians if they only knew.

The boulevard cutting across Thebes City's upper town, which overlooked the teeming city center and the extensive harbor and shipyards, was almost empty. At this hour, government officials were in their offices, and the residents of the mansions were either enjoying their gardens or overseeing their businesses.

They reached the Presidential Palace gates in a matter of minutes. There, a Theban official greeted DeCarde with the deference usually reserved for a visiting head of state, or so Rianne thought. But she was sufficiently self-aware to realize DeCarde's revelation that he was more than just an envoy might have colored her perceptions.

By old imperial standards, the palace wasn't particularly large or ornate. Built after the Great Scouring, its lines were functional and modest, as befit a republic that barely clung to early industrial technology and struggled to rebuild. The ground floor held only a few reception rooms of varying sizes and offices, primarily those of the President and his closest advisers. The upper floor, closed to the public, was the President's private residence.

DeCarde, old soldier that he was, spotted the security dispositions and personnel with little difficulty, even though they tried hard to blend in with the background. Threats of political violence were nonexistent for now. Yet, as Thebes expanded and absorbed less advanced populations, they would increase, along with the need to tighten protection around the republic's leaders. But that was for another day.

Once inside, DeCarde was pleased to see the palace had been retrofitted for electricity, including locally manufactured incandescent filament lights. Nothing as grand as the embassy now boasted, of course. It was supplied by its own miniature fusion reactor and been upgraded by the Marine garrison's construction engineering specialists to accommodate a full defensive array.

The palace, one of the first to be electrified, was supplied by a larger fusion plant, also imported from Lyonesse, which fed a growing percentage of Thebes, one street at a time. Meanwhile, the electrician trade grew by leaps and bounds as demand for people capable of wiring the city exploded. DeCarde looked forward to studying the social disruptions such a quick evolution entailed, but the latest reports from Abbess Rianne for the Lyonesse government had been optimistic.

Giving the locals advanced tech without letting them grow into it went against the spirit of Jonas Morane's plan. But DeCarde was among those who believed needs must now that the Hegemony was aware of Lyonesse's outpost on Hatshepsut. It had gone from easy-going early Void Mission stage to post-industrial awakening against the advice of many in the senate, the Order of the Void, and the citizenry at large in just over two years. However, if the sped-up program worked, DeCarde could see more reclaimed worlds propelled back to modernity in under a generation.

As they approached an open door, Raney pulled a folded sheet of plasticized paper from his tunic and handed it to DeCarde. Then, Freeman's aide ushered them into a spacious office whose tall windows overlooked the bay and the Thebes Archipelago's inner sea.

A gray-haired, dark-complexioned man in his fifties, with a broad nose, intelligent brown eyes, and a firm chin, rose from behind a simple wooden desk and came toward them. He was shorter than DeCarde, but stockier and gave the impression of hidden strength beneath the simple white shirt and trousers, clothing appropriate for Thebes' equatorial climate, even on the nation's leader.

The aide stopped halfway and bowed his head. "Mister President, Ambassador Currag DeCarde, representing the government of the Republic of Lyonesse, is here to present a letter of credentials signed by President Aurelia Hecht."

Abbess Rianne and David Raney stayed by the door as DeCarde stepped forward to meet Freeman. When both were three paces apart, DeCarde bowed his head.

"Mister President, it is my great honor to represent the Republic of Lyonesse to the Government of the Theban Republic as ambassador plenipotentiary."

He straightened, unfolded his credentials, and formally offered them to Freeman, who took the sheet and read it silently.

"Welcome to Thebes, Ambassador DeCarde," Freeman said once he finished and looked up. "I hope your stay here will be pleasant and fruitful for both our republics."

"Thank you, Mister President."

"You know," Freeman gestured at the settee group surrounding a low table to one side, "I dug through the ancient archives to find out how one receives an ambassador and what one does with a letter of credentials. Please take your ease. Can I offer you coffee, tea, or maybe chilled juice now that they equipped the palace with a refrigerator?"

"Juice would be fine, sir."

"Abbess, please join us while our aides confer."

"Thank you, Mister President."

Raney and Freeman's aide vanished as they settled in around the table.

"I know you've only been here two days, but what do you think of Thebes City?" Freeman asked.

"My first impressions? Warm, clean, with bracing sea air, and a sense of energy and purpose, Mister President."

Freeman's chuckle came from deep within, like the rumble of a volcano.

"Diplomatic to a fault. But the city has its less salubrious sections, where criminality is a fact of life and poverty is still very much endemic. The harbor, which looks wonderful from up here, smells like a rotten fish explosion at low tide. And Thebes

City is the most modern, most advanced on the planet. Wait until you see Mazaber."

"Abbess Rianne was telling me about it on the way here."

Freeman chuckled. "I pity the poor souls who'll set up a priory there."

"Do you also pity those who'll establish a Theban embassy?" DeCarde gave Freeman a crooked smile.

"Oh, for sure. But they'll be well remunerated. Rianne told us about the need to unify Hatshepsut under Theban leadership and prepare it for the return of this Hegemony, which also survived the Great Scouring. As a result, we have no difficulties finding eager volunteers. The idea of having our own National Guard troops — trained by your Marines — provide security for our emissaries also helps attract would-be diplomats."

An attendant entered with a tray carrying three glasses and a thermos jug. He placed the tray on the low table and glanced at Freeman.

"Thank you, Chris. We'll serve ourselves."

The man bowed his head. "Yes, Mister President." Then, he turned on his heels and left while Freeman reached out and poured a serving of rich, golden liquid into each glass.

"Sea apple juice, a local specialty made from native fruit that used to grow wild on the islands." They picked up their glasses. "To your health, Ambassador, Abbess."

"And yours, Mister President." DeCarde took an appreciative sip. "Delightful. I'll have to make sure the embassy kitchen keeps a good stock of this juice."

"So," Freeman settled back in his chair. "You think this Hegemony is a potential threat serious enough to accelerate Hatshepsut's reconstruction? I understand from Abbess Rianne that this is not Lyonesse's normal procedure."

DeCarde put down his half-empty glass and also sat back.

"We now know its full name is the Wyvern Hegemony, according to the report filed by *Seeker*'s captain, who was hailed by their ships in a star system next to the old imperial capital. If you'll permit me a brief discourse, sir?" When Freeman made a go-ahead gesture, DeCarde said, "For over a thousand years, humanity was united in a single purpose — to expand across the galaxy. Sovereign star systems joined under the imperial crown were free to experiment with various political and social systems and find what suited their people best. We were at peace with each other for most of that time, something unprecedented in human history. Then, that blackest of black swan events happened — Stichus Ruggero seized the throne and turned the empire into a repressive police state. By the time his descendant Dendera, a true sociopath if there ever was one, became empress, it was all but over. We fractured into a million shards because nothing created by humans lasts forever. We are mortal, and so are our creations."

DeCarde paused and reached for his glass. "Did you ever hear the adage that hard times create hard people, hard people create soft times, soft times create soft people, and soft people create hard times?"

Freeman nodded. "I saw a reference in one of Abbess Rianne's tomes."

"By Dendera's day, our species was soft and ripe for one of the periodic upheavals that mark the turns of history. Except this one was without precedent. Apocalyptic. With most of humanity slaughtered. That, sir, can never happen again. Lyonesse thought it alone had survived intact. Yet now, we find the shards of human civilization coalescing around two separate entities whose first contact ended in one kidnapping citizens of the other. But even if they hadn't committed what is, in essence, a hostile act, our fear is a permanent state of tension and even conflict between disparate visions of what humanity's future should be. After over two centuries of separate evolution, we must surely differ in our aims, outlook, and philosophy, maybe irreconcilably so, especially if the Wyvern Hegemony — an ominous name — is based in the old empire's core. They could well have kept many of the Ruggero era's worst characteristics if Wyvern survived more or less intact."

"Then why not open lines of communication with the Hegemony? Send someone like you on a diplomatic mission aboard a civilian starship and find out who they are and what they plan."

DeCarde shrugged. "Because we're not sure we can hold our own if they respond with gunfire. The task force that visited Hatshepsut two and a half years ago was fairly strong. We rarely send that many large ships on a voyage of discovery. Which begs the question, what else do they have that can counter us if they feel aggressive rather than conciliatory?"

"And once you consider yourselves strong enough?"

"I don't know."

Freeman leaned forward.

"What if they think the same? Wouldn't that mean both the Republic of Lyonesse and this Hegemony are chasing their own tails instead of sniffing around each other to see what they have in common?"

"Possibly, but the reigning theory in some quarters is based on the name Hegemony, which carries rather negative connotations of one state's politico-military dominance over others, and their taking of our Brethren. For many on Lyonesse, it makes them natural enemies of our republic."

"A word that dates back to distant antiquity and one unfortunate act, perhaps done out of fear, and you'd see our species remain divided? Even hostile to each other?"

"Not I, Mister President. But I'm just an extension of my government and enact its policies."

—17—

Lannion
Lyonesse System

"You read Commander Byner's mission report, I trust?" President Aurelia Hecht looked around the conference table at her cabinet secretaries, the Vice President, the Chief of the Defense Staff, and the head of the Order of the Void.

A tall, slender, dark-haired woman in her late sixties with penetrating brown eyes framing a patrician nose, Hecht seemed a throwback to the aristocratic elegance of the imperial era, even though none of her ancestors ever held a title of nobility.

Each nodded as she met their eyes. None would dare attend a cabinet meeting without reading the background material sent by the President's chief of staff.

"Now, we must decide what we do with the knowledge the Wyvern Hegemony, as advertised by the commander of the task force that spotted *Seeker*, begins in the Torrinos system. We can assume their capital is the old imperial capital, and at the very least, they probably own the systems connected to Wyvern by a single wormhole transit. Along with Torrinos, two of them, Dordogne and Arcadia, were important and heavily populated back in the day. If they escaped total destruction, they might well have been quickly rebuilt. But we still know very little. Next to nothing, if truth be told."

"Then I don't see why our posture should change, Madame President," Vice President Derik Juska said. Of an age with Hecht and equally regal in appearance and demeanor, with thick, wavy gray hair, a finely sculpted face, and intelligent eyes, he had a deep voice that registered exceptionally well with voters. "Keep building up Hatshepsut and securing our wormhole network branches until we can withstand a large-scale attack. We cannot be anything other than in a position of power when we meet them face-to-face. Lyonesse's progress must be preserved at any cost, especially if the Hegemony is a reactionary state rather than a progressive one like ours. And allow me to believe they are that."

Hecht thought she could almost hear Admiral Norum's eyes roll, though the Chief of the Defense Staff kept a straight face. In his late fifties, with blond hair mostly turned silver, deep-set blue eyes, and an angular, craggy face, he wasn't impressed with most of the people around the cabinet table, least of all the Vice President.

Over the last two years, Juska had positioned himself as leader of what Norum called, in private and only within her hearing, the supremacist faction, which believed Lyonesse had the sole right to reunite humanity. In truth, they weren't even a faction. At least not an organized one.

But Juska worked behind the scenes with various special interest groups that had sprung up since the Hatshepsut incident, such as Lyonesse First and Reunification Now. It might be a big part of his platform when he ran for the top job in a few years.

Repressing a smile, she said, "That could be a perfectly reasonable course of action."

Sister Gwendolyn, the *Summus Abbatissa*, or supreme abbess of the Order of the Void, raised a long-fingered hand that suited the tall, lean, seventy-something woman with the narrow face and piercing dark eyes.

"May I propose an alternative?"

Hecht nodded. "Please go ahead."

"Why not send an envoy in a civilian ship to the Torrinos system? Have the ship emerge from the wormhole, broadcast a friendship message, and announce our desire to open diplomatic relations with the Wyvern Hegemony. They tried to speak with Commander Byner. I'm sure they'd respond to our ambassador. And if not, we've lost nothing by trying. Besides, they might return our Brethren if we ask nicely, and who knows what they've learned about the Hegemony. Admiral Norum's intelligence staff would be delighted to interview them upon their return home."

"But consider what we will give up in return," Secretary of Defense Vern Reval said. A career politician who had inspired little trust among the military's senior ranks, he'd seemingly hitched his career to Juska's coattails in recent months and was becoming one of the hardliners.

"And that would be?" Gwendolyn asked in a sweet, reasonable tone, the one most feared by novices and senior Brethren alike. "The idea we're reasonable, compassionate people who prefer talking to shows of force?"

Reval didn't roll his eyes. Not quite. But Gwendolyn's knowing smile said it all, at least for those, such as Hecht, who understood her sibylline expressions — or thought they did. She could read him like a book and knew fully what he thought of her intervention.

Still, it was no secret around the cabinet table that she thought little of the SecDef, as he liked to be known. Gwendolyn was one of the more outspoken public figures decrying the allure of chauvinism whenever the supremacist faction raised its head.

"You misunderstand me, Abbess. We would give up the element of surprise, one of the most important principles of war. By remaining distant, aloof, and mysterious, we give the Hegemony something to worry about. What if they're stronger than we are? They hold an advantage if their forces are concentrated where ours are strung out along the wormhole network. Best we don't give them the chance to find out before we're in a better military position."

"With due respect, Mister Secretary, I hear you speak in the language of conflict when conflict among factions within humanity across the stars almost wiped out our species. Shouldn't we try something different instead of doing the same thing that didn't work before?"

A brief frown creased Reval's forehead while a few around the table fought to keep from chuckling. Hecht and Norum exchanged a quick glance, but otherwise remained expressionless.

"You misunderstand me, Abbess. I don't rule out diplomatic overtures, but only once we're sure we can speak from a position of unmistakable strength. It avoids misunderstandings that could, in fact, lead to open conflict. We know our aim isn't subjugating another star-faring society, but we must be capable of resisting it if it tries to subjugate us. Thus, we should remain mysterious until we're ready. And as Secretary of Defense, I can tell you we still have work ahead of us before we can meet the Hegemony openly."

"Right." Hecht raised a hand. "We have two very different opinions on the table. Does anyone have something else to propose?"

When no one answered, she said, "I'll reserve my decision for later. In the meantime, our current posture will remain. We have enough to keep the republic busy without setting off on a diplomatic track absent defined goals and no idea what success might even look like. If their outer limit in our direction is Torrinos, and ours in their direction is Hatshepsut, there are a lot of star systems in between, including a few with habitable planets that one of us will eventually reclaim a few decades from now."

"Speaking of keeping us busy, Madame President," Derik Juska raised a hand. "And somewhat to the point, considering the existence of the Wyvern Hegemony."

"Yes?" Hecht knew what was coming.

"Vern informs me *Serenity* is on the verge of completing her post-refit trials and performing splendidly. She'll be ready for a long-range mission by next week. One of the new replenishment ships has also become available — the one capable of carrying a miniature antimatter cracking station. I think it's time we decided on the matter of an expedition to Earth. Reclaiming it will only strengthen our position as humanity's leading state."

"A long journey for two or three ships."

"Shorter than the one Jonas Morane made with ships worn down by the rebellion against Dendera. He came from the other side of the old empire. While not in the precise middle, Earth is perhaps half the distance if the expedition keeps to the main wormhole branches instead of the outer ones, like President Morane did."

"If major wormholes haven't shifted in the last two hundred years," Admiral Norum interjected. "A few of our more intrepid merchant explorers reported at least three in the Coalsack and adjoining sectors in the last five years."

Hecht clamped down on her irritation. It was a sore point between her and the Vice President and more than a few cabinet members. She saw little point in sending an expedition whose sole aim was to plant Lyonesse's flag on what could only be a ravaged world. The Wyvern Hegemony, if it landed there as well, might simply raise its own. If they didn't land colonists. Wyvern was much closer to Earth than Lyonesse, which was at the furthest end of the old empire's sphere of control. Oh, Juska would raise the same old excuse — Lyonesse must remap as much of the wormhole network as possible. And as if on cue, he did.

"All the more reason for a survey expedition into the heart of the old empire before the Hegemony launches one," Juska replied.

What irritated Hecht as well was Gwendolyn's ambivalence. The latest of her Order's mystical sisters, with what many considered extraordinary ability, had stoked the obsession to reclaim Earth espoused by several supremacist groups in recent times. And they formed a growing percentage of Juska's supporters.

Before first contact with the Hegemony, the Earth obsession had been confined to a fringe, the same fringe that had pursued vague visions and dreams since the days of Abbess Marta, the Order's greatest visionary, seen by some as a prophet. But knowledge of another surviving society with faster-than-light starships that might usurp Lyonesse's role as humanity's guiding light had driven what Hecht thought of as a strange little cult into something that could shift public policy.

A pained look crossed Sister Gwendolyn's lean features as if she could sense Hecht's annoyance at the subject, one they'd discussed in private too often.

"I'm afraid the subject will gain fresh and more pressing attention once word about Torrinos gets out, Madame President. You may safely expect Sister Elana to experience other visions that will undoubtedly be seen as prescient by those who believe the Almighty is shaping Lyonesse's destiny."

"Sometimes we could do without mystics, prophets, and visionaries, Abbess," Hecht replied in a weary tone, knowing she voiced the opinion of Admiral Norum and many of the cabinet secretaries around the table.

"Some within the Order might agree with you, I'm sure. But the Lannion Abbey has been home to a sister with special talents continuously since Abbess Marta, and that's probably a sign the Almighty wants us to heed what they say, even if we don't always understand."

"How about preventing Sister Elana from creating a ruckus once she hears about the encounter in the Torrinos system?" The Secretary of Justice asked.

Gwendolyn gave him a sad smile. "I could no more prevent Elana from speaking about her visions than you can prevent the newsnets from criticizing this administration. There will be renewed interest in an expedition to Earth. Count on it. Many people consider Lyonesse's mission to reunite humanity a sacred one, which we cannot let slip into the hands of something called the Hegemony, which abducted eight of our Brethren and hasn't returned them. Once it's known that this entity's full name is Wyvern Hegemony and has naval units and wormhole traffic control buoys in a star system one wormhole transit from the old imperial capital, I'm afraid the sentiment will intensify and spread."

Hecht let out a soft sigh of resignation. "So, you're saying I might as well keep a step ahead of public opinion and send a survey expedition to remap the most direct wormhole network branches between Lyonesse and Earth."

Gwendolyn nodded. "In essence. Even if those convinced Lyonesse has a sacred mission aren't more than a vocal minority at the moment, their voice and their influence are rather large and growing, as some around this table would know better than me."

"I don't enjoy the idea of government policy being driven by passing notions."

"This is no passing notion, Madame President, but, in retrospect, a rather foreseeable result of the belief in Lyonesse as the savior of humanity. The existence of the Wyvern Hegemony simply coalesced a decades-long growth in sentiment around a single, understandable cause. If followers of the Almighty in the Infinite Void believed in saints, I can assure you there would be pressure to canonize Jonas Morane and Sister Gwenneth by now."

Hecht's face hardened imperceptibly. "So basically, the push to claim Earth is a religious crusade."

"Not quite, but we ignore these social movements at our peril, and the sentiment Lyonesse must not lose its place as the one who'll reunite humanity is spreading. Fast. Call it a newly revived nationalism in response to the knowledge we're not the sole survivors. Whether a crusade is in the name of the Almighty or the secular state doesn't make much of a difference in the end. Few rulers throughout history have successfully stemmed the tide of either version. Once an idea, no matter how wrong-headed, takes root, it becomes well-nigh impossible to extirpate without major societal upheaval. Better take the lead and nudge that idea onto a less dangerous path."

The people around the cabinet table, men and women chosen for their acumen, career record, and integrity, watched Hecht with undisguised interest as she absorbed Gwendolyn's words. The Order of the Void's *Summus Abbatissas* were considered the conscience of the republic since its early days, and their opinions were always carefully considered.

They were the undisputed experts of the human mind, mass psychology, and psychohistory, all of which had served successive presidents well in charting Lyonesse's course back to the stars.

"In other words, send a survey expedition into the heart of the old empire and remap the wormhole network, all the way to Earth if possible."

Gwendolyn nodded. "It would help defuse in advance what could become disruptive developments within Lyonesse society, now we know more about what many, including around this table, consider our rivals rather than our long-lost siblings."

Hecht turned her gaze on the republic's military commander. "Admiral?"

"We have to remap the main wormhole branches anyway, Madame President. The people of Lyonesse can't expect our intrepid merchant explorers to constantly take the risks, even though we owe them a debt of gratitude for the work they've done so far. As the Vice President said, *Serenity* is fresh out of refit and available for a long voyage. She can either go alone since, by anyone's reckoning, she has the autonomy to reach Earth and return via the direct route with a healthy reserve. Or we can add a replenishment ship fitted with one of the new deployable miniature antimatter cracking modules — *Provider* is available — and perhaps even a frigate or a corvette to round off a small task force. I would suggest a corvette that can land, such as *Defiant*. That way, we can be assured everyone has plenty of fuel to come home interstellar if the wormhole network throws them nasty surprises. I think we can spare three ships for a good cause without creating insurmountable issues elsewhere."

"How long can you spare them?" Hecht asked.

Norum smiled. "For one Void Ship rotation, Madame President. And I know just who I'll appoint as commanding officer of the survey mission — Al Jecks. He was in the Hatshepsut system aboard *Serenity* when the Hegemony abducted our Brethren and has seen their ships with his own eyes. He's due for one more rotation as *Serenity*'s skipper before putting up his fourth stripe."

"Give it to him now. That way, there will be no discussion about seniority between him and *Provider*'s captain."

Norum sketched a salute between old comrades. "Aye, aye, Madame President."

"How soon can the task force leave?"

"A week. You can announce it this afternoon if you like. I'll warn the three skippers about their new mission when we're done here."

—18—

"You're sending us where?" Al Jecks, who'd been on leave after a successful post-refit operational readiness evaluation, asked with more than a hint of incredulity when Admiral Norum announced their mission.

Jecks, a tall, wiry man in his early forties with a shaved head, black mustache, and intelligent dark eyes, studied his superior intently as if searching for signs Norum was joking. He, Commander Edith Leung of *Provider,* and Lieutenant Commander Yannick Petrov of *Defiant* had been summoned to join the Chief of the Defense Staff in the Lannion Base Officers Mess private dining room for a last-minute lunch meeting.

It was fortuitous the three starship captains were on the ground and available that day. Leung was on ship's business at Navy HQ while Petrov's *Defiant* sat on the Lannion Base tarmac alongside another Frater class corvette, and Jecks lived a quick aircar hop further up the coast.

"It's just another survey mission, Al. One that merely has Earth as a turnaround point."

While Norum recounted *Seeker*'s discovery and an edited version of the discussion around the cabinet table, Jecks' eyes wandered to the far wall. There, the portraits of each Chief of the Defense Staff hung in what was commonly known as a rogue's gallery, beginning with that of the Lyonesse Defense Force founder, Jonas Morane. Since the private dining room was, in practice if not officially so, reserved for the incumbent, two centuries of admirals and generals staring at them felt apt.

When Norum noticed Jecks' gaze, he correctly divined the younger man's thoughts and chuckled.

"No, you won't be retracing Admiral Morane's route."

"Thank the Almighty. If I recall correctly, they passed through at least one rogue wormhole. Who knows how many of them are out there by now?"

"It'll be the direct route as per the old imperial sailing instructions. Of course, you might face a detour or two, and, if in your judgment, Al, the safety of the ships and crews call for a turnaround before reaching Earth, then so be it."

"Meaning I'll be in command?"

"Yes, and by President Hecht's decree, your promotion to captain is effective now, not once you're back from your last cruise in *Serenity*. I can come aboard and present your new rank in front of the ship's company, or we can do it in my office."

"What's your preference, sir?"

"In *Serenity*. That way, I can speak with the crew in person before your departure. I'll hop over to *Provider* afterward and speak with Edith's people. And I'll be visiting *Defiant* before you lift, Yannick."

Lieutenant Commander Petrov, dark-complexioned, with thick black hair and a lean, youthful face that belied his age, nodded. "We'll be glad to pipe you aboard, sir."

"As will we," Leung said. Of an age with Jecks — they'd been Academy classmates — and just as rangy, she wore her dark hair in a short bob that framed a narrow elfin face with prominent cheekbones.

"Good. The President will make the announcement on the public newsnet stream at fifteen hundred, which gives you time to get word to your crews before the mission becomes public knowledge. A full set of orders will come through in the next day. You can start taking on extra supplies right away. Starbase Lyonesse and Base Lannion logistics departments will be told you have priority right after the President speaks. Load your holds until there's not a cubic centimeter of space left. And now, let's eat."

Moments later, mess personnel carrying cold lunch plates entered the private dining room, proof Norum's aide had been listening in on the conversation from his perch outside the closed door.

After the servers had left, the conversation naturally turned to the survey mission, and Norum was pleased that the three captains displayed growing enthusiasm after their initial hesitation. The discussion eventually touched on the socio-political aspects and Sister Elana's visions. And though they understood the reasons behind President Hecht's decision to finally authorize the expedition, none of them were believers.

Nor did they think a symbolic claim on Earth could give Lyonesse an edge over the Wyvern Hegemony in any way, shape, or fashion. But then, naval officers were realists who understood the universe was harsh, and impersonal. Norum didn't think any of them, nor many in the entire Defense Force, were Lyonesse supremacists.

They didn't linger over dessert. Norum understood they were impatient to speak with their first officers and get word of the expedition spread among the crews before it became public knowledge. He climbed to his feet, immediately imitated by Jecks, Leung, and Petrov as the dining-room door opened again and his aide appeared.

"The car is waiting, sir. We have just enough time to get back."

"Thank you." Norum looked at each of the captains in turn. "And you're no doubt impatient to get moving as well. Thanks for joining me at the last minute. We'll speak again soon."

"Sir." Jecks, as senior among them, snapped to attention, imitated by his colleagues.

When Norum was gone, a crooked smile cracked his previously serious mien.

"I can't tell if it'll be an epic voyage of rediscovery, but as my last outing in *Serenity*, I couldn't have asked for more interesting."

Leung nodded. "Ain't that the truth? By the way, congrats on the fourth stripe. Well deserved."

"Yes, congratulations, sir." Petrov held out his hand. "If you don't want to deal with the base's communications section to call your ships, *Defiant* is just a short walk down the runway."

"We'll take you up on that, Yannick. Thanks. It'll allow us to chat on the way without being overheard. We might as well use the time to discuss standard operating procedures."

Leung chuckled. "Should I be frightened by how fast you've slipped into task force commander mode, Al?"

Jecks leered at her.

"Oh, be terrified. Once we're out of subspace radio range, I'll be the sole authority after the Almighty."

"Maybe I should ask the admiral to move my posting out of *Provider* up by a year."

Jecks nodded at the door.

"And miss the fun? Let's give *Defiant*'s signals chief something to talk about in the mess tonight."

***

"I can't believe Sister Elana's sibylline pronouncements, and those of every other mystic sister before her, finally found traction with the republic's government. I'm sure the shard of Sister Marta that lurks behind Elana's consciousness is thrilled."

Jecks looked up from his cup at Sister Bree, *Serenity*'s counselor, and chief medical officer.

"What was that?"

Bree, an athletic, late forties brunette with shoulder-length hair, a soft round face dusted with freckles and mischievous green eyes, had cut her leave short and rejoined the ship along with everyone else who'd been enjoying liberty. Her first stop after dropping her bag off in her quarters was Jecks' day cabin, where she'd spent many an hour enjoying tea and discussing various subjects with him while the ship was in hyperspace.

"You never heard the story of our mystics? I'm surprised. Your mind generally is a fount of oddball knowledge."

"Not so much about the Order. You keep secrets better than Defense Force Intelligence."

She grimaced.

"We don't actually keep secrets, but there are things we simply won't discuss with outsiders lest we appear a little too fey for the republic's good."

Jecks winked at her.

"That ship sailed two hundred years ago."

"And yet here we are, sailing aboard the Navy's ships." Bree sat back and took a sip of tea. "Anyway, there are some sisters whose talent surpasses the others. Those are the ones whose third eye is at least partially open."

She tapped her forehead with a slender index finger.

"An inner eye that can see matters of the mind and the soul. We can only open it briefly and catch glimpses of what hides from normal sight, like that which lives in our subconscious. Apparently, when a sister with the ability dies, she can leave a small shard of herself in the subconscious of another."

She sipped her tea again.

"The first recorded instance since the fall of the empire was Sister Heloise who touched Abbess Marta moments before her death at the hands of Admiral Zahar on Yotai. At the time, she was merely Marta Norum, the ancestor of your current Chief of the Defense Staff, but she became one of the most powerful and mystical sisters ever. Marta could unerringly find other sisters with the potential to be like her and trained them herself, even after she became *Summus Abbatissa* of the Order.

"When Marta died, she was holding the hand of a younger sister with a partially open third eye, and a shard of Marta's essence — including a bit of the shard Heloise left — took up residence in her subconscious. That sister eventually passed a bit of herself and the cumulative bits of her two predecessors to the next in line at death, and so on until today."

Jecks pursed his lips in thought.

"You're saying there are what? Half a dozen or more dead mystics living in Elana's attic, having a grand old time sending her visions? But if those bits of dead sisters inhabit the subconscious, how would Elana and the previous leading mystics know?"

"Because when a sister like Elana opens her third eye, she can see the bits of mental energy her predecessors imprinted on each successive generation's subconscious. Briefly, as I mentioned, just enough to see part of them never really died. It's also that third eye which supposedly gives our mystics their visions."

"And do you believe this is true?"

Bree shrugged.

"Even after over a thousand years of work by the Order's best researchers, we still understand only a fraction of what the human mind can do, so anything is possible. That we sisters are, to one degree or another, empaths is beyond doubt. Our friars have a bit of our abilities as well. We can't read minds, but we can sense moods, anguish, pain, joy, and hesitation — the things of the soul that differentiate us from intelligent machines. And we can use our talent to heal, teach, protect, and help.

"Besides, the idea of a third eye has existed for millennia. It's not something the Order invented, so I think it probably exists as those who've opened theirs claim. But with visions and prophecies, let's just say I'm as skeptical as the next person. The mystics don't have a track record that proves they're prescient. Yet, since the visions aren't clear, perhaps we simply don't interpret most of them correctly."

"Why did I never hear of the third eye before?"

Bree gave him a mysterious smile.

"Because it's one thing we don't discuss, not even among ourselves, mainly because the vast majority of us cannot open our third eye, me included. Otherwise, I wouldn't be serving aboard a Navy ship. We keep those who can close to home where they help with research and treating people who suffer from serious mental disorders."

Jecks nodded with understanding.

"Like those exiled to the Windy Isles for life — the incurable criminal sociopaths, for instance."

"Just so. Sister Marta was among the first who worked intensively with them and developed approaches still in use today. More importantly, she discovered what didn't work or made things worse and imposed a list of forbidden techniques. For example, she discovered that pushing a sister to open her third eye when she wasn't ready could utterly destroy mind and soul."

"I see." Jecks studied her for a few seconds. "Out of curiosity, why are you so open with me about this?"

"Because I feel we might stir up ghosts of the past and it's perhaps best you realize what some of them are."

"Based on Elana's visions?"

She grimaced again.

"Something about what she said after hearing of Torrinos and our expedition's goal left many of us at the Lannion Abbey wondering about the future."

Jecks' eyebrows shot up. "Do I want to hear?"

"Probably not. Besides, Abbess Gwendolyn has placed an embargo on Elana's latest pronouncements. They're getting a little too eerie."

"Aha! You do have secrets, after all."

A wry smile lit up Bree's face. "It seems so."

"Well, I'm glad you made it back before Admiral Norum's visit."

"Ah yes. Should I congratulate you on your promotion now or when he pins on your new rank insignia?"

"Since I'm already being paid as a post captain, whenever you wish."

"In that case, congratulations. It is well deserved. Once our upcoming cruise is over, do you know where you're headed?"

"Defense Force HQ as Director, Future Naval Capabilities under the Deputy Chief of the Defense Staff."

She must have read something in his tone or expression. "Is that a good assignment?"

"Not bad, but still a desk job. I consider it my penance for five years as a Void Ship captain, the most sought-after command assignment in the Lyonesse Navy. So long as I don't trip over my own feet, chances are good I'll get command of a squadron in one of our outlying star systems after three or four years shuffling projects, proposals, and anything else dropped on my desk by the good idea fairy. If I'm lucky, maybe I'll take over from Lucas Morane at Hatshepsut."

Bree let out a soft chuckle. "Why do I think you prefer spending your life away from Lyonesse?"

"This is a new age of exploration, or rather of rediscovery. I'd rather be out there doing my part in it than riding a desk in Lannion."

"Someone must." Bree's eyes crinkled with mirth at Jecks' vehemence.

"Then someone should be posted to HQ instead of me."

Before she could reply, the day cabin's communicator chimed. "Bridge to the captain."

"Jecks."

"Admiral Norum's shuttle just landed on the starbase. I've warned the side party to assemble in the main airlock and will send the crew to the hangar in a moment."

"Thanks. I'm on my way. Jecks, out." He downed the rest of his tea and stood. "You're welcome to join me."

"I'll join the rest of the crew, if you don't mind."

At that moment, the public address system came to life.

"All hands, now hear this. The Chief of the Defense Staff will arrive shortly. Except for those designated to remain at their posts, crew members will now form up on the hangar deck. That is all."

Jecks put on his sky blue beret with the Navy's double-headed condor and anchor insignia.

"See you later, Sister."

Surprising him not in the least, Jecks found his cox'n, Chief Petty Officer First Class Lara Fast, a thin, tough, gray-haired veteran of Void Ships waiting for him, her cane of office, a silver-tipped, highly polished length of tough Lyonesse wood tucked under her left arm.

Since this was a working rather than a ceremonial visit, Jecks, Fast, and the side party wore Navy blue shipboard uniforms like the rest of the crew — trousers tucked into calf-high boots, high collared, waist-length tunic over a white sweater, and the ubiquitous Defense Force beret. Other than gold rank insignia at the collar, the only adornments were qualification badges and the ship's crest on the right breast, over the name tape. That crest showed a stylized, eight-winged Lyonesse lightning fly in silver surrounded by a circle of gold, eight-pointed stars, and *Serenity*'s motto, *Lead the Way*. It symbolized a Void Ship's mission — to lead the republic back into the old empire.

When they reached the spacious main starboard airlock, they found the eighteen spacers under the combat systems chief petty officer, CPO2 Garnet Gill, and the bosun, CPO2 Reed Ahane, already in formation, prepared to receive their visitor. The spacers were armed with standard plasma carbines, while Chief Gill also carried a cane of office tucked under his left arm, but one slightly less ornate than Chief Fast's. Ahane, as befit his duties of the moment, held a silver bosun's call hanging from a silver chain around his neck in his right hand.

A few minutes later, Admiral Norum's aide, wearing a toned-down version of the gold braid cord over his battledress tunic's left shoulder, appeared in the gangway tube. Gill called the side party to attention and had them shoulder arms while Chief Ahane raised his call to his lips. Jecks and Fast came to attention in unison at the former's whispered command. Seconds later, Norum came around the corner five paces behind his aide, who stopped on the station side of the airlock to let his admiral step aboard.

Chief Gill ordered a present arms while the bosun's whistle trilled the appropriate call for a Chief of the Defense Staff boarding a Republic of Lyonesse warship. Jecks had raised his hand to salute in synchronization with the side party and held it there until the whistle stopped as the chief called the shoulder arms.

"Welcome aboard, Admiral," Jecks said, taking one step forward. "Would you care to inspect the side party?"

"With pleasure, Captain."

"The rest of the crew, or at least those not standing watch at designated positions, is assembled on the hangar deck, sir. We set up a small dais for you if you wish to address them."

"Excellent." Norum halted in front of Chief Gill and returned the latter's salute, then slowly walked down one rank and up the other, stopping a few times to exchange brief words with crew members. At the end, he and Gill exchanged salutes, then Norum fell into step beside Jecks, with the aide and the cox'n following them as they made their way aft to the main hangar deck.

As soon as they appeared in the hangar's starboard inner airlock, the first officer, Lieutenant Commander Yulia Salmin — tall, muscular, with short sandy hair and intense blue eyes — called the ship's company to attention. Under Jecks' guidance, Norum headed for the improvised dais, climbed it, and faced the formation.

"Ship's company, to the Chief of the Defense Staff, general salute." Salmin and the officers raised their hands to their brows in a crisp, snappy movement that made the cox'n nod to himself in satisfaction. Norum returned the gesture and held it for a few seconds until Salmin called attention.

"Let's get on with the formal part first, since you're already in the right position for the occasion. Captain Jecks, front, and center." Norum stepped off the dais.

"Sir." Jecks marched up and halted to face Norum

"Attention to orders. Commander Allan Ricardo Jecks is hereby promoted to the rank of post captain. He will remain as commanding officer of the Republic of Lyonesse Void Ship *Serenity*." Norum stepped forward and removed the metallic commander's rank insignia from Jecks' uniform collar. "Hand."

When Jecks held out his left hand, Norum gave it to him, either as a souvenir or to present to his first officer at the end of the cruise when her promotion to commander was due. Then, he reached into his tunic pocket, produced a rank badge with four stripes topped by the Navy's executive loop, and pinned it on Jeck's collar.

"Congratulations, Captain. Well deserved." They shook hands while *Serenity*'s crew, led by Salmin, applauded. When the cheers died away, Norum jumped on the dais again. "Please stand the crew easy, Commander."

Once she'd done so, he let his eyes roam over the assembled men and women, the Navy's best because only the best earned much-coveted Void Ship billets.

"I won't ask if you're ready for the cruise of a lifetime because I know you are." Norum's voice carried across the vast space, echoing off serried ranks of cargo shuttles, personnel transporters, and combat dropships. "Your post-refit readiness evaluation score is all the proof I need. Well done. In a few days, *Serenity*, *Provider*, and *Defiant* will spearhead a new survey mission into the heart of what was once humanity's greatest empire and the Commonwealth before it. And when I say heart, I mean what was once the Home Sector, with our species' world of origin at its center — Earth. But you already knew that from your divisional officers' briefings over the last few days."

Norum paused for effect, meeting many a gaze.

"I envy each and every one of you. This will be the longest, most exciting voyage of rediscovery since Lyonesse returned to the galaxy and began making President Morane's dream a reality. You'll be mapping wormhole branches that haven't seen a starship in over two centuries and passing worlds cut off from the rest of humanity since the empire's collapse. And if you reach Earth, you'll be the first people from Lyonesse to do so in a very long time. No one can tell what awaits you out there, but whatever that may be, I know you'll prevail and return with a wealth of data that'll keep astrographers busy for years to come.

Fair winds and following seas, my friends. Lead the Way." He let the sound of the ship's motto fade, then said in a conversational tone, smiling, "I'll answer any questions you may have for the next few minutes, then I'm off to speak with your comrades in *Provider*."

— 19 —

"We can thank the Almighty our usual suspects didn't try to light up the admiral with impertinent questions," Chief Fast said as she sank into one of the chairs facing Jecks' desk with a sigh of relief. Salmin and Sister Bree were already seated, having arrived a few minutes before the cox'n, who'd had a quick word with the divisional chiefs about Norum's visit.

Jecks smiled. "He did mention our crew came across as the strong silent types compared to some he'd known in his time aboard starships. I think he suspects me of having ordered our people to stay quiet."

"Just as well he pinned your new stripes on before his speech," Fast said in a low growl. "But I'm happy with the visit and told the divisional chiefs so."

"How about you, Yulia?"

"No complaints. Admiral Norum isn't a high-maintenance CDS, so there's that."

"Sister?"

"The mood was positive and relaxed. I'd say our people are ready for the challenge."

Jecks smiled at her. "Is that the Sister of the Void or the psychologist speaking?"

"A bit of both."

"No doubt. I think it went well, so thank you for ensuring *Serenity* put her best foot forward. Now, we can turn our attention on high-tailing it out of here and into the unknown."

"Not that we'll reach the unknown for a while," Salmin replied. "I assume we're topping up antimatter fuel reservoirs in the Micarat system?"

"I was thinking Takeshi. That'll give us more of a reserve once we leave the last outpost in that section of the network behind us. We'll give Micarat a quick hello in passing. Rear Admiral Barca is one of my former skippers and an all-around good guy. He'll welcome a brief chat and be saddened if I didn't call."

"Will you convene a captain's conference in person before we sail?"

Jecks nodded. "As soon as *Defiant* joins us. I believe she's due to lift off tomorrow after the admiral says his farewells."

"Private supper in your quarters or a wardroom meal after?"

Jecks thought for a moment. "Let's make it private. That way, the three wardroom presidents can discuss something for their members without us captains in the way."

Salmin, the wardroom President because of her post as first officer, nodded. "Probably a good idea. I figure a get-together in one of the starbase wardroom's private spaces will do. Cocktails and nibblies, a strictly informal getting-to-know-you."

"Why do I think you already discussed this with *Provider*'s first officer?"

She gave him a friendly smirk.

"Because you know I'm always three steps ahead of the game, which is why you've kept me on as your number one."

"All right. Anything else we should discuss right now, or can we go back to our regularly scheduled duties?" When none of them answered, Jecks said, "Thank you."

***

"She looks almost brand new." Commander Edith Leung looked around *Serenity*'s bridge with appreciative eyes as Jecks gave her and Petrov of *Defiant* a quick tour before heading to his day cabin, where they would discuss the proposed standard operating procedures and hash out anything else.

"The yard did a good cleaning job after digging out her worn innards. I'll say that for them. But joking aside, she can still match the newest ship coming off the slipways even after almost fifteen years in space. That's how well built she is. Yet she's the last of the current Void Ship class. Once *Gwenneth* launches and sets the new standard in two years, *Serenity*'s generation will retire from service one after the other while you and I also retire, Edith. I daresay Yannick will enjoy what's coming more than us."

Leung snorted with derision. "I might retire, but if you don't trip over your own toes during your tour at Navy HQ after this cruise, you'll be wearing stars and bullying Yannick mercilessly."

"Not even in my wildest dreams." Jecks ushered them through the door connecting the bridge to his day cabin. "Yesterday was my last promotion ceremony, which is just as well. Once the Navy hands me retirement papers, I can move to an outpost and make myself useful helping the locals rejoin galactic civilization.

Why don't we sit around the table? Coffee, tea, or something else to sip on?"

Leung shook her head. "I'm already overdosing on caffeine. So long as you're serving a decent wine with supper..."

"I am. How about you, Yannick?"

"I'm good too, sir."

"Then let's go over the proposed SOPs. As you might have noted, being smart naval persons, I adapted them from the standard task force protocols HQ likes its far-flung squadrons to use."

Leung smirked. "The notion had crossed my mind, especially since we'll be the furthest flung squadron in the entire fleet."

"Comments?"

They worked their way through the SOPs over the course of two hours, during which Jecks formed his private opinion of Leung and Petrov's thought processes. Both were, of course, highly competent. Otherwise, they wouldn't be commanding starships. Most naval officers never earned that honor. But Jecks wasn't under the illusion they, and he for that matter, were selected for this mission because they were the best of the best. No, Admiral Norum chose them because their ships were available, nothing more.

He knew Leung from way back and could remember her quirks as a midshipman and junior officer, but that was long ago. People changed as they came up the ranks. Most improved their positive traits and worked on the negative ones. Others let career aspirations get the better of them and turned into different people. So far, he could still recognize the quick-witted woman with an off-beat sense of humor he knew at the Academy. She was perfectly at ease with Jecks and Petrov and had no problems expressing her views, which were invariably insightful.

Petrov was an unknown quantity, however. Younger by a decade and the most junior in rank of the three captains, he was soft-spoken — when he spoke at all. Petrov let his seniors do most of the talking and debating. Jecks might have ascribed it to natural diffidence, but timid officers lacking self-confidence didn't earn starship commands. No, Jecks figured the younger man was letting experienced captains take the lead while listening and absorbing as much of their hard-won knowledge as possible. Having met the sort who were overly self-confident, a few to the point of obnoxiousness, he was okay with Petrov not opening his mouth much.

Jecks glanced at the antique clock adorning the day cabin's sole sideboard. It had been a gift from the crew of his first command, the corvette *Prevail* — third of its name — when he turned her over to his successor and took on the duties of commanding officer, Lyonesse Defense Force Basic Training School upon promotion to commander.

Besides the hours in ancient numerals he knew were referred to as Roman, the clock's face bore the stylized silhouette of an armored figure riding a four-legged beast of burden. He'd never investigated the clock's provenance. Still, every time he held it in his hands and scrutinized every visible surface, he felt as if the precision instrument was ancient beyond anything he could imagine.

"How about we call it a day? I think we're all on the same frequency and can test our procedures between here and Takeshi before heading into the Great Unknown. Or at least wormholes that haven't been transited in over two centuries."

"Considering my stomach is making insubordinate demands, and you've likely stocked up for the cruise, I'd say we repair to your quarters and sample your private provisions," Leung said. She winked at Petrov. "Right, Yannick."

The younger man allowed himself a slight grin. "No arguments here, sir."

"So be it, but the meal will come from the ship's galley. I don't lay in special provisions since my logistics department head and *Serenity*'s chief cook are top-notch. Everyone here eats well." Jecks grinned at Petrov. "You may wish to make a note of that."

"No worries, sir. *Defiant*'s galley is the equal of any in the fleet. When I was a middie, one of the crusty old chiefs teaching basic told us a happy ship was a well-fed ship, and that stuck with me."

"Good, because once we reach the limit of our survey trace, we'll be on reconstituted rations until we dock at a Lyonesse starbase again. And it takes skill to make those taste like fresh."

Petrov's smile broadened. "Been there, ate that, sir. A corvette can patrol farther than its fresh food lasts on account of the antimatter fuel to stasis cargo ratio the naval architects somehow buggered up."

A comical grimace twisted Jecks' face. "Oh, don't I know it. I had *Prevail* longer ago than I care to remember. We ate many a reconstituted meal."

***

"Starbase Lyonesse Traffic Control, this is the Void Ship *Serenity*. Commander Task Force One-Oh-One speaking."

"Traffic Control here. Good morning, sir," a mellifluous female voice replied.

"Good morning. Task Force One-Oh-One will depart as per the sailing schedule, with *Defiant* undocking and breaking out of orbit first, followed by *Serenity* and then *Provider*. We will assume a course directly for the hyperlimit and jump to the wormhole terminus in synchro."

"Yes, sir. That schedule is on the board. You are priority one for undocking and departure over a thirty-minute window beginning in five minutes and can proceed at your command."

Jecks, seated in the bridge command chair, leaned back, smiling.

"Task Force One-Oh-One understands we are priority one beginning in five minutes and for the thirty minutes after that. *Defiant* will commence undocking procedures in five minutes."

Almost immediately, Petrov's voice sounded over the bridge speakers.

"*Defiant* acknowledges and has initiated countdown to undocking procedures."

"Traffic Control understands *Defiant* has started the countdown to undocking procedures as number one on the departure schedule. From all of us in Starbase Lyonesse, Godspeed and good luck. We look forward to your safe return."

"Thank you," Jecks replied. "Task Force One-Oh-One, out."

He knew every spare video pickup on the orbital station would transmit his ships' departure for the benefit of Defense Force HQ on the surface and probably President Hecht's office. They likely even listened in on his brief exchange with traffic control just now.

Which gave him an idea.

"Signals, can you patch us into the base's open video feed? I wouldn't mind seeing what we look like from a spectator's point of view. They must have a composite stream for HQ going. See if you can find it and hook in."

"Consider it done, sir," the communications petty officer of the watch said.

The primary display lit up with four separate feeds just in time to see *Defiant*'s docking tube retract. Then, the large clamps holding her to the docking arm opened, and she began moving sideways under the pressure of tractor beams pushing her away to a safe distance. Though half *Serenity*'s size, the corvette still looked magnificent as she lit her thrusters and gracefully arced away from the station and Lyonesse. When her bow steadied on the planned course, *Defiant*'s sublight drives lit up, and she began accelerating toward the hyperlimit.

Jecks had chosen to observe the officer of the watch go through the undocking and departure evolutions rather than do it himself. He'd made it his policy long ago that the lieutenants and sub-lieutenants in *Serenity* would get all the practice they could overseeing maneuvers, both simple and complex. Instead, he focused on the video feed showing his ship as she left Starbase Lyonesse's embrace, turned her bow toward deep space, and fired her sublight engines.

By the time *Provider* followed suit, the spectacle seemed almost anti-climatic, though the replenishment ship's departure was as slick as *Defiant*'s. He half expected one last farewell from HQ, perhaps Admiral Norum himself, but the radio remained stubbornly silent. They were off and likely wouldn't speak with Lyonesse again until they reached the first subspace relay on the return voyage. For some reason, he felt a sudden but mercifully brief pang of homesickness before the excitement of one last adventure aboard a Void Ship seized his imagination again. It left him with nothing more than keen anticipation at seeing what was out there.

***

"Would I be right in guessing you'd rather be aboard *Serenity* right now than here with me?"

President Aurelia Hecht turned her head and gave Admiral Farrin Norum a knowing smile. Both had been watching the broadcast from Starbase Lyonesse on the presidential office's wall-sized primary display from the comfortable settee group around a low, marble coffee table.

"I'd take the most junior bosun's mate billet to be heading out in her." He glanced back at Hecht. "As would you."

"True. There's an atavistic urge to head into the unknown imprinted on our species' genetic code. It's how we created an interstellar empire with countless inhabited star systems after decoding most of our home world's secrets."

"And lost it in an orgy of killing unmatched in our history." Norum let out a soft sigh. "Still, I'd rather be out there with Task Force One-Oh-One discovering what little is left than here."

"Ditto. But our time in deep space has passed. To everything there is a season, and a time to every purpose under the heaven."

Norum let out a soft grunt as his eyes tracked *Serenity*'s departure arc.

"Ecclesiastes was always my favorite chapter in the Almighty's Book. If only for the wisdom hidden in its verses." He paused, as if to gather his thoughts, then resumed in a solemn tone, "Or ever the silver cord be loosed, or the golden bowl be broken, or the pitcher be broken at the fountain, or the wheel broken at the cistern. Then shall the dust return to the earth as it was: and the spirit shall return unto God who gave it. Vanity of vanities, saith the preacher; all is vanity."

"I never took you for that deep a religious thinker."

Norum gave her a crooked smile.

"Something about us returning to Earth now, at this point in human history, rekindled my appreciation for beliefs ancient even before our forebears reached for the stars.

"All go unto one place; all are of the dust, and all turn to dust again," Hecht quoted in a soft voice. "Don't ask me where that came from. It simply did."

"I see I'm not the only one whose imagination was captured by words recorded when no one could even conceive of humanity leaving Earth." He chuckled softly. "Though perhaps right now, I can better understand the impulse that led us — citizens, government, Order of the Void, and Navy — to send Al Jecks and his crews back to the cradle of humanity."

Hecht gave Norum a strange look. "Let's hope the vanity that birthed this impulse to rediscover Earth will not doom their souls."

"And now I definitely don't want to ask where that came from."

— 20 —

"So far, so good." Al Jecks gave Lieutenant Ginny Retief, his navigator and current officer of the watch, a pleased smile when she confirmed they had come out of the wormhole in the Parth system after a long series of transits.

The network had taken them from Lyonesse through the uninhabited Broceliande and Drumelzier systems to Arietis, the first of the republic's recolonized worlds, then via another uninhabited system to Micarat, followed by Yin and Takeshi, all three of which had also been reclaimed and garrisoned.

During imperial times, a wormhole connected the uninhabited system, ISC651000-3, to Yin, obviating a detour via Micarat. But it had shifted over the previous century and a half and led nowhere useful. The enforced detour added an extra transit and partial star system crossing, but they reached Parth quickly enough, nonetheless. The route was well established, buoyed, and supported by a series of subspace relays.

"Contact the Parth Mission and see if they need anything from us. Otherwise, we'll cut across to Wormhole Three."

"Aye, aye, sir."

"And then we can finally begin our actual survey." He cocked an amused eyebrow at the first officer sitting to his left. "Took us long enough to reach the start line."

"You know," Yulia Salmin turned her chair so she could face him, "I've been wondering how the republic will govern a large interstellar polity from the back of beyond once we've reclaimed more than just the nearest sectors. It takes a starship three wormhole transits from Lyonesse simply to reach the nearest junction. At least Wyvern has four wormhole termini, three of which link it directly to major star systems. And Wyvern was, if not at the heart of human space, then near enough to rule over all those stars during centuries before discovering stable wormholes."

He gave her a shrug.

"We move the capital elsewhere, to a more central location, and Lyonesse reverts to the sleepy little backwater it was during the imperial era. It wouldn't be the first time. Earth ruled during Commonwealth days, and when the Commonwealth died, Wyvern became the new capital."

"There's a theory which supposedly has been around for a long time, sir. No one knows how long," Lieutenant Retief said. "It posits that humanity, or at least a large part of it, has been governed by an empire — though it was called by many names — that never ended since it was founded in Rome at the start of the common era. This empire merely changed hands and capitals throughout history. Physical borders, politics, language, or ethnicity didn't define it though. No. It was characterized by the unchanging mentality of the elites who've ruled over our species ever since Emperor Augustus of Rome."

Jecks scratched his chin, eyes narrowed in thought.

"I think I read about the idea of an empire that never ended years ago in a rather obscure political philosophy context. Can't say it made much of an impression. Did you research the subject, Ginny? You sound like you know more than most people."

She gave him a faint smile.

"A bit, sir. It caught my imagination when I first came across it in a political science class. I wanted to point out that the seat of empire changed from time to time as the balance of power shifted between human polities before the Faster-than-Light Diaspora — Rome to Byzantium, then to Madrid, after that to London, then Washington, and so forth. With the Diaspora, the seat of empire shifted to the newly created Commonwealth's capital, Geneva, until the founding of the interstellar empire moved it to Draconis on Wyvern. Or at least that's what the theorists say. One might argue the seat of empire moved from Wyvern to Lyonesse over the last two centuries. And it will move again when the eternal elites decide a large wormhole junction will allow them to exercise power more easily over human space."

Salmin gave the navigator a searching look.

"If the theory has some truth to it, and there's nothing to say it doesn't, maybe the seat of empire never really left Wyvern or hasn't yet. If the latter, then maybe we are in the midst of the next shift."

"Or Wyvern retains supremacy if the empire that never ended is destined to remain there for the foreseeable future." Jecks made a face. "Mind you, I'm not sure the idea holds water. Human nature is such that elites of every society throughout history will behave in roughly the same way, treat ordinary citizens the same way, and have more in common with each other than the people over whom they rule. The exercise of power is an immutable constant, and it inevitably corrupts those who wield it, or perhaps it mostly attracts those who are morally corrupt in the first place."

Before Retief could reply, the signals petty officer of the watch raised his hand.

"A reply from the Parth Mission, sir. They say thanks for the offer, but they're good. A supply ship from Micarat came through three weeks ago. And they wish us a pleasant survey expedition."

"Wormhole Three it is, Ginny. Set her up, and let's get out of here."

Jecks jumped to his feet. "I'll be in my day cabin. Care for a cup of tea, Yulia?"

"Sure." Once they were in the privacy of his office, she asked, "You seem happy we won't swing by Parth. Is it impatience or the idea of so many souls leaving their mortal remains there over thirteen hundred years since it first became a prison planet?"

"Impatience mostly. I visited Parth a few years ago. Hot, humid, and overgrown in the habitable zone. Freezing cold in higher latitudes, not much left of the past. The locals have regressed to preindustrial levels, likely in the space of a single generation, and most are descendants of prisoners. They were rather aggressive toward the mission at first — there's still a battalion of Marines guarding our installations. Not a place where shore leave is an option.

"Besides, I found it depressing as heck. Especially a place called Desolation Island, where the current inhabitants' ancestors were exiled for life, meaning they were the second worst of the worst, not quite bad enough to deserve execution. They spiraled back into the stone age and will attack anyone landing on their shores. Desolation Island makes our Windy Isles look like compassionate detention. No, I don't much care to revisit. The Brethren and Marines there must be tough or unimaginative."

"Or both."

The door chime pinged, and Jecks bade it open, admitting Sister Bree.

"Join us for tea, Sister. We were just discussing all the souls whose mortal envelope died on Parth, a place of perdition long before there was an empire."

"A choice assignment for the Brethren, though. Precisely because those who remain still suffer in a place of perdition and need our help more than any others in our expanding republic."

"Having visited both Hatshepsut and Parth, just to mention our furthest missions on the two main wormhole branches, I know I'd rather be posted to the former."

Bree smiled.

"And I the latter. You knew Brethren in reunification missions are volunteers, right? When they volunteer, they provide their first, second, and third choices, and we always have more wanting hardship postings than there are positions available."

"Testing themselves in the service of the Almighty," Salmin said in a soft tone, as something she'd heard long ago resurfaced from the depths of her mind.

"Just so. Of course, the volunteers are merely a small tranche of the entire Order. We must still fill our assigned positions in the Defense Force, in health care and teaching institutions on Lyonesse and the Coalsack Sector worlds opened to colonization and run all of the abbeys and priories. As the republic has grown, so have demands on the Order, and recruiting isn't always easy, as you might know from your own Service's experience. Our reach is outstripping our population growth, and we didn't have a large base to begin with."

"Hence lifting natives of fallen star systems back up the technological ladder in a single generation or less — instant population increase for the republic. Unless they decide they don't wish to join us once they achieve self-sufficiency."

A mysterious expression briefly appeared on Bree's delicate features.

"I don't think that'll happen. By the time they're ready for the wider galaxy, they'll be tightly tied to us by more than just trade and other prosaic issues. Have no fear. One of a Brethren mission's goals is turning local populations into enthusiastic citizens of Lyonesse through teaching, good works, and other forms of influence."

Salmin opened her mouth to comment but was cut short by the officer of the watch announcing *Serenity* would go FTL shortly. When Lieutenant Retief's voice faded away, Sister Bree spoke first.

"You were about to say something concerning Servants of the Almighty conducting influence operations like your Defense Force Command and Staff College teaches them, right?" An impish grin lit up her face. "Monastics and members of religious orders have been engaged in such activities since the beginning of civilization, Commander. Maybe even earlier. You could say we invented the concept long before military leaders caught on to its usefulness in every environment and under any condition."

Jecks snorted. "Figures."

The final warning — three klaxons — sounded, and they placed their coffee mugs on the table, knowing the momentary disorientation of passing into hyperspace might generate inadvertent spills. Then, the universe twisted itself into a psychedelic pretzel, at least that's what Jecks perceived. He'd never asked what others saw. But the moment was short-lived, and after shaking off the feeling, he drained his cup.

"Well, folks, now that we're FTL again, I'll be joining Chief Ahane's aikido session on the hangar deck. Either of you care to join me?"

—21—

Celeste Mission

Friar Shakku, now wearing the same battledress uniform and carrying the same field gear as Major Dozier's Marines — minus power weapons — stuck his head into the main office.

"I'm off on the reconnaissance sweep now."

Sister Maryam looked up from her workstation and gave him a wry smile.

"I'd say have fun, but I know you're overjoyed to wear a uniform again and leave the minutiae of running this place in my and your deputy's hands."

"Jealous that I'll make first contact with people upriver?"

"I'll confess to a touch of envy. But since I didn't do a hitch in the Corps, the envy isn't born of nostalgia for a time when life was so much less complicated."

"Then why?"

"You're off on vacation from setting up a large mission in unknown territory in record time while I'm desperately searching for locals we can train as hospital orderlies to help us deal with the ever-growing inflow of patients from every settlement within a hundred kilometers."

"It won't be all boat rides and cocktail parties with village elders. We will be roughing it and might even bump up against locals who believe in sky demons like those in Angelique."

Maryam made a face, but before she could reply, Major Dozier appeared.

"Ah, there you are, Friar. B Company is almost ready." He examined Shakku in silence from top to bottom before nodding with satisfaction. "Haven't forgotten the basics, eh? Good stuff. What were you again?"

"Infantry sergeant — squad leader, D Company, 1st Battalion, 4th Marines."

"Then you'll be reliving your glory days. Not that we expect you to kick ass and take names. But hauling a ruck through the rain forest is just as crappy whether you're a grunt or one of the Almighty's soldiers."

Dozier gave Shakku a hearty slap on the shoulder before heading downhill to the newly built landing where B Company was preparing the boats under Centurion Harald Brock's impassive gaze.

Maryam and Shakku exchanged glances once Dozier was out of earshot, and the friar said, "My deputy will deal with Major Dozier. Have no fear."

"I'm actually becoming somewhat inured to his rather crude but hearty, fellow-well-met persona. Let's just say his people getting the hospital up and running without a hitch bought him a lot of goodwill."

"Glad to hear it. I'd hate to come back and find the battalion had an unexpected change of command."

Maryam waved him away.

"No worries, now go before they send a full search party for their chaplain-diplomat."

"Stay well."

"I intend to."

Shakku headed for the landing — in the nick of time, as it turned out. Most Marines were already loaded with only Centurion Brock, his first sergeant, and a handful remaining on shore. Dozier and Brock were having what appeared to be a light conversation from a distance, but Shakku knew from experience they were discussing and confirming last minute items. Try as anyone might, a few details of lesser importance always arose late in the preparation process.

The boats, which looked very much like starship escape pods with a watercraft's lower hull, bobbed contentedly along the floating dock, most of their passengers inside the housing that occupied the above-water part save for a one-meter-wide walkway running along the gunwales around the craft. However, unlike escape pods, they were gray rather than white, and their skins could turn into chameleons at the flick of a switch. Carrying fifteen per boat, the expedition numbered nine craft, two per platoon, and one for company headquarters.

Shakku saw no apparent weapons, but they didn't need heavy ordnance. The Marines could unleash enough firepower from within the boat through firing ports and from the deck to ward off the most determined attack by natives. Hydrodynamic drives fed by miniature fusion reactors and controlled from the cockpit beneath a blister at the front of the housing propelled the craft at speeds not seen on Celeste in over two hundred years.

Fifteen Marines in each, plus their kit, the collective gear, and the consumables such as the all-important rations and ammunition, meant tight quarters at night but comfortable cruising during the day. Lashed together, they would transform into a perfectly defensible temporary forward operations base while foot patrols headed away from the river to check inland locations considered of interest, based on aerial and orbital imagery. Of course, each platoon carried its own complement of small drones that could scout the way ahead for dozens of kilometers and stay virtually invisible to both casual observers and modern sensors.

Brock and Dozier raised their hands in greeting, and the former pointed at the boat bearing the marking 2-9 and known for the duration of the sweep as Two-Niner, which was the company commander's callsign.

"Load up, Friar. We're just about ready to cast off."

Shakku, face split by a grin exuding pure joy, sketched a salute. "Aye, aye, Skipper."

He glimpsed Brock and Dozier exchanging salutes as the last Marines headed for their boats before stepping below decks to stow his gear in the cozy compartment. One of Brock's troopers pointed out his assigned cot on the starboard side, and he dumped his rucksack on the foam mattress, followed by his tactical harness. Then he clambered back into the fresh air to witness their departure into the great, if not quite so mysterious, unknown.

Drone overflights had given them plenty of information about the people living upriver, but nothing beat human eyes, ears, and noses on the ground. And nothing could ever replace a human being when contacting isolated communities founded by the survivors of the Great Scouring two centuries earlier.

Shakku met Brock and First Sergeant Yaphet Chelmsford on deck and took a seat beside them on top of the housing near the cockpit blister as two Marines per boat released moorings and fed the synthetic ropes onto their hidden spools.

"Nothing beats a ground-level view of the countryside, eh, Friar?" Brock said in a good-natured tone. "Drones can't smell out strange doings, let alone see into the hearts of strange folk."

"So here we are, heading into the once known," Chelmsford rumbled in his deep basso voice, "pushing back the old frontier."

A big man with a square face, hooded eyes, shoulders that could hold up the world, and hands like hams, Brock was as open and even-tempered as he was strong. Chelmsford, dark-complexioned but as large and squarely built as his centurion, came across as fiercer but was equally competent. Shakku had watched both hoist equipment and material alongside their troopers as they built the mission, without losing sight of the goings-on so that it was as if they were everywhere at once on top of putting their muscles to good use.

"Ain't it the truth?"

Shakku grinned back at them, happy to be pulling away from shore, headed into the continent's dark heart alongside the best Colonial Marines in the Hegemony. Like old times, except he was no longer a simple squad leader but the patrol's civilian chief, who'd decide which human settlements they'd approach and how.

And he'd make first contact armed only with a smile and his finely honed ability to read human beings. Not one as intense and defined as that of a talented sister like Maryam, to be sure. But she and her colleagues were needed at the old priory, where they were building on the initial goodwill of the locals with all their strength and harden the Hegemony's beachhead so a disaster such as Angelique couldn't happen again.

The little flotilla, moving in sync as one under the direction of Two-Niner's pilot, headed for midstream and turned its bows eastward, where low hills covered by vegetation of Earth origin marched in serried ranks on either bank. Distant mountains framing the broad Harmonie River lowlands carved out of the planet's crust eons ago, clawed at the deep blue sky a hundred or more kilometers away. Shakku recalled reading that the entire river zone was a rift valley slowly widening as the underlying tectonic plates moved away.

"Beautiful weather for it," Chelmsford remarked. "Gotta make sure the sensor operators and the mark one eyeball crew don't lose focus and start thinking this is a pleasure cruise."

Shakku glanced at the cockpit blister, where a Marine seated behind the pilot stood sensor watch, looking for threats or unusual readings ahead and to both sides. In addition, four troopers sat topside on each boat, watching for subtle signs even the best sensor-fed tactical AI could miss.

Soon, a drone would lift off from one of the boats and put eyes on the river beyond the upcoming bend. And just as the thought occurred to him, a tiny object lifted off from Two-One-Alpha, the boat carrying number 5 Platoon's leader and half of his command and sped ahead so fast Shakku lost sight of it within moments.

"There she goes." Chelmsford jerked his chin in the drone's direction.

"If you want to see what it sees, Friar," Brock said, "Just flip down your helmet visor and dial the visual feed to channel one-oh-seven. It's reserved for whichever recon drone is clearing the way."

Shakku did so and found his stomach fluttering while his brain adjusted to the bird's-eye view of the river over a kilometer ahead. He knew they weren't expecting trouble or unusual sights this close to Grâce and the mission. Dozier's Marines had conducted daily patrols out to almost fifty kilometers in every direction. At the same time, tethered sensors floating a few hundred meters above the mission's operations center gave the duty watch a long-range image of the surroundings.

The Order and the Hegemony Government had jointly taken the lessons of Angelique to heart and demanded the Corps equip the battalion with every piece of gear that could conceivably be of use, religious scruples, and fiscal parsimony be damned.

Compared to the local sail and oar-driven boats, Brock's little flotilla moved at a fast clip, even facing into the current, and a quick glance aft proved they'd attracted a fair number of spectators. Shakku was sure the Grâce elders would speak with him or Maryam soon to get fast watercraft for their fisher folk. They were undoubtedly eager to climb back up the technological ladder as fast as they could, and Shakku wondered, not for the first time, whether the measured pace used by the Old Order Brethren and their Republic of Lyonesse wasn't too stodgy.

After all, these were humans only two centuries removed from the most advanced civilization in the known galaxy. Surely, they could go from sailing skiffs to hydrodynamic drive boats in less time. Of course, it meant skipping over every other electricity generation method straight from nothing to miniature modular fusion reactors.

He flipped up his helmet visor, though his eyes kept staring ahead, seeing but not seeing.

"What's up, Friar?" Brock asked. "You look like you're a hundred light-years away."

"I was thinking about the long-range plan of raising Celestans to the Hegemony's technological level and wondering whether it's too long. They've already seen a lot of what we can do in a short time, and now our boats, moving up current without oars or sails, and they rely heavily on fishing out in the gulf."

"Isn't the idea making them self-sufficient?" Chelmsford asked. "Can't do that if we just give 'em stuff produced by our factories."

"True. But we based that on the experiences of the Old Order related by the Brethren abducted from Hatshepsut. They don't show up with a full military contingent and all manner of tech that might arouse the curiosity and perhaps envy of the locals before establishing themselves as indispensable members of the community. I think it likely that the Angelique disaster was in part triggered by showing too much too soon."

"And we're doing it again, except with people who haven't regressed into stone age savagery."

Shakku gave the first sergeant a thin smile.

"Just so. And with even more people and more tech. Asking the folks in Grâce and the surrounding settlements to wait for a generation or more before they can fish using our sort of boats, hunt with power weapons, and work with power tools, big and small, just like us, might be too much."

"Should I understand a Friar of the Order, and the most senior Wyvern Hegemony civilian in the Celeste system is questioning the Colonial Service's approach?" Brock asked with an amused smile.

"You understand correctly, Centurion," Shakku replied in a dry tone. "Our Order almost single-handedly crafted the Colonial Service's protocols concerning native populations, and we Servants of the Almighty err as much as any other human. The more I think of it, I wonder whether we drew the right lessons from the Angelique disaster. Santa Theresa was perhaps too easy and made us believe any fallen population would go along with our plans."

He gestured over his shoulder.

"Look at how many are watching us speed up current. It's been like that since day one. They're not stupid people, nor are they simple. We've shown our hand from the get-go, and now they want to play. No one has said so, but it'll come sooner than you think. Put yourself in their shoes.

"We have gear that would make their lives immeasurably simpler, safer, and more prosperous, and they know it. I figure keeping to the Colonial Service timetable won't end well. Not here, not with the approach we took. Yes, the goal is self-sufficiency, but in what? Producing miniature fusion power plants? Not in this decade or the next. But we can give them those power plants and help them set up their own production of simple tools that are nonetheless well beyond anything they can imagine."

Shakku shrugged.

"Boats? Same thing. Give their fishing industry a leg up to save on crew requirements and reorient the people thus freed to the new production lines. Same for agriculture — modernize their processes and farm equipment and reduce the need for farm workers who can be used elsewhere. In other words, put Grâce through a sort of industrial revolution now, not when they've learned enough to put the pieces together themselves."

Chelmsford let out a soft snort.

"And make them dependent on us not just for knowledge or medical services, but everything. Piss off the friars and sisters, and there won't be a replacement fusion plant coming from Wyvern to keep the village lit at night. Disobey them, and when a hydrodynamic boat drive breaks, there won't be any spare parts available until the next ship arrives. Sneaky, Friar. Admirably sneaky. Do it that way, and you'll be a colonial governor in everything but name."

"Oh, I know, Sergeant. And it's not my first choice, but the Archimandrite and the Colonial Service gave me broad powers to avoid another Angelique disaster. And gut instinct tells me the protocols laid down back home, in a cozy office, won't work. They would have if we'd landed as a small group of Brethren, without troopers and heavy gear, and lived simply while teaching. It's what the Old Order did on Hatshepsut. But President Mandus insisted on ensuring the natives couldn't overrun a mission again. Bad for morale back home, I hear." Shakku gave Chelmsford a sad look. "And so, we now face a similar situation as Angelique, but with more sophisticated people whose generational memories recall much of life before the Great Scouring."

"Governor, the Friar Shakku." Brock chuckled. "It has a certain theocratic ring. Will Sister Maryam be your lieutenant governor?"

"She'll be the first who tells me I'm mad when she hears of my plan."

"But she can't disobey?"

Shakku shook his head.

"No. The hierarchy is clear. Not even the assembled Brethren on Celeste can vote me out of office or curtail my powers. Only Wyvern can. Not that I'm worried. Maryam will sense the same hunger in these people as I do, only better. So can all the sisters. Once she takes a moment to reflect on what she's picked up and the logic of assuaging that hunger instead of starving it and seeing our relationship take a wrong turn, she'll be fully on board. The idea may have occurred to her already, and we've not had time to discuss it."

"I gotta say I'd be more comfortable with your course of action, Friar," Chelmsford said. "We have the stuff. We can get more from home, so make 'em happy little Hegemony citizens as soon as possible. The last thing we want is shooting the buggers if they decide they'd rather help themselves. Lots of good, hardworking folk in that place and the others in the vicinity. We Marines don't make war on civilians, so best if we keep the civilians from making war on us, right?"

"From your lips to the Almighty's ear, First Sergeant."

— 22 —

That night, the flotilla moored in the middle of the river a hundred kilometers upstream of Grâce after briefly visiting a few settlements already in contact with the mission. The subtropical forest had closed in on the lazy ribbon of water after the last of the known villages, leaving little space for accessible shores, let alone beaches, and choked off the light.

Shakku could sense a change in the mood of the Marines riding sentry duty topside — what might have felt like a pleasure cruise at first became a genuine patrol. They sensed the potential for hidden peril on either shore, a few paces from the river, where eyes couldn't see beyond the thick curtain of vegetation.

He'd read that the greenery's distant ancestors once grew between what the ancient history texts termed as Earth's Tropic of Cancer and Tropic of Capricorn. Whatever those were. Even he made little sense of the terminology. But he knew the denser forest could hide perils sensors might miss among the riot of exuberant vegetation and wild animal life.

The smells, the sounds, and the subliminal vibrations were so different from those around Grâce that they might as well be on a different planet. But he felt no impending danger, even though sleep was elusive. Thus, Shakku spent more hours than he liked topside, sitting in silence in the darkness with the rest of the Marines standing watch.

And when the Hour of the Wolf came, he found himself more alone than at any other time in his life, wondering whether the future of an entire world hung on his decisions, particularly that of tossing aside the plan and following his instincts, something he'd never done.

Then, when the night sunk into its darkest phase, tiny bright sparks lit up on either bank like miniature fireworks, weaving in and out without rhyme, rhythm, or purpose. Fireflies, whose distant ancestors had been brought to Celeste from Earth during the first intensive terraforming attempts.

Shakku watched them dance, mesmerized, lost along a river light-years from both his home and that of the fireflies' distant ancestors. When their delicate streaks of light died away, he climbed to his feet, gave the two Marines standing guard on deck a silent wave, and headed into the pod where Centurion Brock, First Sergeant Chelmsford, and the rest of B Company Headquarters troopers snored peacefully. He climbed into his narrow bunk and fell asleep at once, content with his decision and the good omen of dancing fireflies on either shore.

***

Toward noon the following day, they reached the first precontact settlement, a village of a few hundred inhabitants built across the Harmonie from a ruined imperial era town. Like Grâce and the others along the coast, it comprised one and two-story wood houses with attached barns and kitchen gardens, surrounded by a three-meter-tall palisade of sharpened vertical logs. A short wooden jetty thrust out into the river while boats, most of them turned upside down, lay atop the rocky banks. Fields surrounded the settlement, and Shakku saw many people hard at work, tending seedlings, pulling weeds, and working a primitive portable irrigation system taking water from a nearby stream before it tumbled into the Harmonie.

They had observed it for some time the previous day thanks to drone overflights and saw no evidence the inhabitants might be hostile. In fact, Shakku suspected word the Grâce Priory had new tenants made it this far. Maybe someone even came downriver and checked if the rumors were true.

While the rest of the flotilla moored in midstream, Two-Niner cautiously approached the jetty as people gathered on the shore, wondering what these strangers with boats that had neither oars nor sails might bring. A bareheaded Shakku, wearing the Order's dark robes over his battledress, stood in the bow, feet spread apart, hands joined in front of him, watching the locals. When the boat was a few dozen centimeters from the jetty, he jumped off with a light spring in his step and took three paces forward while Two-Niner backed out to rejoin the other boats.

Alone on shore, Shakku waited patiently for the villagers to approach him. Or ignore him if they so wished. He might have changed his mind concerning the rate of change they'd impose on Grâce and the surrounding communities, but not a settlement's right to refuse contact.

A bearded man of advanced years — white hair, seamed face, hooded eyes — came through the palisade's open riverside door, staring at Shakku as he walked with a determined step, two younger men at his back. They wore the same homespun clothing common downriver and were likely younger in years than they appeared, thanks to hard lives scratching the soil and roaming the countryside for sustenance.

"So, the rumors are true," the old man said in a deep voice roughened by the years and an accent thickened by two centuries of isolation from mainstream humanity. "Servants of the Almighty reclaimed the Grâce Priory."

"My name is Shakku, sir, and I am indeed a Friar of the Order, head of the mission that now occupies the priory."

"Oh, aye?"

"May I ask your name and that of your community?"

The old man studied Shakku for a few moments with suspicion. "Why are you here, Friar?"

"My companions and I are traveling the Harmonie River to meet as many people as possible."

"And why would you be doing that?"

"Our aim on Celeste is helping rebuild what the Mad Empress destroyed during the Great Scouring. And, in doing so, improve the lives of Celestans. The Order of the Void Reborn and our government on Wyvern sent us. Both wish to reunite the humanity rent asunder by the empire's downfall." Shakku didn't know whether the old man and his people had kept enough memories of the past to remember when humans traveled across the stars.

"Oh, aye?" He repeated. "And why would you be helping rebuild a fallen world? What are we to you who come from the stars?"

"Our fellow human beings, deprived of their birthright."

The old man scratched his beard, eyes narrowed.

"Mighty fine words, Friar. Will you make us worship your Almighty in exchange for your help?"

Shakku shook his head.

"Your beliefs are of no concern to us, only your humanity. And if you don't want our help, we will not insist. People are free to choose their own paths."

"And what will this help entail?"

"At first, the knowledge that was lost by your people — medical, agricultural, animal husbandry, that sort of thing. Also, knowledge about small industries you might have, such as cloth-making, leather work, and metal work. We will also provide you with medical care by sending a team at regular intervals or for emergencies."

The man nodded. "At first, eh? Then what?"

"We will help you trade with other communities for things you need but can't produce. And in time, grow a network of like-minded communities striving to recapture what you lost."

"I see. Again, fine words, Friar. And if I say no, you'll just leave?"

Shakku inclined his head. "Indeed. At this very moment, if you wish it. And no prejudice will come to you and your people. You'll always be welcome at the Grâce Priory and in the communities that are working with us."

A woman, roughly the same age as Shakku's interrogator, pushed through the growing crowd and headed for them, scowling. Thin, sharp-faced with long, white hair twisted into a thick braid and clear, intelligent blue eyes set in a face prematurely aged yet curiously ageless in some respects, she reminded the friar of a few elderly sisters he'd known.

"Enough, Albrecht. Show the friar some hospitality and discuss his offer over a cup of tea." She stopped beside Albrecht. "My name is Helga Yossai, and the man who's been questioning you with such impertinence is my husband, our headman. Welcome to Beausejour, named after the city of our forebears across the river, Friar Shakku. And yes, we're interested in what you offer. Only this stubborn man of mine is so suspicious about everything. He'd question his own reflection in the water for looking so shiny."

Albrecht glared at his spouse and growled something Shakku couldn't make out. Her swift reply, equally unintelligible, startled him, but he turned to the friar and bowed his head after a few seconds.

"Would you take a cup of tea with me, Visitor from the Stars? I apologize for my manners, but we see few strangers here, let alone those from so far away."

Shakku returned the bow. "I'd be honored, Headman Yossai."

***

Several hours and many cups of herbal tea later, Shakku made his goodbyes to Albrecht Yossai and stepped into the midday sunshine. Curious villagers — at least those with no immediate duties — watched him cross the small central square and head back toward the river, carrying an oral agreement he'd recorded in Yossai's own voice for transmission to the priory.

As he reached the river gate, he heard light footsteps behind him, and sensing someone wished to speak with him privately, he stopped at the foot of the empty jetty to wait.

"A word with you, Friar?" Helga Yossai asked when she caught up with him.

"Certainly."

"I knew Albrecht wouldn't speak of it since he considers any mention a bad omen, but you might figure out what's going on. None of us here will approach the site." She seemed nervous and glanced back at the village gate several times while speaking. "It started a year or so ago. Maybe a little longer, but definitely less than two years."

"I'm listening," Shakku said to encourage her when she hesitated.

"We send hunting parties into the hills regularly. A few men with lances, bows, arrows, and long knives. Game is abundant beyond Old Beausejour, in all those valleys and glens." She jerked her chin at the ruins on the far bank. "There was something hidden they glimpsed recently. A structure overgrown by vegetation; one we'd never stumbled across before. It's covered in glowing white symbols and writing as if there was light within, which attracted the hunting party's attention. Not that anyone dares stay nearby when darkness falls, so we don't know. The area is familiar to our people, even though it's at the furthest limit of our range toward the north, so some think the symbols and writing weren't lit until recently; otherwise, we'd have seen it before. Our village has been here since after the Great Scouring. But no one could say for sure."

"Can you tell me where I might find this structure?"

Yossai shook her head.

"No. Our trackers can find their way into any part of our range and reach it again, but only on the ground, by following trails and markings left by generations of hunters. It's a half-day walk — five or six hours — for young, healthy men. That's everything I can say about distance. But you'll find it by heading straight away from the river and due north. A word of warning, Friar.

Albrecht isn't the only one who considers the structure a bad omen. It was found not long before rumors of sky demons occupying the ancient Angelique Abbey wafted down the river from where the savages live, deep in the interior. Many believe there's a connection, though we don't debate the matter."

Shakku nodded once. "I see. No worries. I won't mention our conversation to anyone. But why tell me this now?"

"There are no such creatures as sky demons, Friar. Only humans come from the stars to retake Celeste. Like you. Who should I inform if your arrival on this world seemingly causes strange things?" She let her words hang between them. "Well, we are simple folk, living a hard life. It doesn't take much to trigger the imagination after growing up with stories of the world that was before the Great Scouring. And about souls destroyed by the evil empress. This is why my Albrecht was so cautious with you earlier. He's responsible for our community and won't risk us lightly."

"Yet you're not as suspicious. Is there a reason?"

She gave him a wan smile.

"I can tell much about people and suss out those who have evil intent. You're a good man, Friar. A saintly man who wishes only to help others."

Shakku returned the smile.

"Thank you, Helga. For convincing your husband and for telling me about this strange thing."

"May the Almighty watch over you, Friar." She bowed her head in a quick birdlike movement and turned back toward the gate.

When Shakku glanced out at the river again, he saw Two-Niner heading toward him at a walking pace, its pilot hedging his bets on when the friar would reach the end of the jetty. As it turned out, the boat was a second behind Shakku, which allowed him to simply step aboard without its hull touching the rickety wooden structure.

"So?" Centurion Brock asked as Shakku settled beside him near the pilot's blister.

"They signed on with us, but not without some doing."

As the flotilla resumed its progress upriver, he related the conversation with Albrecht and his private chat with Helga afterward.

"I think the settlement's headwoman has the innate abilities to become a sister. The Old Order Brethren told us that wild talents aren't unusual in fallen populations, and their recruitment can help build up our numbers. Not Helga Yossai of course. Or at least not soon. But I'd like to follow up on this mysterious structure that perhaps started glowing around the time the first Colonial Service reconnaissance team surveyed Celeste before the re-establishment of the Angelique Abbey. And no, they couldn't give me clear directions. Their trackers can find it again, but I don't want to use them."

"A low-level drone sweep then," Brock replied. "One of the big birds with heavy-duty sensors. They can detect minute artificial power emissions. If that structure started glowing after two centuries, then something that woke up recently is powering it from within. Maybe the survey's sensor sweep triggered it. If I recall the briefing, they covered the entire planet to remap it. One stray ping on a slumbering receiver, and good morning, Celeste."

Shakku cocked a skeptical eyebrow.

"After over two centuries?"

"Easily. Solar collectors to keep it trickle-charged. Or thermal exchange. Or even a miniature fusion reactor. If the demands on the reactor are minimal, its fuel could last longer than you might think. We haven't evolved the technology much in two centuries, that's true, but by the end of the imperial era, they'd refined it as far as humanly possible." Brock stomped his foot on the boat deck. "The power plants in these boats won't need replenishing for a few years. In fact, we'll wear out moving parts before the reactor runs out of fuel. Same for the ones powering the priory. If we brought enough from Wyvern, we could electrify every settlement we've visited and have twice as much again in reserve."

The friar gave Brock a questioning look. "You know a lot about the subject."

A grin split the centurion's face.

"I may be a Marine by vocation, but I'm an engineer by education and profession, as are the other officers in the battalion. The command noncoms and senior sergeants, by and large, are engineering technicians or technologists in one specialty or another. They might call our military trade pioneers after the old infantry troops trained as sappers, but we're capable of much more. Only our junior ranks can really be compared to the pioneers of yore, and they'll become technicians and technologists as they go up the ranks and broaden their education. It's amazing what you can do with Marines if you think of them as more than just infantry grunts."

"I shall keep that in mind, Centurion. And now, I should send a report back to the priory. I'll add a notation for Major Dozier to sweep a thirty square kilometer area north of the river opposite the Beausejour village with one of your sensor drones."

"How about I do that, Friar? Marine to Marine? It'll just be easier for everyone." Brock's disarming smile took any hint of criticism from his words.

Shakku inclined his head.

"Fair enough. I haven't worn a uniform in longer than you've been in the Corps and probably won't get the idea across as efficiently."

—23—

Three days later, after recruiting several more settlements as they crept deeper into the continent, though each with greater difficulty than the previous one, they reached a village several hundred kilometers further upriver from Beausejour. It was visibly more primitive and less welcoming than the earlier ones. And in contrast to the latter, it was built among the ruins of a small town called Embrun on the old maps, rather than on a site untainted by the Great Scouring. Dense forest loomed beyond the fields and on the river's far bank, giving the area a rather gloomy aura. Or so Shakku, with his heightened senses, thought.

The inhabitants wouldn't let him land, and thus he spoke from the bow of Two-Niner bobbing a few meters offshore. Several locals immediately made what he knew was a sign to ward off evil, and his ears picked up mutterings about sky demons returning. After a few minutes, the headman, a big shaggy, bearded individual wearing a mix of leather and homespun cloth, pointed toward the river and shouted at Shakku to leave and never come back in heavily accented Anglic words rendered almost incomprehensible by his gravelly voice.

Shakku bowed his head in acknowledgment and made a hand sign to the pilot while keeping his eyes on the increasingly hostile crowd. Almost at once, the boat smoothly slipped backward, away from shore to rejoin the flotilla in midstream, while Shakku took his usual seat next to Brock and Chelmsford.

"No buyers, Friar?" The latter asked.

"Did you see them make warding signs?" Both Marines nodded. "I also heard the words sky demon used by several people. And that makes me fear we might be entering Baune's heart of darkness, epitomized by the inhabitants of Angelique."

"Do we turn back?"

"Not just yet, Centurion. We're coming up on the mouth of the Sanne River, and I'd like to visit the settlements just upstream from its confluence with the Harmonie. If we center the heart of darkness on Angelique and consider its outer edge to be here, then the Sanne skirts the perimeter. We may find takers along its banks. At the very least, I'd like to see the condition of the people with my own eyes and hear them with my own ears."

"It's your call." Brock passed on the orders, then turned back to Shakku. "Tell me, Friar, your term heart of darkness, is that a flight of fancy or something else?"

Shakku raised his hand, palm facing downward, and wiggled it from side to side.

"Yes and no. I can't quite remember where I came across the term, but I think it fits what we face here. Angelique, whose history during the imperial and Commonwealth eras wasn't wholesome, sits at the heart of this continent. In the years before the Great Scouring, it was already a place of darkness for a large swath of its underprivileged inhabitants — a majority of the population, by the way. So many died there during the fall, and since then, our first mission to Celeste being merely the most recent, that the very earth around the city still resonates with the imprint of their deaths."

Shakku gave Brock and Chelmsford a grim look.

"As far as we know, it is the most primitive, superstitious, violent, and ignorant part of Celeste, or at least the continent of Baune, since we've not explored the lesser continents yet. Therefore, it is Celeste's heart of darkness, both spiritually and metaphorically."

The first sergeant let out a soft grunt.

"Then tell me this, Friar. Why did your people choose Angelique for their first mission on this world when they must have known about the darkness you say is baked into the soil?"

Shakku shrugged.

"We were overconfident. Arrogant even. A classic case of hubris. It was the densest population center on the planet, and our leaders thought they could overcome the darkness by bringing the Almighty's light and elevating as many people as possible in short order. But they forgot Nemesis, winged balancer of life, dark-faced goddess, daughter of Justice. She always punishes the frivolous insolences of mortals. And thousands died. All of ours and many locals."

Brock scratched his chin.

"A few rods from God, and your heart of darkness is only a bad memory, Friar. Based on the after-action report I read, I figure neither you nor anyone else can save the Angeliquans."

A wintry smile tugged at Shakku's lips.

"Destroy Angelique to save it?"

"To save us further misery and death down the road. Marines don't sign up for colonial duty to get killed by irredeemable savages in faraway places."

"Yet only the Almighty can know whether they are irredeemable or whether we can bring them out of their savagery. It is not for us to make that call."

"You're the one who calls Angelique the heart of darkness, Friar," Chelmsford said. "Me, when it gets too dark, I enjoy lighting things up. If you've never seen what a penetrator rod does when it slams into the ground at terminal velocity, you'll be surprised at the intensity of the flash. Multiply that by a few dozen and no more heart, no more darkness. The end."

"I think we can let the Angeliquans live out their lives undisturbed for now. If they don't attack us, we won't attack them. And in time, as civilization spreads across Celeste once more, the great-grandchildren of today's wildlings will find their way back into the light."

"You're the boss, Friar. The savages stay beyond our perimeter, we're good."

They fell silent for a long time, enjoying the sun, the sights — ruins, many smothered beneath a blanket of vegetation lined the banks on both sides — and the fresh air. Finally, Chelmsford pointed at a dip in the river's northern bank.

"And that, if I'm not mistaken, is the confluence with the Sanne."

"You would be right, Top," the pilot said.

"Recon drone heading in," the sensor operator added.

As he watched the little machine disappear, Shakku realized that the subtropical forest had closed in on both banks again, dense, green, and slightly menacing, a wall of life that could conceal many perils from even their sensors. It was as if humans had never tamed this little corner of Baune, yet the Celestans had thoroughly domesticated it long before the Mad Empress' reign. Long before there was an empire, in fact.

The flotilla turned to port one boat after the other and entered the Sanne, whose water, flowing from the distant mountains, lazily co-mingled with the Harmonie. Though nearly as broad as Baune's longest river at the confluence, the Sanne quickly became narrower and darker thanks to the thick vegetation overhanging the banks and, in many places, tall trees growing in the shallows atop complex root arches. With the sun already well past its zenith, shadows were creeping across the channel, and a brief chill enveloped Shakku as Two-Niner passed through a patch of shade, even though the air temperature remained pleasantly warm.

Although Embrun wasn't that far behind them, it was as if they'd entered another world once the Harmonie River vanished behind a bend.

"Not much evidence left of human habitation, is there?" Chelmsford asked no one in particular. "I figure there were farms, fields, houses, docks, all sorts of stuff on both banks of a river that can serve as a highway for skimmers and water transports."

Shakku glanced at him.

"It doesn't take long to erase visible traces of civilization in a place teeming with aggressive vegetation. I bet if we run archeological surveys with the drones, we'll find signs of many ruins beneath that greenery. But that'll be for another time, once Celeste is back within the fold, and we can devote energy to researching what happened here over the past two centuries."

"Sir, the drone spotted something on the right bank, a hundred meters ahead, past the next bend. Take a look."

Both Brock and Chelmsford lowered their helmet visors. Shakku, whose tactical gear sat on his bunk below, tried to get a glimpse of the sensor operator's display through the cockpit blister.

"What the hell?" Chelmsford turned to Brock. "Are you seeing that, sir?"

One of the company HQ Marines appeared in the hatch and silently handed Shakku his helmet. He had it on, visor down, and connected to the drone's feed within seconds. The latter's video pickup was aimed at a less densely wooded stretch of shoreline where small boats could easily be pulled out of the water and up a muddy slope.

There, a macabre sight waited for them. Three human skulls, with bits of flesh and hair still attached, sat atop two-meter-long, evenly spaced wooden poles. The one in the center wore what was unmistakably a Wyvern Hegemony combat helmet.

"It looks like we've found the actual boundary of your heart of darkness, Friar. That helmet could only have come from the Angelique Abbey."

Another chill coursed through Shakku's body, and he said, "Get everyone below deck and turn us around, Centurion."

"You expect an attack? The sensors would have picked up human life signs." Brock glanced at the operator. "Anything?"

"Sir, both banks are so full of life we're having a hard time getting clean readings a few meters beyond the tree line directly on either side. Further ahead, it gets worse. Could humans be hiding beyond the bend, where the drone is? Maybe, if they're not wearing or carrying metallic objects or anything else that might give off an inorganic reading."

Brock turned to Shakku again.

"What's up, Friar?"

"There's evil here. I can't say whether it stems from the skulls, a human presence, or an echo of the past. But those skulls are a warning. If we go ashore on the east bank of the Sanne River, we enter their territory, and they will attack us."

"The Angeliquan savages who murdered our people."

Shakku nodded.

"Yes. I know we're still far from the city, but hunter-gatherers can roam a wide area, especially by boat. If we'd gone further up the Harmonie, we'd have seen more warning signs."

"Let 'em try us," Chelmsford growled. "They'll merge with the Infinite Void before you can say boo."

"I'd rather avoid loss of life, theirs as much as ours, if possible. Please turn us around, Centurion."

"Wilco."

Brock gave out the order, and the lead boat swung around moments before clearing the bend. Shakku's unease stayed with him for a few kilometers, then dissipated like a bad dream come daybreak, and he remained silent, grateful that the Marines weren't speaking either. Maybe their subconscious had picked up something of what the friar sensed and told them the flotilla was better off heading back — what they might call a gut feeling.

As the Harmonie came back into sight at dusk, Brock finally broke the silence.

"Do you want to go upriver a bit and see if the Angeliquans planted more skull totems to warn the unwary? Now that night is falling, we hold an advantage they can't match." He tapped his helmet's visor to indicate its night vision capability.

"No. Let's mark this area as the furthest limit of our activities for the time being and return to base."

"Suits me just fine, Friar. There's something wrong with a place where people go from faster-than-light star travel to marking their boundaries with human skulls that still have bits attached in the space of two hundred years."

"It can happen in a fraction of the time, Centurion. Less than a generation, depending on the circumstances. If you can get your hands on a history of the imperial prison planet, Parth, go to the section covering Desolation Island, where those exiled for life were sent. Most went from FTL travel straight back into something approximating the iron age. Apparently, the worst of the worst formed stone age level tribes whose brutality rivaled the Angeliquans. Of course, that's an extreme case. But even now, the veneer of civilization remains fragile and much too thin."

"I'm not sure I want to read something so depressing if truth be told." Brock glanced over his shoulder at the Sanne slowly vanishing into the darkness. When he turned back, he asked, "Shall we stop just past Beausejour where they can't spot us and go look for that structure? I'll call operations in the morning and see if they've uncovered its location."

Shakku shrugged. "Why not?"

"And we'll moor mid-river for the night, a few kilometers past the last village. That way, if there are bad guys in the forest, we'll see them coming from a distance."

"A good precaution."

Chelmsford let out a soft grunt.

"Or we could keep going downstream with just enough forward motion to steady the boats. Have double the troopers on deck at all times. Less sleep for everyone, but it'll put more distance between the friar's heart of darkness and our immortal souls."

Brock considered it for a moment, then shook his head.

"I don't think it's necessary. That last village — Embrun — doesn't look like it's under threat from roving bands of wildlings. Otherwise, their palisade would be a lot stronger than it is."

The first sergeant nodded.

"True. Moor midstream, it is."

Shakku, who no longer picked up an eerie menace, didn't mind either way, but the Marines surely still heard echoes of the gut feeling that sent them away from the Sanne River and its grisly territorial markers. Yet he couldn't quite regain his usual serenity thanks to a persistent sense of unease, as if Angelique's circle of darkness was still expanding, driven by ghosts spawned from a place where evil had imprinted the very soil.

It had to be more than just the thousands who died violently in and around the old abbey. Perhaps something dire happened during the Great Scouring, more than just the destruction caused by the Mad Empress' Retribution Fleet. But they'd likely never find out.

— 24 —

"I'm glad the operations center had the drone drop off a homing beacon," Shakku said in a low voice to Brock while the Marines walking point checked out yet another animal trail intersection. Meanwhile, they and the rest of the patrol, half of B Company — the other half was guarding the boats under First Sergeant Chelmsford — knelt on either side of the faint path, even-numbered troopers facing left, odd-numbered troopers facing right.

All wore full armor, gloves, tactical harness, small packs, and helmets with lowered visors — not a bit of bare skin showing — even in the growing heat, thanks to swarms of insects whose distant ancestors came from Earth and saw humans as walking buffets. Shakku was the only one not carrying a loaded carbine or wearing a sidearm on his belt. He only had his knife. But beyond that, he was indistinguishable from the Marines.

"You and me both, Friar. Oh, we'd have managed by dead reckoning once ops gave us the coordinates, but a patrol can drift over the course of fifteen kilometers in dense forest and waste time searching for the target at the other end. I'd like to be back in the boats by dark."

"We will." Shakku's lips found the end of the water tube snaking into his helmet, and he took a quick sip from the bladder in his small pack, happy he didn't need to open his visor for a drink. Everyone in the patrol carried two liters of water, two days of rations, water purification straws, first aid kits, and spare ammunition — apart from the friar.

Sunlight flickered through the tall treetops here and there, but the spongy ground, covered by decades of decaying vegetation, lived in a permanent twilight during the day. Small critters flitted around them, curious about these new, never seen before intruders who carried a human scent but not a human appearance under their tactical gear. That larger animals watched from deep inside the undergrowth was a given. Still, the biggest predators on Celeste other than humans, knew better than to try their luck with the Marines.

Shakku's biggest worry was meeting a hunting party from Beausejour. He'd rather no one knew they were checking out the structure that made the villagers nervous. But the chances of a wildling band coming this far west were next to nil, for now.

The point men reappeared and made hand signals indicating the intersection was clear and the path they were on continued in the right direction. At Brock's gesture, the Marines stood and resumed their march deeper into a forest that had grown over what was once an expanse of fields, farms, and small hamlets, judging by the almost invisible remains of walls, foundations, and fences they passed at regular intervals. But Shakku sensed no darkness. Not even sadness. Humanity's greatest works eventually decay and are reclaimed by nature, no matter where. Only artifacts out in space or on airless worlds have a chance of outliving the species that created them.

Around noon, Shakku decided he'd brave the teeming insects for a bite to eat and fished a ration bar from a front pocket on his harness. He unwrapped one end, raised his visor, and took a quick bite before lowering it again. No tiny biting or blood-sucking creature made it inside. Shakku finished his meal without giving a piece of himself to the small wildlife and was mildly surprised when the column stopped once more.

"We're here," Brock whispered as he dropped to a knee beside the friar. "The point men are checking the area for tangos."

"You're sure?"

"They saw the structure hidden beneath a fine blanket of greenery and sent back video. Without the glowing symbols, it would have lain undiscovered for a few more centuries — or longer if its power collectors failed. Which they would have eventually."

"And the symbols?"

"Anglic letters and numbers. They make no sense now, but once we've dug it out, we should be able to determine what it says and what it is." Brock fell silent and tilted his head to one side as a voice came over the company network.

"Two-Niner, this is November Two-One. Nothing other than animal life signs in the immediate area. No recent traces of human activity. Energy readings from the thing are faint, barely above background radiation, but unmistakable."

"Roger. Two-One and Two-Two, spread out."

Almost at once, the Marines from number 5 Platoon ahead of Shakku and Number 6 Platoon behind him stood and vanished into the forest to set up a secure perimeter around the object. A few minutes passed while he listened to the muted sounds of troopers making their way through the undergrowth. Then Brock tapped him on the shoulder.

"Shall we?"

They followed the faint trail left by the Marines walking point and entered an overgrown thicket. There, hidden beneath a blanket of vines and surrounded by thorny undergrowth, stood what appeared to Shakku's eyes as a monolith approximately two meters high, four meters wide, and a meter thick. What little they could see of the slick surface confirmed it was of artificial origin and not a natural rock polished by eons of rain.

And, as advertised, they could make out faintly glowing Anglic letters and numbers. Shakku could understand how it might have remained undetected for so long. It was indistinguishable from a natural terrain feature at only a few paces' distance without the glow.

"Want us to clear it, Friar?"

"Hmm?" Shakku, who'd been more deeply immersed in his thoughts than he figured, shook his head and glanced at Brock. "Yes. Otherwise, we won't know what this is."

The centurion pointed at two of his Marines, then at the structure. Both nodded and got busy ripping off the vines and slicing through the thorny bushes. Strong arms and laser tools made quick work of the green blanket, leaving Shakku and Brock standing in front of what was obviously a monument covered in names and what looked like military unit crests. Letters and images glowed softly in a blueish hue while names dissolved after a few seconds to be replaced by fresh ones.

"It's a war memorial," Brock finally said, pointing at a date near the top, "commemorating a battle fought on Celeste during the empire's Formation War against the remnants of the old Commonwealth twelve hundred years ago. I've read accounts of those fights. Rather than surrender, Commonwealth officials and military leaders self-destructed their defensive positions so they could kill imperial troopers by the tens of thousands. Looks like this one is for the Battle of Eliason."

Shakku glanced at Brock. "The old maps we have don't show a place called Eliason."

"Indeed, they don't, but I suspect we're standing on the site of the Commonwealth government's last redoubt in the Celeste star system. They obviously erected this to commemorate the imperial personnel killed during the battle. I remember reading about a similar one on Earth, overlooking the site where Geneva once stood, and on a few other core worlds which sided with the Commonwealth instead of acceding voluntarily to the empire."

"To commemorate the dead and remind all who pass here that such murderous battles among humans should never occur again," Shakku said in a soft voice.

"Someone forgot to tell Dendera."

"I understand she never left Wyvern during her lifetime, and Wyvern joined the nascent Empire of Sovereign Star Systems right at the outset, so there were no battles fought on its surface during that period."

Brock didn't immediately answer but kept staring at the names appearing and disappearing on the slick silver-gray surface.

"I wonder how many dead this commemorates."

"More than you can imagine, Centurion. Now that it's no longer slumbering, there must be a way of interrogating the monument."

"Right." Brock pulled out his battlefield sensor and aimed it at the slab. After a few seconds, he let out a soft grunt. "I'm pulling in data. Names, ranks, units. An endless stream of them. Most died on the same day in the Battle of Eliason."

Another minute went by. Then Brock shook his head.

"Forty-three-thousand-five-hundred and five Imperial Ground Forces members — the equivalent of three divisions — died in a single instant on that one day when the Commonwealth holdouts wiped Eliason off the map with an antimatter demolition device."

"Appalling. Why do we keep killing each other in such unimaginable numbers?"

Shakku took a few steps forward without conscious thought, dodging the remains of the undergrowth removed by Brock's Marines, and laid his hand on the monument. He withdrew it almost at once, as if the slick surface had scalded him, and let out an audible gasp. After a moment, he stepped back, eyes fixed on the shimmering names.

"What is it, Friar?"

Shakku held up a restraining hand, asking for a moment alone with his thoughts. Brock, who'd come to know the friar over the course of the sweep, figured something momentous had just happened and held his tongue.

Finally, Shakku took a deep breath and let out a long, heartfelt sigh.

"That monument appears to be what our mystics call a soul window, a memento mori resonating with the echoes of the dead. I could sense the souls whose violent death was imprinted on the very ground on which they built the memorial when I touched it. It was a sensation beyond anything I've experienced. I'd suggest Maryam come here and do as I did, but the experience might overwhelm her, seeing as how she's so much more sensitive to ripples in the Infinite Void."

He turned to Brock.

"This is a powerful place that will affect any human with a working sense of empathy. You might feel nothing if you touch the memorial, nor will your Marines, but being in its vicinity will touch your subconscious and alter your mood. I suggest we re-drape it with living vines and leave. Once our expansion reaches this area, we can rededicate it to its original purpose — remembering the dead and warning that humanity cannot survive too many bloodlettings of that magnitude."

"As you wish, Friar."

Brock gave the orders, and within five minutes, the patrol was retracing its steps to the Harmonie River and their boats. If they'd felt something, Shakku couldn't say. No one spoke, as was proper during an operation in unknown territory. But when they reached the boats and cast off, the Marines were as subdued as they'd been after exiting the Sanne and leaving its grizzly territory markers behind.

"There are too many dead around us, Friar," Brock said as they sat in their usual spots, watching the sun kiss the far horizon. "Killed because of a thirst for power or a mindless yearning for revenge. How many did Dendera's Retribution Fleet massacre again?"

"According to the Lyonesse Brethren, around ninety percent of our species, an incomprehensible genocide."

"Let's hope humanity's current leaders heed the ghosts of the past and don't extinguish the remaining ten percent in a mad rush to reclaim the imperial crown."

— 25 —

Hatshepsut

"You're not serious, Ambassador." Lieutenant Colonel Salmin didn't quite glare at DeCarde after the latter announced he would be aboard the Thebes Republic's first and only steam-powered Q ship to sail through the Saqqara Islands' Central Passage. But almost. "We've tamped down pirate depredations in the last year. However, this expedition will attract their attention like nothing else."

"Which is precisely why I want to observe how we go about eradicating the problem once and for all. You know how it is, Tom — you can take a Marine from the Corps, but you can never make him anything else." DeCarde smiled at the younger man. "Besides, it's time I visited Aksum since we'll soon be opening consulates in Mazaber and other coastal cities, and I'd rather not swoop in aboard one of the Hatshepsut Squadron's dropships. I'd rather keep those for recalcitrant city elders."

A sardonic smile lit up Salmin's square, honest face. Just as most of his line, he was a stocky man with short, dark hair, hooded brown eyes, and a keen mind. "You mean the Thebans will open diplomatic missions, which we will use as forward operating bases?"

"If you like. Thebes and Lyonesse are virtually indistinguishable with Hatshepsut being a bulwark against Hegemony incursion in our sphere. We will need places to stash your troopers if the Theban diplomats feel a need for the ultimate argument."

"We can use dropships for that."

"Too visible. You know what the ancient definition of diplomacy is, right?"

Salmin smirked. "It's a way of prolonging a crisis?"

"That too. But I mean the one that goes diplomacy is saying good doggie to an aggressive canine while searching for a rock."

"And my battalion is that rock."

DeCarde nodded.

"Just so. The Thebans will soon have their own means of projecting force, but you remain my ultimate argument on this planet."

Salmin sketched a salute. "Yes, sir. And you know how I enjoy arguing."

DeCarde made a face.

"Don't remind me, Tom. You were the most vocal company commander in the battalion during my tenure as CO."

"But was I wrong more than half of the time?"

"No, you were right most of the time." DeCarde climbed to his feet. "But then, so was I. Which is how we both ended up on

Hatshepsut, the republic's most important outpost. How about you introduce me to whoever will command the Marine detachment aboard *Vigilance*?"

"That would be Command Sergeant Alvar Virtanen, 1st Troop, A Squadron."

"Your senior sword?" DeCarde gave Salmin a knowing look. "Is he the Virtanen I remember from when I had the 3rd Battalion?"

"Yes, sir."

"Excellent choice, then. He was in the top five percent of noncoms at the time."

"And still is in the top five percent in the entire 21st. He'll be commissioned as a centurion once our tour here is over." Salmin gave DeCarde a smug look. "I know better than to send anyone but the best on this sort of mission."

"I wonder who taught you that. By the way, I still have a reserve commission and have been doing my annual qualifiers, so you can equip me as an anonymous Marine without desecrating the regimental crest of the 21st. I don't plan on traveling in ambassadorial style."

Salmin frowned at DeCarde. "Diplomats can keep a toe in the Corps?"

"And the Army, and the Navy. We don't advertise it and only mention the matter if required. But it means we can legally issue orders to Defense Force units on outposts if we deem it necessary to further our mission."

"Is that why they promoted you to colonel in the reserve after leaving active duty?"

DeCarde tapped the side of his nose with an extended index finger.

"It makes me not only the most senior government official in the star system, but since my promotion predates Morane's, I'm also the most senior military officer."

"Convenient — for a proconsul." Salmin gestured at his office door. "After you, sir."

"It is that, but let's keep it between ourselves, Tom."

"Oh, there was no need to say so, sir. I can figure things out on my own these days."

DeCarde gave him a sideways grin. "How fast they grow up."

"I'd give you the time-honored Pathfinder reply, sir, but since you still outrank me…"

They walked out of the headquarters building and into the blindingly bright midmorning sunshine and quickly rising temperature. The 3rd Battalion, 21st Pathfinder Regiment, occupied a standard Lyonesse instant base, built with containers dropped from low orbit by one of the Navy's transports. The battalion's Marines had erected it on a piece of unused shoreline just outside Thebes City leased to Lyonesse by the Republic of Thebes government for more than what the rocky, infertile land was worth.

A trio of flags fluttered in the cooling offshore breeze from metal posts rammed into the earth between the HQ doors and the large parade ground at the center of Marine Corps Base Hatshepsut — those of Lyonesse, the Defense Force, and the 21st Pathfinders.

The parade ground, an open expanse of stone smoothed by construction lasers, was surrounded by the squadron buildings, the kitchen and mess, the supply stores, and the armory, a hulking structure occupying most of the base's western end. A second row of buildings behind the squadron offices housed the barracks, while an enclosed range and simulation center sat behind the armory. A wire-topped berm surrounded the entire installation, even on the north side, where the land gave way to a three-meter drop onto a rocky shore washed by endless waves.

DeCarde's keen eyes spotted troopers wearing dun-colored battledress practicing weapon drills in the armory's shade.

"Natives?" He asked.

Salmin nodded. "Theban Marine noncom candidates going through the small arms specialist course."

"Power weapons?"

"Yep. And they're doing as well as any civilian back home would after completing basic. The nucleus we're training will run their own recruit and basic infantry schools under our oversight in a year or so. Perhaps even less. I figure five years, and the Thebans will have a solid cadre that can take over responsibility for ground defense from us. But they'll still need a few of our officers and command noncoms for a while as their people progress up the ranks and gain experience. The expedition to Aksum will be the first actual operation for their most experienced people, noncom candidates who've completed the small arms course and have been assessed as ready for the section leader's course, after which they'll become sergeants."

"Do you think we can make the locals fit for the Lyonesse Defense Force without putting them through our schools?" DeCarde asked, eyes on the troopers as he and Salmin made their way to A Squadron HQ.

"We're putting them through the same syllabus, changed for local conditions and level of technological knowledge. Those are smart people, sir. They're keen on regaining what they've lost and, as a result, are learning faster than most recruits back home do. It's as if they're trying to bridge a two-century gap during an eight-week recruit course. The noncom candidates are even keener sponges."

DeCarde chuckled.

"Their government is highly motivated to take over the entire planet with our help. I'm sure that factors into the enthusiasm."

Salmin let out an indelicate snort. "When did you become so cynical, sir?"

"Am I wrong?"

The Marine laughed as he pulled the door to A Squadron HQ open.

"No. No matter what world and how long since they last saw off-world strangers, people are people. I like the Thebans. They're good folk. But they'll eat this planet alive once we let them loose. The difference between here and Aksum is like night and day. Never mind the other continent, Sylt, where the capital used to be. Only stone age nomads left there. The Brethren tried approaching a band after flying in on a Navy shuttle and almost didn't make it out alive. After you, Mister Ambassador."

They found themselves in a short corridor with several open doors. Its cream-colored walls, though bare, were spotless, as was the gray floor. When Salmin ushered DeCarde through the door marked Troop Leaders, the sole occupant, a tall, muscular, thirty-something man with dark hair going prematurely gray at the temples, sprung up from behind his desk. He wore the dun-colored garrison uniform mandated for tropical duty and combat boots of the same hue. His shirt's sole adornments were Pathfinder wings, a name tape, and command sergeant rank insignia — three upward-pointing chevrons, three downward facing rockers with crossed swords in the space between.

"Sirs." Command Sergeant Alvar Virtanen barked out. "Welcome."

"How are they hanging, Sergeant?" DeCarde asked, smiling, as he stepped forward, hand outstretched.

"Same as when you had the Third Herd, Colonel. One beside the other." They shook enthusiastically, and Salmin could see Virtanen was glad to see his old CO again. "I hear you're the republic's ambassador around here."

"You heard right, and I want to see something of the countryside from your perspective and that of the locals."

Virtanen glanced at Salmin. "Sir?"

"Ambassador DeCarde is coming with you aboard *Vigilance* for the Central Passage clearing expedition and the trip up to Mazaber."

"Roger that, sir. Ambassador, it'll be tight quarters aboard the Q ship. No VIP racks and such. Much more primitive than what we're used to aboard starships."

DeCarde waved Virtanen's comment away. "I'm a Marine."

The noncom nodded. "Understood, sir. Welcome aboard."

"Get the Ambassador fitted out in full kit, weapons included. No rank insignia. He'll be an incognito idler and extra rifleman. And since I know you're wondering whether it's legal, the Ambassador is still on the officers' reserve list."

"And I do the annual weapons qualifications, like a good reservist. My last was six months ago, so I'm good in that respect."

"Yes, sir."

"Thanks. Got a moment to talk to me about the expedition and the troopers you'll be leading into action?"

A grin split Virtanen's craggy features.

"For you, Colonel, I got lots of moments." He gestured at a chair in front of his desk. "Grab a pew."

"Since I already know everything, I'll leave you in the sergeant's expert hands, Ambassador."

"Want me to drop by your office on the way out, Tom?"

"How about you stick around for lunch in the mess, sir? Maybe Virtanen can take you around his unit and let you meet the rest of the troopers."

"It's a deal."

Once Salmin was gone, Virtanen called up a map projection of Hatshepsut and settled behind his desk.

"So, let's see. I have thirty-one Marines in my outfit, prime troopers with not a single slacker, barracks lawyer, or dumbass in the lot. They also gave me sixteen Theban Marines, guys who are candidates for sergeant once we're back, in other words, the best of the lot. The idea is to get them blooded before taking the sergeant's course. My four sections now have eleven bodies instead of seven since I've sprinkled them around instead of forming a Theban-only section. We've been working with them for the last two weeks, both here, in the training area in the interior, and aboard *Vigilance* herself. I gotta say I'm impressed. Not a mouth breather in the bunch. They're almost as squared away and snappy as my own."

DeCarde knew it was high praise coming from a career Pathfinder command sergeant who believed no one could ever be as good as the Marines of the 21st.

"Gear?"

"On top of the regular individual, squad, and section weapons, we're bringing plasma cannon and grenade launchers. The Thebans now have radios on their ships and can talk with home from wherever. We're also bringing surface to orbit commo if we need long-range support. There's plenty of ammo for everything since we don't have to hump it and some diving gear. You heard about the imperial corvette that crash-landed in the water? Well, since we're passing over it on the way to Mazaber, we'll stop and check it out up close."

"Interesting. How about the Theban Marines?"

"The only difference between the locals and us is unit badges. We equipped the Thebans with Lyonesse battledress, tactical harness, helmet, and small arms. Doing anything else wouldn't be right since they'll be at our side during the expedition. Mind you, I think the idea is getting them set up on Lyonesse Defense Force pattern gear as the supplies come in from home, and eventually giving them what they need to produce some of the simpler pieces right here. Make 'em part of us, right, Colonel?"

"That's the goal. So how is the expedition going down?"

—26—

An embassy car dropped DeCarde off at the foot of *Vigilance*'s gangway in a section of the port now fenced off as a Theban Defense Force naval base. The ambassador, wearing an unmarked Marine Corps uniform, took a pair of issue duffel bags from the car's cargo compartment. Then, he gave the driver a silent nod and headed up to where a Theban petty officer stood under the side-to-side awning.

From outward appearances, *Vigilance* looked like nothing more than the most modern of Thebes' miraculous steam-powered cargo ships which had cut travel time between the Theban Archipelago and Aksum in half. Slightly larger than the barquentines that once made up most of Thebes' merchant fleet, she was flush decked, save for fake cargo hold hatches, between the low forecastle and the aft superstructure. The latter sprouted wing galleries on each side of the bridge and was topped by twin smokestacks and an antenna array.

In deference to the tropical waters she plied, the shipyard painted her hull above the Plimsoll line and her superstructure a blinding white while the stacks were black. And though she'd not been launched long ago, the relentless attack of saltwater was already leaving rust streaks below the hawseholes and scuppers. A limp Theban flag hung from a staff at her stern — black sea eagle centered on a background of a broad red, horizontal stripe edged by white bars.

But even though she resembled the refurbished wooden cargo ships coming out of Theban yards as fast as they could be converted to steam, *Vigilance* was no merchant vessel. She hid Lyonesse-designed multi-barrel calliopes and rapid-fire canons on either side beneath hinged hull plates, as well as forward and aft. They fired chemically propelled rounds whose manufacture was by now within Theban capabilities.

She also carried ammo, extra crew, modern radio gear, and Command Sergeant Virtanen's mixed Lyonesse-Theban Marine troop. Her captain was an officer in the newly created Theban Navy, an old hand of the Aksum trade by the name Lars Fenrir, whose escape from the Hegemony raiding party more than two years earlier had become the stuff of legend among Theban seafarers.

When DeCarde reached the top of the gangway, he found himself face-to-face with Fenrir himself. *Vigilance*'s captain wore the khaki Theban Defense Force uniform with shoulder boards almost identical to those of a Lyonesse Navy captain — four gold stripes topped by an executive curl — and the sky-blue beret adopted by Thebes from its Lyonesse patrons.

Only the insignia on the beret differed, though both versions incorporated the ancient anchor symbol. Fenrir looked the part of the master mariner, with a tanned and well-weathered face framed by short, sun-bleached hair and an equally short beard, albeit shot through with silver strands.

"Permission to come aboard, Captain?" DeCarde, carrying a bag in each hand, couldn't salute but bowed his helmeted head.

Fenrir returned the courtesy by raising his right hand to his eyebrow in a gesture halfway between casual and parade ground formal.

"Permission granted. Ambassador DeCarde, welcome aboard the Theban Republic's premier, and so far, only dedicated warship."

DeCarde took a step forward, dropped one of his bags, and stuck out his hand.

"I've heard a lot about you, Captain. All of it good. Hiding your three-master from the Hegemony, then disguising it as a four-master, was a stroke of genius."

Fenrir shrugged as if embarrassed by DeCarde's praise and replied in his rough voice, "If you can't adapt out in the wild, you might as well stay home and fish from the end of the pier."

"It's much the same up there." DeCarde nodded at the sky.

"I hope I'll get to see it one day."

"You will, Captain. I'll make sure of that."

And DeCarde knew he'd do so. Part of his campaign to solidify Lyonesse's control over Thebes involved taking leading citizens up to Hatshepsut Station on carefully planned excursions and showing them what was coming. Provided they cooperated with Lyonesse. He'd take President Freeman up first once the expedition was back in Thebes. And since Fenrir was the Theban Navy's de facto commander, at least until Thebes commissioned more large ships, he wouldn't be far behind Freeman.

"Ah, there you are, sir." Command Sergeant Alvar Virtanen, bareheaded and wearing a dun-colored, lightweight tropical field uniform, appeared seemingly out of nowhere. "Let me grab that."

He reached for the duffel DeCarde had dropped to shake Fenrir's hand.

"No need. I'm incognito, remember?" DeCarde quickly picked up his bag. "Just show me to my bunk, and I'll get out of the heavy gear."

In keeping with Marine Corps practice, he'd donned his full armor, with harness and helmet as the easiest way of transporting the items to the ship.

Virtanen gave DeCarde a broad grin.

"As you want, Trooper. Come along, then."

"If you'd like to join me on the bridge afterward, Mister Ambassador, and watch our departure?"

"With pleasure, Captain."

The sergeant led DeCarde through an open steel door, down a set of stairs, and along a passageway running fore and aft beneath the fake cargo hatches to a set of doors marked barracks.

"You'll be bunking with me and my HQ section, Colonel. A little more space than the troop berths. This ship has functioning heads too, so no sitting over the downwind gunwales and letting it rip right into the ocean."

The ten-meter by ten-meter compartment was as austere as advertised. Steel framed canvas bunks stacked three high, ran along the forward and aft bulkheads while lockers stood against the inboard one. The only natural light and ventilation came from portholes piercing the hull above a pair of tables and a dozen chairs which provided the sole recreational amenities. But with everything painted white, it didn't feel suffocating.

"That one's yours." Virtanen pointed at a bottom bunk. "And your locker has your name on it. I'll let you get organized and check on the troopers. When do you want to inspect the ordnance and fighting positions?"

"Maybe once we're underway?"

"Roger that, sir. By the way, are you okay with us going bareheaded? The crew doesn't wear a lid when they're at sea. Mind you, they're a bunch of civilian mariners wearing brand new Navy uniforms."

"It's your command, Sergeant. Whatever you choose is fine."

"No lids it is, then, sir."

With Virtanen gone, DeCarde found himself alone in the compartment and quickly stripped off his combat gear — it was warm and getting warmer below decks. He replaced his battledress with the same lightweight tropical field uniform the sergeant was wearing. Then, DeCarde stowed his clothing, equipment, and weapons in his assigned locker with proper Marine care and precision, a habit that hadn't left him when he left the Corps. Should Sergeant Virtanen wish to inspect it, he'd find no cause for complaint.

Satisfied, DeCarde made his way up into the superstructure and the bridge by following the neat and obviously brand new signs marking each stairway, door, and hatch, and the arrows showing the way to the primary nodes.

The bridge, an airy compartment with windows on three of four sides — forward, port, and starboard — sat at the very top of the superstructure. DeCarde had taken the interior stairway, though exterior ones connected to the open-air bridge wings that allowed unobstructed views from bow to stern and stopped at the top landing, short of the coaming. He caught the eye of the duty officer, another lean, tanned mariner with a seamed face, this one wearing Navy lieutenant stripes on his shoulder boards.

"Permission to enter the bridge?"

"Granted, Mister Ambassador, sir. Captain Fenrir said you have the privilege of the bridge at all times. He's in the chart room. My name is Razul. I'm the fourth officer."

"A pleasure to meet you, Lieutenant."

"Likewise, sir. If you have questions, please don't hesitate."

DeCarde wandered into the bridge, hands clasped behind his back, and studied the mechanical instrumentation panels, the compass, the various levers and wheels, including the big, spoked ship's wheel which controlled the rudder, and the other devices necessary to sail a steamship across oceans. Among them were the new and vital ship-to-ship and ship-to-shore radios.

He recalled from the briefing notes that Thebes was already redeveloping much of the industrial era technology when the first mission arrived, including the Sterling engine, which served as auxiliary power aboard wooden sailing vessels. Many of the latter had been or were in the process of conversion to more powerful steam engines of Lyonesse design, making the Stirlings obsolete.

Vigilance, however, was something new. Locally built with Lyonesse's help, it was the first metal-hulled ship in Hatshepsut waters for over two hundred years. Moreover, it was fully electrified and boasted electric lighting, fan-driven ventilation, heating, and, most importantly, electric-motor-driven calliopes and rapid-fire guns hidden behind retractable camouflage plates.

Granted, the locals might not have been able to design and build her so quickly on their own, not for another few years, maybe even a decade or more. But according to the reports, they had no problems handling and maintaining her — at least during the shakeout cruises over the last few weeks. And her construction had triggered another industrial leap forward.

But it would take a while before the next of her kind came off the slipways. And for a reason more challenging to resolve than most — the lack of workers. Farmhands and others displaced by the rapid modernization of agriculture had filled many of the shipyards' needs and those of other nascent industries, but there were never enough people. And that meant inflationary pressures were making themselves felt, something which, if not corrected, could lead to discontent, even unrest, in a population experiencing a rate of change like no other in recorded history.

The coming year would prove delicate, especially with the planned expansion to Aksum, where most of the planet's non-Theban population lived — apart from the stone age nomads on Sylt. But DeCarde didn't plan on wasting efforts there, not before Thebes had the rest of Hatshepsut in hand under his guidance.

"Ah, Ambassador," a voice behind DeCarde cut short his contemplation of the planet's future. "Just in time. I was doing a last check of the tides table. We'll cast off momentarily. The merchantmen are already anchored in the harbor, waiting for us to lead them out into the open ocean. If you'd like to watch from the port-side wing, you'll get the best view of the castoff procedure."

"Thank you."

DeCarde stepped out into the sunshine, wishing he'd at least brought up his bush hat, but it was too late now. He felt the background vibration of the steam engine become more noticeable and louder and saw the gangway pulled aboard by a party of *Vigilance* sailors. Moments later, at a signal he neither heard nor saw, dockyard men by each of the mooring bollards released the Q ship's ropes, which vanished up hawseholes in seconds while the shallow, muddy water beneath the stern suddenly boiled up as the propeller shafts engaged.

Then slowly, majestically, *Vigilance* moved along the pier, her bow pointed toward the outer harbor, and her deep horn blared three times, startling DeCarde. Once free of the inner harbor, the Q ship picked up speed as she turned due west for the main channel leading out of the vast archipelago, whose islands were remnants of a continent submerged long ago when Hatshepsut's extensive icecaps retreated. By now, the planet had little more than small, circumscribed polar regions.

DeCarde, happy for the growing breeze but feeling the sun's glare, gratefully retreated into the bridge.

"As sweet an evolution as I've ever seen, Captain," he said, smiling at Fenrir.

"Aye, thank you. But we've been maneuvering in and out of harbors with Stirling engines for a long time, so it's old hat. We just have to remember our new steam engines put out a lot more power, and a little spin of these huge propellers can go a long way." Fenrir scratched his beard. "Mind you, I've been told of a hydrodynamic drive that does away with propellers and makes harbor maneuvers even easier."

"They exist, and you'll see them on Hatshepsut in due course, but they need what we call a fusion reactor to power them. The dynamo spun by your steam engine to provide electricity for the ship wouldn't even wake up a hydrodynamic drive, let alone get it to suck in water at one end and spit it out at the other. If you like, I can show you how it works."

"I'd like it once we're out in the open ocean and it's watch after watch with no course changes. This isn't the time for cyclones or other nasties. A clean three days to the Saqqaras once we clear the archipelago, and then we'll test her mettle." Fenrir gave DeCarde a calculating look. "You figure we'll wipe the filth off the face of the planet?"

"Probably not, but your ship will send a good number of them into the Infinite Void during our outbound trip, and on the way back, we can send Sergeant Virtanen and his Marines to hunt the rest."

"From your lips to the Almighty's ears, Ambassador. Mind you, compared to the ship I commanded the last time I took the Central Passage and left hundreds of corpses in my wake, *Vigilance* is a destroyer of all that dares bar her way."

DeCarde clapped the Theban on the shoulder. "This will be the last time the Saqqarans present a threat to Theban shipping. I can guarantee that. Once we're done, the Central Passage will be as safe as Harbor Avenue in downtown Thebes City."

Fenrir scoffed.

"I gather you haven't navigated Harbor Avenue after nightfall, Ambassador. If you do, ignore the offers, keep your hand on your wallet, and get the hell out of there as quick as you can."

"I'll keep that in mind. And now, if you'll permit me, I'd like to see the ship's armament and the fighting positions for the Marines. Sergeant Virtanen will be my guide."

"Enjoy the tour, sir. By the way, your sergeant is a rather impressive man. The Theban Marines attached to his troop can't say enough of him."

DeCarde smiled.

"Glad to hear it. When I was a Marine, I had the privilege of being Alvar Virtanen's commanding officer back in the day. Since then, he's only become a more fearsome fighter and leader of men."

"You were a Marine, then? Figures. Every second Lyonesser I meet served in your Defense Force, including the Brethren, like Chief Administrator Horam."

"Service is a way of seeing other worlds, growing as an individual, and experiencing new things before settling into a civilian career." DeCarde's lips twitched. "Of course, some of us take longer to settle than others, but a fair percentage of our young people sign up for a three to five-year hitch after school. It teaches them discipline, hones their sense of initiative, and develops intestinal fortitude."

Fenrir let out a chuckle.

"Intestinal fortitude. I like that. One day our youngsters might do so as well, but at the moment, everyone who can work is needed in the new industries."

"Indeed. Well, in a few years. With that, I'll join Virtanen below decks."

DeCarde sketched a salute and vanished into the stairwell, leaving a pensive Fenrir to stare at where he stood. Then, the mariner shook himself and picked up his binoculars. Time to check on the three merchant steamers who'd sail under the Q ship's protection. They'd better be raising anchors by now.

—27—

When DeCarde entered the troop HQ section compartment, he found Virtanen waiting for him.

"My people are settled in and are raring to resume action station drills. Something about fighting a sea-going, steam-powered Q ship is just nuts to my Marines. And the Thebans? They can't get enough of anything, period. Ready, sir?"

"Take me on the grand tour."

They started with the starboard midship battery, whose camouflage plate was in the closed position, hiding its contents. It boasted a twelve-millimeter, six-barrel calliope — DeCarde remembered reading the weapons were, for an unknown reason, called Gatling guns long ago — and a rapid-fire one-hundred and five-millimeter cannon. Between them, they could sink anything that floated on Hatshepsut and even breach stone walls should any defended town on Aksum prove hostile.

Virtanen slapped the calliope.

"When this baby goes off, it's as if the Almighty is standing by your ears, tearing the Infinite Void apart. Four thousand rounds a minute if we want to empty the ship's ammo lockers. We have ball and high explosive, both with one in five tracers. Granted, it's not plasma, but will make mincemeat of the Saqqarans or anyone else stupid enough to try us on. Electrically powered, though, so if we lose the generators, that rate of fire becomes zero rounds a minute. Both guns are controlled from over there." He pointed at a thick window behind them. "One crew per. Ammo is gravity fed from above via those tubes and spent casings are funneled below for recycling. Waste not, want not."

Virtanen showed DeCarde the inside of the control room, then said, "The port-side battery is a mirror image of this one."

"In that case, no need to visit it. How about up in the bow?"

"Follow me, sir."

They headed forward and climbed up the starboard stairs to emerge in another enclosed compartment, this one with a single calliope sitting silently at its heart.

"We're in the forecastle right now, sir, which exists solely for that fire-breathing machine. It can shoot forward, across a sixty-degree arc, and on each beam. Mind you, it'll stop if the gunners switch from front to side, so it doesn't shoot off the corner pillars. The control room is on your left, same setup as the starboard battery, minus a canon controller. Ammo is gravity fed from above, spend casings collected from below. Aft looks the same except it occupies the rear of the superstructure's second level."

"What's next?"

"The firing positions for embarked troopers." Virtanen headed for a door at the rear of the gun compartment and spun its locking wheel. When the door swung open, bright sunlight hit the deck, relieving the gloom.

As they walked out, the sergeant pointed at stairs leading to the forecastle's second level.

"Three shielded firing positions on each side, capable of taking our largest portable weapons and the calliope's ammo locker in the middle. Care to go up?"

"Not at the moment."

"The rest of the shielded firing positions are in the aft superstructure. Two sections can cover three hundred and sixty degrees." They stepped off along a deck that was pitching as *Vigilance* cut across waves coming through the passage between Thebes' main island and its eastern neighbor. DeCarde could see three columns of smoke in a tight column behind them — the merchantmen who'd traded masts for steam engines. They'd make the crossing to Mazaber in record time, now that the Central Passage could be risked because of their iron-hulled escort.

But none of it was possible without Lyonesse scrapping the principles established by President Jonas Morane and fueling Theban progress up the technological ladder at a high rate. Case in point, the four steamers now headed for Aksum couldn't even make it across the ocean without the dry fuel pellets to fire up their boilers.

And those came from a prefabricated plant whose modules were built on Lyonesse and assembled on Hatshepsut by the technicians who brought it across the stars aboard a naval transport. There wasn't enough wood, coal, or petroleum in the Theban Archipelago for an entire steam-powered fleet, let alone combustible natural gasses.

"What are your fire control protocols?" DeCarde asked as they neared the outside starboard ladder leading up to the bridge wing.

"My troop sergeant and I are on the bridge with the captain during operations, while two troopers monitor battlefield sensors from the bridge wings. The sensor situation isn't ideal, but we didn't have time to mount a set permanently and wire it to the generators. That'll be for the next cruise. I control the large guns while Gus Hightower oversees the small arms. We do everything via the troop radio network. Considering the sort of opposition we might face, it'll work just fine. If someone comes up with an iron-hulled, armed pirate ship, we might need to rethink the command-and-control setup."

DeCarde noticed Virtanen's tone and choice of words made it clear he wasn't seeking his former CO's approval or even counsel, another sign of his growth as a professional and his evident self-confidence.

"Have you practiced with the ship running at sea?"

Virtanen nodded. "During the final shakeout cruise. Captain Fenrir runs a tight ship. There's usually only him, the officer of the watch, a petty officer at the helm, and a signaler, meaning there's plenty of room for Gus and me. I'd be even happier in a fire director's nest up top, but that could give the game away. Maybe one of *Vigilance*'s descendants might have a proper remote fire control system run from a combat information center below deck."

"I doubt there will be many more Q ships, let alone dedicated ocean-going warships."

It only took Virtanen a few heartbeats to catch on.

"Because Hatshepsut won't be disunited long enough to need them, right?"

"Yep. And once this place has a single government, the only war and Q ships in this system will be up there." DeCarde pointed at the sky. "Ours, and ours alone."

***

"There are the islands of perdition known as the Saqqaras, Ambassador." Fenrir pointed at dark humps slowly creeping over the western horizon, their tops kissed by the rising sun when DeCarde entered the bridge after breakfast a few days later. "We'll be passing *Cimarron*'s wreck at the passage's entrance by midafternoon, which means anchoring nearby for the night. I must confess, I'm still not quite used to the speed we can travel nowadays."

DeCarde gave him a questioning glance. "Why anchor? Is the navigation that dangerous?"

Fenrir squinted at the distant island and shook his head.

"No. It'll be a clear night, and that's the only thing we need, especially since we don't depend on wind or an underpowered Stirling engine. The Saqqarans — they're the risk. We might not see them coming until it's too late."

"Sergeant Virtanen and his Marines will pick them up the moment they launch boats, no matter how dark it is."

Fenrir turned toward DeCarde and gave him a skeptical look.

"They have a Void Sister's instincts?"

"They have night vision visors attached to their helmets and sensors that can pick up human life signs from a distance."

The mariner shook his head. "This new-fangled stuff is hard to remember. Whatever next?"

"May I offer a suggestion, Captain?"

Fenrir made a go-ahead gesture with his hand. "Please."

"Let the merchantmen anchor before entering the passage, near this *Cimarron* you mentioned, and we keep going so we can attract the Saqqarans. They attack, we wipe them out, and the cargo ships then follow us through."

"What if the Saqqarans don't attack us?"

"Then, when we reach the other end, we turn and come back for a second run. If they don't try that time either, the cargoes go through, and we assume they're smart enough to avoid *Vigilance,* or this nasty narcotic I've heard mentioned has done the job for us."

Fenrir scratched his beard, then nodded.

"Fair enough, Ambassador. We'll do it that way. Less time wasted hanging about."

"Now, does this wreck marking the entrance to the passage have a story, or did it come about through bad navigation?"

"Oh, aye, there's a story alright, and it's nothing to do with pirates. It happened over twenty years ago when I was a junior master's mate in *Morningstar*, schooner. We were outbound to Mazaber and using the Central Passage. It was still safe then. *Cimarron* had been overdue in Thebes on her return from Mazaber when we left, and therefore her owner asked us to keep a lookout. We saw no evidence of her in the Passage or along the Aksum shore, nor was she in port in Mazaber. If she'd crossed our wake, we would have seen her. The navigable channel along Aksum isn't that wide. Three weeks later, when we came back through the Passage, we found her wreck where she is now, beached, masts collapsed, spars and ropes in complete disarray."

"Driven ashore by a storm, perhaps?"

"No. There were none during the entire six-week period. As far as anyone can tell, she disappeared after leaving Mazaber and reappeared at the Passage's eastern end after we'd gone through westbound. I took a landing party and found her holds full, personal possessions stowed, hammocks rolled up, her log and ship's books in the captain's desk, the purser's money still where it should be. The last entry in the log stated she'd spent the night at anchor on the western end of the Passage, waiting for daylight — before we reached the Saqqaras on our way to Mazaber. Back then, even without pirates, many captains preferred doing the Passage during daylight hours.

"We offloaded everything and brought it home for the owner, but no one ever heard from the crew again, and no one knows what happened. Most of us consider *Cimarron* cursed and won't approach her. Too many unanswered questions. If the Saqqarans drove her aground, why didn't they plunder her? If they attacked, where are the remains of the crew? And why, when we crossed the Passage westward, did we not see her wreck, nor come across her sitting at anchor on the far side?"

"A fascinating mystery, Captain."

"Oh, this world hides more mysteries than you would guess. I've always said we've been out of sync with the rest of the universe since the Great Scouring."

"Some would say of humanity itself is out of sync after ninety percent of it died thanks to the last empress' madness."

Fenrir let out a soft grunt. "No doubt. All those souls wandering the Infinite Void, looking for mischief or vengeance. At least that's what the Brethren might say. I haven't asked."

"I can do it when we're back. Abbess Rianne and I get along with each other, even though I'm not much of a believer."

"She gets along with everyone. Nice that the Order let her stay in charge after that damned Hegemony abducted the rest of the Lyonesse Brethren save for her and Horam. Both were aboard my ship at the time."

"I know. I've heard the story in great detail."

“No doubt. And now, if you’ll excuse me, I must confer with the other captains about our proposed plan. They may wish to anchor further out, away from *Cimarron*. It doesn’t get too deep for our anchor chains until about two kilometers offshore from the easternmost island.”

—28—

"I'm surprised there's that much left of the schooner," DeCarde said, peering at *Cimarron* through Fenrir's binoculars. "Over twenty years?"

"Aye, and that's another mystery we can't explain. Mind you, she's sheltered from the waves there, and this part of the islands hasn't seen a typhoon in longer than I can remember, but she's still made of wood, and the salt water isn't kind."

"Could I take a boat and a few Marines to check her out?" DeCarde lowered the binoculars and looked straight at Fenrir.

"With due respect, no, sir." Fenrir didn't even hesitate. "It's considered bad luck among us. More than a few of my crew and those in the merchantmen will think you might bring *Cimarron*'s ill fate back aboard with you. I can't afford that sort of thing, and I will invoke my rights as senior captain and sole master after the Almighty, if necessary."

DeCarde, who heard the vehemence in his words, if not still mild tone, raised both hands in surrender. He could always press a Navy dropship into service and mount his own expedition later.

"Fair enough, Captain. Your ship, your rules."

"Thank you for understanding."

DeCarde raised the binoculars to his eyes again and studied the weathered hull lying on its side on a pebble beach. But this time, something stirred in his subconscious, as if a mysterious wreck that could survive the passage of time, tides, and seasons. disquieted him. The DeCardes had always possessed what was often called a touch of the second sight, sensitivity to people and the environment that made them not only superb military officers but known for having a gut instinct without peer.

Command Sergeant Virtanen and Sergeant First Class Hightower's arrival snapped DeCarde out of his reverie. Both wore battledress, armor, tactical harnesses, and helmets and were ready to set up their fire control center for *Vigilance*'s sail through the Central Passage.

"My troopers are in position, sir," Virtanen said, eyes on Fenrir. "You can raise the camouflage plates whenever you wish."

"Good. Let's see if the savages take the bait."

The sun was halfway to the western horizon when *Vigilance* left the wreck behind and entered the winding Central Passage proper while the cargo vessels anchored offshore. As he watched their progress, DeCarde wondered whether the Saqqarans, confronted with an iron beast bereft of masts, would even try piracy.

It had been two years of slim to nonexistent pickings while Theban ships went north, around the top of the island chain. A much longer route to Aksum, but one the Saqqaran boats couldn't handle. It wasn't so much as a passage but open ocean with no land between the northernmost island and the polar ice cap, where waves and wind ruled without mercy.

The Q ship's forward motion slowed to a crawl as she nosed into a channel where verdant tropical vegetation choked the shores. They were, in military parlance, dragging their skirts to tempt an unwary foe instead of plowing through at a speed oar-propelled boats couldn't match. Besides, the sun would vanish shortly after eighteen hundred hours local time with the suddenness typical in the tropics, more or less when *Vigilance* was halfway through the Passage, where it was at its narrowest.

It appeared eerily peaceful to DeCarde — warm, tropical air, laden with scents both fair and not so pleasant, avian creatures wheeling and cawing overhead, and the river framed by impossibly green trees and undergrowth. A paradise compared to many worlds Lyonesse now claimed as its own, such as dry, ancient Arietis, where life only thrived in abundance at the bottom of a rift valley.

Vigilance chugged ahead, her propellers spinning at reduced speed but still roiling up the muddy waters of the Passage. The steward came up with a jug of coffee, and DeCarde helped himself once everyone else had taken their share. He was slowly becoming accustomed to the caffeine-rich brew, a staple on Hatshepsut where the plant took root with enthusiasm long ago. Despite many attempts, it never grew on Lyonesse, and over two centuries, coffee first became myth, then legend after the last beans were ground and brewed. Tea, which grew in abundance, became the preferred drink while it slowly vanished on Hatshepsut.

But sipping the bitter black liquid along with the bridge crew and Virtanen's Marines while the sun's last rays gave the jagged peaks a greenish glow felt oddly appropriate to DeCarde. Yet there was still no sign of Saqqarans bent on resuming the piracy that drove Theban ships to take the longer northern route.

"Last light," Virtanen commented as the sun's rays died away, leaving the Central Passage a darkened slick oozing between impenetrable walls. "If they're going to try, now's the time."

Vigilance's interior and position lights — red, green, and white — were off, as they would aboard any ship crossing pirate-infested waters. She was nothing more than a shadowy mass slicing through the water to the muffled sounds of her steam engine and propellers.

The bridge instruments emitted a soft glow, visible to the duty watch, but no one else. To DeCarde's eyes, it was as if a previously unknown primeval darkness had fallen over the planet. He'd spent most of his life within sight of light, natural or artificial, faint as it may be. And here he was aboard the most heavily armed surface vessel on Hatshepsut, gliding through the night, looking for battle. He'd traveled through more absolute darkness aboard a starship, with nothing beyond its hull but the emptiness of space. Still, he felt hemmed in by a mass of life invisible to the naked eye, a sensation that tickled his subconscious and made him preternaturally alert to any disturbance.

"Contact." The whispered voice of the starboard sensor operator came over the radio net, cutting through DeCarde's musings. "Over a hundred human life signs ahead of us on the northern shore; distance approximately fifteen hundred meters, around the next bend."

"Same place as last time," Fenrir muttered. "We saw them off with what we had back then, but it was a close-run thing. If Friar Horam hadn't been aboard? No telling how many would have died."

"Correction. Over two hundred life signs," the operator said.

"Best we open up the batteries, then." Fenrir gestured at the officer of the watch. "Give the word to unmask."

A minute passed, then several thumps coursed through the hull, followed by soft squeals as crew members unlatched and hoisted the camouflage panels out of the way to reveal *Vigilance*'s awesome firepower.

"The life signs are leaving shore and spreading across the Passage."

Fenrir glanced at DeCarde.

"Same damned technique as before, too. They're in for a shock once they realize how high my freeboard is compared to a trading schooner or barquentine."

"Haven't they been watching us since we came into sight of the islands?"

"Sure. If they've assembled, we've been under observation for hours, but they've never seen a ship like *Vigilance* before and can't appreciate her size."

A flicker of light appeared around the bend, then another and another, until the entire passage was on fire.

"Torches. I was wondering how they'd manage an attack in the dark."

"Aye. By now, a sailing ship, even with her Stirling engine running, can no longer turn around and avoid them."

The Q ship, her bow now outlined by the dancing red glow coming over the tongue of land at the heart of the bend, kept a steady pace while the Marines, Lyonesse, and Theban checked their weapons one last time.

The troop radio came to life again with Virtanen's voice.

"This is Niner. Bow calliope will engage at my command. Everyone else, hold your fire until I give the word."

"Bow calliope acknowledged. We are racked and ready."

An eerie chant arose from the waiting pirates, something birthed by the furthest depths of Hades. As *Vigilance* came around the bend, a hair-raising tableau unfolded — boats tied together side-by-side blocking the Passage, each adorned with long poles from which hung human heads.

The boats carried from eight to ten men, one of whom held a lit torch and the remainder weapons of every kind. They wore bits of leather, fur, and castoffs obtained by scavenging wrecks or attacking ships that came too close, mostly Aksumite fishing vessels, prospectors, and explorers, since the Thebans had given the Central Saqqaras a wide berth in recent times.

To a man, they had long, braided hair and beards and wore what could only be bones and bits of mummified human flesh — ears, noses, fingers, genitalia. Bloodlust, hatred, and something so savage contorted their faces, that DeCarde felt a shiver run up his spine. These were no longer human beings by any measure he could find. At least not the sort with whom one could reason.

"They're looking worse than ever," Fenrir said. "Drugs must be — what the hell?"

"Looks like someone sold them weapons."

Hundreds of primitive chemically propelled slug throwers appeared, their large-bore barrels aimed at *Vigilance*.

"Aye, and if I find that someone, he'll hang. Feel free to shoot first, Sergeant Virtanen, before they do so."

"Yes, sir. Bow calliope, you will strafe the line of boats from port to starboard in one continuous burst. Niner-Alpha, individual Marines to pick off survivors."

"Niner-Alpha, ack," Sergeant Hightower replied.

"Bow calliope, ack.

"FIRE."

A sound akin to rending cloth drowned out the chanting Saqqarans as tracers reached for the boats. Many tracers. DeCarde had to remind himself that for each round he saw, there were another four he didn't. Against wooden watercraft, the high explosive rounds would have been wasted, but even so, the heavy twelve-millimeter slugs were ravaging hulls and men alike.

How many survived the first burst, DeCarde couldn't say, but the barrier broke apart as boats sank and their occupants spilled into the water, chanting replaced by howls of rage and pain. The torches fell one by one and died away while the Marines in the forecastle and atop the main superstructure picked off anything that moved with three-round bursts.

Here and there, torches had fallen into boats, creating little fireships that might have threatened a wooden schooner, but before DeCarde could remark on it, squad automatic weapons targeted and sank them by ripping their remains to shreds.

It was over in a matter of moments, leaving nothing but dead bodies and debris.

"No more life signs on the water," the starboard sensor operator reported. "Still forty or so along the shore."

"Transmit range and direction to the starboard battery."

"Ack."

"Starboard battery, once you're dialed in, you may open fire with both weapons, one calliope strafe, one five-round salvo from the canon. Wipe 'em out."

"Starboard battery acknowledges."

A few seconds passed, then another line of tracers ripped through the night, accompanied by the thumps of the canon, turning a fifty-meter stretch of shoreline into an inferno. Trees transformed into flying splinters and clods of earth shot up into the night sky.

"What say the sensors?" Virtanen asked.

"A few life signs left."

"Canon, one more five-round salvo."

"Ack."

When the rain of debris tapered off, the sensor operator came on again and said, "Target destroyed."

"That takes care of the immediate threat," Fenrir said in a voice tinged with awe. "Two hundred plus fighting-age males gone will cripple the tribes living along the Passage, but there are still thousands and thousands of them on the islands north and south of here."

"So long as they heed the lesson and stay away from piracy, they can live however they want."

"But they won't, Ambassador." Fenrir scratched his beard again. "I figure it'll either take them dying off from the drugs they're being fed by Aksumites, or the Marines, yours and ours, hunting down every last one. Until then, convoys using the Central Passage will need us or ships like *Vigilance* as an escort or carry their own guns and Marines. Otherwise, it'll be the Northern and Southern Passages. But the seas there won't be so difficult in steamships, nor take as much time as sailing, especially against the prevailing winds."

"What now, sir?" Virtanen asked.

"I figure we anchor here for the night and see if any more of the buggers show up. At dawn, the merchantmen can come up the channel and join us."

"Then we'll stay unmasked, and I'll leave a one in two watch at every fire position and the sensors. We might as well put spotlights on the water all around us for good measure."

Fenrir nodded. "Let's do it. Officer of the watch, stand down from action stations and prepare to set anchor a hundred meters further west, where the channel is straight. Once that's done, go to anchor watch."

"Aye, aye, sir."

"The prevailing current is west to east," Fenrir explained for DeCarde's benefit. "Once we get away from this floating charnel house, the remains of the dead won't surround us."

DeCarde was tempted to ask about the souls of those who died so violently lingering around this place instead of merging with the Infinite Void. But a moment of reflection told him it might be ill-advised. Besides, who knew whether they even had souls? He'd certainly sensed nothing human in them.

After an uneventful night, the three merchant steamers, sailing one behind the other, finally came into view late the next morning. Fenrir ordered the anchor up and the camouflage plates down, and by dusk, they emerged from the Passage into the shallow, reef-filled Aksum Sea. Already they could make out the continent's coastline in the distance, and Fenrir ordered the convoy to anchor well beyond the range of Saqqaran boats. Nevertheless, each ship kept an enhanced night watch, with *Vigilance*'s Marines and their sensors covering them.

— 29 —

At dawn the following day, the cargo ships raised anchor to complete the rest of the journey by themselves. *Vigilance* would spend the day anchored near the sunk imperial corvette offshore from where New Aden once stood before heading for Mazaber as well.

Within a few hours, the Q ship sat near a broken stretch of land that bled into the shallow waters, shattered by orbital strikes. They'd left nothing behind but ruins blending so well into the surrounding landscape that the city might as well never have existed.

DeCarde, leaning against the railing on the port-side bridge wing, studied the shore, wondering why he experienced such a deep sense of unease. Were the souls of those murdered by the Mad Empress' Retribution Fleet still lingering here? Or was he sensing a distant echo of that horrific day when Hatshepsut, presumed to be in revolt against the empire, became a mass grave?

A sudden urge to walk the land where New Aden once stood seized him.

"Captain, could I beg you for a boat? I'd like to go ashore?"

Fenrir, sitting in the captain's chair, turned a stern look on DeCarde.

"This is a cursed place, Ambassador."

"Nonetheless, I would do so. Lyonesse Marines can handle the boat if your crew isn't inclined to confront the ghosts of the past."

"Oh, my crew will take you ashore, Ambassador. I'm more concerned with what will happen to you after they do so."

"I'll bring a few Marines with me, Captain. Something demands I pay my respects to the souls who perished here while Sergeant Virtanen's divers examine the imperial starship sunk beneath us."

Fenrir gave DeCarde a fatalistic shrug.

"Very well. I'll have a boat readied."

The moment DeCarde's foot touched the raw, blasted stone beach, a faint but unmistakable jolt ran through his body. New Aden had been the second-largest city on Hatshepsut, with over a million people calling it home. And they died in a fraction of a second. Yet an echo of that mass murder still lingered in the soil. No wonder the Hatshepsut natives thought it cursed and refused to go ashore.

A pair of Lyonesse Marines climbed out of the boat with him while the other two remained aboard, and DeCarde wondered whether they sensed anything — sorrow, eeriness, a faint jab at the subconscious — or if he was alone in that respect. He'd encountered no one outside the Order of the Void who had the family sensitivity, but a few places still left a mark on even the least sensitive people, provided they had a soul. Those who didn't wouldn't feel a thing, not by walking over this ground, nor while murdering innocents in job lots like the Mad Empress' admirals.

He and his escort walked up a slope covered in struggling bushes, sea grass, and other hardy native species where New Aden's harbor once cut a half-moon into the jagged coast. The rain of destruction from above had obliterated it just as it turned the city into a ravaged landscape where little grew atop the ruins even over two hundred years later. It was indeed a place forgotten by the Almighty.

DeCarde stood at the top of the slope and let his eyes roam, looking for anything recognizable, a trace that this had once been a major imperial city. But in vain. Unwilling to spend hours walking around under the increasingly harsh sun for reasons he couldn't even define, DeCarde turned around and headed back toward the boat.

Once Lyonesse controlled Hatshepsut, maybe he or his successor could place a monument to the dead here, but New Aden would never be rebuilt. It was now hallowed ground.

As the boat pushed away from shore, DeCarde glanced at its twin, designated as dive tender, now moored several hundred meters ahead of where *Vigilance* sat at anchor.

"Let's see what's happening over there, Corporal."

The Marine at the controls nodded once. "Yes, sir."

Too young to have been in the Third of the Twenty-First in DeCarde's day, he nonetheless must have heard stories because he behaved as if the latter was a bona fide serving colonel in the Lyonesse Marines rather than a civilian who was more bureaucrat than diplomat.

They tied to the diving tender where a pair of Marines monitoring field sensors sat, attention focused on the heads-up displays inside their helmet visors.

"How's it going?" DeCarde asked.

"They're checking the underside of the wreck right now, sir. From what we can tell, she's the River class imperial corvette *Sanne*." The Marine rattled off a hull number. "She's still pressurized, though we can't pick up any residual energy traces. No clear sign of damage, so there's no knowing how she ended up in the water unscathed this close to the spaceport."

DeCarde stared at the massive shape beneath the boats for a few moments.

"Tell the divers they're not to try any of the airlocks, just in case. That's a war grave down there, and we can't disturb it."

"Yes, Colonel."

Word of his former Marine status had definitely made the rounds, and the troopers likely saw him as one of their own, albeit a senior officer. DeCarde didn't correct the lance corporal.

"Thank you."

DeCarde watched as silver fishes shaped like men flitted around the wreck beneath them, shimmering in the refracted rays of the sun, until they finally surfaced. The first to hook his arms over the dive tender's gunwales removed his rebreather mask and grinned.

"Heck of a nice dive, sir. You should try. I figure it wouldn't be too hard raising *Sanne* to the surface by mechanical means. She strikes me as being close to neutrally buoyant. Once her upper hull is exposed to fresh air, tractor beams from a few synchronized lifters can haul her out and put her onshore."

"And then what?"

"Sir?"

"Never mind me, Sergeant. I visited where New Aden used to be and got a nose full of grim history. How about we leave *Sanne* where she is, declare her a war grave, and put a memorial marker on shore?"

Virtanen hauled himself over the gunwales. "Sounds like a good plan, sir. Let's let whoever died inside her rest in peace."

***

Vigilance pulled into Mazaber harbor only a few hours after the three cargo ships dropped anchor offshore, thanks to her powerful steam engine and twin propellers. In DeCarde's eyes, the town — for it didn't merit the title city — was just as decrepit, noxious, and filled with idlers as reports said.

"Captain."

"Ambassador?" Fenrir turned away from overseeing his officer of the watch nose the Q ship along the harbor front to a mooring that let her cover the merchantmen.

"I understand the individual running this place has his own palace. Can we see it from here?"

"You mean whoever sits at the head of the table? None of them own the place. They just rent it with tax money until a stronger pretender shows up." Fenrir pointed at a clump of gray stone buildings on a rise that barely poked above Mazaber's rooftops a kilometer inland. "If that's who you want, he lives over there — the place with the multiple red roofs and a curtain wall to keep out unwanted peasants looking for their share of the take."

"Then please anchor us so they can clearly see one of our batteries from the chieftain's palace once it's unmasked."

"You plan on intimidating the current incumbent?"

DeCarde shook his head.

"No. I'll merely point out the advantages of submitting to Theban rule, first among which would be a continuance of the current state of affairs in Mazaber under a new planetary administration, one enforced at the point of modern automatic weapons."

Fenrir gave DeCarde a strange look.

"Isn't that a little undiplomatic?"

"Think of it as a bit of gunboat diplomacy, an ancient art enjoying something of a revival. I figured while I'm here, I should introduce myself and start the process of establishing a Theban foothold on Aksum."

The mariner appeared skeptical but merely grunted.

"I suppose we must start somewhere if we want to regain the stars."

DeCarde gave Fenrir an amused grin. "That's the spirit, Captain."

"Colonel?" Sergeant Virtanen appeared in the bridge doorway. "We just received a message from Starbase Hatshepsut over the Lyonesse network. A starship, tentatively identified as a cruiser, with Wyvern Hegemony markings, came out of Wormhole Two a short while ago. She went FTL on an inward-bound course."

PART III – REVENANTS

—30—

Hatshepsut

"The course this cruiser took going FTL will bring it to Hatshepsut's hyperlimit, Mister Ambassador, unless it drops out of hyperspace between Hatshepsut and the wormhole, something that wouldn't make much sense. Why they're heading here, we can't tell. Surely they must have figured we'd station ships in this system after their incursion and that a single cruiser wouldn't make much of an impression." Captain Lucas Morane gave DeCarde a skeptical look.

The latter was in the troop HQ compartment, where Command Sergeant Virtanen had set up the surface to orbit communications terminal.

"Then they want something other than to fight us for possession of Hatshepsut. Last time, the Hegemony sent an entire battle group on a reconnaissance. They'd dispatch at least that number if they harbored aggressive intentions."

Morane nodded. "Sure, but a ship of that size can still wreak havoc on my squadron."

"If it's here on a one-way mission, which I doubt. They know that while we're at the end of our supply lines, they've outstripped theirs by a few hundred light-years. Anything more than superficial damage could maroon them." DeCarde frowned in thought. "No. Something tells me they're on the same mission as *Seeker* was when she entered the Torrinos system — to see what we're doing. I suggest that when this cruiser drops out of FTL, you take the usual precautions but without powering up targeting sensors, then hail its captain. After all, they tried hailing *Seeker* rather than target her when she appeared on their sensors in Torrinos."

"Fortunately, there's enough of a buffer between the hyperlimit and Hatshepsut's high orbit to give us plenty of reaction time. Okay. I'll stay weapons tight and keep my ships at a distance unless the intruder goes hot, and we'll let events unfold. If you like, I can send a shuttle to fetch you. We have at least eight hours."

DeCarde shook his head. "Thank you, but not right now. I'll be entertaining the current strongman running Mazaber later today and convince him he's better off continuing to govern the city under our, or rather Theban rule rather than find himself ousted by superior firepower."

Morane chuckled. "Gunboat diplomacy in action. Does our government approve of such measures?"

A wink. "I'm an ambassador plenipotentiary, Lucas. As far as this planet is concerned, I am the Republic of Lyonesse government. However, dealing with matters beyond

Hatshepsut's atmosphere is your remit. Let me know how it pans out the moment you can."

"Sure thing."

"DeCarde, out."

Once the ambassador's image faded away, Morane ensured the initial report was off to Lyonesse via the long chain of subspace relays. By the time it reached Navy HQ, the intruder would have dropped out of FTL at the hyperlimit, and they'd know why it came.

***

"Ops to the captain."

A surge of adrenaline coursed through Lucas Morane's nervous system as he looked up from the weekly fuel expenditures report. It could only be the intruder. The timing was spot on.

"Morane here."

"Contact at the hyperlimit. One ship, cruiser size, same markings as the contact at the wormhole terminus, not hiding its emissions. Even has running lights on to make sure we can't miss it."

"Open a channel on the old imperial emergency band. If we're still monitoring it, so are they. I'm on my way."

The walk from his office to the Hatshepsut Station's operations center was a brief one — three paces across Deck Five's central corridor. As soon as he entered, the officer of the watch stood, relinquishing the throne-like command chair, and stepped aside.

"We're broadcasting, sir. Ships and station are on standby to raise shields and power weapons. The other orbitals are ready for an emergency shutdown."

"He's decelerating and beginning a turn to starboard, away from us," the sensor petty officer reported. "Shields are down, weapons are cold, and we're not picking up targeting sensor pings."

"What the heck is he playing at?" The officer of the watch asked in a low tone.

"Incoming signal from the Wyvern Hegemony cruiser *Aethon*. Audio and video."

Morane glanced at the signals petty officer. "Put it on the primary display."

Moments later, he found himself face-to-face with a dark-haired man whose hooded brown eyes set in a craggy face studied him with polite interest. He wore a uniform like Morane's, including identical gold captain's rank insignia at the collar.

"My name is Evan Kang, Captain. I command the Guards Navy ship *Aethon,* and I'm here on a peaceful mission."

"Jonas Morane. I'm the commanding officer of the Republic of Lyonesse Navy's Hatshepsut squadron. Why are you here?"

"My government sent me to return the Lyonesse citizens abducted by Task Force Kruzenshtern over two years ago. All eight are in good health and eagerly anticipating their repatriation. And since I won't insult your intelligence, sir, we're also charged with finding out what you've been doing here in the meantime. As you may have noticed, my shields are down, and my weapons are unpowered. We've begun our turn back to the hyperlimit and will head home as quickly as possible."

"We can see that. Our shields and weapons are unpowered as well."

Kang nodded. "Indeed, sir. Since I cannot place my ship at risk so far from our space, we will launch a civilian pattern shuttle with the eight Brethren aboard. The craft has more than enough autonomy to reach Hatshepsut and land. Its control node is unlocked and will accept your navigation commands. Please conduct a thorough scan before taking it aboard one of your ships or landing it on Hatshepsut."

Morane frowned at Kang, wondering whether he was truthful or setting a trap. But the Wyvern Hegemony officer's face was as open and honest as any he'd ever seen.

"Can I speak with one of the Brethren?"

"Certainly. We expected your request. They've been listening in on our conversation from the shuttle. Please go ahead, Sister Hermina."

Kang's face vanished, replaced by a thin, gray-haired woman with sharp features, deep-set eyes, and the ageless features of a Void Sister.

"I am Hermina, formerly prioress of the Thebes Mission, Captain. The eight of us are, as Captain Kang said, healthy and eager for home. We spent the last two years living among the Hegemony's offshoot of the Order of the Void. They treated us as any Wyvern Brethren, save for not being allowed to leave."

Morane saw the officer of the watch, who stood beyond the video pickup range, give him thumbs up, then point at a picture of Hermina on a side display, confirming it was indeed her as far as the intelligence AI could tell.

"Welcome back, Sister." Morane inclined his head. "Captain Kang, if you'll launch the shuttle on a course toward Hatshepsut, I'll send one of my corvettes to intercept it after you go FTL. Does that suit you?"

"Perfectly, sir. Now that we've arranged to repatriate your citizens, I'm charged by my government to offer yours an apology for their abduction. It was not planned but a spur-of-the-moment action by the officer in charge of the expedition, based on our astonishment at finding an outpost of another star-faring human society. For over two centuries, the Wyvern Hegemony believed itself the sole survivor of the Mad Empress' genocide. Our government realizes that doesn't excuse what was done and recognizes your republic's sovereignty over Hatshepsut and any other star system you may have reclaimed. It also hopes you'll recognize the Hegemony's sovereignty over the star systems we're reclaiming peacefully. If your government wishes to open diplomatic relations at some juncture, you need only send a ship to Torrinos again and have it announce your intentions."

As Morane processed Kang's words, he could only think how annoyed DeCarde would be that he wasn't here to speak with the man. But there was no point crying over a missed diplomatic opportunity. DeCarde could review the recording as often as he wished and make his own recommendations to his superiors back home.

"Noted, Captain. I will send a full copy of our conversation to my superiors on Lyonesse."

"And I mine on Wyvern. If I may launch the shuttle now?"

"Please go ahead."

"Thank you for your forbearance, Captain."

"Speaking beats shooting at each other. I hope you have a pleasant voyage home, Captain."

"Thank you, sir. Kang, out."

The moment his image faded, Morane stood and turned to the officer of the watch.

"Send *Bassus* to pick up the shuttle and raise Ambassador DeCarde on a private channel. I'll be in my office."

"Aye, aye, sir."

"Also. send a copy of my conversation with Kang to the captains and Colonel Salmin."

The sensor petty officer raised his hand.

"They launched on a course for Hatshepsut, sir. It's broadcasting a beacon on the old imperial emergency channel. I can detect several life signs aboard. No abnormal energy readings."

"Make sure *Bassus* takes extensive scans before hauling it aboard."

***

Once DeCarde had digested the recording, he let out a soft groan of dismay.

"What a missed opportunity for a diplomat such as myself. But, for what it's worth, you did splendidly, Lucas. I'm eager to debrief the returning Brethren and learn more about this Wyvern Hegemony and its self-proclaimed peaceful coexistence goals."

Morane cocked an amused eyebrow at him.

"You sounded just a little sarcastic there, Ambassador. Could it be you don't believe the Hegemony wishes for a harmonious relationship with Lyonesse? That their offer to open diplomatic channels is crap?"

"I likely mentioned this before, but at its core, diplomacy is the art of saying nice doggie until you can find a rock."

A bark of laughter escaped Morane's throat.

"Cynic."

"Oh, I didn't coin the aphorism. It was ancient even before our long gone thousand-year empire came into being."

"So, you think the Hegemony wants to make nice while they build up their strength, and once they surpass us, we'll be at the receiving end of interstellar gunboat diplomacy?"

DeCarde nodded.

"That is the most likely outcome."

"And what makes you so certain?"

"We've been doing it ourselves for a long time, Lucas. And if we do it, they'll do it because we share the same heritage. I have no doubt the Hegemony understands nations don't have friends or allies. They have interests, and those change." DeCarde raised a hand. "Oh, I'll recommend we open diplomatic relationships and then use our embassy to gather intelligence about them, just as they'll use theirs in the same way. The only thing worse than having a competitor's representatives at the heart of our state is not having our own people at the heart of his."

Morane shook his head in mock despair.

"You used to be an honest Marine. What the hell happened that turned you into a flinty proconsul?"

"The realization that if I stayed in the Corps and made general, my life would become one of insufferable boredom behind a desk in Lannion." DeCarde gave Morane a knowing look. "Think about that, seeing how your next assignment will come with a star and a desk at Navy HQ."

"I'm glad you think I still might be promoted, which is doubtful, but yeah, that desk at HQ isn't a great incentive. Anyway, what should we do with the returned Brethren, considering the former leaders of the Hatshepsut Mission — Sister Hermina and Friar Metrobius — are among them?"

"Land them in Thebes and let them live with their own until they hear from the Motherhouse. Returning to ordinary monastic status after time in a leadership position is normal for the Void Brethren. They'll submit to Abbess Rianne and Chief Administrator Horam without question."

"Right. I'll see that *Bassus* sends the Brethren to the surface in one of her shuttles. The one gifted to us by the Hegemony is coming aboard the station, so we can conduct a detailed examination. They'll have made sure it's sterilized, that's a given, but we can learn things about their shipbuilding practices. And I'll send my intelligence officer to debrief them after they have a chance to re-acclimatize."

"If you can have me picked up wherever I'll be at that time, I'd like to sit in on the debriefing. *Vigilance* will stay in Mazaber for a few more days while I finish making arrangements."

"And how did your meeting with the current strongman go?"

DeCarde chuckled. "My good friend Sven Ironclaw? It was a lovely cocktail party beneath a striped awning on *Vigilance*'s main deck. Very posh for Mazaber."

"Clean stemware would be posh for Mazaber. Wait a minute — Sven Ironclaw? Is that for real?"

"I'm pretty sure his mother named him Sven. But the Ironclaw moniker?" DeCarde raised his hand, palm facing downward, and rocked it from side to side. "Still, he's as big and mean as you might imagine. It's a job requirement around here. In any case, he enjoyed the firepower demonstration put on by our Marines and can see the advantage of allying himself with Thebes, especially if it means his Theban friends will ensure no unexpected regime change occurs in Mazaber."

A grin split Morane's face.

"Hah! Your buddy Sven never heard that quip about nations having neither friends nor allies, only interests."

"No, and I won't educate him on the matter lest he realize that there will eventually be a regime change, one we expect since we'll engineer it. Sven is a cunning man who excels at betraying and knifing his opponents in the back, but he's desperately naïve about politics and diplomatic relations."

"So, when will you establish a full Theban embassy to keep Mister Ironclaw in power and under control?"

DeCarde gave Morane a noncommittal shrug.

"That is still to be negotiated. If I can get the terms I need from Sven, I'll speak with President Freeman over the radio. Should he agree, I'll ask for your help flying the diplomatic staff and Theban Marines here. There is no sense wasting a week at sea during which Sven can fall from power or decide that on second thought, he doesn't like the terms."

"No problems."

"Okay. I'm sure we'll speak again in the next couple of days."

"No doubt, and when we're done here, I'll call Abbess Rianne and tell her she can expect eight more Brethren for evening services. Cheers, Mister Ambassador."

"Until next time."

—31—

Wyvern Hegemony Starship Alkonost

"I believe we found the Pacifica system, Captain." *Alkonost*'s navigator, Lieutenant Ulf Ragnarsson, a tall, bearded redhead in his late thirties, grinned at Derwent Alexander over his shoulder. "The star's spectral class matches, and we've found seven planets, one of them in the habitable zone."

Alexander, sitting in the bridge command chair, let out a theatrical groan. "Finally. I was beginning to believe it no longer had any wormholes. Plot a course to the planet in the habitable zone. Let's confirm we're in the right place and, if so, see what the last two hundred years have wrought on humanity's first extrasolar colony."

"On it, sir."

"And when ready, execute." Alexander climbed to his feet. "Officer of the watch, I'll be in my day cabin."

Once alone in his private sanctum, Alexander drew a cup of coffee from the urn and sat behind his desk with a soft sigh. Red dwarf after red dwarf, none of them with habitable planets or self-contained habitats had become tedious. It only took one wormhole on the critical path to shift, and navigation was thrown off by a dozen light-years or more.

As a remapping exercise, it was valuable, and HQ would be pleased with *Alkonost*'s progress. But he didn't have many more wormhole transits left before he had to turn back. Yet if this was Pacifica, and the wormhole to Earth hadn't shifted, they'd make it.

Of course, if this was Pacifica, he could attempt an interstellar crossing and still not reach the limits of his autonomy, provided they could find Sol, the star around which Earth orbited. The empire had relied so much on the wormhole network that interstellar navigation atrophied in the last half-century of its existence.

The jump warning came before his thoughts could leap into a rabbit hole and take him on another round of wondering how humanity had ended up where it now was — decimated, smashed into a thousand shards, yet rediscovering its past because, without that, there was no future. And already two factions were vying for the same goal.

***

"No doubt about it. This is Pacifica. The surface configuration corresponds to what's in our database. But it took a real beating from the Mad Empress' ships." Lieutenant Ragnarsson reported with a somber expression. "The major centers are only ruins, as are the power generation nodes — not a single one still showing so much as a stray emission the sensors can detect through the background radiation. What's left of hydroelectric dams is barely visible after over two centuries of erosion. If there are human life signs, they're much too dispersed and hidden among other life to be detectable from this altitude."

"Another bloody wasteland, courtesy of a corrupt, power-hungry idiot who should have been strangled at birth. Too many of them have graced our collective history since the first humans came together as more than mere family units."

He heard a throaty chuckle behind him — Sister Taina.

"Don't hold back, Captain."

Alexander turned his chair and smiled at her.

"On that subject, never. It's where survey missions hit you in the gut. Reading and hearing about the Great Scouring in school is one thing, but seeing a planet that once boasted over a billion inhabitants laid waste? That's reality shaking your soul with a vengeance."

"Will you set foot on Pacifica?"

"If our orbital survey finds something of interest, such as remnant populations in sufficient numbers to warrant a Void Mission or artifacts Wyvern might want to know about. It'll take around thirty to forty hours in low orbit before we have enough data." Alexander jumped to his feet. "Buy you a cup of coffee, Sister?"

"Certainly."

But before Alexander could take a single step, the intercom came to life.

"CIC to the captain."

He leaned over and touched the arm of the command chair.

"Captain here."

"Officer of the watch, sir. Sensors just picked up what seemed like a ghost at the hyperlimit on an approach from what should be Wormhole Pacifica Five."

"Another sensor ghost? The old core sector seems to teem with them." Alexander searched his memory for details on Wormhole Five and failed. "Where does that lead?"

"Depending on the branches, either the old Imperial Shield, Cascadia, or Rim Sectors."

"Could it be a Lyonesse ship running silent?"

"Sure," the CIC officer replied. "But that would mean they've made quite a detour."

"Who else could it be, here at the heart of human space?" Alexander glanced at Taina and frowned.

"Non-humans who finally noticed the largest, meanest empire in this part of the galaxy self-destructed. And who remember our old tactic of running silent."

"We're trying to regain contact with the ghost, sir. If it's real and not our sensors seeing things."

"Good. Captain, out."

Once in the day cabin, Alexander drew two cups of coffee from the urn and handed one to Taina, who'd taken her accustomed chair across from his desk.

"You think non-human sentient beings who escaped the Mad Empress' death throes are creeping into the old empire, looking for signs something survived? If I recall correctly, we'd surpassed the Shrehari in size and population long before the Ruggero Dynasty seized the throne, never mind the various single and multiple star system polities in the Shield Sector and what used to be the Protectorate Zone."

Taina took a sip of her coffee and shrugged.

"Wyvern kept FTL capabilities, as did Lyonesse. Why not the Shrehari or others? The fact we've not seen a trace of non-humans in the wormhole network doesn't mean they haven't been there all along. Our Hegemony's population barely suffices to retake the neighboring systems, and I daresay Lyonesse is in the same position. How much less capable of claiming former imperial star systems would non-human polities be, considering their home worlds are thousands of light-years away? And yet, anyone who can travel FTL and find wormhole termini may come and go as they please without leaving traces." A small smile. "Except for this ghost and the one in the Celeste system. If it's a starship, do you think they spotted us?"

"From the hyperlimit, considering we're not trying to hide? Almost certainly. Anyone who can travel FTL, whether they use the wormhole network, should be capable of picking up our emissions without difficulties."

"Then let's hope they're curious explorers like us and not beings bent on conquest."

Alexander sat back and sighed. "You know what gets me, Sister?"

"No."

"We could have been doing this two hundred years ago and reclaimed human space once the dust settled on the Mad Empress' evil deeds."

"Yes, but the trauma was such that our ancestors preferred closing in on themselves and preserving what remained. Unfortunately, inertia set in." She made a face. "Human nature. Despite trying for thousands of years, social engineers still haven't been able to change it and never will."

Alexander scoffed. "Social engineers. Heck of an oxymoron."

"And yet they endure, even in the Hegemony, where they've been busy behind the scenes keeping the population quiescent and obedient. Hasn't worked, has it? The moment President Mandus let us loose, we regained the independent spirit of our distant forbears who first colonized this part of the galaxy."

"And—"

"Bridge to the captain."

Alexander leaned forward and touched his desk. "Captain here."

"We found something of interest on the surface, sir."

"Already? That was fast."

"It's a faint power emissions source that appeared after our first survey scans reached the ground. May I send you the video feed?"

"Go."

The day cabin's primary display came to life with an orbital view of Pacifica. More precisely, an area marked Hadley, the former star system capital, now nothing more than a field of ruins overrun by vegetation. A small red dot appeared north of Hadley on a promontory that overlooked the entire region.

After a few seconds, the video pickup zoomed in on the dot at a speed that left Alexander and Taina feeling queasy for just a moment. When it stopped, the effect was as if they were suspended a few meters over the surface by a tractor beam.

"What are we looking at?"

"An artificial object about seven meters long, a meter and a half thick, and based on the shadows, about three meters high. Vines cover much of it, but there appear to be glowing markings on its vertical surfaces."

"A monument?" Alexander and Taina exchanged glances. "Why would a monument release detectable emissions after being pinged by our sensor sweep?"

She gave him a mischievous smile.

"You mentioned a discovery of interest might draw you to the surface, Captain. I believe this qualifies."

"Probably. It's the first unscathed human construct we've found so far, but the survey is still young."

***

"That's it, Captain. We're done. The next step is focusing on areas of interest, but other than the monolith, damned if I can figure out what those are," Lieutenant Ragnarsson said after dropping into the chair across from Alexander's day cabin desk beside the one occupied by the first officer, Reena Prince. "There are no significant human life sign concentrations. In fact, it would surprise me if there are more than a quarter-million people on the surface."

"Out of a population of what? Over a billion just before Dendera's genocide?" Alexander shook his head. "Unbelievable. Let's find the largest concentration and send Centurion Lee's troopers to scope them out. And I will visit the monolith myself. Sister Taina will want in on that."

"Sir." Prince gave him a hard look. "Captains shouldn't lead landing parties."

Alexander returned her stare with a smile.

"I won't be leading a party, Reena. The sister and I will merely be tourists surrounded by either a section of Centurion Lee's Marines or a detachment of bosun's mates equipped for hazardous environments."

"If you must," she growled.

"Oh, I must. And so does the sister. That's a piece of humanity's past. I'd never forgive myself for not touching it with my own hands. We'll discuss it along with Centurion Lee's reconnaissance at eleven-hundred."

***

"It's a memorial," Taina said when she caught sight of the monolith. "Dedicated to the dead of the empire's Formation War."

The ship's pinnace had landed in a small clearing atop the truncated promontory only a few dozen meters away. Charred vegetation indicated a recent forest fire, perhaps caused by lightning.

"How do you know that?" Alexander asked, eyes on the structure. "We can barely see the inscriptions."

"I can sense echoes of souls who died violently. Memorials built on or near ground where large numbers perished often conduct vibrations from the Infinite Void."

"But why from something that happened over twelve hundred years ago?"

Taina, who wore naval battledress like Alexander and the rest of the landing party, albeit without tactical harness and sidearms, glanced at him.

"The monument obviously predates the Great Scouring, and the last widespread loss of life on the core worlds before then resulted from the Commonwealth's death throes."

The petty officer in charge of the landing party walked up to Alexander and Taina.

"Should we clear off the green stuff, sir?"

"Please."

As the gently glowing inscriptions appeared, Taina nodded.

"It's indeed from that era. Many people died when the Pacifican government decided resisting was better than submitting to imperial rule after Earth fell." She turned to the petty officer. "If you scan the memorial, you might catch a data stream."

The man inclined his head as he retrieved his battlefield sensor. "Sister."

"Why do you think it's emitting?" Alexander turned his eyes on Taina.

"Because, if you look carefully, you'll see the names on the memorial change every few seconds. It's dedicated to so many lives that they can't all be shown simultaneously, so why not provide visitors with a complete roll call if they desire? Someone obviously built it to remind people on Pacifica of the horrendous costs of civil war."

"I see. Amazing, the monument is still intact and fulfilling its purpose after so long, and all it took was a scan from orbit to reawaken it. A shame there's nothing like that on Wyvern. It might have reminded the Ruggero Dynasty of their duty to preserve humanity rather than feed crazed ambitions."

Taina smiled at him.

"Wyvern didn't experience any undue loss of life twelve centuries ago — it was at the center of the imperial movement."

"And of its destruction."

"Sir." The petty officer turned around. "I've downloaded a large data packet containing over seventy-thousand names along with personal details, units, date of death, that sort of thing. Seems like most died on the same day."

"Killed during the siege of the last Commonwealth redoubt?" Alexander asked Taina, who'd clearly taken the time to research Pacifica's history in greater detail than he had.

"Probably. Many Commonwealth diehards couldn't bear the idea of facing new masters intent on cleaning up centuries of corruption and incompetence, the sort that already triggered a pair of murderous civil wars, and who'd gleefully fight a third, so they could maintain their privileges. If we ever reach Earth, we should find a similar memorial near where Geneva, the Commonwealth capital, once stood."

"We will, Sister, and—" At that moment, Alexander's surface to orbit radio lit up.

"*Alkonost* to Captain Alexander, First Officer here."

"Alexander."

"Our sensor ghost from the other day turned out to be very real indeed, sir. He fired thrusters and sublight drives to turn and head back for the hyperlimit. We picked up a nice emissions profile and good imagery, and there's no way it's a Lyonesse ship. Granted, their shipbuilding will have diverged from ours, but form follows species and function, and well over fifteen hundred years of human design won't have been erased so quickly. That was a non-human starship. The power curve is so dissimilar from ours, it reflects a vastly different design. We're still running the visuals through the database to see if we can come up with a reasonable approximation. Yet, we lost so much during and after the Great Scouring that identifying the species might be impossible."

"Any markings?"

"None we could see."

Alexander thought for a moment, eyes narrowed.

"Try hailing them on normal and subspace frequencies, identify us, and advise them this star system belongs to the Wyvern Hegemony. Even if they pick up the message, they probably won't understand, but it's worth a shot. And please note their departure vector. I'd like to know which wormhole they might be taking."

"Aye, aye, sir. That was it."

"Alexander, out." His gaze rested on the monument again for a few seconds, then he glanced up at the clear blue sky. "We definitely waited too long if non-humans are prowling star systems which belong to us by right and are still inhabited by our species. And sadly, we have neither the population nor the industrial base to re-establish ourselves as undisputed masters of those systems within a single generation."

He glanced at the petty officer. "If you've finished capturing the data, let's head back to the ship."

"Done, sir." The petty officer let out a sharp whistle. "Mount up, folks. Shore leave is over."

***

"They didn't answer, though whether they don't listen on the same frequencies as us or because they can't understand our language is up for debate, sir."

Commander Prince took her usual chair in Alexander's day cabin, where he and Taina had repaired after shedding their battledress and tactical gear. "But their course will bring them to Wormhole Four, which will take them to the Sol System and Earth if it hasn't shifted."

"Damn." A frown creased Alexander's forehead. "I don't like the idea of a non-human visiting Earth ahead of us."

"Not just any non-human." A grimace spread across Prince's features. "We figure, based on design, that it could well be Shrehari."

"Weren't they having a dynastic problem that triggered a deadly civil war during Dendera's reign?"

Taina nodded.

"That's what the histories say. Their empire self-destructed at about the same time as ours, though we do not know whether the government went full genocide on its own people as well. Nor can we tell whether our collapse triggered theirs. Some would posit the abrupt end of mutual trading relationships had something to do with it, considering how much went back and forth between our spheres after centuries of peaceful coexistence."

"I see." Alexander nodded, then came to a decision. "Once Centurion Lee and his people are back aboard, we'll—" The door chime interrupted him. He glanced at this desk's inlaid display. "Speaking of the good centurion, he's arrived. Enter."

Lee stepped across the threshold and came to attention.

"I'm here to report on the results of our reconnaissance, if you have a moment, Captain."

"You arrive precisely on time. Grab a cup of coffee and take a seat."

"Yes, sir." Lee helped himself, then dropped into the chair beside Prince. "Nothing we can pinpoint as a suitable site for a Void Mission, sir. Seems like pretty much everyone adopted a nomadic lifestyle, following game and the seasons around the major continents. A straight up Wyvern colony in a nice subtropical location will do better than a mission. Let it grow and spread for however long, then bring the nomads in. It might take a few generations, but there's no fast option here, unlike Celeste or Santa Theresa. Not enough warm bodies to convert. At least not in one spot."

"Is there a point in watching for a longer period?"

Lee shook his head.

"Not that I can figure, Captain. We might drop a few autonomous surveillance sensors to watch potential game trails, as it were, and pick them up on our return trip, but setting my troopers up in observation posts for a few weeks won't get us any further. This isn't nice and neat like the area on Celeste we watched before the new mission arrived. These people really took a tumble down the technological ladder."

"Alright, then." Alexander slapped his desktop with the fingertips of both hands. "As I was about to say when you arrived, my plan is to head out as soon as we can and your findings make that possible. We'll drop a few sensors wherever you think they'll be most useful. We'll also deploy a small satellite constellation to augment those sensors and monitor Pacifica's surroundings out to the hyperlimit. It's the only way we have of marking Hegemony territory. I want to follow that perhaps Shrehari ship since it might be heading in the same direction as us. Comments or questions?"

When Lee and Taina shook their heads, Prince said, "I'll get the sensors and satellites organized, Captain. We should be ready to break out of orbit within the hour."

"Putting us only a few hours behind the intruder."

— 32 —

Republic of Lyonesse Ship Serenity

"No doubt about it, sir. This is the Farhaven System. The star's spectral class matches perfectly, and there's a blue planet in the habitable zone, along with ten others that aren't suited for our sort of life. The distribution between rocky planets and gas giants corresponds with the old navigation database." Lieutenant Retief glanced over her shoulder at Al Jecks, sitting in the bridge command chair.

"Which means we've finally arrived in what was once humanity's core sector, the worlds colonized during the First Migration," Jecks said with an air of satisfaction. "And no charted wormholes gone rogue between Lyonesse and here. By the way, I trust everyone is familiar with what happened here during humanity's first interstellar civil war? If not, I suggest a brief perusal of the historical database."

"Oh, yes." Sister Bree made a face. "It set the tone for the next fifteen hundred years, during which we fought three more genocidal civil wars. It's a wonder our species still even exists."

"I wonder whether Fort Wagner is still standing or whether the Retribution Fleet wiped it off the face of the planet." Lieutenant Commander Salmin spoke in a soft, contemplative tone. "If only to spite the Imperial Marine Corps. Mind you, our Marines no longer formally observe the battle's anniversary. But, my brother Thomas, the colonel — he has the 3rd of the 21st on Hatshepsut — says they still consider Fort Wagner a shrine to the Corps' loyalty and heroism. And they raise a glass to the 3rd Regiment's bravery every December 2nd."

"We'll find out soon enough how the Mad Empress' murderers treated the fort. Ginny, plot a course to Farhaven and get us synced."

"Aye, aye, sir."

"Here's hoping we come across more survivors than just a few scattered nomadic bands," Sister Bree said.

"Or any. The number of empty worlds we found was depressing," Salmin replied. "It'll take us centuries to repopulate them, and, in the meantime, any star-faring species can take what's ours by right and make it theirs."

"Such as the Hegemony?" Bree asked, smiling mischievously.

"At least they're human, and if we represent half of our species, they're the other half. We have encountered no non-humans in the last two hundred years. But that doesn't mean they're not navigating the wormhole network or even interstellar space and discovering we vanished from most worlds, leaving them open to colonization by the first comer." Salmin gave Bree a sad look. "And judging from our history, that means there will be war.

Perhaps not in our day, but in our children's and grandchildren's time."

"A discouraging thought."

***

"Farhaven is as bereft of emissions from advanced technology as every other planet we passed." Chief Petty Officer Second Class Gill swiveled his seat to face Captain Jecks, now occupying the CIC's command chair. "Every city, town, and village is gone, flattened and covered by a carpet of vegetation. But one piece of Farhaven is still standing."

He turned back to his workstation, touched the control screen, and an aerial view of a star-shaped structure atop a hill appeared.

"Fort Wagner," Jecks said in a half-whisper.

"Seemingly untouched. No power, of course, like the rest of the planet, but you can still see the grave markers if you look at the slopes. For some reason, vegetation hasn't taken over, as if someone is still tending the place."

"According to the footnotes of a Fort Wagner history published around five hundred years ago, they laid bio-engineered grass during the imperial era, Chief. It doesn't grow beyond a few centimeters in height and will allow nothing else to live there. Reduces maintenance."

"Impressive. I guess Dendera's killers figured destroying a shrine which stood for so long was bad luck."

Jecks shrugged.

"Whatever their motives, I'm glad they left it intact. First Officer?"

"Sir."

"I'll be visiting Fort Wagner with a landing party, which will make a painstakingly detailed survey. I'm sure our Marine siblings will be glad for news of their shrine." He paused. "Let's make it one better. Once the site's been cleared of threats, anyone in the task force who'd like to pay their respects can go stretch their legs, and commune with fifteen hundred years of history. Other than landing parties, most of our folks haven't left their ships since we departed from Lyonesse."

"Understood."

"Signals, link in the other captains so we can discuss plans."

***

Al Jecks and Sister Bree stepped off the pinnace and onto a remarkably intact landing pad at the base of Fort Wagner's gentle slopes. Almost at once, Bree let out a soft gasp.

"What?"

"This is a place of enormous power," she replied in a low, strangled voice. "The likes of which I've never encountered before. The essence of those who died here left an indelible imprint in the landscape."

"Perhaps that's why it survived the Second Migration War, the empire's Formation War, and Dendera's Great Scouring."

Jecks' tone held a faint hint of facetiousness, but Bree nodded, her eyes taking in the rows of graves beneath the fort's low berm.

"It is possible. We still know so little about what makes us human, what energies we absorb during life and release upon death. And how the manner of death affects those released energies." She turned her head and gave him a wan smile. "What you would call the soul. Perhaps whoever attacked Farhaven during those civil wars felt a subconscious compulsion to avoid damaging this place lest they unleash something incomprehensible."

Jecks and Bree stood for a moment longer in the warm morning sun, ears picking up only the soft rustling of leaves in the breeze and the distant trill of birdsong. The clean, gentle aroma of healthy natural surroundings without a trace of human artifice tickled their nostrils in a way they'd never experienced. If it weren't for the silent figures of men and women in Lyonesse Navy battledress slowly walking among the graves or on top of the ramparts, they might have believed themselves alone on a world abandoned by humanity.

"Are you okay, Sister?" Jecks asked after a while.

"Yes. Something merely startled me. There's no threat here, not after so long. Even the imprint of evil stemming from the atrocities committed by Farhaveners against defenseless loyalists has dissipated." She paused. "What I now sense is sadness and solemnity. Shall we go up?"

They took the stone path that led from the landing pad occupied by half a dozen shuttles, two from each ship, to Fort Wagner's sole entrance, a chicane zigzagging through the indestructible berm that sheltered the remaining above-ground structures.

"We should have brought a Lyonesse Marine Corps flag with us," Jecks remarked, indicating the bare pole at the center of the fort with a nod. "Based on the histories, a Marine flag flew there night and day, above an eternal flame and the spot where the 3rd Marine Regiment buried the ashes of its colors the night before the ultimate battle. The last iteration must not have survived as well as the rest of the site after the garrison evacuated."

Bree laid a hand on his arm.

"Make it a formal flag raising ceremony with an honor guard and a band, even if it's a virtual one. The spirits guarding Fort Wagner would be pleased, as would our Marine comrades back home once they see a recording. It'll do wonders for morale."

"A fine idea, Sister. We'll do as you say."

Those were the last words they exchanged for quite a while as they walked between the grave markers laid into the ground before entering the fort itself. In Jecks' eyes, a man who'd been born on a planet colonized during the last two centuries of imperial rule, the dates inscribed on the markers were incredibly far in the past. No human had even set foot on the worlds currently claimed by Lyonesse when these Marines died, nor did his species know of other sapient beings back then.

Inside the berm, the fort was surprisingly clean, as if the permanent garrison had left a few days ago. Even their barracks and offices, which were unlocked and still furnished, gave the impression they'd just left on a field training exercise for a week or two.

Of course, the eternal flame at the flagpole's base no longer burned, since there had been no one to tend it for generations. But the silver plaque marking where the 3rd Regiment's commanding officer had buried the ashes of the regimental colors still shined dully, its surface free of dirt and corrosion. The same held true for the plaque marking the entrance to the underground bunkers, where the bodies of several thousand loyalists, mainly children, the elderly, or others incapable of fighting, lay entombed after being massacred by Farhaven rebels when they finally took possession of the fort. Those who could fight had died alongside the Marines until none remained.

As they stood before the memorial listing the names of the Marines and loyalists who died during the Farhaven rebellion,

Jecks said, "There hasn't been a 3rd Regiment on the Marine Corps order of battle since the day it died here. Did you know that, Sister? Not the Commonwealth's, nor the empire's, nor ours. And I suspect the Hegemony doesn't field one either."

"Yes. I read that somewhere. It was a tradition any unit wiped out with no survivors would never be reconstituted, with its name and title placed on what they called the supplementary order of battle."

Jecks nodded.

"The tradition is still part of our heritage, though Lyonesse hasn't suffered that sort of loss yet and hopefully never will." He glanced at Bree. "Had enough for today? We'll be back to rededicate the fort tomorrow."

"Give me a few minutes longer. I feel I'm not quite done communing with those who died here."

He nodded.

"This place has that sort of effect on you, doesn't it? I'll read out the actual wording used during the remembrance ceremony tomorrow. We might as well do this in the time-honored fashion."

"You have the full text?"

"When I realized our navigation plan would take us through the Farhaven System, I dug it out of the Command and Staff College archives, just in case."[1]

***

"Very moving ceremony, Captain." Lieutenant Commander Salmin snapped off a salute as Jecks, Chief Petty Officer Fast,

---

[1] See Appendix – Fort Wagner

Sister Bree, and the twenty-strong honor guard, all save for Bree wearing Navy dress uniform, marched down the shuttle's aft ramp. "There wasn't a dry eye on the bridge, and I daresay anywhere else in Task Force 101. The honor guards from *Provider* and *Defiant* did their ships proud too. I don't think you'll be paying for drinks in Marine Corps messes for as long as you live after they see the recording."

"Let's hope the flag lasts until we post a permanent garrison here. A shame we couldn't relight the eternal flame. Still, that power source engineering rigged ought to keep the flag lit up at night for a long, long time. And with that, we're done here. Get the task force ready to break out of orbit while we change."

"Yes, sir."

A few hours later, as Task Force 101 reached Farhaven's hyperlimit, the jump klaxon sounded throughout *Serenity,* and the CIC crew braced itself for the momentary disorientation. But just as the hyperdrives began spooling up, the sensor chief let out a puzzled grunt.

"What the—"

Then, the universe twisted itself into a pretzel, and the ship left normal space. Once he recovered, the CIC officer of the watch turned to Gill.

"You were saying before we rode the vomit comet?"

"Sensors picked up a pretty solid ghost at the hyperlimit, sir."

"Hegemony?"

Gill shook his head.

"No. Their ships are identifiably human and not that different from ours regarding the basics. This one wasn't human. Not even close."

A blurry image appeared on the primary display, along with sensor readings.

"I'll say, Chief. Never seen the like before. And the emissions curve is way off from what we know about Hegemony ships." He tapped the command chair's control screen. "CIC to the captain."

A few seconds passed. "Jecks here."

"Sensors picked up a quasi-ghost seconds before we went FTL. I'm forwarding the image and data to your day cabin. We can't make out what it is, but it's not Hegemony. The intelligence AI is working with the readings and our database to figure it out, but our information on non-human shipping is over two centuries out of date and pretty sparse."

Jecks didn't immediately reply though he kept the link open. "Tell you what, something about it makes me think our old friends, the Shrehari, might finally have noticed our thousand-year empire vanished and are looking for us."

"The Shrehari?"

"Tell the AI to focus on that species first."

"Aye, aye, sir."

"Jecks, out."

Gill chuckled. "Figures the skipper would suss it out first, the amount of history he's memorized."

"Let's see if the intel AI agrees. The skipper knows history, but the AI can run through more data in a second than the human brain."

—33—

Celeste

"Friar Shakku, got a moment?" Major Dozier stuck his head into the chief administrator's tiny office. "We may have a bit of a mystery, courtesy of an envoy from a settlement south of here, on the coast, which we visited, a place called Antibes. It sits about ten kilometers south of the old imperial city by the same name flattened during the Great Scouring, across a wide but shallow bay."

"Sure." Shakku dropped the weekly supply consumption report and sat back. "What's the story?"

He'd been fully immersed in the minutiae of administering a Void Mission on a fallen planet since their return from the upriver sweep. As a result, he'd paid less attention than he should to the Marines and his first contact teams extending the mission's zone of influence up and down the coastal plain.

"The man showed up at the main gate, wanting to speak with the friar in charge about twenty minutes ago. Something about ghosts in the mountains east of his village, strange lights at night, stories about animals and people vanishing. Been plaguing them for a while now — he can't be precise, mind you — and after we visited, the Antibans decided we were the folks who could figure out why and make it stop. Apparently, we, or at least someone not from this world, are responsible. Not sky demon territory, but that of strange people from away."

"And you'd like me to speak with this envoy."

Dozier nodded. "If you would, Friar. It sounds spiritual, and there's not much we Marines can do with that sort of thing. He's in the reception center."

Because the mission was getting so many visitors from the central west coast, Shakku ordered a container converted to a waiting room so that folks couldn't just wander around the complex unsupervised. It was open during daylight hours and staffed by two of Dozier's Marines. So far, troublemakers had stayed away, but it was just a matter of time.

"Have someone escort him here, if you would, Major."

"Sure thing." Dozier sketched a salute and vanished.

A few minutes later, Dozier himself reappeared with a shaggy, bearded, gray-haired man in homespun clothes.

"Elder Goggin of Antibes, Friar."

The Marine ushered Goggin in and left, although Shakku knew one of his troopers was standing by, out of sight, in case of trouble.

"Please sit."

"Aye. Thank you kindly." The old man replied in a deep, firm voice, as he nodded.

Shakku studied Goggin for a few moments before speaking. He had the seamed face and deep-set dark eyes common among people in the region, and his calloused hands spoke of a lifetime of manual labor. But he nonetheless exuded an aura of health even though he was at the far end of middle age by local standards.

"My name is Shakku, Elder Goggin. I'm the chief administrator of this mission. I trust you had a pleasant journey?"

"Oh, aye. Came up the coast by boat. Saves on shoe leather and finding animal tracks through some of the woods between Antibes and here."

"What can I do for you, sir?"

"You can tell us what in the name of the Almighty's been going on in the Louvain Valley. It ain't natural that we know for sure."

Shakku called up a map of the coast on his workstation display and found Louvain, approximately twenty kilometers straight inland from Antibes, which sat on a narrow but fertile strip of coastline at the foot of the coastal mountain range. There was little in the database concerning the valley except it had been inhabited because the orbital scans showed the remains of artificial structures beneath a carpet of vegetation.

"Tell me about these happenings."

"It's been an uncanny place as long as everyone living in the area can remember. Years ago, before my time, people went exploring the valley and were never seen again. Wild animals avoid it, and those who don't get sick. The souls of the dead congregate there on certain nights when an eerie glow seems to emanate from the valley floor. But like I said, it's always been so, and we learned to avoid going near it. However, in recent times, maybe in the last year or so, shooting stars have landed in the valley.

"We could see them come down. Worse yet, those shooting stars would rise again and vanish in the sky after some time. And on nights when that happened, domestic animals vanished; a few people who lived in the woods and worked as charcoal burners disappeared too. There one week, gone without a trace the next, leaving their belongings behind. It stopped around the time you arrived. Then it started up again. There are no more shooting stars that fall out of the sky and come back up, but strange things keep happening. The charcoal burners returned and didn't know they were gone. Can't remember what happened during the two or three weeks they weren't in this world."

When he saw the surprise in Shakku's eyes, Goggin chuckled.

"Oh, I'm not done yet, Friar. One of our intrepid lads, out at night to look at the stars away from town, spied a pair of strange creatures watching us as we slept. They each had two legs, two arms, and one head and wore clothes like your Marines. But those heads." Goggin shook his head. "They weren't human. No, sir. They had ridges over the skull, wide, flat noses, eyes that had no whites, and ruffs of fur running from the top of the skull to the nape of the neck. And they were bigger than most of us."

"How did your lad get that good a look without being seen?"

A grin split Goggin's face.

"He's our best hunter. Can creep up on prey and get within touching distance unseen and unheard. Got amazing night vision too. But mainly because the creatures moved through a moonlit spot along the fringe of trees on a ridge above Antibes. Not woodsmen, them. Too much time spent looking at the fancy gizmo each held in one hand. That was five nights ago. When he reported to the elders, we decided I should take a boat and visit the Brethren from the stars to see what could be done.

"We don't feel safe with strange beings creeping around watching us. Abducting people and animals and the like. The area was tolerable before shooting stars going upwards arrived. Ever since, it's been getting worse. People are afraid, and I hear part of your job is keeping those who come under your protection safe. So here I am, Friar, to ask that you take Antibes under your protection, just like Grâce and the others along the coast, and rid us of those creatures."

Shakku, whose mind had been racing while Goggin spoke, knew without a doubt that another sapient species was on Celeste. The old man's description could only apply to one with whom humanity had fought a war long ago and then enjoyed a thousand years of peace. Even if at first it was peace through superior firepower and then one out of sheer inertia as both empires expanded away from each other.

"We will investigate, Elder Goggin. You have my word on that. And if Antibes wishes to join our league, then welcome. We will send a team as soon as possible and survey your community so we can best decide together how we may help."

Goggin inclined his head respectfully.

"Thank you, Friar."

"May I show you around and offer you a meal?"

The man scratched his beard.

"A quick tour, but then I must hurry home. The tide and the winds will be favorable to my boat's departure sooner than you might think."

***

Major Dozier and Sister Maryam stared at Shakku with astonishment and disbelief after relaying Elder Goggin's tale and his suspicions.

"The description fits," Shakku said. "Assuming they solved their dynastic issues quicker and without murdering hundreds of billions of their own, why wouldn't they be venturing into what once was our sphere? They're curious about what happened to us. We were respectful neighbors and trading partners for what? Well over a thousand years? And then we just stopped visiting."

Dozier grunted.

"But why the furtiveness? They must know we're here. There could even be one or more of their starships in orbit right now, staring at us."

"Because they're afraid of being caught snooping on a world that's been ours for fifteen hundred years? Who knows what the current government's policy is? They, like us, are a predatory species, and when predators find an empty ecological niche, they will try to fill it. And there are a lot of empty worlds in our part of the galaxy these days. The question is, will they consider planets with remnant human societies, even if they're preindustrial, as being empty? Or will they bypass them? And do they even have enough population, ships, and other means of rapid expansion? We certainly don't. I would venture they're on an exploration journey, one with the aim of uncovering what happened to our empire without attracting the attention of those who, like us, lost no technological advancements."

"And if they discover they're now the biggest empire in this quadrant?" Dozier asked.

"Then, for starters, we might not recover the systems we owned in the old Rim Sector, the ones they invaded during the

Commonwealth Era. In any case, we must reconnoiter the Louvain Valley and do it in a way that won't betray our interest."

"Our options are limited. We have the satellites *Yatagerasu* placed into orbit; we can use our drones or send a patrol." Dozier rubbed his chin as he frowned. "Tell you what, let's start with the satellites. Get some good aerial imagery and see if there's evidence of activity. It's the least intrusive method. Meanwhile, since this town wants in on our scheme, let's send a delegation of Brethren along with a half company to establish the relationship. That way, if the intruders are watching, they'll know our area of operations is closing in on theirs. It might convince them Celeste is coming back under Wyvern's control."

Maryam nodded.

"I agree. The last thing we need is confrontation. If these are explorers, they'll either make themselves known or make themselves scarce once they suspect we're aware of their presence. Depending on how long they've been on Celeste, they might even have observed our mission and will have seen our starships. But I think we have two mysteries centered on the Louvain Valley, which may or may not be linked. One is the intrusion by non-humans, the other is the valley itself or what it used to contain before the Great Scouring."

Shakku inclined his head. "Just so. But investigating the second will have to wait for the resolution of the first."

"Tell you what," Dozier said. "I'll have my folks go through the satellite data for the last few weeks and see what they picked up in and around Antibes and Louvain. Who knows? We might have evidence of shuttles flying nap of the earth now that Goggin's shooting stars no longer take off and land. That's how we creep up on settlements."

"Very well. Let's proceed with the imperative of avoiding confrontation at any cost. If there's a ship in orbit, we can vanish in a flash at the slightest provocation."

— 34 —

"So, this is where you saw the creatures?" Centurion Brock studied the wood line where the young hunter had lain in wait a week earlier. He'd taken half of B Company as escort for the Brethren delegation to Antibes, leaving Chelmsford and the other half behind. Soon after arriving, he'd asked Elder Goggin for a guide up onto the crest overlooking the little town.

"Aye, sir." The youth nodded, pointing at a spot between large tree trunks with little undergrowth. "The creatures weren't much as woodsmen, that I can tell you."

"So Elder Goggin said." Brock turned to the command sergeant leading Number Five Platoon. "Let's see if your troopers can do better and find their trail."

"Yes, sir."

Within moments, pairs of Marines holding battlefield sensors spread out and methodically quartered the area using advanced electronics and their mark one eyeballs. It didn't take long for the first result.

"Up there, in that tree. It's well camouflaged so no one might notice, but that bump is a sensor aimed downhill. Installing it was probably why the intruders were here."

Brock nodded. "Seeing as how they now know we're spreading out, they might have deemed it safer to place remotes so they could watch from afar. I wouldn't be surprised if we found more of these around here and closer to Grâce. Maybe even a few aimed at the mission itself."

"You realize, sir," the platoon leader said, "that these things work line of sight, so either there are repeaters around connecting them to their command node, or there's a satellite in orbit we don't know about. Considering the effort involved, one starship pumping out a stealth satellite is easier than setting up a whole ground-based telecommunications network, especially if the intruders are operating in other spots on the planet."

"Good point. Let's leave that sensor there for now, although we can assume they'll realize we found it whenever they receive the next data dump. I'll warn the major. You keep on looking."

***

"Got 'em," Major Dozier announced with glee as he entered Shakku's office, where he and Maryam took their morning tea. "Both on the satellite recordings and outside Antibes."

He recounted Centurion Brock's findings, then said, "And even though our satellites are geared for weather, communications, and geomatics, rather than surveillance, they occasionally catch other things, even though they're not programmed to warn us about them. Such as unknown flying objects coming in and out of Louvain Valley, hugging the terrain for hundreds of kilometers in a southerly direction before popping up behind the horizon. The last flight out caught by the satellites was the night after the Antiban hunter spotted the intruders. Since then, there's been no activity in the entire area that we could see."

A frown creased Shakku's forehead.

"Then what use is the sensor Brock found?" Before Dozier could reply, the friar snapped his fingers. "They too have one or more satellites in orbit."

"That's our theory. When the next supply or survey ship comes through, we'll have it hunt the thing. I suggest we do a drone overflight of the Louvain Valley as soon as possible and see if we can detect any unusual activities. There's no point in playing coy if they seeded the entire coast with sensors and understand we now know about them."

"Fair enough. Do what you must, Major. Again, no confrontations, please. Just find out what they've been doing in the Louvain Valley and remove any surveillance equipment they might have left. Everything else will have to wait for the next Navy ship."

Dozier grinned. "The joys of being at the end of the supply line. No senior officers are breathing down my neck, but to make up for it, no orbiting starships are there to cover my back."

He sketched a salute and vanished.

Shakku and Maryam looked at each other in silence, sipping their tea.

"What do you think?" The former finally asked.

"They're curious and know they shouldn't be here without our permission. I doubt they have any hostile intent. Like us, they're at the end of their supply line and can't do much harm lest they suffer harm themselves, which will make a voyage home difficult, if not impossible."

"It's still rather unnerving to think a non-human species has been watching us in secret as we reclaim Celeste. I wonder how many more of our worlds they're exploring. And how many of those they're tagging for colonization, notwithstanding a native human population, be it ever so primitive by their or our standards? And consigning that population to subjugation or elimination."

***

Dozier, sitting in one of the operations center's spare seats, perked up when First Sergeant Chelmsford, who was watching the drone's sensors, announced, "Entering target zone."

"Sensors on max output. Let's hammer that place from a low altitude. Maybe we'll get more than the orbital survey, and the satellites picked up. Something attracted the intruders to this place."

After fifteen minutes of crisscrossing the valley, the drone flight came to a hover above the vegetation-covered ruins at the foot of a low cliff side and switched over to ground-penetrating sensors.

"Looks like they found an interesting bit, sir."

"Hmm?"

Dozier, who'd been studying the results of the low-level scans, looked up from the holographic projection of the surface mapped by the drones. So far, they had nothing but ruins of what appeared to be a squarely built site, with streets crossing at right angles everywhere. Most building foundations were of equal length and width, and a landing pad overgrown with creepers bordered it on one side. Many of them had been crushed in recent times — the intruders, maybe?

As the intelligence AI reconstituted what the place might have looked like over two centuries ago, Dozier became convinced it could have been a military installation. One that didn't appear on the old maps, meaning a classified site, and yet within thirty kilometers of a sizable seaside town.

"The drone swarm AI thinks there's something beneath the surface or inside that cliff." Within seconds, the tactical holographic projection of the site spawned the schematic of a tunnel behind the collapsed facade of a building that once stood against the rock wall. "Want to bet that's where the intruders were looking for whatever, sir?"

Dozier stared at the growing tunnel network.

"If so, they covered their tracks rather well. We'll need a foot patrol to examine the place and enter that tunnel."

"Centurion Brock is the closest, and he's equipped and provisioned for a long stroll across the countryside. Plus, there's an overgrown road from the coast to the Louvain Valley, whose nearest point is only five kilometers from B Company's current location. They can be there by midafternoon if they push through."

"All right." Dozier slapped his thighs and stood. "I'll check with Friar Shakku. Call Centurion Brock, send him the information on the valley and road, and tell him to stand by for orders. He should leave a section behind with the Brethren visiting Antibes village."

"Roger that, sir."

***

"Transfer to the Colonials, they said. You'll see new worlds, they said. They didn't say that we'd see them on bloody foot." Trooper Pavel Harris grinned at Centurion Brock as the latter watched his half company prepare to move out. "Would have been nice if the Colonial Service left us a few dropships or some hover barges."

"The best way to travel and see the sights is on foot, Harris," Brock replied, knowing by the Marine's playful tone that he was grousing in the time-honored manner typical of every military service since the Roman Legions. "Besides, who'd maintain aircraft, let alone spacecraft around here?"

As per the new standard operating procedures, they'd brought their combat armor, a load of ammo, and rations for a week aboard the boat flotilla that had taken them and the Brethren delegation along the coast from Grâce at a speed Elder Goggin would have envied, despite wind and tide. Curious as the villagers were when they first disembarked wearing only battledress, combat harness, and helmets, and carrying sidearms, now that the Marines were transforming into carapace-clad creatures from another era, they'd attracted a respectful audience watching from a distance.

The armor, part protection, and part exoskeleton allowed them to move at a pace impossible for even the fittest human who wasn't so equipped to keep insects away and prevent the Marines from overheating or becoming chilled. But the suits didn't make their wearers invincible against primitives, given enough attackers with no fear of death, as the Marines at the Angelique Abbey discovered before they died.

"The crews that come with them, sir," Harris replied with the air of someone explaining the obvious. "And when they're not tinkering with their flying toys, they can serenade us with some imperial era classics."

"Okay, Harris. I'll let you make that proposal to HQ when we return home. But right now, there's a mystery waiting in those mountains, and the only way in is riding the bipedal personnel carrier."

They found the old road half-buried beneath dirt, creepers, and rotting vegetation within half an hour of leaving Antibes village, and were in the first valley by midday, eating up the kilometers without stopping. The countryside was peaceful as can be, with birds and small animals everywhere among the lush vegetation on either side of them.

Though nothing grew through the old roadbed, tall trees with massive boughs created a tunnel pierced by small shafts of sunlight that captured dancing dust motes and insects. Brock found it strangely calming even though the half company moved as a combat patrol in potentially hostile territory rather than making a non-tactical forced march.

As Chelmsford had figured, they crested the pass that led into the Louvain Valley by midafternoon and stopped while Brock and the two platoon leaders studied the target. The drone swarm was still hovering above Louvain, though a few hundred meters up, and would be invisible if not for helmet visors keyed to mark its position so it could, among other things, serve as a line of sight tight beam communications relay.

Brock switched on his radio's transmit function. "Zero, this is Two-Niner. We have eyes on the target and on our air support, over."

A few seconds passed, then the ops duty sergeant's voice came on.

"Two-Niner, this is Zero. Acknowledged. Nothing has changed since you received the last data packet. No traces of anything other than animal activity. Niner has cleared you to head in at your discretion."

"Two-Niner, roger. Out."

Brock resumed his study of the semi-crumbled facade on the cliff face across the narrow valley floor even as shadows from the western ridge crept toward it. Twilight in the Louvain Valley came well before it did on the coast.

Then, he studied the old roadway, looking for signs someone might have tampered with it, even though the drones found nothing unusual. Artificial intelligence, though powerful, lacked the one thing that saved many a Marine over the centuries — gut instinct. And at the moment, his gut told him it was okay.

"All right, let's move."

The patrol wound its way through the road's switchbacks until they reached what was now visibly a defensive berm beneath the dense scrub, confirming Major Dozier's idea this had been a military installation. They saw no trace of a gate or security arch where the road cut through the perimeter, but that wouldn't have survived an aerial strike powerful enough to flatten every single freestanding structure.

When they reached the ruins against the cliff side, the Marines on point at once spotted the tunnel entrance hidden behind a jumble of stone and greenery, thanks to the imagery from the ops center's holographic projection.

Brock deployed one of his platoons in a security perimeter, then sent the other to reconnoiter the tunnel, one small step at a time, scanning for tripwires and other assorted hazards left behind by the intruders. But the first twenty-meter segment, cut into the stone with laser drills, was bare. No signs, no markings, no artifacts. Yet they found evidence that there had been things affixed to the walls and ceiling — lights, perhaps, and conduits — which were carefully removed at some point.

They reached a junction with another tunnel, and the platoon leader sent one section down each branch. Both quickly came upon airlocks whose doors hung open. Beyond, they found more corridors, empty rooms, more airlocks, and stairs headed in both directions, but no contents. Still, they recorded plenty of anchor points and many places where the walls and ceilings weren't discolored as if objects covering them had been removed recently. Those spots were circular, rectangular, square, linear, of every geometric shape, but not irregular and therefore unlikely to be random.

By the time a tapestry of stars shone on the Louvain Valley, the platoon emerged from the underground complex none the wiser, save for one thing.

"This is all we found, sir," the platoon leader knelt beside Brock and his colleague and held out a dark, shiny scrap of plastic. "There are markings on it, but damned if I can figure out what they say."

"Dropped by the intruders, perhaps." Brock took the scrap and turned it over in his hands. "No matter how well you police an area, some bit of trash or other always escapes notice if your first sergeant is in a hurry."

"I figure the intruders stripped whatever was in there — power conduits, light fixtures, etcetera. We might never know what this place was used for during imperial times."

"The multiple airlocks might give us an idea, though. I don't think it was an armory or a supply depot, let alone an ammo dump. Which leaves us with a research facility."

The other platoon leader let out a soft grunt.

"Something that could be hermetically sealed off from the outside through multiple layers of protection."

Brock nodded. "The only sort of research needing that containment level I can think about offhand is biological, chemical, radiological, or genetic. Nasty stuff no honest Marine wants to face. But why would the intruders strip it bare?"

"Beats me, sir."

"Me as well. Let's set up camp for the night while I speak with the major. But not here. This area doesn't feel right."

"Roger that, sir. If you hadn't said it, I would have." The command sergeant looked around. "It wasn't a good place. Not if the imperials were doing the sort of research you mentioned."

"We'll climb back up to the saddle between the valleys. There are a few flat spots that'll do just fine." Brock climbed to his feet and took a few paces away from the cliff wall and its tunnel network as he raised the operations center.

***

"Interesting." Friar Shakku, eyes on the holographic projection of the suspected research facility, stroked his chin as he digested Centurion Brock's report. "Show me the scrap of plastic again."

Major Dozier called up its image on the operations center's primary display.

"Definitely non-human, Friar. The writing matches nothing in our database."

"Does your database contain information on non-humans?" Sister Maryam asked.

Dozier shook his head. "No. I suppose HQ didn't deem it necessary to load that sort of data."

"Once our next report reaches Wyvern, I can guarantee the policy will change," Shakku said. "But back to the item. Only one species familiar to our empire used this sort of runic script."

"The Shrehari." Maryam's flat tone made it a statement. "But why would they strip everything from the installation? And how did we miss their activities?"

Dozier shrugged.

"Considering the amount of work involved, I'd say they did it before our mission arrived. Otherwise, we would have noticed something. It's possible they were active in this star system before our first survey ship showed up. Maybe even during the first mission's establishment and subsequent destruction. There are ways of fooling the non-military satellites the Colonial Services places into orbit, especially when it's far from a complete constellation. Our current orbital setup has blanks, both in terms of coverage and programming. A half dozen scientific satellites simply won't suffice for defensive purposes."

"But why this installation and why now? We didn't even know it was there."

"I daresay our surveys weren't exhaustive, Sister. If you haven't noticed, the Hegemony is in a hurry to reclaim as many worlds as possible before Lyonesse takes them."

She snorted with amusement.

"Wait until the people back home hear there's a third party showing interest in Celeste. That'll make the Presidential Palace jump."

"Could be the non-humans did an exhaustive survey and gave special scrutiny to anything that looked like an old military or research installation hoping to find useful intelligence. Why strip it?" Dozier gave her a lopsided grin. "Why not? They discovered what was being done there before the Great Scouring and figured they either needed to replicate it or make sure we never found out. Who knows what Dendera's government was up to? She and her followers committed the worst crimes against humanity in recorded history. That isn't up for debate. Why not research bio or genetic weapons forbidden by law, things that'll target specific segments of our species or even non-humans? And why not do so in an innocuous place within a reasonable distance of a minor city? No one would suspect it."

Another shrug. "Not that we'll find out anytime soon, or ever. The Louvain installation isn't on any map; whatever was behind those airlocks is gone, and if the intruders are still watching us, there's nothing we can do until the next ship arrives. But if I had to bet on it, I'd say they'll be gone soon, if not already. We arrived a little too early for them, and they were forced to wait while *Strix, Alkonost*, and *Yatagerasu* were in orbit. But once those left, they finished their work. I doubt they'll stick around for long in case another of our ships shows up without warning. We had no clue when we arrived and therefore weren't looking, but now, we can tell the next arrival there might be hidden satellites in orbit and even a ship or two loitering at the hyperlimit. And they know it."

"What are your plans now, Major?" Shakku asked.

"In the morning, I'll have Centurion Brock do a ground-level search of the entire installation, then return to Antibes village. Meanwhile, we'll continue the search for hidden sensors in our vicinity. Everything else will have to wait until my report reaches Wyvern and the higher-ups decide on the next steps."

— 35 —

Wyvern Hegemony Starship Alkonost

"That's where it all began," Lieutenant Ulf Ragnarsson said in a reverent tone as a small blue planet appeared on the bridge's primary display. "No doubt about it — Earth, the cradle of humanity. We're the first Hegemony citizens to set eyes on it in over two hundred years."

"Captain to the CIC."

"CIC, officer of the watch."

"Any sign of our possibly Shrehari intruder?" When the CIC didn't immediately reply, Alexander chuckled. "I know, big universe, tiny ship. He might not even have taken this wormhole, but doubled back to Pacifica once we crossed the event horizon. Still, my gut instinct tells me he's here."

"Yes, sir. And no, sir, we're not picking up anything." The officer of the watch paused and added in a droll tone. "Yet."

"That's the spirit. Alexander, out." The excitement at being the first to remap the way to Earth definitely seemed infectious. "Ulf, plot a course for that little blue planet."

"Yes, sir. With pleasure. I never thought I'd hear that order in my lifetime."

"And while you're at it, let's see the system's other planets."

"Certainly. Wait one."

Within moments, a ringed planet appeared, a gas giant whose banded outer atmosphere had a yellowish hue. Countless moons, bright dots of reflected light, swarmed around it.

"Saturn, the second-largest planet in this system," Alexander said with awe in his voice. "Over eighty moons at last count, which was long ago. Named for an ancient Roman god, like the rest of Sol's planets save for Earth."

The image dissolved, replaced by an orb featuring distinct latitudinal bands with turbulence and storms at their boundaries.

"And that would be Jupiter, the largest. It also has over eighty moons. I wonder whether its legendary red spot still exists. It was a storm larger in diameter than Earth."

"Honestly," Commander Prince said in an unimpressed tone, "I'm having a hard time seeing how they're anything special. We have planets like that in our star systems."

Alexander grinned at her over his shoulder. "Killjoy."

She smiled back. "Someone has to keep a grip on reality."

Lieutenant Ragnarsson jerked his chin at the display. "Mars. Where our ancestors set up the second off-world colonies after those on Earth's moon and came across the first non-terrestrial life forms — bacteria."

A reddish world now filled the screen, one with white polar caps and darker areas covering large swaths of the surface.

"They conducted the first terraforming experiments there as well. All were failures, of course, but they provided valuable lessons. I wonder whether the domed colonies still exist." Alexander glanced at Ragnarsson. "Is Mars in a suitable position to swing by on the way in?"

The navigator studied his plot. "Both are on this side of the sun, so only a quick dogleg, sir. A few hours at most."

"Cancel the course to Earth. We'll stop off at Mars first. I'm curious about the fate of the Mars colonies."

"On it."

Prince chuckled. "It must be nice to indulge your curiosity, sir."

"My orders include surveying former imperial worlds, and survey I shall."

***

"Looks like the Mad Empress' killers wasted little ammunition on the Mars domes, Captain," the sensor chief said once the images and scan results appeared on the primary display. "A few punctures in each, and that's it. Left the inhabitants to die of suffocation."

"Some might have survived in the underground portions." Alexander rubbed his chin as he studied the shattered domes of the capital, Nerio, and the darkened city beneath. "I seem to recall reading that something like two thirds of each city was below the surface."

"They didn't survive until the present day, sir. No higher life signs of anything on the planet. It's probably back to bacteria only, and we can't pick those up from orbit."

"Any thoughts of landing a team, sir?" Commander Prince asked.

Alexander hesitated for a second or two and shook his head. "Tempting as it is, we'll leave that to the archeologists who'll eventually make their way here in a few decades. I'd rather spend as much time as possible surveying Earth and its moon. Let's spend a few hours orbiting Mars, mapping the entire surface, before we head inward to our objective."

Prince gave him a sardonic grin. "Impatient?"

"Yes. Of course I am, like everyone else aboard." He hesitated. "Besides, this place feels a tad depressing. Humans inhabited Mars for over thirteen hundred years. Now there are nothing but ghost cities on its surface, doomed to vanish in time, leaving no trace of what once was. Lieutenant Ragnarsson?"

"Sir."

"Plot a course for Earth."

"Already done and laid in, sir. It'll be a quick jump."

Alexander rubbed his hands. "Officer of the watch, execute. And Commander Prince?"

"Yes, sir?"

"Rig the ship for silent running. I want to come out of FTL as quietly as possible, in case an intruder is loitering around Earth."

***

"Nothing, sir. If there's a ship within the hyperlimit, its emissions are better dampened than the previous sensor ghosts, or we're at the wrong angle and distance to pick it up, unlike the one in the Pacifica system."

"Thank you." Alexander sat back and rubbed his chin. "What the heck? This is our star system and no one else's. If a non-human ship is hanging around, let them see us. Up systems, and head for Earth orbit."

"Aye, aye, sir."

"And give me a view of Earth that'll fill the primary display. I want to enjoy this approach. In the meantime, check if anything is left on the moon. As I recall, there were no inhabited sites by the middle of the imperial era, but automated industrial complexes were still operating during the Ruggero Dynasty."

With a contented smile on his face, Captain Derwent Alexander, Wyvern Hegemony Navy, studied the limpid blue planet that had birthed his species, pleased *Alkonost* was the first Hegemony ship to visit it after all this time. It might at least earn him a footnote in the history of humanity's second expansion across the stars.

"Beginning the surface scan of Earth, sir," the sensor chief reported.

By the time they completed their first orbit around the planet, it was obvious nothing much had survived the Great Scouring, similar to Pacifica. The night side was black where, based on images in the database, cities once lit up coastlines and river valleys. Nor did the sensors pick up any artificial power emissions, except a tiny, faint source, exactly like that of the Formation War monument on Pacifica.

"And that," Alexander said in a subdued voice as he studied the southwestern end of Lake Geneva on the primary display, "was where the old Commonwealth capital once stood. This means the memorial we're detecting is the original one, dedicated by Imperial Marines once resistance across human worlds ceased. It's still standing, reminding passers by of the cost of civil war. And it's the only undamaged artifact of human origin left on Earth."

***

Republic of Lyonesse Starship Serenity

Al Jecks shook off the emergence nausea and turned his eyes on the CIC primary display, looking for a closeup of the small blue planet that spawned his species. And he found it at once. Just as the ship's sensors detected, they were not the first to revisit it.

Chief Gill raised his hand.

"Captain, there's a starship in orbit, not even trying to hide. Configuration and emission signature make it Wyvern Hegemony. A cruiser, based on the size and the comparison files brought back from the Torrinos system by *Seeker*."

"The task force is running silent," Lieutenant Commander Salmin said from her usual post on the bridge. "Unless they were watching the precise patch of space where we dropped out of FTL, they shouldn't have spotted us."

"I guess it stands to reason we'd find a Hegemony ship here. This is their backyard."

"Um, sir."

Jecks, who'd known Gill for many years, knew that tone. It meant what he was about to hear next wouldn't be welcome news.

"Yes?"

"I found a sensor ghost at the hyperlimit a quarter of an arc to our starboard on a course around Earth. He's well hidden, but there's a little emission stream, nonetheless, probably stemming from wear and tear after a long time in space. Resembles what we picked up in the Farhaven System."

Jecks and the combat systems officer exchanged a glance. "He's not Hegemony or Lyonesse. That's a given."

"Shrehari," the latter said in a flat tone. "We're the only ones of us around, and another Hegemony ship wouldn't be running silent at the hyperlimit. That's a bit far to provide close support."

"Has to be Shrehari. Could be the one we spotted in the Farhaven System, and he booted it here ahead of us." Jecks paused, eyes on Earth's image. "Or he was trailing that Hegemony cruiser. If we found one, why wouldn't there be others exploring our space? And since the Hegemony is closer to what once was, and still could be the Shrehari Empire, it stands to reason there might be more than a few of their ships surveying this part of our former empire."

"Do you think the Hegemony cruiser is aware of the intruder?" Salmin asked.

"It's possible, but if I picked up something that seems like a Shrehari ship near Earth, I'd go to silent running and hide in one of the Lagrangians while watching what he does." Jecks shook his head. "No. My gut tells me the Hegemony folks don't know they have a stalker."

"With our arrival, make that several stalkers, sir," Salmin replied. "But we can't remain silent forever. Either we twiddle our thumbs waiting for the cruiser to finish his business and leave, or we light up and tell him about what we think is a Shrehari ship. The first option won't be tenable if he's here for a while."

"You think we should go up systems and hail our fellow humans?"

Salmin made a face.

"You know how the old saying goes, sir. I against my brother. I and my brother against my cousin. I, my brother, and my cousin against the world. Or, in this case, we and our Hegemony siblings against the galaxy. As a bonus, if we light up, the intruder will see four human-built ships instead of one and realize trying any shenanigans might be risky."

Jecks turned his eyes on Bree, sitting in her accustomed place at the back of the CIC.

"What's your opinion, Sister?"

"We would learn more by making overtures to representatives of the Wyvern Hegemony this time around than by hiding as we did at Hatshepsut when we first learned of their existence. Remember, the Hegemony commander in the Torrinos system tried to speak with *Seeker* instead of raising shields and powering weapons." She smiled. "And you have full discretion, since we're well beyond any ability to speak with HQ."

"Which is hidden at the ass-end of the universe, as my first cox'n used to say." Jecks rubbed his cheek for a few seconds. "Right. Here goes nothing. Signals, make to all ships, up systems, and open a link on the old imperial emergency band. Make sure *Provider* and *Defiant* are connected. I want their captains to witness this. Then, I'll contact them myself."

—36—

Wyvern Hegemony Starship Alkonost

"Captain, three contacts just lit up at the hyperlimit."

Alexander turned toward his sensor chief. "What?"

"They look like human designs, so maybe Lyonesse." A pause. "No shields, no signs of weapons powering, and no targeting sensor pings."

"Shall we go to battle stations?" Commander Prince's hologram, floating by Alexander's right elbow, asked.

"No." The word came out before Alexander even had time to think. "The last thing we want to do is fight this far from home. We'll match their actions, no more."

"Sir." The CIC signals petty officer of the watch raised her hand. "Incoming link on the old imperial emergency band. The Republic of Lyonesse Void Ship *Serenity*, Captain Al Jecks, commanding, requests a link with the captain of the Wyvern

Hegemony cruiser in orbit around Earth and informs him that we are not alone in this system. A Shrehari ship appears to be loitering in silent running at the hyperlimit."

"What?" Alexander and Taina exchanged an alarmed look. "Accept the link, and if there's video, put it on the main display. And find that Shrehari ship."

Within moments, the image of a lean-faced man in his early forties with a shaved head, black mustache, and intelligent dark eyes appeared. He wore Navy blue battledress with the four stripes and executive curl of a post captain on his collar.

"I'm Al Jecks. I command both the Void Ship *Serenity* and the 101st Task Force, including the replenishment ship *Provider* and the corvette *Defiant*. Our mission is to remap the wormhole network between the Republic of Lyonesse and Earth."

"Derwent Alexander, Captain, of the Wyvern Hegemony cruiser *Alkonost*. I'm on the same sort of mission as you are, but as you can see, without escorts. Now, what's this about a Shrehari ship running silent at the hyperlimit? We've picked up strange sensor ghosts several times, and in several star systems since leaving Hegemony space, ghosts we also believe could be Shrehari."

Jecks raised an extended index finger.

"Stand by for directions to the ghost's current position, Captain. He's leaking emissions like someone who's been out on patrol a little too long. Then you can see for yourself."

A few seconds later, the sensor chief raised his hand. "Got the data, sir. Scanning now."

"So, Captain Jecks, what will we do now?" Alexander asked with a faint but recognizable sardonic smile.

Jecks shrugged. "As far as I know, Wyvern and Lyonesse aren't competing powers, let alone adversaries."

"True."

"Although your lot abducted Void Brethren from Hatshepsut."

Alexander snorted.

"That was the doing of the mission controller, a Commission for State Security colonel named Crevan Torma. Like every other starship captain assigned to the Colonial Service for survey duty, I read the file. Our people in *Repulse* took good care of yours, and I have that from my current first officer, *Repulse*'s second officer at the time, who cared for their well-being. They received VIP treatment aboard her ship and were taken under our Void Reborn Brethren's wing."

"Don't take this the wrong way, but why should I believe you?"

"The abduction was a reaction to discovering we were not alone in surviving, nothing more. We have no reason to harm Void Brethren or anyone else. I'm sure my government will return them when possible. And now that we know of each other's existence and see we're not much different, we should talk." Alexander tapped his rank insignia and pointed at Jecks. "After all, we wear almost the same uniform. Even if we don't fly the same naval ensign, we speak the same language and descend from the same ill-fated Imperial Navy. Though I'll concede your Void Ship, though recognizably of human design, differs from anything we build. Why that name, by the way?"

"A long story, Captain Alexander. It goes back to the years after the empire's collapse, when every surviving ship of the Order of the Void's fleet sought refuge on Lyonesse, bringing the survivors of various purges, pogroms, and massacres. In the following decades, we used Order of the Void Ships to scavenge, explore, rescue, and reconnoiter. From then on, every class of ship built by Lyonesse specifically to venture alone into the wilds of the old empire was called a Void Ship. *Serenity* is merely part of the latest flight designed by our yards."

"Sir." The sensor chief raised his hand. "Got the bastard right where *Serenity* put him. Looks a lot like the ghosts we picked up along the way here. Leaking a bit more, though, so I'd say the Lyonessers are right — it's been out on patrol for too long."

Alexander glanced from his chief back to Jecks. "So, what next?"

Jecks sat back in his command chair and eyed his Hegemony counterpart with a calculating gaze.

"How about we light up the Shrehari as a first step and tell him he and his friends aren't welcome in imperial space? He doesn't need to know the empire is gone and that we serve two different surviving governments, both hard-pressed to reclaim even a fraction of what our species once owned. Ever play poker, Captain Alexander?"

The latter chuckled.

"Our Navy forbids gambling aboard Hegemony ships, but yes. I enjoy a friendly game now and then, strictly for bragging rights. And I know the concept of bluffing. Who gets to speak with the Shrehari on behalf of a united humanity?"

"What's your date of rank based on the old universal calendar?"

When Alexander told him, Jecks grinned.

"You draw the duty, sir. Your date of rank is two standard years ahead of mine. However, it doesn't mean I'm placing myself under your orders."

"Of course not. May I suggest you join us in orbit before tickling the Shrehari's skull ridges? It'll make our pretend unity seem more believable." When Jecks didn't immediately reply, Alexander added, "If you're worried about underhanded business, keep in mind that while we're not as far from home as you are, we still can't play silly buggers and expect to make it back. I'm not quite at the outer limit of my allowed wormhole transits, but almost. A few wormhole termini shifted in this sector over the last two hundred years, making my voyage home just a tad longer than it would have been before the Mad Empress unleashed her Retribution Fleet."

Jecks nodded.

"As my first officer reminded me, there's a proverb about my brother and me against the rest of the universe, and I don't like the idea of non-humans creeping about in our space, whether it be Wyvern, Lyonesse, or not yet reclaimed by either."

"Agreed. I don't know about you, but since I'm beyond my HQ's reach, I have full authority to deal with matters at my discretion. You?"

"The same." A pause. "So, Captain Alexander, do we form an alliance of human naval forces and eject the Shrehari from this star system before jointly exploring Earth?"

Alexander nodded. "We do. Any other course of action would be illogical. I will formalize the matter with a log entry."

"As will I."

The two captains considered one another in silence for a few heartbeats while their respective first officers realized both men were taking each other's measure and liked what they saw.

"In the spirit of mutual trust and cooperation, once we're rid of the Shrehari, I'd like to invite you aboard *Alkonost* for dinner so we can talk face-to-face. Or if you'd rather invite me aboard your ship, that's fine as well." A smile tugged at Alexander's lips. "Or we could meet halfway in our respective shuttles and share a meal in the center of the docking tube."

Jecks let out a bark of laughter.

"That might be a little too odd even for me, and as my first officer can attest, I'm one of the less conventional captains in our Navy. Let me just ask you one question, Captain. Do you still have any wine left in your private stock? Because it seems like my officers drank mine dry."

Alexander nodded.

"A nice red Draconis Grand Cru, one of our better vintages." He sensed Taina gesturing just beyond his line of sight. "Hang on, my ship's counselor wants to say something. What is it, Sister?"

"I would enjoy meeting *Serenity*'s senior Void Sister. If she would be amenable, perhaps I can entertain her while you entertain Captain Jecks."

Alexander turned back to the latter. "What does your ship's counselor say? I assume she's sitting by your side, listening in, just like ours."

Jecks glanced to one side for a few seconds, then said, "Sister Bree accepts the invitation with pleasure, Captain."

"Excellent. But first, let's get rid of that intruder. As soon as you join us, I'll prod him."

***

"Alright." Captain Derwent Alexander, Wyvern Hegemony Guards Navy, squared his shoulders as he took the bridge command chair. "Are all ships linked in?"

"Yes, sir," the signals chief replied. "Interestingly enough, their communications technology and the primary frequencies they use don't differ from ours. Interoperability won't be a problem from that angle. And my counterpart in *Serenity* sounds like a nice guy who knows his stuff."

"We all belonged to one big Navy before the Mad Empress tore humanity apart," Commander Prince remarked in a wistful tone. "I'm glad we can still work together for the common good of our species two centuries later."

Alexander glanced at her and smiled.

"As a wise man once said, there's nothing like an external threat to unite, however briefly, those who would compete for supremacy. But if we develop this bit of cooperation into something more lasting so Hegemony and Republic can co-exist in peace, then so much the better."

"From your lips to the Almighty's ear, sir."

"Let's hope he'll help the Shrehari realize four to one are bad odds."

Alexander turned to his signals chief. "Ready?"

"Yes, sir. Tight beam transmitter zeroed in and tracking. If his communications system follows real space physics, he'll realize we're calling."

"Then put me on."

"Go ahead, sir."

"Shrehari vessel, this is the Imperial Starship *Alkonost*, Captain Derwent Alexander, commanding. You are in our space without permission. Cease hiding and respond." He glanced at the signals chief. "Put it on a loop."

"You think they'll understand Anglic?" Jecks asked.

Alexander shrugged. "Doubtful, but neither you nor I can translate messages into Shrehari."

"A glaring oversight by both our commands. Still, who'd have thought we would find them snooping around in our star systems while we were conducting our own surveys?"

"It's been a long time since any human spoke with them. We forgot we weren't the only star-faring species in this part of the galaxy during our respective time of isolation."

"True." Jecks sat back in his command chair. "While we're waiting, mind telling us how Wyvern survived?"

"It almost didn't. By the way, four of the old imperial core worlds made it — Wyvern, Arcadia, Dordogne, and Torrinos. Simply put, the admirals of the 1st Fleet revolted against Dendera at the last minute and stopped an out-of-control Retribution Fleet before it could wreak utter destruction on our four planets. Draconis, the old capital, was destroyed during the fighting, wiping out the remains of the imperial government and killing Dendera. Those same admirals then set up a military dictatorship to ensure what remained would survive and began rebuilding." Alexander made a face. "We lost nothing, but we fell into a stasis that kept us in our star systems under said dictatorship until the Hatshepsut matter woke up our current government. You might say your republic is responsible for our Hegemony returning to the stars."

"I see. Do you want a thumbnail sketch of Lyonesse's history, or did the abducted Brethren tell the tale?"

Alexander nodded.

"They did. In great detail, perhaps as a way of touting your republic's superiority over our formerly ossified state. But we're catching up." He gave Jecks a crooked smile.

A woman's voice unexpectedly filled the ensuing silence. "Captain Alexander, this is Edith Leung of *Provider*. Pardon me for stepping in, sir. May I ask, is the Hegemony still a military dictatorship?"

"Yes and no. Our former head of state, the Regent, abandoned all military titles and uniforms and is now a civilian President, theoretically co-equal with the other two members of the new Executive Committee. One member is our head of government, the Chancellor, and the other is the head of the Order of the Void Reborn, who has the title Archimandrite. Call it a first step in returning to constitutional rule. Previously, senior Guards and the bureaucracy members formed a conclave that elected the Regent for a defined term of office from among Guards officers wearing four stars. After the experience with Dendera, we consider the idea of a ruler for life anathema.

"Any Regent who refused to step down would have been immediately arrested and likely executed without trial. The conclave still has an interim role in supporting the Executive Committee, but the idea is to turn it into a senate. Whether that senate will have elected members hasn't yet been discussed. In short, our government arrangements at the very top are in flux since we found out about you."

"Fair enough, sir. Thank you."

"I'm sure we'll have plenty of time to exchange information on our respective political arrangements while surveying Earth, Commander Leung."

"I hope so. We have two hundred years of catching up to do."

"Indeed—" Alexander saw the signals chief raise a hand. "Yes?"

"We're receiving a reply, sir. It's incomprehensible."

Alexander turned back to Jecks. "Are you getting this?"

The latter nodded. "Yes. I guess the Shrehari forgot their translation database at home as well. Ah, he just lit up. At least he seems to understand the intent of your message."

"And we finally get a good look at him. CIC, are you seeing this?"

"Yes, sir. That's a Shrehari, alright. The hull architecture closely matches what they fielded during our imperial era, and the markings are definitely Shrehari runes."

Jecks nodded. "My people concur."

"One mystery solved. And we can get that message translated when we reach our respective homes."

"Sirs," *Alkonost*'s combat systems officer said, "the Shrehari lit his drives and is turning away from Earth. No signs of raised shields or powered weapons."

Alexander snorted. "Our counterpart over there figures it's time to make himself scarce. Hopefully, he'll let his high command know he encountered an imperial task force in Earth orbit which didn't appreciate their presence."

"And he just went FTL outbound in the general direction of Wormhole One," the combat systems officer reported.

"Which still leads to Pacifica, in case you were wondering, Captain Jecks. He could be the one whose trace we picked up there. Where he'll go from that system is anyone's guess. A wormhole in the multi-transit branch between Pacifica and Celeste shifted, leaving him dozens of potential escape routes in red dwarf systems." Alexander paused, then smiled. "Or he could look for more of his kind and return in greater numbers."

"Doubtful, but we'll remain alert." Jecks cocked an eyebrow. "Now, you mentioned something about a Draconis Grand Cru?"

"And a meal, though I'm at a loss which one of the three it should be. What clock are you keeping in the Lyonesse Navy? Surely not Wyvern Coordinated Universal Time like us after two centuries on your own."

Jecks shook his head.

"No. We use our own UTC based on the Lyonesse capital, Lannion. It's currently fourteen thirty-five aboard my ships."

"And sixteen-twenty here, so not far off, amusingly enough. Supper it is, then. You and I have much to discuss. When can you come aboard?"

"In ninety minutes?" Though Jecks kept an impassive face, Alexander knew *Serenity*'s captain was just as impatient to meet his opposite number as he was.

"We'll be ready to receive your shuttle on our hangar deck in ninety minutes, Captain."

"Until then."

"*Alkonost*, out."

Jecks' image faded as the signals chief gave the all-clear signal, meaning the links with *Provider* and *Defiant* were also cut.

Alexander stood and glanced at Taina. "Join me in my day cabin, please."

Once the door closed behind them, Alexander asked, "What are your thoughts about Jecks?"

Taina, who seemed a bit tired, dropped into her accustomed chair across from him.

"I sensed caution, which is understandable, intense curiosity, also not unexpected, but no hostility or intent to deceive. I'd say Captain Al Jecks is what you believe yourself to be, Derwent. A professional, conscientious Navy officer who'd rather seek peaceful solutions than confrontation."

"Glad you can confirm my gut instinct about him. He strikes me as a likable sort."

A mischievous smile lit Taina's face.

"You realize he and his Void Sister are likely having the same discussion at this very moment."

"I hope so."

—37—

Wyvern Hegemony Starship Alkonost

Derwent Alexander and Sister Taina, standing behind the hangar deck control room's thick transparent aluminum window, watched the sleek white pinnace with unaccustomed markings pass through the force field. The roundel was a silver anchor superimposed on a golden double-headed bird clutching a scroll inscribed *We Shall Prevail* while the words Republic of Lyonesse ran along the upper part of the pinnace's hull above the insignia and an alphanumeric registration number ran below it along with the name of its mother ship, RLS *Serenity*.

As it gently settled between the facing rows of *Alkonost*'s shuttles, the space doors closed, and the hangar deck petty officer released the inner airlock. Moments later, ten spacers with carbines at the shoulder arms position marched through, led by the bosun who held a silver whistle in her right hand.

Alexander and Taina followed as the bosun dressed her side party in two precise ranks of five by the airlock and then took position on their right flank while the former approached the pinnace.

When the pinnace's aft ramp dropped, and Al Jecks appeared, trailed by Sister Bree, the bosun gave the present arms and raised her whistle to her lips. The trill of the side call echoed through the cavernous compartment while Jecks marched up to Alexander, halted, and raised his hand in a crisp salute.

"Permission to come aboard, Captain."

Alexander returned the compliment with equal precision. "Granted and welcome, Captain."

They shook hands while Taina and Bree formally bowed their heads. Both wore the same dark robes, making it virtually impossible for a casual onlooker to tell who was Order of the Void and who was Void Reborn. Even the captain's shipboard uniforms were so similar — the rank insignia being a case in point — they could have belonged to the same navy if it weren't for Jecks wearing a blue beret and Alexander a black one.

"If you'll follow me." The latter gestured toward the inner airlock.

They fell in step beside each other, the sisters behind them, and as they passed the side party, still at the present arms, both saluted. Once in the passageway, Jecks said, "A lovely reception, Captain. Thank you."

"Do you still practice the fine art of side parties and bosun's whistles in the Lyonesse Navy?"

"Oh, do we ever. I had our Chief of the Defense Staff come aboard just before leaving, and he received a similar welcome, except scaled up for a four-star."

"Glad to hear it." Alexander glanced over his shoulder as they reached the aft lifts. "You might as well go ahead with your guest, Sister Taina."

"Yes, Captain." Taina smiled at Bree and gestured toward the starboard lift door as she touched its call screen. "I thought we might talk in my quarters, which are one deck below the captain's."

Both the port and starboard lifts arrived, and their party split in two.

"Your ship seems familiar yet different," Jecks said as he and Alexander stepped out a few decks higher. "It's an eerie sensation."

"We kept much of the imperial era's styling."

"And we made a deliberate break, although it seems rather superficial, all things considered. I guess form truly follows function, even for starships."

Alexander ushered Jecks into his private quarters' sitting room, where a table for two had been set, and a bottle of Draconis Grand Cru waited on a sideboard, breathing.

Jecks looked around. "Nice. Two compartments?"

"Plus private heads. Rank hath its privileges."

"So, it does. I'm going to miss those."

Alexander gestured at a chair as he reached for the wine bottle. "Is this your last cruise?"

"Yes. With a staff job at the end of it. You?"

"Same." Alexander poured, then took the other chair and raised his glass. "Do you still have toasts of the day, Captain?"

"How about you call me Al?"

"In that case, please call me Derwent or Der if you prefer."

Jecks nodded. "Pleasure. As for toasts of the day, yes, we do."

"What day is it today on your calendar?"

"Monday."

"Funny that — same here. In which case, may I propose we toast our ships?"

Jecks raised his glass as well. "Our ships."

They took a sip, and Jecks made appreciative noises.

"Nice. Very nice. Lyonesse isn't the sort of place where one can grow quality grapes. Many things we humans took with us to the stars don't grow there. It's a great place but hardscrabble in some respects."

"Most of those things grow on Wyvern, though. The wine from its grapes is the best in the Hegemony." Alexander raised his glass again. "Which is why I suspect our distant ancestors chose it as the empire's capital when Earth surrendered the title. Or was made to do so. Your health, Al."

"And yours, Der." Another sip. "You spoke of mysteries — plural — earlier. I'm curious."

"Monuments dating back to the empire's Formation War." When Jecks cocked a questioning eyebrow, Alexander related the story of the memorial on Pacifica. "And there's another one here, on a hilltop just south of where the old Commonwealth seat of government used to be by the shore of Lake Geneva. But unlike the one on Pacifica, which remained dormant until it picked up our sensor sweep, this one was live and radiating emissions when we arrived, meaning someone or something woke it up. Or it's been live non-stop for centuries."

"Interesting. How is Pacifica, by the way?"

"Scattered human life signs, no undamaged structures except for the memorial, lots of debris in orbit. Like every other world the Hegemony surveyed in the last two years. Earth doesn't seem much different, but we've only had time for one full scan. Did you find anything interesting on your travels?"

Alexander took a sip of wine and settled back in his chair.

"Same as you. Destroyed worlds everywhere. Some are entirely depopulated and ripe for colonization by whoever gets there first. We stopped off at Farhaven. Does the name still resonate in the Hegemony?"

At that moment, the door chime rang.

"Ah, here's our meal. Enter." Two spacers, each carrying a tray, stepped in and silently served the two captains. "It's the same thing everyone else aboard is having, but my food preparation people are top-notch. Even after weeks away from home, we eat as if we were ashore."

One spacer smiled and nodded. Then, their job done, both vanished again.

"You were mentioning Farhaven. Yes, it still resonates somewhat. Our Marines observe the anniversary of the Battle of Fort Wagner. Not in the way they did before the first Ruggero emperor forbade military ceremonies that didn't exalt his glorious rule. How about your Marines?"

"The same. I held a commemorative service while we were there to rededicate the memorial and hoist a new flag since the old one vanished long ago. I'll send you a copy of the video we took."

As they ate, Alexander and Jecks compared notes, their voyages, and their respective navy's traditions, discovering they had so much in common that the differences were, as Jecks eventually put it, utterly negligible. By dessert, after finishing the bottle of Draconis Grand Cru, they began planning a joint exploration of Earth and a joint flag raising at the Geneva Monument, claiming the cradle of humanity for both Lyonesse and Wyvern as a sort of co-dominion.

—38—

Once alone in Taina's quarters, the two sisters, sitting face-to-face across a small table, studied each other in silence so long that anyone but a Void adept would have become excruciatingly uncomfortable. But they were using more than just their eyes. After a bit, both relaxed by common accord, and a smile appeared on Bree's face.

"Well met, Sister. Your spirit in the Almighty is as strong as mine."

Taina inclined her head. "Indeed. We both belong to the Infinite Void."

"Is it true our Brethren taken from Hatshepsut are in good health? And that a secular official ordered the abduction without prior approval by the head of the Void Reborn?"

"You may test my mind, Sister. It is true. I personally met with them at the New Draconis Abbey and learned much about how

Lyonesse approaches fallen worlds. They will return to you, with our apologies, of that I have no doubt."

Bree held Taina's gaze for almost a minute, then nodded. "You speak the truth, Sister."

"Always between those of us who serve the Almighty." Taina paused. "A thought occurs to me. Or rather a question. Did the head of your Order, I assume it is still a *Summus Abbatissa*, provide instructions should you meet one of us?"

Another smile. "Did your Archimandrite? A quaint title, by the way. You'll have to explain how a friar came to head the Order of the Void Reborn, but not right now."

A nod. "He did. Those of us traveling beyond the Hegemony were to ensure our captains strove for peaceful dialog if we met any of you."

"Our instructions were the same, almost word for word. Now that we know of each other, our leaders are concerned we don't turn what should be a reunion into a confrontation, notwithstanding what happened on Hatshepsut."

"Neither of us incurred casualties, and you may ask Commander Prince in person about how we treated your Brethren in *Repulse*. She will not lie."

Bree waved away Taina's suggestion. "There is no need. Did you influence your captain when we made our presence known?"

"I may have nudged him and given him extra resolve, but Derwent Alexander is not a man prone to gratuitous violence. He's highly intelligent and well-read and understands how humans can make a total mess of things. I know he's genuinely pleased to greet your captain as an ally rather than a competitor. But I must keep this place's ghosts from burdening his subconscious too much. And you?"

"As I'm sure Al Jecks will tell Captain Alexander, *Serenity* arrived at Hatshepsut when your task force was in orbit. We remained in silent running until they left, so this is not his first encounter with Hegemony forces. Since then, he's developed his own outlook on the matter of two human polities seeking to regain lost worlds, based on his keen understanding of the past and of human nature. He needed little nudging to take the road of peace and cooperation. But I'm also sheltering him from the imprint of the past on this world, so his mind remains unperturbed." Bree paused for a second. "Unfortunately, not everyone in the Republic of Lyonesse shares our views about peaceful relations."

A crooked smile twisted Taina's lips. "You have your own supremacists, I gather?"

Bree nodded. "We do. They're fired up by our current once-a-generation mystic sister, who some claim is a prophet or a visionary or someone with the gift of precognition. Not that she's a supremacist — she's too unworldly for such things. But the Lyonesse First adherents use her words for their own ends."

"We had our own prophet, many decades ago, before my birth, a Sister Jessica who said, among many other fey and vague pronouncements, that the two halves of what was rent asunder will reunite. Few pay attention to her visions nowadays, but Archimandrite Bolack is a believer. However, he doesn't broadcast it for fear our version of your Lyonesse First people seize on Jessica's words to foment a crusade that will lead to clashes with your republic." Taina's smile vanished. "I fear the unofficial alliance between our captains might not be well received by everyone when we get home, let alone formalized on a government-to-government basis. At least not honestly."

"Agreed. Sadly, the actual work of setting humanity on a peaceful path won't be done by those of us who venture out into the unknown, or rather the once known."

Taina bit her lower lip. "I shouldn't say this, but I'm one who devoutly hopes we reunite as equals and rebuild together. Yet even some highly placed people who should know better and heed the Almighty's guidance would undoubtedly see peaceful relations with Lyonesse as a way of gaining time until our strength surpasses yours and we can dictate terms."

"Not that this is a comfort, but we have plenty of those as well. People who believe our sacred mission to preserve human knowledge against the long night of barbarism has morphed into leading all of humanity now that we avoided the long night and dawn might be nearing. They want the same thing — gain time until no one can overcome our strength, especially not the Wyvern Hegemony."

The sisters gave each other knowing looks, and Taina said, "Hopefully, news of the Shrehari roaming through what both our governments consider their sacred heritage will have a salutary effect on the supremacist nonsense."

"The idea that if we don't hang together, we will hang separately? It might be a difficult principle to teach politicians with short term outlooks."

Taina sighed. "Not just politicians, unfortunately."

"Then you and I should make a pact, here and now. We recognized each other as kindred souls the moment we first met. Let us work toward our common goal — turning Wyvern and Lyonesse away from the path of competition and onto that of cooperation until our societies mature sufficiently to accept reunification as equals."

"Agreed."

She stretched her hand out to Bree, and when the latter took it, both closed their eyes, sealing the pact as only trained and talented Sisters of the Void could. By opening their souls to each other.

"Shall we join the rest of the Void Brethren serving in *Alkonost* for the evening meal?" Taina asked once they ended their silent communion.

—39—

Wyvern Hegemony Starship Alkonost

"We got what we could from orbit after three days of four starships surveying every square centimeter." Alexander sat back in his day cabin chair, eyes on the primary display showing Jecks in his day cabin aboard *Serenity*. "But damned if I can figure out where we concentrate our ground surveys. The old imperial ecologists finally have their wish. A mostly depopulated Earth returned to a wild state where nature flourishes in the absence of humans."

"It's a bloody park, that's what it is. A preserve no one visits, no one can enjoy, let alone appreciate. Not that the remaining preindustrial societies have time to contemplate the exquisiteness of the Almighty's creation while the planet is sinking into another ice age. And I'd be wary of calling those particular old-timers something as scientific as ecologists. From my readings, they were zealots whose credentials one could describe as questionable."

"True." Alexander nodded. "If I recall correctly, some even advocated restoring other worlds to their original state along with Earth, meaning ninety percent of humanity had to vanish. Well, they got their wish on that. Not that we have any of the sort in the Hegemony these days. Or if we do, they're staying damned quiet so they don't attract the attention of the Commission for State Security. Our government has little patience with loud, intolerant people upsetting the social balance."

"We have a few of them. But no one pays attention, not when the focus is on growth and expansion. Only inward-looking societies where every need is met can afford to tolerate activists of any stripe. What is it a thinker once said about them long ago?" Jecks scratched his chin. "Ah, yes. Activism is a way for useless people to feel important, even if the consequences of their activism are counterproductive for those they claim to be helping and damaging to the fabric of society as a whole."

Alexander smiled. "I must remember that quote. My friends in the Commission for State Security will probably frame it and hang it in every one of their offices."

Jecks shivered theatrically. "I still can't fathom an advanced society employing something like your State Security organization. It seems so primitive and coarse."

"No arguments here. Fortunately, their attempts at placing officers aboard every starship and in every unit faltered. And now that our government is returning to civilian control, it won't be proposed again, thank the Almighty."

"Maybe you can suggest your President turn the Commission back into what it was, a proper Constabulary whose sole role is investigating interplanetary crime."

Alexander grinned. "We'd have to first delete the entire political crimes section in our criminal code."

"Ugh." Jecks made a face. "The problem with political crimes is that they're whatever the governments want them to be. We've had attempts at criminalizing dissent, meaning whatever speech and ideas the powerful don't like back home, but we roundly slapped those who proposed such laws."

"They'll be back. But enough commiserating. What do we do about boots on the ground exploration?"

"Divvy up the continents between our four ships and let each captain decide where to focus for a week. Then we share everything and head home. Any preference?"

Alexander thought for a moment. "I'll take the Americas."

"Nice choice. I'll take Europe and Africa, *Provider* can take Asia, and *Defiant* can take Oceania and Antarctica."

"Once we're done, I'd like us to copy what you did at Fort Wagner — rededicate the Formation War monument overlooking Lake Geneva. Hold a joint ceremony and hoist both of our flags, music and all. Our cox'ns can get together and plan it. Video of the event will create a row back in New Draconis." Alexander smirked. "And hopefully make the people in power think about where they're taking us."

"Oh, and in Lannion as well. Yes, we will end our mission that way, my friend. Remind humanity's leaders there's more that brings us together than keeps us apart."

***

"That was a lovely meal," Sister Taina said in a wistful tone once *Alkonost*'s pinnace cleared *Serenity*'s space doors and turned aft toward its mother ship. "A shame we'll probably never meet again in this life."

"Oh, I wouldn't be too sure of that," a contented Derwent Alexander replied. "But Al Jecks does set a splendid table, and it was nice to finally meet Edith Leung and Yannick Petrov in person. Good people. How about the Void coven's private dinner?"

"Coven?" Taina snorted with amusement. "You mistake us for those who pretend to be something they're not."

"Witches?"

"Deluded folk. There is no such thing as witches. Never was. To answer your question, the Old Order Brethren do not differ from the Void Reborn at heart, which I already knew from spending time with our Lyonesse guests in the New Draconis Abbey. We're but one half of a whole that deserves to heal."

"I daresay we naval officers found the same sort of kinship." Alexander fell silent as he parsed his thoughts. "A shame Earth was no different from any other fallen world we've visited. Apart from the atavistic memories of our species' planet of origin — sights, sounds, scents, and the sense we were on our true home — there's nothing that differentiates it from any other human world destroyed by the Retribution Fleet."

"Except the original Formation War memorial overlooking Lake Geneva, the model for the others on worlds that suffered mass casualties because the Commonwealth elite refused to surrender."

Alexander nodded. "Other than the memorial. I think we did our ancestors proud with the joint ceremony, though. And the flag raising."

Taina smiled at him. "Without a doubt. Maybe we even put some ancient ghosts to rest."

"Ghosts angry that after a thousand years of peace and stability, we damn near wiped our species out — yet again? I sure hope so. But I think they won't rest easy until we come together as one without quarreling. Too bad Sister Jessica's vision didn't specify how we would reunite. And where that movement would start. Otherwise, we could claim it was coming true." Alexander let out a soft sigh. "You know, I'll miss Al Jecks. I found it easier to speak with him on so many subjects than with my Guards Navy peers."

"Because he's both so much like them, but not part of the same structure and hierarchy. I daresay he thinks the same. Sister Bree and I also found common ground I'd be hard-pressed to explore with most of my Void Reborn Brethren."

"Good. The more of us who see a future without conflict, the better our chances of making it so."

"Tell me something, Derwent."

"Yes?"

"How did your subconscious perceive Earth?"

Alexander thought about her question for a good long while, then said, "I suppose it made me sad, just like Pacifica and Celeste after contemplating the death and destruction. But you know what? After the memorial rededication ceremony, it was as if someone had lifted a weight from my soul."

"Then maybe the ghosts of Earth truly are now at peace."

***

"Well, this is it, Derwent." Al Jecks gave his counterpart and now friend a sad smile as they made their farewells over a private channel, each alone in his own day cabin. "I've enjoyed our joint survey and how we made common purpose. Hopefully, our political masters will approve."

"Our political masters will have a fit at hearing the Shrehari are surveying our star systems before we can even reclaim them." Alexander grimaced. "But once they get over the initial scare, they'll revert to type, I'm afraid."

"True. Still, one can always pray they'll listen to reason and open honest lines of communication between Lyonesse and Wyvern rather than pursue costly dreams of unattainable supremacy. You're heading straight home?"

"Yes. We'll stop at Celeste, check on the mission, and then at Santa Theresa. Now that we've remapped the wormhole branch, it won't be as long a trip. You?"

"Oh, definitely, though my trip will take longer. I'm thinking about replicating, at least in part, Jonas Morane's voyage across the empire with the 197th Battle Group's remains. A sort of memorial to the courage and determination of his people, if you want. We'll reach Lyonesse long after you've docked at Wyvern. And on that note, it's time we break out of Earth's orbit."

"Fair winds and following seas, my friend." Derwent Alexander raised his hand.

"To you as well. It's been fun. *Serenity*, out."

The display darkened, leaving Alexander to stare at nothing, wondering how the Hegemony government and his superiors would perceive his actions. Finally, he stabbed his communicator with an extended index finger.

"Captain to the bridge."

"Officer of the watch here, sir."

"Break out of orbit and set a course for Wormhole Earth One. We're going home."

—40—

Wyvern

"You called us, sir?" Brigadier General Crevan Torma, with Sister Ardrix on his heels, appeared in the open door to Admiral Godfrey's office.

"Yes. Come in, both of you, and sit. We've just received a subspace message from *Alkonost*. She's in the Santa Theresa system on her way home from Earth. Captain Alexander's mission report is intriguing, to say the least, and we must discuss how we should deal with his findings and his actions before Admiral Benes and I decide what we'll tell the President in two hours. The future of our path back to the stars may well depend on it."

"How ominous," Ardrix said as she took her accustomed chair across from Godfrey alongside Torma.

"I read the executive summary, but since you two are responsible for our discovering Lyonesse's existence and triggering the Hegemony's rebirth as an interstellar power, it's only fair we watch Derwent Alexander's full report together."

Godfrey touched his desk, and the primary display on the wall to his right lit up with the Wyvern Hegemony's phoenix and sword. All three turned toward it and settled in comfortably while the crest vanished, replaced by Alexander's open, honest face.

"The following is Wyvern Hegemony Guards Navy Starship *Alkonost*'s survey mission report from when she left Celeste to her arrival in the Santa Theresa system on the return trip. Concerning our primary objective, finding the wormhole branch to Earth and surveying it, mission accomplished."

Godfrey, Torma, and Ardrix exchanged appreciative looks but remained silent as the report delved into the details of the journey. When Alexander's face faded out, replaced by the Hegemony's sigil, Ardrix let out a soft whistle.

"There is so much to unpack that I barely know where to begin."

"How about we start with the reaction to news the Shrehari have been exploring human star systems for who knows how long?" Torma suggested in a tone that could be interpreted as mildly droll. "I believe the President, the Executive Committee, and the Hegemony's senior leadership will experience an intense, collective nerve spasm. Especially when they hear the addendum from the Celeste Mission about Shrehari picking a former imperial research station clean of everything, including the last bit of wire, *while our people were there*."

Godfrey smiled at his inspector general.

"There's no way of softening the blow on that point, Crevan. I foresee the President and the Service Chiefs asking for a more rapid expansion of our fleet. That will be followed by the Chancellor bemoaning a radical increase in defense spending because it will trigger another inflationary cycle since our workforce and production capacity are already proving insufficient. No." Godfrey shook his head. "I'm not so much worried about the reaction to news of the Shrehari.

"Considering we've been at peace with them since a century before the empire's formation, I doubt they'll try annexing worlds with human populations. Until I see proof to the contrary, I'll chalk up their intrusions as curiosity about our fate. And I will make sure every damn ship in the fleet carries a Shrehari language database from now on. What a missed opportunity. I'll send their message to Naval Intelligence and get a translation before Sandor and I speak with the President, but I suspect it'll be nothing more than excuse us for trespassing."

"You're right, sir. The Shrehari won't be our biggest problem, not in the short term. No, the more immediate and bigger problem will come from Derwent Alexander and his Lyonesse counterpart making nice and claiming Earth as a co-dominion on behalf of both governments. There will be many high-ranking individuals in our government who'll cast a jaundiced eye on unauthorized diplomacy carried out by a naval officer who exceeded his orders. I know the belief will be that Wyvern acknowledged Lyonesse as an equal rather than asserting her primacy as the legitimate heir of empire."

Ardrix nodded. "Crevan is correct. And it gets worse. Consider the video of the memorial rededication ceremony and the symbolism of the double-headed condor and the phoenix, two mythical birds some believe closely related, side-by-side. The only visible differences between the honor guard from *Alkonost* and that from the Lyonesse task force were the color of the berets, the insignia on them, and the pattern of the weapons they carried. The rest — uniforms, rank insignia, drill movements, commands — were virtually identical. A Shrehari observer would almost certainly have concluded they were part of the same armed forces. Something they obviously did when *Alkonost* painted their ship with her tight beam comms emitter."

Torma let out a soft snort. "Most Hegemony citizens wouldn't be able to tell the difference, either. And they won't when the video leaks, which it will. Once that happens, a large swath of the population, at least those who pay attention, will realize two hundred years of separation made little difference. Though we live in polities with disparate government systems, we're still the same species, with the same interests, longings, ambitions, and beliefs. Most folks will think we were once united and should become so again, especially if the Shrehari are eying our space with predatory glee. And they won't care how we do it. Alexander and his counterpart playing nice is just the thing to make them feel warm thoughts."

"Which won't please the supremacists," Ardrix said. "Not even within my Order, where many believe the Void Reborn should absorb the Old Order and bring it into the present."

"An interpretation of Sister Jessica's prophecy, which could be incorrect."

Godfrey let his eyes rest on each of them. "So, what advice do Admiral Benes and I give the President? Crevan?"

"We know she's prepared to open formal diplomatic relations with Lyonesse, as per the message passed to their people in the Hatshepsut system by Evan Kang when *Aethon* dropped off the Old Order Brethren."

"On her terms, not Derwent Alexander's terms."

"Clearly, sir. But disavowing Alexander would send the wrong message. We're not strong enough to act on the desires of those who want reunification with Wyvern reigning supreme. Lyonesse most probably isn't strong enough either. That leaves us with no choice other than being nice while we consolidate our position."

Godfrey made a wry face. "And while they consolidate theirs."

"Furthermore, nothing that happened on Earth limits the government's freedom of action now or in the future, unless those who object to Alexander's impromptu alliance corner the President with demands of disavowal."

Ardrix chuckled. "Vigdis Mandus isn't the sort who gets cornered."

"No, perhaps not in the literal sense, but by creating a stink, those who want Wyvern to reign supreme will force her hand. Best if she outmaneuvers any opposition by declaring her public support of Alexander's actions, thanking him personally, and seeing he makes this year's commodore list. At the same time, she should send a diplomatic delegation aboard a civilian starship to Hatshepsut and announce publicly she's done so. That'll make any dissenters seem foolish if they object too loudly."

"But it won't make them go away." Godfrey rubbed his chin, eyes narrowed in thought, as his gaze wandered to a favorite painting hanging on the opposite wall. It depicted one of the good emperors decorating a naval rating in front of his shipmates on what used to be the imperial parade ground at the heart of old Draconis. "Thank you for that. Your advice matches what I've been thinking. I hope Admiral Benes will agree."

"He's no Wyvern supremacist, as far as I can tell, sir," Ardrix said.

"Indeed, but perhaps only because he knows we won't be strong enough to assert ourselves for several generations." Godfrey turned his eyes back on her. "Now that there are Shrehari in the mix, the political equation has shifted. How far and in what direction? Only time will tell."

Godfrey's office communicator chimed at that moment, and he glanced at the call screen.

"Speak of the devil, and he appears." A quick touch and Admiral Benes' face replaced the Hegemony sigil on the primary display. "Hello, Sandor. I was discussing Derwent Alexander's report with Crevan Torma and Ardrix."

"Hello, Johannes. And hello to you too, Crevan and Ardrix. You've decided on recommendations for the President by now, I suppose?"

"We have. But I'm curious about your thoughts before I tell you ours. Would you prefer Crevan and Ardrix to leave us in private?"

"No. After all, they're our resident experts on Lyonesse."

"Until Captain Alexander gets home, sir," Torma said.

"Did you know he was the sort who'd enter an informal alliance with what many in the armed forces consider our competitors, Sandor?"

Benes let out a bark of laughter.

"You give me too much credit as a visionary. No. But I knew he would take the most sensible path in any situation. I'm not surprised he acted as he did. By the way, he and that Jecks character did a good job at the Formation War memorial above Lake Geneva. The Chief Petty Officer of the Navy will approve once he sees the video and will give *Alkonost*'s coxswain a Bravo Zulu that'll land on the latter's next performance evaluation. By the way, I'm surprised there are more of those on the old core worlds."

"Wherever Commonwealth diehards took as many imperial troops with them as possible. Too bad we forgot the lessons immortalized by those monuments. So, your thoughts on recommendations for the President."

"Get ahead of the inevitable debate about Wyvern's place as leading human reunification, declare what Alexander did on Earth as supporting government policy, then reach out to Lyonesse and formally cement the friendship Alexander and Jecks developed. Send a diplomatic mission to Hatshepsut in a few weeks once their task force is back home and the Lyonesse government can decide on their next steps."

Godfrey chuckled. "It seems we're in complete agreement. That bodes well, especially since Vigdis embodies the old quip that the true measure of intelligence is the ability to change. I suppose we might as well put our own choice for ambassador forward and get ahead of the Chancellor, who'll have his candidate, someone beholden to him personally." He glanced at Torma. "What would you say if I propose we recommend Crevan lead the diplomatic mission as ambassador plenipotentiary? We know we can trust him implicitly — he has no personal ambitions, he's a loyal servant of the Hegemony, and he will tread where even the bravest fear to go if it's for the good of Wyvern."

"Sir?" The word came out slightly off-key as if Godfrey's suggestion stuck in Torma's craw.

"Oh, we'll transfer you to the inactive reserve list and you'll become a civil servant answerable directly to the President, since she'll take over relations with Lyonesse in person." Godfrey glanced at Benes, whose eyes were dancing with amusement. "What do you think, Sandor? Get ahead of the game and put our man in place. We can always make him a major general once his time as ambassador is over."

A frowning Torma sat up even straighter than before, something Godfrey didn't know was possible.

"Sirs, with due respect, I ordered the abduction of eight Lyonesse Brethren. I'm hardly the sort of person they'd want back on one of their worlds."

Godfrey waved Torma's objections away.

"We returned them with our apologies. You treated them with respect. And they learned much about us during their stay, so no harm done. These things happen."

Ardrix reached out and touched Torma's forearm.

"I can't think of a better choice for the good of the Hegemony. And I volunteer to accompany Crevan as his chief of staff."

"Can the Order put your status as Sister of the Void on the inactive Brethren reserve?" Benes asked.

A brief peal of laughter wafted across Godfrey's office.

"We don't place Brethren on the reserve list, but I can be temporarily relieved of my vows for a specific purpose, so long as that purpose is for the betterment of the Order. And that's something only Archimandrite Bolack can authorize."

"One step at a time, Sandor. We agree about proposing Crevan as ambassador?"

"Definitely. Better our dour State Security investigator than one of the Chancellor's ever so slick deputy secretaries, someone who knows his or her path to glory is assured by keeping Conteh happy."

—41—

Lannion
Republic of Lyonesse

"Madame President." Admiral Norum took one step into Hecht's office and bowed his head instead of saluting since he was bareheaded.

"What brings you here at this late hour and under such a cloak of secrecy?" She gestured at the chairs in front of her desk.

"We just received a full report from Captain Al Jecks. He is, or at least was, in the Parth system when he pushed it into the subspace network. You'll be happy to hear Task Force 101 reached Earth and is on the way home in good order. No injuries, let alone fatalities, and no damage to the ships other than wear and tear. And a hell of a story. Fortunately, Jecks coded his transmission for my eyes only."

Hecht gave him a curious stare. "Fortunately?"

"You'll understand once you listen to his entire report, Madame."

She glared at him. "What did I tell you about formalities between us when we're alone, Farrin?

"Sorry. Aurelia." Norum's expression showed no contrition as he retrieved a data chip from his tunic pocket. "Can you put the contents of this on your office display, please?"

Hecht held out her hand. "Give here, you incorrigible formalist."

An hour later, as Al Jecks' face faded from the office display, Aurelia Hecht sat back in her chair and let out a long sigh.

"Wow. Okay, now I get why you're glad it was for the Chief of the Defense Staff's eyes only. That's bloody explosive. The Shrehari playing around in our space?"

"Right now, it's more accurate to say the Hegemony's space," Norum replied with a sardonic smile. "Or rather their immediate neighborhood. Nice rededication ceremony at the Geneva Formation War memorial, though. I thought the Wyvern people looked sharp in their black berets."

"The only immediately visible difference between their personnel and ours," Hecht growled. "Same uniforms, rank insignia, drill movements, commands. That'll cause waves in the cabinet and the senate."

"Finding out that a competitor you'd love to hate isn't much different from yourself always does. Watching their and our flags flying over the memorial will rile our Lyonesse First adherents, though. And if you're not careful, they can cause a lot of trouble."

"No need to warn me, my friend. I expect a blow-up once Captain Jecks' actions become common knowledge. I daresay some of the more radical Lyonesse First loudmouths will accuse him of treason, among other nasty things."

"Loudmouths who don't understand we're in no position to run roughshod over the Hegemony and declare ourselves the legitimate heir of the empire, especially since the people on Wyvern surely believe they're the heirs and we could only be junior partners in the reunification effort. We may never become sufficiently strong to dictate terms because they're doing as we are — rebuilding, expanding, reoccupying old imperial star systems. And that political calculus must account for the Shrehari. By the way, I'm having their message translated by intelligence as we speak."

Norum scratched his cheek as he contemplated his old friend.

"Move tonight, Aurelia. Stay ahead of the troublemakers. Release a communique that summarizes Jecks' report and enthusiastically endorses his actions on Earth. Paint a rosy picture of Jecks and his Hegemony friend Alexander as they surveyed Earth together — comrades in arms, brothers, that sort of thing. Too bad Al's just got a promotion because giving him a step up early on the strength of his achievements would have been perfect public relations. Maybe I can find him a plum assignment for his tour ashore.

"And announce you're sending a full diplomatic mission to Wyvern. After all, they left the door open when they returned our Brethren healthy and unharmed and filled with useful intelligence about the Wyvern Hegemony's society, its politics, and their Order of the Void Reborn."

"Since we're making government policy on the fly, without cabinet involvement, let alone the senate's advice and consent, who should lead our delegation to Wyvern?"

A knowing smile lit up Norum's face.

"Currag DeCarde. He's a servant of the republic and not his personal ambitions. He can be on his way within days aboard one of Hatshepsut Squadron's ships. According to his last report, he launched the Theban expansion into Aksum and Thebes itself is modernizing as fast as humanly possible. Most importantly, the Theban government willingly accepted the guidance of a Lyonesse proconsul who promised them the stars. I'd say most of his work there is done. Another ambassador, who doesn't have quite as powerful a personality, can take over now."

"Yes, I read that report. Bringing the Theban President and his senior officials up to visit Hatshepsut Station was a stroke of genius. They now know what's almost in their grasp as long as they keep working with us. Very well. Currag DeCarde, it shall be. Prepare orders detaching one of Hatshepsut Squadron's corvettes as a diplomatic courier. I'll write up credentials and confidential instructions for DeCarde."

"And the communique?"

She nodded. "And the communique, with Martin's help. But before anything goes out, I'll have to brief the Vice President and the cabinet. Otherwise, there will be a lot of sore faces around the table, whether or not they're Lyonesse First sympathizers."

"Early tomorrow?"

"Yes. But not too early. I'll call a cabinet meeting for eleven-hundred hours. That'll give me enough time to get everything done and enjoy a good night's sleep."

***

Aurelia Hecht saw Vice President Derik Juska's face harden with growing anger as he and the cabinet secretaries watched Al Jecks' report. By the time they reached the joint memorial rededication ceremony, with the republic's double-headed condor flag flapping in the breeze beside the Hegemony's phoenix, she thought he was working himself into a case of apoplexy.

Had he genuinely become a Lyonesse First believer? She'd always figured him as more of a pragmatist who was using the movement to expand his political base and differentiate himself from rivals when the presidency became vacant.

At the conclusion of the report, Juska turned a harsh glare on Admiral Norum.

"What the hell was Jecks playing at on Earth? The President and her cabinet make policy, not some junior post captain with delusions of grandeur. His actions could jeopardize the republic's future dealings with the Hegemony."

Juska spat out the last word as if it were a foul-tasting morsel of food.

Hecht mentally rolled her eyes. It was going to be as unpleasant a cabinet meeting as she feared.

"What would you rather he'd done, Mister Vice President? Trigger an interstellar war over who claims Earth? Never mind, we're in an even worse position than the Hegemony to enforce such a claim."

Juska's nostrils flared as he clamped down on his anger.

"Take care with your tone, Admiral. You serve at the pleasure of the republic's Executive Branch."

"Yes, sir."

Those who knew him well understood Norum was not contrite, but after staring at him a few seconds longer, Juska turned back to Hecht.

"My apologies, Madame President, but I fear for our future if commanders on missions beyond our subspace network engage in unauthorized diplomacy according to their whims and without a full understanding of the second and third-order effects."

"What's done is done, Derik. Our job is dealing with what happens next. The following is a communique I will issue this afternoon. It presents this administration's intentions concerning our future relations with the Wyvern Hegemony. I will not debate the communique's wordings or contents. It goes out as is. If you cannot, in all conscience, support my policies, I would ask for your resignations forthwith."

Hecht indicated the cabinet room's primary display.

"Listen carefully because you will support me fully and with no mental reservations whatsoever if you stay. And if afterward you do not understand why I've decided on this policy, then perhaps I should reconsider your continued fitness as cabinet secretaries."

Norum watched the startled, alarmed, and even resentful expressions in the eyes of the men and women around the table. Aurelia Hecht, like Currag DeCarde, was a forceful personality at the best of times, but she'd never been this harsh and direct with people she'd handpicked save for the Vice President.

They watched a recording of her issuing the communique in silence, though more than a few glanced at each other several times. When her image faded, Hecht looked around the table.

"Captain Jecks' report and what you just saw are embargoed until I release them. Any government official or Defense Force member who leaks the slightest bit before then will be dismissed with prejudice and no appeal. And if any of you have friends or acquaintances sympathetic to the Lyonesse First movement," she held Juska's eyes for a heartbeat, "please tell them I will not brook any opposition to my policy about the Wyvern Hegemony. Our constitution gives the President sole authority over relations with other states. That clause hasn't been needed so far, but it is now in force. And until further notice, I am my own foreign affairs secretary. Questions?"

When no one said a word or so much as twitched, Hecht stood. "Thank you."

Then, she swept out of the room like a battleship of old under full sail. The moment she vanished from sight, the cabinet secretaries, clearly repressing words they couldn't speak within hearing of the Chief of the Defense Staff, President Hecht's closest friend and confidant, filed out one after the other until only Norum and Juska remained.

"Tell you what, Admiral," the latter said in a conversational tone that couldn't mask his anger. "If I become the next President, your term as CDS is over. And none of your recommendations as a replacement will get the job. Nor will said replacement sit at the cabinet table as if he or she was more than a mere servant of the administration, who takes orders and carries them out instead of playing gray eminence and whispering policy proposals in the President's ear. Because that's you, isn't it — Aurelia's intentions, the wording of her communique, and the rest of the bullshit?"

"Believe it or not, Mister Vice President, I merely took Captain Jecks' report to her last night. She decided based on what she heard and set her policy vis-à-vis Wyvern by herself." Norum adjusted his blue beret on his head. "By the way, sir. You won't become the next President. I can guarantee that. Cozying up to the Lyonesse First nut jobs now will sink any chance you have. It may be two centuries since humanity self-destructed. However, the citizens of our republic still remember, and they have no appetite for confrontation when there's the possibility of peaceful cooperation. So, what if there are two human states going forward? So long as they're friendly toward each other, our species will flourish once more. Jeopardizing even such a possibility? Now that's what I call treason, sir, not against Lyonesse but against humanity. Have a good day."

Derik Juska stared at the cabinet room doorway for a long time after Norum's departure, wondering whether that faint feeling in the pit of his stomach was because Hecht and her pet admiral had just done an end-run around his political ambitions. But he'd become Vice President because he was a scrapper, someone who made quick work of his opponents, and both Hecht and Norum were yesterday's news. Their terms of office would end while his rise continued.

— 42 —

Hatshepsut

"Sir, a ship came through Wormhole Two a few minutes ago. She's broadcasting a beacon on the old imperial emergency band, identifying herself as the Wyvern Hegemony Diplomatic Transport *Eirene*. Her captain requests permission to approach Hatshepsut, so Ambassador Crevan Torma may speak with the Republic of Lyonesse's senior government official in this star system."

"Ambassador?" Jonas Morane's eyebrows shot up. "Wasn't the man who abducted the Brethren a police general called Crevan Torma?"

"I can look it up if you want, sir," the operations center duty officer replied.

"Don't bother. Tell him he can jump inward but stay at the hyperlimit until he gets further instructions."

"Yes, sir."

"Morane, out."

He sat back and stared at the display showing Hatshepsut in all its glory below them. Funny that a Hegemony ambassador showed up not long after Ambassador DeCarde received orders to head for Wyvern and present his credentials to their President. Synchronicity? Or a message from the Almighty? But since he was still here, Morane supposed DeCarde was the senior Lyonesse government official who should speak with this Torma.

"Communications."

"Sir," a voice replied moments later.

"Get me a link with Ambassador DeCarde. If he's not available, leave a message that I would like a moment of his time as soon as possible."

"Yes, sir."

Only five minutes had passed when DeCarde's face appeared on Morane's office display.

"Your call sounded urgent, Lucas. What's up?"

"Seems like the Hegemony is a few steps ahead of us, Ambassador. There's a civilian transport from Wyvern inbound, carrying their ambassador. A man by the name Crevan Torma."

"Brigadier General Crevan Torma? Sister Hermina's captor?"

"No rank was given, sir, but he wishes to speak with the senior Lyonesse government official in this system."

DeCarde nodded. "To arrange for safe passage, no doubt. Well, his unexpected arrival solves a few problems. When the ship drops out at the hyperlimit, by all means, hammer it with your sensors and either allow it to dock or enter orbit. I'll come up with my staff an hour before they arrive. Once they're here, invite Ambassador Torma and his staff aboard the station, where he and I will discuss arrangements."

"Yes, Ambassador."

A calculating smile tugged at DeCarde's lips.

"How'd you like to send that corvette to Lyonesse instead of Wyvern?"

"I'd be much happier."

"Let's see if Torma is a man who'll take a few risks in the service of his government."

Morane's eyes lit up.

"You propose taking his ship back to Wyvern while my corvette transports him to Lyonesse?"

"Or part of the way there if we can arrange for someone else to take him on once he reaches the Coalsack. That way, you won't be short a ship for long."

"A most excellent idea, sir."

DeCarde tapped the side of his head with an extended index finger and winked.

"That's why we ambassadors get such a magnificent salary in the republic's service."

Morane chuckled. "I think it's more the crafty old Marine Pathfinder at work than the diplomat."

"As my former sergeant major used to say, if it's a dumb idea and it works, it ain't dumb."

***

Eirene's main airlock opened with a loud sigh, and Crevan Torma stepped out into a large docking tube whose austere appearance clearly marked it as multi-use here on a station at the far end of Lyonesse space. He still wasn't quite used to his formal, high collared dark business suit, nor had he become accustomed to Ardrix wearing a feminine version of it rather than monastic robes or a Hegemony uniform.

A naval officer with captain's stripes on his collar appeared at the station end of the tube and saluted him, a gesture he returned with a measured bow of the head.

"Ambassador Torma, I'm Lucas Morane, commanding officer of the Lyonesse Navy's Hatshepsut Squadron. Welcome aboard my station."

"Thank you for your courtesy, Captain." He gestured at Ardrix. "This is my chief of staff, Ardrix Moore. I bring five additional envoys with me, but they'll remain aboard *Eirene*."

Torma had been a tad nonplussed when Ardrix showed up for work with a last name and wearing civilian clothes after being temporarily relieved of her vows before leaving Wyvern. He'd never considered the Brethren once had such things, but she'd been born into the Moore family of New Draconis.

Morane inclined his head toward her in greeting. "Welcome, Envoy Moore."

"Thank you, Captain."

"If you'll follow me, Ambassador Currag DeCarde and his chief of staff are waiting to discuss your respective appointments in my conference room."

"Respective appointments?" Torma asked, falling into step beside Morane.

"He's currently the Lyonesse ambassador to the Theban Republic, Hatshepsut's leading state, but has just been named the republic's ambassador to the Wyvern Hegemony. Your arrival here is quite fortuitous."

A faint smile crossed Torma's lips.

"My government hoped I would arrive after yours had digested the 101st Task Force's survey report and decided it would expand on the cooperative spirit shown by our respective captains."

"If I may ask, sir, is this your first visit to Hatshepsut?"

This time, Torma's smile was anything but faint.

"No, as I'm sure you're aware. Ardrix and I have old acquaintances here — unless they went elsewhere after their repatriation."

"All eight are still here and have resumed their duties."

"Good to hear, Captain. They may have been involuntary guests, but we hold them in high esteem, not least for the grace and serenity with which they accepted their temporary change of circumstances."

They took circular stairs up two decks, then walked down a corridor as bare as any other part of the station they'd seen so far. Nothing more than alphanumeric designators on various doors broke the monotony, and Torma couldn't identify what lay behind them. Finally, they reached an open one, and Morane ushered them through.

"Ambassador DeCarde," he announced formally, "may I present Ambassador Torma and Chief of Staff Moore, representing the Wyvern Hegemony. Ambassador Torma, Ambassador DeCarde and Chief of Staff Hermina Ruttan."

A fit-looking, middle-aged man wearing a suit not that different from Torma's climbed to his feet, imitated by a similarly dressed woman whose familiar face elicited a smile. Another example of synchronicity?

Both ambassadors shook hands while their respective chiefs of staff sized each other up, eyes dancing with suppressed amusement.

"I believe you know my chief of staff?" DeCarde asked as he invited Torma and Ardrix to sit at the conference table with a hand gesture.

"She was a guest at the New Draconis Abbey thanks to our actions."

Hermina snorted. "A prisoner in a gilded cage more like, General. And you, Ardrix, did you renounce your vows and can no longer be called Abomination?"

"I've been relieved of them temporarily so I could serve Ambassador Torma, but I still belong to the Order. And you?"

"The same. Ambassador DeCarde sought me out when he was appointed to Wyvern and suggested I join his staff. My *Summus Abbatissa* approved and lifted my vows for the duration."

DeCarde smiled expansively.

"Diplomacy is always easier when the people involved have prior connections, no matter how tenuous, don't you think, Ambassador Torma? The idea of appointing a Sister of the Void as a principal staff member to both our delegations will help as well. The fact our superiors came up with it separately bodes well."

Torma smiled back.

"I know Chief of Staff Ruttan's friends will welcome her back with open arms on Wyvern. And you, sir, will be equally welcomed by President Vigdis Mandus as the representative of Lyonesse. After what Captains Alexander and Jecks accomplished together, she looks forward to receiving the republic's representative."

"And it will please President Hecht to receive you, Ambassador Torma. Your arrival now is extremely fortuitous."

"How so?"

"May I suggest we simplify our transportation arrangements in the spirit of our navies' cooperation on Earth?"

"Please." Torma gestured at DeCarde to explain.

"I was to take one of our ships, and you were to make the entire trip aboard yours. How about I travel in your ship with my delegation? Meanwhile, you and yours take the one put at my disposal by Captain Morane?"

Torma nodded. "A brilliant notion, Ambassador. I wholeheartedly approve."

"Then, if *Eirene* is ready for the return voyage, I'm impatient to reach my new post on your world. I know Captain Morane's designated ship can leave at any time."

"In that case," Torma turned his smile on Morane, "I can only thank you for your courtesy and hospitality, however brief it is. We can shift over as soon as your ship is ready, sir. And I'll speak with *Eirene*'s captain the moment we're finished here. She'll depart at your convenience, Ambassador DeCarde."

"Excellent. A good start to what I hope will be a long and fruitful relationship between our people."

"In that vein, we translated the Shrehari message recorded by our people, and my government asked that I pass it along to your government."

DeCarde inclined his head. "A gracious gesture. We also translated it. I'm curious if our respective analysts came up with the same wording."

"This is our interpretation." Torma, who'd clearly memorized the message, intoned, "I am Commander Greth of the Imperial survey cruiser *Qal Vuch,* and I apologize for intruding into space claimed by our old ally, the glorious human empire. I will depart immediately."

"We still use the same translation database, it seems. I wonder what the Shrehari made of finding our respective ships navigating star systems they found empty or sparsely populated by preindustrial societies."

Torma shrugged. "I couldn't say. Perhaps one day, a human ambassador will travel to their home world and re-establish diplomatic relations. Then we might know."

"Indeed. I'm impatient to get on with my voyage to your capital, Ambassador. Unless there are other matters we should discuss, I suggest we swap starships and head out."

—43—

Lannion
Republic of Lyonesse

Ambassador Crevan Torma and his chief of staff, Ardrix Moore, sitting on a patch of grass, watched the sunset over the western Middle Sea from a vantage point high above Lannion. The armed forces base was several kilometers to the west, its polished cliff side still bathed in light while the tarmac, where three of Lyonesse's intriguing corvettes sat in silence, slowly welcomed the twilight.

"A beautiful world in its own right, isn't it?" Ardrix said in a soft voice. Like Torma, she wore light yet elegant civilian clothes and was unrecognizable as a Sister of the Void temporarily relieved of her vows.

They chose this spot not just for the vista it offered but also because they could speak openly without being overheard.

Somehow, after seeing the state of Lyonesse technology compared to that of the Hegemony, Torma didn't entirely trust their Wyvern manufactured portable jammers to block the unseen eyes and ears their hosts had undoubtedly set in both the residence and the embassy office. Out here, the jammers would more easily frustrate spy gear working from a distance.

"Yes. But no more or less so than Wyvern." Torma turned his head toward her and smiled. "Though the people are rather different in many ways. Did you notice not everyone in President Hecht's cabinet is pleased by our arrival? Vice President Juska in particular, I'd say."

"Oh, I noticed. In more ways than one." Ardrix gave him a knowing smile. "Juska definitely dislikes us and would rather we spontaneously disintegrate. The Defense Secretary as well."

"They must be supporters of this Lyonesse First movement we heard about."

She nodded.

"Supremacists, yes. I daresay they'll be our greatest adversaries and will look for ways to disrupt our efforts to establish long-term, friendly relations."

Torma let out a soft sigh.

"I'm just waiting for someone to point out Wyvern had the poor taste of sending a retired political police general as an ambassador and a Void Sister who also worked for State Security. That should go over well in a place where the citizens take pride in their constitution and its limits on government."

Both he and Ardrix had spent their time aboard first Morane's corvette, then a frigate detached from the Yotai Squadron, studying everything about Lyonesse in those portions of the ship's database made available by the captains. Several Lyonesse ideas and practices left them, whose people had lived in a military dictatorship for two centuries, slightly bewildered. Others proved there was nothing new under the sun, whichever sun that might be.

"It is what it is, Crevan. If the Lyonesse media, politicians, or citizens verbally attack our embassy or us for who we are or what we represent, we can only maintain a dignified facade and let President Hecht deal with matters. After all, opening diplomatic exchanges with the Hegemony is her administration's policy. We only speak for our President, not ourselves."

"I wonder how Currag DeCarde and Hermina are getting on in Draconis."

"Probably with fewer doubts, worries, and questions. President Mandus will not allow open differences of opinion concerning her policies. Besides, Hermina knows Wyvern and DeCarde struck me as the quintessential soldier-diplomat, a man who can weather all indignities while using any means necessary to carry out his government's goals."

Torma chuckled. "You got that from a brief meeting?"

"I could sense a forceful personality, the sort I've met before." She glanced at him. "You're not much different, Crevan. Perhaps not as smooth, but that's just a matter of habit. Give it a few weeks among the locals, and you'll match DeCarde in most ways. Our superiors made no mistake when they chose you as the Hegemony's first ambassador to Lyonesse, even if you don't quite believe it." A chuckle. "You know, something tells me your past as a police general will be more of a help than a hindrance with those who count around here. Not to mention, it gives you a mysterious aura among people who don't actually understand what the Commission for State Security is."

"You mean I'll give the earnest citizens of Lannion a darkly delicious frisson of danger? I doubt it. But as you said, it is what it is." He glanced at the walled compound sitting halfway up the hillside in one of Lannion's poshest neighborhoods. "Mind you, the villa they gave us as a residence is lovely and well suited for the receptions we need to host. They could have done a lot worse. I'm sure if Vice President Juska had his way, we'd be setting up shop in a rundown farm with a leaky roof and bad plumbing on the outskirts of town. And they gave us a chancery in a prime spot across the street from Government House, protected by the age-old extraterritorial protocols."

"Oh, President Hecht is serious about establishing relations strong enough to avert war if our interests clash. So is Admiral Norum — another powerful personality similar to Currag DeCarde and you. Juska? Less so."

"Have you spoken with the local Brethren yet?"

"Yes. They're cautious around me. Hermina made a full report from Hatshepsut and certainly dubbed me the Abomination, even if she hasn't used that term to my face for some time. But they were reasonably friendly, nonetheless. I have a standing invitation to attend services, use their libraries, and visit with the Lannion Brethren if I need a respite from my diplomatic duties. Obviously, they have unspoken motives and aren't just acting out of kindness to a fellow Void Sister, however schismatic she might be."

Torma laughed. "That'll be a common refrain during our entire stay — they want to know about us as much as we will research them. After all, diplomatic delegations have been engaged in intelligence gathering since time immemorial. DeCarde and his envoys will be subjected to the same."

Ardrix made a face. "Except his chief of staff already learned about our Order of the Void."

"And is that such a bad thing?"

"No. It's much harder to engage in open warfare with someone you understand intimately."

Torma snorted. "Tell that to my friends whose marriages have failed."

She glared at him. "On a state-to-state basis, funny man. People who see themselves reflected in others will hesitate before picking up a weapon. The problem is when a non-negligible percentage sees little to no commonality. Lyonesse has them. We have them. And if neither government pays attention, or worse yet, if they become part of the government, they can precipitate another catastrophe."

"And part of our job is finding them, then work on changing their views, or if that's not possible, figure out ways of neutralizing their influence." Torma sighed again. "A tall order."

"Keep in mind you have an asset whose specialty is the human psyche. Theoretically, the temporary lifting of my vows doesn't absolve me from obeying the strictures placed on us sisters. But in practice, by living as Ardrix Moore, I'm much less constrained by my conditioning. Don't ask how that works. I don't understand either, and I won't tell anyone back home when we return, let alone the sisters here. I daresay Hermina is in the same position. They chose us as our respective ambassador's chiefs of staff instead of the usual secular bureaucrats for a reason."

"Both Presidents want to make sure they hold the best hand possible when negotiating with each other through us."

"Precisely."

"Make sure you don't get caught mind meddling, though. The locals might consider such activities contrary to our diplomatic status."

Her smile returned. "At the risk of sounding immodest — yes a sister usually doesn't brag — my work with the Commission has given me an insight into the human mind that is rather different and mostly unknown here. I tried a few techniques on the Lannion Brethren, and none of them could sense my presence."

Torma studied her profile against an eastern sky slowly turning a deep magenta. "Is the Archimandrite aware of this?"

She nodded. "He hoped I would prove more capable than the Old Order sisters. Not only so I could help you influence the Lyonesse government but also plant the seeds of a new single Order under his leadership, helped by an army of sisters whose abilities match mine."

"Why? Does Bolack have ambitions of his own?"

"Everyone at the top does — Mandus, Conteh, Bolack, the Service Chiefs, the senior bureaucrats. All dream of a new empire, a reunited Order, and a return to the Golden Era that marked the empire's first few centuries, when everything was possible." She gave him a mischievous look. "In accordance with Sister Jessica's prophecy, not that of the local mystic."

"Just like those running the Lyonesse government."

"Yes." Ardrix plucked a blade of grass from the ground and studied it with her usual intensity, but Torma sensed her mind wasn't on the tiny scrap of native vegetation. "How will this end, do you think?"

Torma shrugged. "As the Almighty intends? I'm no more of a visionary than anyone else. But as a mere human being, I have hope for our species. You?"

"I think we'll be okay in the end, ambitions notwithstanding."

"Why?"

"Because my inner eye can make out the first hint of dawn."

APPENDIX

THE BATTLE OF FORT WAGNER

The colony Farhaven was in full revolt against the government of humanity's first interstellar federation. It was the time of the First Migration War, which birthed a new compact between Earth and its soon-to-be sovereign colonies. The Marines of the 3rd Regiment, sent to quell the bloody uprising on Farhaven and protect colonists loyal to the government, had been fighting with increasing desperation for over six weeks, cut off from reinforcements and resupply, harried by the rebels at every turn and with no safe harbor. The countryside had turned against them, and a rebel army of fifteen thousand strong was hunting them down. In those six weeks, the regiment lost nearly half its strength to rebel ambushes and raids. They had no means of dealing with the wounded, and those who fell into rebel hands died a horrible death.

Shortly before noon on December 1st, the Regiment's rearguard finally broke contact with the rebel army's lead elements, and the survivors of a desperate retreat, protecting over four thousand loyalists, men, women, and children, streamed into Fort Wagner, the last government stronghold on the planet. Bereft of artillery, armored vehicles, and every other tool of modern warfare, they carried only small arms and crew-served portable weapons. At two in the afternoon, the gates of Fort Wagner slammed shut, and the overlapping rings of mines, obstacles, and compacted earth berms were closed. The long retreat was over because the 3rd Marines had no other place to go. Fort Wagner would be their last stand.

Shortly after eighteen hundred hours, the rebel army, counting on the momentum of their headlong pursuit, attacked Fort Wagner with little preparation. The garrison, every Marine who could shoot along with armed colonists, repulsed them easily. The rebels withdrew, leaving hundreds of dead and wounded lying on the grassy slopes beneath the fort. At midnight, a second attack, as badly planned and executed, also broke against the 3rd Regiment's fierce determination. But ammunition stocks were dropping fast, and the defenders' numbers slowly dwindled because of casualties. By now, the Marines knew it was only a matter of time. Twelve thousand against less than fifteen hundred, odds of ten to one, would overwhelm them.

Two hours after the second attack, a party of rebels, under a flag of truce, came to offer Colonel Greeson, commanding officer of the 3rd Marines, terms of surrender. The Regiment would be permitted to march out of the fort with their weapons and baggage and occupy the nearby Tranto spaceport unmolested so that they may await transport off-planet. They made no mention of the four thousand loyalists, survivors of rebel massacres, and other atrocities. Unwilling to condemn his men one way or the other, Colonel Greeson took the unusual step of holding a Regimental Council.

At oh-four-hundred, the surviving company and battalion commanders, first sergeants and sergeants major, as well as the regimental staff and regimental sergeant major, assembled in a large underground bunker. There, Colonel Greeson presented the rebel offer. He did not state his own preference but instead called upon each of the assembled Marines to vote in turn, from the most junior to the most senior. Command Sergeant Yolanda Turnik was the first. Before saying yea or nay, she asked Colonel Greeson what would happen to the loyalists if the 3rd Marines surrendered. When Colonel Greeson didn't reply, Sergeant Turnik said, 'If we abandon the loyalists to save our skins, we break our oath and sully our honor. I would rather die. We stay.' One after the other, the members of the Regimental Council echoed Sergeant Turnik's sentiments. When Colonel Greeson, as the most senior, cast the final vote, it was unanimous. The 3rd Marine Regiment would not leave without the loyalists. That decision was presented to the loyalist leaders, as was a bald estimate of their survival chances, which were nil.

At daybreak, Colonel Greeson met with the rebels and rejected the terms, as they didn't include the loyalists. When the Colonel and his party entered the fort again, they knew it was for the last time. Three hours later, Fort Wagner was subjected to a murderous assault which the defenders, reinforced by volunteers among the loyalists, repulsed at substantial cost. Sporadic bombardment and sniping continued as the sun rose in the sky revealing a scene of death and desolation around the fort. Rebel bodies were piled up by the hundreds on the slopes and along the tree line beyond. But inside the fort, the situation was just as bad, and Colonel Greeson knew the end was near.

At fifteen hundred hours on the afternoon of December 2nd, the surviving Marines assembled for the last time as a regiment in the fort's courtyard. There, under the watchful gaze of his troops, Colonel Greeson burned the regiment's colors so they would not fall into rebel hands. He placed the ashes in a steel case along with the unit's war diary and buried them at the foot of the flagpole. Then Colonel Greeson ordered the regiment's battle flag nailed to the mast. It would not come down until the 3rd Marine Regiment was either victorious or wiped out.

At five o'clock, as the sun-kissed the horizon, the rebels launched a massive assault on Fort Wagner with every available soldier. Their casualties were beyond anything previously experienced on Farhaven, yet they finally broke through by sheer weight of numbers. Valiantly, the surviving Marines fought on, some with nothing more than the bayonet at the tip of their rifles. Slowly but surely, the regiment died, each trooper taking three rebels before succumbing, defiance still echoing loud around the central courtyard. The last platoon, ten Marines under the command of Second-Lieutenant Rudy Westphalen, held the entrance to the underground complex where the remaining thirty-five hundred loyalists, mostly children, the elderly, and the wounded, sought refuge. For nearly half an hour, the last platoon kept the rebels at bay, turning the courtyard into a charnel house.

Soon, however, Lieutenant Westphalen's little command numbered five troopers, himself, and no more ammunition. In an act of desperate courage that will live forever, Lieutenant Westphalen ordered his men to fix bayonets. Then, shouting the regiment's battle cry, Faugh a Ballagh, the last survivors of the 3rd Marine Regiment charged the astonished rebels. They died in a hail of bullets at twenty minutes past six in the evening. What followed will be remembered as one of the darkest acts of savagery committed since humanity spread across the stars. The rebels slaughtered each and every loyalist, turning the underground bunkers into immense mass graves.

The men and women of the 3rd Marine Regiment died rather than break their oath and stain their honor forever. We will not forget their courage. We will always live up to their example. At the going down of the sun and in the morning, on this day, as on every other day of our lives, we will remember them.

Three days after the rebels took Fort Wagner, losing over four thousand troops in the effort, a relief column of two full regiments landed on Farhaven. The rebels, drained and bruised by the stubborn 3rd Regiment, were quickly defeated. When the full extent of the massacre at Fort Wagner became known, the commander of the 4th Marine Division ordered every rebel soldier tried and executed for war crimes, smashing the rebellion on Farhaven forever. The 3rd Marines and the loyalists were avenged. To this day, at Fort Wagner, their memory lives on, and it will do so for as long as there are Marines to remember.

About the Author

Eric Thomson is the pen name of a retired Canadian soldier who spent more time in uniform than he expected, both in the Regular Army and the Army Reserve. He spent his Regular Army career in the Infantry and his Reserve service in the Armoured Corps. He worked as an information technology specialist for several years before retiring to become a full-time author.

Eric has been a voracious reader of science fiction, military fiction, and history all his life. Several years ago, he put fingers to keyboard and started writing his own military sci-fi, with a definite space opera slant, using many of his own experiences as a soldier for inspiration.

When he is not writing fiction, Eric indulges in his other passions: photography, hiking, and scuba diving, all of which he shares with his wife.

Join Eric Thomson at http://www.thomsonfiction.ca/

Scan to visit the site.

Where you will find news about upcoming books and more information about the universe in which his heroes fight for humanity's survival.

And read his blog at https://blog.thomsonfiction.ca

If you enjoyed this book, please consider leaving a review on Goodreads or with your favorite online retailer to help others discover it.

Also by Eric Thomson

Siobhan Dunmoore

No Honor in Death (Siobhan Dunmoore Book 1)
The Path of Duty (Siobhan Dunmoore Book 2)
Like Stars in Heaven (Siobhan Dunmoore Book 3)
Victory's Bright Dawn (Siobhan Dunmoore Book 4)
Without Mercy (Siobhan Dunmoore Book 5)
When the Guns Roar (Siobhan Dunmoore Book 6)
A Dark and Dirty Wary (Siobhan Dunmoore Book 7)

Decker's War

Death Comes But Once (Decker's War Book 1)
Cold Comfort (Decker's War Book 2)
Fatal Blade (Decker's War Book 3)
Howling Stars (Decker's War Book 4)
Black Sword (Decker's War Book 5)
No Remorse (Decker's War Book 6)
Hard Strike (Decker's War Book 7)

Constabulary Casefiles

The Warrior's Knife
A Colonial Murder
The Dirty and the Dead

Ashes of Empire

Imperial Sunset (Ashes of Empire #1)
Imperial Twilight (Ashes of Empire #2)
Imperial Night (Ashes of Empire #3)
Imperial Echoes (Ashes of Empire #4)
Imperial Ghosts (Ashes of Empire #5)

Ghost Squadron

We Dare (Ghost Squadron No. 1)
Deadly Intent (Ghost Squadron No. 2)
Die Like the Rest (Ghost Squadron No. 3)

Made in United States
North Haven, CT
29 September 2024